GW00858014

Stories for Homes

Volume Two

Edited by Debi Alper and Sally Swingewood

ISBN-13:978-1979289276
ISBN-10:1979289271

This anthology has been created by a community of people. As well as the authors and editors, volunteers have been responsible for proofreading, cover design, layout and formatting, promotion and social networking, website updating, events organisation, finance and liaising with the charity.
https://storiesforhomes.wordpress.com
https://www.facebook.com/StoriesForHomes
https://twitter.com/storiesforhomes
Cover design by
http://www.headandheartpublishingservices.com/
Cover Artwork © Sally Swingewood 2017

All funds from the sale of this book go to the housing and homelessness charity, Shelter.
Registered charity in England and Wales (263710) and in Scotland (SC002327)
http://www.shelter.org.uk

Dedication

*This anthology is dedicated to the victims and survivors
of the Grenfell Tower fire, 14 June 2017.
You will never be forgotten*

CONTENTS

FOREWORD

At the time of writing the UK is an unsettled place. Successive national ballots have exposed a divided population, a country which has no common goal, no common sense of identity. And the concept of 'home' is central to our collective crisis.

When the Stories for Homes project began in 2013, 'Brexit' was not a word. Now it is amongst the most inflammatory in the English language, causing brutal rifts between families and friends and prompting a huge escalation in reported hate crimes. European citizens who have made their lives here do not know if they can continue to call it home. UK citizens who live in Europe are in the same uncertain position.

Alongside this the UK has seen a weakened currency, rising food prices and swingeing cuts in social care. Promises for more affordable housing and a new generation of social housing have not materialised. Bills to improve the lot of private renters are routinely overturned. Improvements to existing housing stock are slow and often cosmetic.

The feeling of inequality, of a privileged class that does not care about ordinary people, crystallised when Grenfell Tower, a 24-storey tower block in Kensington and Chelsea – the richest borough in London – was destroyed by fire in June 2017. Official figures give the numbers of people who died at 80, but the real figure will probably never be known, due to the shocking intensity of the fire. It soon emerged that one factor in the devastation was the use of flammable material in the exterior cladding. Safer cladding would have cost more. Financial savings were prioritised over safety. This block, like so many others which are home to the poorest people in our society, had no sprinkler system. It did not have sufficient fire exits. Fire safety tests had not been carried out as required. Alarms were inaudible from many of the flats.

Residents knew their homes were potential death traps but their concerns had been ignored for years. A blog written back in 2013 warning of the dangers resulted in the blogger being sent a legal letter, accusing him of defamation and harassment. He was not the only protester who was threatened for voicing fears. With chilling prescience, the Grenfell Action Group wrote in November 2016: 'It is a truly terrifying thought but the Grenfell Action Group firmly believe that only a catastrophic event will expose the ineptitude and incompetence of our landlord.'

Following the disaster, checks across the country revealed hundreds more blocks with the same flammable cladding as Grenfell Tower, as well as missing fire doors and various other serious issues. In one area people were forcibly moved out for emergency remedial work. In others, the decision to tell residents was delayed because no one knew quite what to do. And this is about a single identified issue.

Meanwhile, one group of people has lost their homes entirely and others will be waiting months for theirs to be made safe. Where do they go? This country already has a shortage of homes available to ordinary people. Housing lists are so long that those in need are routinely told they will never be housed and will have to find another solution. Some of the traumatised Grenfell residents were originally offered homes in

Manchester, hundreds of miles from 'home', with warnings that they would be considered intentionally homeless if they turned down this offer.

Some of those who own homes in nearby luxury developments have been publicly appalled at the idea of Grenfell survivors being moved into the 'social housing' element that is legally part of every new build. Some have gone as far as saying they will move out if survivors are housed there. No one expected to see refugee families in the shiny new block with its private swimming pool, sauna and spa. Such places are intended only for the rich.

Shelter, the charity which Stories for Homes supports, cites three main criteria for housing: safety, stability, affordability. The UK is currently failing its citizens on every point. Now is perhaps a good time to remind everyone that we are all only one or two major life events from homelessness. This crisis is not about other people. It is about all of us. We all have a duty to raise our voices and demand immediate change.

Sally Swingewood and Debi Alper

TED BONHAM

The Life This Is

I don't know, maybe 1 should tell you a story? It'll distract us for a bit. I know you think my stories never go anywhere but, well – it's not as if this story does go anywhere, it's just – it just somehow feels significant for some reason. At least for me.

It would have been five or six years ago. Back when Sarah and Joe were first living together in that tiny flat they used to share in Withington. They had a system back then. Well-practised, unconscious almost. Sarah rolled a joint whilst Joe made the tea. It was always that way round because Joe only smoked cigarettes when he was drunk and had found he wasn't very good at spliff-making sober. Sarah had taken up smoking to fill the long weekends of her rural teen years, continuing to roll her own all through college and university, so that it came to her now as naturally as writing her own name. In fact, if she wasn't concentrating she sometimes spelt Williams with three l's.

Joe and Sarah would still have been second years at Manchester University at this point, Joe studying physics, Sarah philosophy, and they managed to fit a couple of hours of day-time TV in most afternoons. The process began just as a perceptible increase in volume and saturation of colour on the television indicated the first of a series of advertisements for high interest loan companies and cholesterol-reducing sandwich spreads.

And so Sarah looks over to Joe just as the ads break in and asks him quietly to 'put kettle on, love,' and Joe creaks up out of the old floral armchair, preparing for the arduous three metre journey to their scruffy little kitchenette. He isn't being facetious when he turns back to ask Sarah if she's 'putting a brew on' too, the vocabulary of tea-making long having been muddled with that of weed smoking. And so, at his prompt, she leans forwards to gather together the relevant materials from the cup-ringed mess of a coffee table as he, pausing briefly to glance out through the window at the ever-grey Manchester autumn, heads towards the kettle.

He rubs his eyes. I remember, his eyes often itched back then, whether due to pollen, tiredness or pollution. So he rubs his eyes and then picks up the kettle, which is cheap, obviously, and some years old. He checks the water level. He doesn't like to waste water and can tell by eye, by the weight of it almost, the exact amount needed for their two mugs. It is an amount just slightly over the worn-away minimum indicated on the clear plastic guide. Limescale gives him selective blindness as he tops up the water from the constant dripping tap. He tried to stop it once, the dripping, took a Philips head screwdriver to removing the handles and replacing the washers in the taps. But he's convinced it only made the dripping worse. He doesn't notice that he hasn't quite shut the lid right before he clicks the kettle on and moves to rinse out two mugs.

They each have their own mug. An ill-matching but comfortable pair. His is large, once white, with a centred 'Starbucks' logo and a hairline fracture running down its entire length near the handle. A mug for swigging from, a quality that he feels far outweighs the vulgarity of its branding. Hers is a little smaller, 'more ladylike,' she would say, like when she has to order twice as many halves as he orders pints from the good-looking barman at the pub on the corner. It is printed with the name 'Emma' in a simple pink font (they don't know an Emma). These are their mugs, inherited from nobody knows where, and with the high and low water marks of a life-time of hot drinks staining their interiors. There are other mugs in the cupboard, but they're seldom taken out except for guests. Instead, Joe uses a stained and faded J-cloth to wipe off the worst of the drips, noticing as he does so a faint lipstick mark on the smaller one that provokes a smile.

The noise of the steam rattling the lid of the kettle alerts Joe to the need to secure it properly. Next, he digs out two dusty tea bags from the almost empty jar. The kettle clicks itself off. He places a tea bag in each mug and, after a short pause for the water to go off the boil (he read somewhere that boiling water scalds the tea), he fills each from the kettle. He then heads back across the living room to the fridge in the alcove to fetch the milk. He notices Sarah as he passes; she is focusing on her lap, ignoring the latest life changing JML product being demonstrated on the screen. Her fingers work, pulling gently at the tobacco and laying it out just so. Joe opens the fridge door and takes out an almost empty carton of semi-skimmed. He checks the date on the label and then sniffs the dregs.

Tripping slightly over an unevenness in the floor beneath the carpet, Joe returns to the two patiently waiting mugs. His eyes barely bother to scan the always cluttered surfaces for a teaspoon. Instead, he fishes the two teabags out with the ends of his guitar-calloused fingers, squeezing each in turn against the side of the mug to strain out the last of the colour, if not the flavour. He slightly scalds his fingers in the process, but this doesn't seem to bother him as he gingerly places each teabag on the precarious pile overflowing a small, chipped saucer next to the sink. He splits the last of the milk between the two mugs and tentatively sips his own. Small white bits can be seen floating on the surface as he heads back to sit down just as *Come Dine with Me* begins again and Sarah sparks up the joint. He hands across her mug and she balances it on the arm of her chair with a quiet, 'Cheers, love.' He settles back into his armchair and smiles again because she does.

And then, well, that's it I think. I mean, that's what I remember of what happened. I'm not sure why, it just somehow seemed significant, you know? One of those little moments that stays with you for some reason. Or that you rewrite in your memory until it becomes significant for you. One of that group of memories and ideas that all seem somehow linked together. Those events that come to mind when I think about home.

What? No – No, I'm fine. Just a bit cold maybe.

LEIGH FORBES

Coming Home

I hope it's going to be all right, but I'm nervous. Really, really nervous. See, I'm going home today, to my old man and me kids, and I'm excited and stressed and scared all wrapped up in one.

I'll tell you right away I've been in the nick, but I ain't saying no more than that, because you'll have judged me enough already. If you really want to know, my kids are polite and cleanly dressed, and my husband's got a job, and we never claimed nothing we're not entitled to. Whatever else you think, I'm no scrounger. We're a decent family. You have to know all that to start with.

You also have to know whatever I've done, I was trying to make things better. Kevin worked all day and night and never saw his family. We never had no money, and we just rowed all the time. I knew where it was going, but I love my husband, and I didn't want the kids to lose their dad – so they ended up losing their mum instead, which was dumb. And even though I got it wrong big time – and I know it was wrong – I thought I was just doing my best for my kids. I've always tried to do me best, see. Apart from being away, of course; but I didn't have no say in that in the end.

Kev was a star. He stepped right up to the mark, though he struggled at the start; he couldn't find Jessie's lunchbox that first day, and I weren't there to tell him where it was, so she went to school with her sarnies in a plastic bag. I felt more guilty about that than anything. I'd never seen how the humiliation would spill on them too. Just never thought about it. Too wrapped up in me own mess.

But they've been all right. Jessie really took to playing mum. Not that I was much of a rôle model before – I get that now – but she taught her dad how to cook and keep things tidy, and she must have been a big help to him, what with everything else. Even when she started big school. We thought she'd go all stroppy spending every day round them teenagers and their hormones, but it's made her more responsible, more grown up. I hope it's going to be OK now I'm coming home. I don't want to cramp her style.

Little Tommy's OK. He's so full of Good that kid, and all this stuff with me just seems to pass him by. The social worker said it'd come out later, but we'll just have to wait and see, won't we? For now, he's my little ray of sunshine, such a joker. I hope I can cope with him getting up to his tricks all the time. I've seen him every week, of course, but it's not the same, and he was just a little toddler when I left, hardly talking or anything – though always full of giggles for his mum. Now he's a chirpy 5-year-old, and he'll look all grown up in his school uniform (Kev said he was desperate to wear it today), and he never stops rabbiting on. I mean never. And I'm worried I'm going to find all the noise hard to handle, because I've been used to things being more quiet, you know?

But I do really love my kids, and I know they love me. I hope it'll be OK.

And Kevin? I kept wondering if there's been anyone else. He's a good man, but it's been a long time, and I'd understand if he didn't love me anymore. But he's always just seemed sad, and he wouldn't be sad if he had a bit on the side, would he? He'd be cheerful... and smug. And he wouldn't need to wait for me – he's got grounds after all. But he never said nothing about divorce. He always just said we'd get through somehow.

And we're nearly through. The first bit anyway. The next bit'll be hard too, I ain't pretending it won't. But that can wait.

Right now, I'm thinking about the party food they've done. Kev said it was supposed to be a secret, but he wanted to warn me, in case it was too much on my first day back, then he just blurted it all out. Said he just meant to get a cake, but the kids kept putting stuff in the trolley and he hadn't the heart to tell them to put it all back. Not when Tommy kept saying, 'And this is for Mummy too.' He'd had a shock when the woman said how much at the checkout, but it was too late then. Tommy had the whole thing planned, right down to the chocolate fingers set round the cake, like rays of sunshine.

Not long now. I'll be there soon. I wouldn't let them come and meet me on the bus. I reckoned it'd be a bad start if I couldn't find my own way home. 'If you can find it,' Kev had joked, and I laughed because I didn't want him thinking he'd upset me. But it's no joke for me. That's another thing you have to know: I've taken it all seriously – which is why I'm coming home now, not when I should've been. I've learnt new skills while I've been away too. I'm a seamstress now, which feels odd; I weren't really nothing before, except a mess. Now I've got a job lined up on the other side of town, and I'm going to walk there and back every day. Not because we can't afford the bus, but because I'm looking forward to walking two miles in a straight line.

I'm passing the pub now, and wondering if a drink would steady my nerves. I've never been much of a drinker – which is just as well, given the rest of it – but I know they wouldn't blame me if I stopped for a quick one. I cup my hand over my eyes and peer through the grimy window. It looks warm in there. I could just have one, couldn't I? To calm me down a bit.

But I'm thinking about the old sheet Kev said they'd had out of the cupboard, and the glitter paints he got Jessie for her birthday. Tommy did the writing, Kevin said – took him ages, because he wanted to make sure he had all the right letters in the right order. Jessie did the stars and swirls and everything else. Except the smiley faces. Tommy did those too. Like I said, he's full of the good stuff that boy.

They wanted to hang it outside, but Kevin wouldn't let them. Felt right mean he said, but he didn't want it reminding the whole street what happened, and he didn't want no one thinking we're smug because I'm coming home earlier than I should. So the banner's inside, draped a bit over the bannister and across the hall to the coat hooks. I can't wait to see it.

I push away from the pub and turn for home. I don't want a drink. I want to see the glittery writing and smiley faces. I want to see my family.

And then I see Sarah Cartright turn the corner ahead of me. She's got her older boy with her… or is it the little one? I've been away that long I can't tell. And suddenly I'm all a fluster. If it's Charlie, I could ask about his football, but if it's Ryan, I'll look a right twit, because Ryan doesn't play football. They're getting closer now, and she's looking at me all odd like. Not unfriendly, just surprised. I clam up.

'Hello, Julie,' she says. 'I didn't know you were… home.'

I feel like an idiot; I haven't even made it home yet.

'You still playing football?' I blurt to the boy, realising too late that he's wearing full kit, including boots.

'Ryan just made the school team.' Sarah ruffles his hair. 'He scored the winning goal in his first match, didn't you, love?'

Ryan cocks his head to one side with a scowl, dislodging his mother's fingers.

'Sorry, we can't stop.' She smiles too brightly. 'But if you fancy a coffee sometime…?'

The offer hangs in the air, and I wonder if I'm supposed to answer. If she means it, I should say yes; but if she's just using it as a way to get away, I should say no. I don't know which.

'I don't really know,' I falter. 'I need to…'

'Sure.' She looks all concerned like. 'Give me a ring, yeah? The boys would love to see Tommy.'

All I can think is how I want to see Tommy too. I mumble something, and scuttle on.

Not far now. I hope it's going to be all right.

The front door's been painted since I left, and there's winter pansies growing in the window box. What else will have changed inside, I wonder. Will it feel like home? My hand hovers on the bell. But before I have time to get my head round it all, the door flies open.

'MUMMY!' Tommy hurtles into my legs, jumping up and down so I have to grab the door frame. Snatching my balance, I reach down and haul him up. God, he's heavy now.

He's already pointed out the banner, and told me about the cake in the lounge and the balloons and the special meal that Daddy's cooking me tonight. ('But that's a secret, so I didn't tell, OK?')

Then Jessie's there in the doorway to the lounge, her eyes wide with fear… and relief.

'Hello, Jess.' My voice cracks with the effort. Shifting Tommy onto the other hip, I free a hand to reach out. She slides under my shoulder and grips me round the middle like she's going to fall off.

'Welcome home, Mummy,' she gulps, which starts me off too; she hasn't called me Mummy in years. And I'm just burying my face in their faces and we're all three of us crying. Except Tommy's giggling too.

I can feel the chill pouring past me into the house, surging round my legs like a flooding river. I can't help thinking the warm air's streaming out just as fast, but I'll keep my mouth shut. I shan't start narking the second I get back. The cold doesn't matter. All that matters is in my arms.

It's Tommy who breaks the moment.

'Say hello to Dad, Mummy.' I notice he's dropped the 'Daddy'. He slips down from my hip and pulls me inside. 'He's been all stressing today. But hurry up. He said we can't have cake until you get home, but now you're home so we can have cake. Yay!'

'Hello, love.' I can't meet Kevin's eye, and find myself looking at my feet and thinking I'll get mud on the carpet, and I should probably take my shoes off.

He steps forward and catches me in a massive hug and his face is buried in my neck. His breath comes out all juddery, and it's all I can do to breathe at all, he's holding me that tight.

'I'm sorry,' I muffle into his shoulder.

'No more sorrys,' he muffles back. 'Just what-shall-we-do-tomorrows?'

'Cake! Cake! Cake!' Tommy is jumping up and down beside us, and with my face squashed sideways I see Jessie reach out and put a hand on top of his head to still him. 'Come on Tom,' she says. 'Let's go and cut the first slice for Mum.' And she hauls him into the lounge.

I pull away from my great hulk of a hubby and hold him at arm's length. I never seen him cry before. Not even when I had to go.

'This has been the real punishment,' I say. 'Being away from you lot.'

And Kev just says. 'It doesn't matter anymore. You're home.'

And finally I know it's going to be all right.

JAN CARSON

The Tiger Who Came Back to Apologise

The baby is finally sleeping. Sophie is pouring herself a coffee. When the doorbell rings she is contemplating a biscuit and, afterwards, a shower. Ideally, she'd like a bath and the chance to dry her hair properly with a hairdryer. Since the baby, such luxuries are beyond her.

The doorbell is an old-fashioned one. It sounds like a small gong struck twice in quick succession. Ding dong. Far too loud for a house containing such a little baby. Sophie keeps asking Graham to take the batteries out. Graham keeps saying, 'Good idea, Soph. I'll do it at the weekend.' He hasn't got round to silencing the doorbell yet, or to hanging the baby's mobile. Graham is the sort of man who requires nagging.

The doorbell makes Sophie start. She spills a tiny slurp of coffee. It leaves a brown stain on her shirt. Later, she will notice it and wonder if it's coffee or just more of the baby's runny poo. She'll sniff at the stain cautiously, like a bloodhound nosing for clues. These days she often finds herself sniffing at unpleasant things.

The doorbell rings a second time. Sophie glances at the baby monitor. She's wearing it on her wrist today, attached with elastic bands. This way it shouldn't end up in the fridge again, or swimming round the washing machine with the baby's vests. The monitor grumbles and flashes urgent red, its tiny dots dancing like the blips on a hospital heart monitor. It falls momentarily silent. Upstairs, in the nursery, the baby is deciding whether to howl or not.

Sophie sets her untouched mug on the counter and bolts for the door. She must intercept the ringer before he makes another assault on the bell. Today she's running on caffeine and a half hour's sleep. No part of her works properly. But, suddenly she is all go. She is meat and muscle; hard, pumping legs, scooting out the kitchen door, past the downstairs loo and along the hall, not even caring about her swollen breasts, lolloping about in their maternity bra. Not even feeling the dull throb of them. Sophie will do whatever it takes to keep the baby sleeping for another hour.

The baby is not a bad baby. He is placid like his father; blessed with the same gummy grin. He is plump. He is adorable. He is like the infant Jesus on Christmas cards, napping in his crib.

The baby does not sleep.

This isn't entirely true.

The baby occasionally sleeps.

For ten minutes right in the middle of *Eastenders*. For a single blessed – but rather inconvenient – hour between three and five. For hours and endless, awkward hours every time Graham's mother comes round for a cuddle. The baby isn't particularly keen on sleep. When he does drop off he holds himself like a hairline fracture. The whole house eggshells round him. Quietly. Gently. On sock-soled tip toes. The slightest noise makes him wake suddenly and scream. The full-lung shriek of him isn't human, more like an industrial machine. Anything can set the baby off. A telephone. A light turning on next door. A dropped shoe. The doorbell ding donging on a Tuesday afternoon.

Ding dong, sings the doorbell for a third time. Sophie hasn't been quick enough. The monitor on her wrist hesitates a half beat then goes hysterical. She doesn't need disco lights to tell her the baby's up. She can hear the loud howl of him coming through the ceiling. But, she's at the door now and it will only take a minute to sign for the parcel, or accept the flyer, or say, in a somewhat strained voice, 'I'm afraid we're not interested in tarmacking the drive at the minute.' Just a few seconds. Then Sophie can go upstairs to the baby, try to coax the sleep back into him before he arrives at that purple-faced point of no return.

Sophie slips the monitor off and gives the door her full attention. The hall is darker than it should be. Something enormous is blocking the light. There is a heaviness in the air. Like the moment just before thunder breaks. Sophie knows it's him. For years she's been waiting to come into the hall and find his orange shadow furring through the frosted glass. She's rehearsed this moment a hundred thousand times. How she will be standing when he sees her? What she will be wearing: a purple dress, a blue sweater, the adult version of black buckle-up shoes? The way she'll say, 'It's you. I always knew you'd come back,' and open the door wide enough to let him in.

Now, the Tiger is here, standing on her welcome mat, waking the baby with his persistent ringing. It is not as she'd planned. Not as she wants it to be.

She steps away from the door, back into the darkened hall. She needs a moment to remember herself.

She doesn't feel like Sophie any more. Since the baby all the hot confidence has dribbled out of her. Like a slow puncture. She no longer believes in her own face. She stares at herself in the mirror now. Tries to smile and can't manage it. Her mouth is a dropped stitch. She looks bewildered. Bewildered is her new look. She is just like Graham. Graham has always appeared bewildered and ineffectual and sort of vague. He is the kind of man who does not have a distinct outline, who begins every conversation with an apology. When they first got together other people said, 'Don't be so hard on him, Soph. He's really nice; so kind, so gentle. You could do a lot worse.' Sophie thought kind and gentle might do for a season, just 'til someone fiercer came along. But the baby came along instead. Now she is stuck with Graham and his vague kindness. It is beginning to rub off on her. There is no force in anything she's done lately. No urgency. She starts to say something and can't remember where it's going. She drops her sentences softly like a sweater you pick up and immediately think better of.

She is not the Sophie she once was. Bold-mouthed. Wide-eyed. Ready to turn the house upside down, just for something to do. She sees herself as the Tiger will see her. The image grates. Here are the fines lines feathering her eyes and here the papery sag of her chin, the lank, ribbonless hair. Sophie is not a bold girl any more.

Perhaps the Tiger won't even recognise her all grown up with breasts and hips, and a small child of her own. He will be disappointed. Sophie knows he will be disappointed. She wants to be different for him but doesn't know how. Still, she tries with her hair. She pinches some colour back into her cheeks. She tucks her shirt into her jeans. The soft pillow of her belly avalanches out. Now, she looks like a fat rectangle: waistless and frumpy. Out come the shirttails in one frustrated tug; better to hide the flab than draw attention to it. There's nothing more she can do without changing. She stands as tall as her heelless feet will permit and opens the door.

'It's you,' she says, forcing her voice confident, 'I always knew you'd come back.'

He is just as big as she's remembered.

'It's good to see you, Sophie,' he says.

He has a slight Yorkshire accent, soft and woolly on the longer vowels. All these years she's had his voice wrong: louder, growlier, more like Liam Neeson. This has been the voice she's always wanted in a man – confident, coiled, almost fierce – and has instead acquired Graham with his nasally Birmingham accent and his need to be always apologising. 'Sorry' for not fixing the doorbell. 'Sorry' for spilling the milk. 'Sorry' for grabbing you with raw lust. So many apologies, when all Sophie's ever wanted is a little wildness, a bit more fury.

'Would you like to come in for tea?' she asks.

The Tiger doesn't answer. Maybe he's gone off tea.

'Or something stronger?'

Sophie's had a six pack of her daddy's favourite beer hidden for years under the sink, right behind the Tiger food. Because she needed a reminder of him. Because she knew he'd eventually come back.

'I don't drink anymore,' he gruffs. Sophie catches a hot whiff of blood, raw on his breath. She hasn't smelt meat in months. Graham is a vegetarian. He won't even allow pretend meat in the house. All the little hairs on her arms come suddenly up. There is a flutter in her chest like something live and frisky is trapped in there, trying to get out. She hopes the neighbours are staring, horrified, through their venetian blinds. She hopes they're getting a good eyeful.

'I'll come in for a second,' he says, 'but I'm not stopping.'

She stands aside to make room for him. This is only habit on her part. What Sophie really wants to do is plant her socked heels on the doormat and let the Tiger rush past her like a wild thing. She would enjoy this immensely. It is so very long since anyone bowled her over. Graham hasn't even tried.

The Tiger bows his enormous head, lifts his enormous paws and slinks inside. He's not used to indoor spaces. He struggles to control his own bulk. Sophie catches the briefest crush of him as he passes. His fur is not fine like human hair but rather rough like the swept ends of a yard brush. It scratches. It leaves marks. His tail collides with the coat rack scattering anoraks and umbrellas. What a mess he is making. Utter chaos. Sophie is thrilled. The Tiger isn't. He apologises, attempts to right the coat rack and accidentally snaps one of Graham's ski poles clean in two.

'I'm so sorry,' he mumbles.

Sophie wants to say, 'Don't apologise. You can destroy the whole house if you want to. I'll help.' Sophie is ready to ruin everything but the Tiger seems a little reluctant.

Crouched beneath the hall lights, she notices he is older now. The fur around his mouth and eyes has lost its fiery redness. It is thinner and flecked with silvery threads like the hair of an elderly man. She can see the cage of his ribs lining through his loose flesh. His breath rattles. He holds his head like it is a drag on his shoulders. He will not look her in the eye. Even when she says, 'What's the matter, Tiger? Come into the living room and have some beer. It'll be just like old times.'

He isn't stopping. He's only come to say sorry.

'Sorry for what?' asks Sophie. She hates how the word sits on his enormous lips, all meek and shrivelled. He might as well be wearing a bow tie or some other humiliating item.

'I'm sorry for coming into your house before,' he says, 'breaking stuff and eating all your food. I was wild back then. I was so selfish.'

'I liked it,' she says, 'It was exciting.'

'It was wrong. It wasn't polite.'

Above their heads, the baby makes a final attempt to be heard. He opens his lungs and shrieks like a fire alarm.

'What's that?' the Tiger asks.

'It's the baby,' says Sophie.

'You have a little one of your own now?'

'A boy. He's four months old.'

'Oh, Sophie,' says the Tiger, 'I'm so pleased to see everything's turned out well for you.'

Sophie could easily shoot the Tiger. Sophie could weep and weep for days. It's not as if she wanted him to eat the baby. Or destroy the house. Or tear Graham into bloody pieces. She only needed to know him capable of it. The Tiger is no longer capable of any fierce action. He is soft and placid. He is vaguely kind. Sophie wonders why she has waited all this time for a Tiger to come. Surely she could have been bold without him. She could have taught herself how to roar.

'I'll let you get back to the baby,' the Tiger says. 'It was nice to see you again, Sophie. Will you pass my apologies on to your mother? Tell her I've changed.'

Sophie nods slowly and opens the door. She can't bear to look at him, so much reduced.

'I'm glad you came,' she says, 'Not today. The first time. The time you destroyed everything.'

The Tiger bows his enormous head, lifts his enormous paws and backs slowly out. Sophie closes the door and listens to him crunching up the gravel path. She feels very angry. She wants to break many individual items but settles for the second ski pole. It will not snap in her hands because she isn't as strong as the Tiger. The fury is all stuck inside her like a hiccough that won't come up. She lets the baby scream for ten more minutes while she finishes her coffee. It is almost cold. It isn't even refreshing.

Sophie lifts the baby from his cot and bundles him into his pram. She pushes him howling, down the street, to the café on the corner. She orders chips, and, with her chips, four fat sausages which she eats slathered in red sauce. Later, when Graham returns from work, she doesn't mention the Tiger or the broken ski pole.

But, she does get right up into his face and say, 'I had meat for lunch, Graham; four whole sausages AND they were delicious.' She does this just to prove that she is still the same bold Sophie, still ferocious, still capable of destroying things.

MICHELE SHELDON

Monsters

Today

There's a half-arsed monster sticking its tongue out at me daring me to step onto his beach. And when I look closer he's surrounded by a gang of them: a rabbit-eared ghost, a toothless troll and a what-you-looking-at-teenager and his gormless girlfriend. This isn't the first time they've tried to intimidate me. They pretty much do it every day.

Yesterday

It was a blue cheese take me to your leader pebble. And I was like, well, what you going to do because you don't have legs and I do. Ha. Ha. Ha. Can't catch me. Useless legless lump. Except I didn't say it out loud because of Dad. So I put my hood up, gave stupid alien face the finger and walked away.

The day before that

I'd come up with a plan to take them by surprise: take a running leap. But the thing is not to look down. Don't ever look down because what could I do if mid-air I see their spiky seaweed teeth snapping away at my arse? A big fat nothing. So I decided always to look ahead. And just as I was feeling all pleased with myself for getting it sorted that's when I saw him. The tide had transformed the harmless green seaweed-haired monster head into the bad-breathed Daesh soldier who gave me ten seconds to run before he started shooting. I turned away fast, screwing up my eyes to get his twisted face out of my head, and ran into town.

Four days ago

I didn't even get close to the beach because dough-faced fat white baldy bad man was blocking the path.

Fuckingdisgustingimmigrantcuntwhydon'tyoufuckoffhome, he shouts from his front door step every time I come out of the mosque.

I wanted to stamp on his pebble doppelganger, watch his face spreading and sticking over the pavement like chewing gum. But I turned away from Mr Shouldhaveletthelotofyoudrown and ran all the way to the harbour.

Five days ago

I glimpsed a brother pebble. I reached out and grabbed the jagged dagger of flint, turning it this way and that, trying to find his handsome face again: Iron Man, a lady with a cat on her head, a deranged-looking giraffe wearing a flowery hat. But my brother had disappeared. Has disappeared. Is disappeared?

A week before

I was eating chips and being hassled to share them with two dazzling white seagulls when I saw my social worker. It was definitely him. Jowls of disdain in profile. I imagined setting them wobbling as he tells me to stop asking about my brother.

I'm trying my best. No, you can't contact them. It has to be through us. Yes. Tomorrow. Definitely tomorrow.

I wrapped up the few remaining chips in the paper, remembering what Miss Debbie, my English teacher, says about students who promise to bring their homework the next day: tomorrow never comes. I took out my phone and messaged him about my brother and asked again why they take money every week for a TV licence when I have no TV.

Two weeks before

I'd only just arrived at the beach when I saw the flat blank grey face of the Home Office solicitor who re-aged me.

I think I know how old I am, I told him.

But we think you're 21.

How can that be? I left home at 13 and arrived in France on my 14th birthday. It's taken two years for me to get an interview. Two years. And I don't even have a solicitor with me.

It's your height.

My father is tall. Over 6 foot.

It's not just your height. It's your demeanour.

My what?

The way you behave. You're too mature for a 16-year-old and your English is too good, your vocabulary in particular.

I wasn't sure whether to take that as a compliment. I put my head in my hands.

Two years, I've waited for an interview, I mumbled. Two years of doing nothing but learning English. And now I discover doing the right thing is the wrong thing.

Kabul is safe now.

I don't come from Kabul.

I mean the whole region is safe now.

Have you been there?

He shook his head, wouldn't look me in the eye.

I couldn't look at him either. This grey-faced man telling me what my country is like. And I wonder how he'd feel about going home if he'd had a gun pointed at his head and heard his father being shot.

I'm sorry but your application for asylum has been turned down. You may lodge an appeal but please consider carefully your chances of success as well as the cost to the UK taxpayer...

Tomorrow

I'm going to be brave. I'm going to grind my boot into these monster faces. I'm going to ignore the long slimy strands of brown seaweed lying over the beach like discarded bandolier bullet belts. I'm going to show them who's boss. Who's King of the Beach. No more standing here like an idiot, my foot hovering. Too afraid to take a step. Too afraid to look up across the water to where the real monsters are waiting for my return.

SHARON BENNETT

Seagull

Today is their anniversary. She sits on the edge of the bench, careful not to let the cake topple between the metal struts onto the path below.

Isn't he heavy? Somebody, a woman, wants to know. Not really. She is used to the weight, and the wobble, as he fidgets around on her head, pecking here and there as he tidies his home. His balancing skills are second to none and when he stands on one leg, he weighs almost nothing at all.

No need to mention the smell. Or the gloopy mess that drips onto her shoulders, and then runs down her back to form a black and white streaked cloak.

At least the screeching has stopped. He has calmed down since that day at the end of the pier when his webbed feet embedded into her backcombed hair. He is quite the hair stylist, as it turns out, teasing her strands every day, one by one, into an impressive nest-do of salt and pepper twigs. She looks better now than she did before.

It's fair to say that she would miss him, if he wasn't perched up there all day and night. Who else would keep lookout and ward off strangers?

Sometimes, wandering through town, she catches sight of their reflection in a window, gets a rare chance to look him in the eyes. She watches as he tilts his head one way, then another and admires the way he changes leg, noticing how the shift in weight makes her nod. Passers-by must think her quite mad, nodding at nothing, but she doesn't care and applauds him anyway. Besides, she looks taller with him up there.

Mind you, he doesn't always stand, she explains to the woman. He settles down when he's tired, and when he does, he fits her head perfectly. Like the sort of hat you spend your life looking for. And at night, when they are both tired, he sleeps on the side of her face, his soft belly covering her ear, so she can hear the sea and the gurgling rock pools of her childhood. Sometimes he stretches out his wings to cover her completely. Then nobody even knows she's there.

She returns to the cake. Although she doesn't want the woman to think they eat like this every day, because they don't. Normally they have chips. They take it in turns. One chip for him, one for her. Him. Her. Us. The ones he wants to save for later, he pokes into her hair, oriental style, turning her into a shuffling Geisha girl. She doesn't mind, he can do what he likes. It's his home after all.

If they don't fancy chips, they do a lucky-dip rummage in the bins. She could explain more, like how he sucks at the droplets from her hair after a rainfall, but the chattering radio on the woman's lapel is distracting her. She is reminded of the day at the end of the pier.

The lady wants to know how many fingers is she holding up.

One less now, as it happens. That's the trouble with a finger that looks like a chip.

MATT BARNARD

The Sound of the East Dry River

The bus sped past and the raw power of it made him shudder and want to weep. He hadn't put his arm out to stop it. He'd seen it turn the corner at the bottom end of the High Street next to Oxfam, and watched it hurtle up the road, the driver obviously trying to make up time. Now he could still feel the air buffeting around him. He sat with his head leant back against the glass of the bus shelter. Beneath him the slippery plastic seat had lost its original chill. It was a dreary day, and he looked around, feeling as if all his senses were newly-opened to the world, the sights, sounds and smells barging in on his mind, clamouring for attention.

Next to him, a woman with a large suede coat sat muttering. 'These drivers, they'll kill somebody one of these days. Mark my words, someone will stick their hand out and the bus will come right on and plough into them, just like that. Mark my words.'

She was saying it to no one in particular, and turned her head away to look into the distance, clamping her lips tight. Jacob looked at her. At this moment, people seemed alien and inexplicable, full of hidden fury, capable of almost anything. Had he come here for this, to this grey country with its skies like smudged charcoal? To end up on a single mattress on the floor downstairs while Esther kept the double bed upstairs. And now – how would he tell Esther?

Something else to blame him for, to screw the hate deeper into her soul.

The police had offered to drive him back, but he'd refused. He didn't want to be suffocated by their condolences any longer. He could see himself through their eyes, an old black man with white hair, fingers cracked from working with his hands, moving slowly like a bewildered cow. Inside he wanted to scream at their professional sympathy and the air of inevitability. Another black kid, another gun.

A shadow loomed in front of him. He looked up and saw a bus waiting. The woman in the coat was already shuffling up to it, her large frame rocking from side to side across the pavement. She got to the door and placed her shopping bags inside, gripped one handle and winched her herself up. Then she showed her pass to the driver and shuffled along inside to find a seat.

The driver looked at him through the open door. 'You getting on, mate?'

He was young, probably the same age as Dwaine, but white, with hair slicked into a sort of messy fin, an earring glinting in one lobe. Jacob looked back at him, then stood up and got on the bus, moving his body as if for the first time, aware of each step, of putting his hand lightly on the yellow handle, feeling its indentations, fumbling in his pocket, lifting his arm to show his pass to the driver. The doors shut and the bus shuddered off as he slid into the nearest free seat. He looked out the window as they drove up through Kentish Town and towards Gospel Oak, questions ringing in his mind.

It had started to go wrong when he announced one evening at dinner that he wanted to go home. He wanted to see the cargo boats in Port of Spain again. He wanted to take Dwaine to Macqueripe and eat boiled corn and roti and baked shark on the beach like he had when he was a boy. Esther looked at him as if he were mad. What did he want to go back there for after thirty years? she'd said. His head must be coming off in his hands, she'd said.

'It's not'ing but island of thieves. And that Basdeo he's the worst. Some Indian boy from Princes Town, think he all smart with his papers, up and running it all. Ah's not going back there.'

Jacob slumped back in defeat, but at night he dreamt of the salty air and smell of bitumen that wafted from the docks across the city. The plumbing business suffered and he stopped going to St Mary's with her. On Sundays she'd put on her smart dress with the flowers and big black hat and ready herself in the mirror, while he watched her from the stairs in his vest, unshaven. She'd mutter about him not coming to church and staying in and drinking Captain Morgan all day, adjusting a scarf or pinning a brooch to her lapel, asking him what sort of example he was setting 'the boy'. Week by week she grew more bitter, more disgusted by him, while the longing for home grew in his belly.

Dwaine was still going with her then, and would look up with serious black eyes, his face full of pleading. After a while he stopped going to church as well. Sometimes Jacob would try to persuade him to go to a QPR game, but more and more Dwaine wanted to go out and do his own thing and Jacob stopped asking. He could feel the boy slipping away, but he watched it happen like a man under water.

One day they got a knock on the door. Dwaine was at the police station after getting in a fight outside a pub in Harlesden. Esther thought she was going to die of shame, and told Jacob over and over, her eyes bitter with accusation. Her boy, a good Christian boy, getting into a fight outside a pub.

When they brought Dwaine out of the cells he seemed like a child again. He was quiet, apologising to them and to the policeman. Jacob wondered when he had grown so large. His neck was huge and he had a man's hands. Seeing his son in a police station should have brought him to his senses but it didn't. After a few days, he watched Dwaine's confidence returning. The episode became a joke between him and his friends, a badge of honour, and Dwaine slipped further into his own dark world, leaving his parents far behind.

The windows of the bus were steaming up. Jacob heard disjointed snatches of conversation from the other passengers, two boys talking about a new computer game, a girl complaining to her boyfriend that her mum wouldn't let her use the car at the weekend. He was struck by a profound sense of sadness and regret for himself and Dwaine and Esther. He wondered how it had ended up like this, and his mind insisted on raking through the ashes of the day. He remembered sitting in an armchair staring at the faded rose wallpaper, a terrible numbness inside him. Esther was at a friend's. She'd said she was going to pray, but he knew she couldn't stand being in the same house as him. Then he heard a rap at the door.

They were polite and told him without messing around. They said that no, they didn't think it could be someone else's boy, someone who looked like Dwaine, but they would need him to come down and make a formal identification. So he went with them. He got into the back of the car and looked at their pink, neatly shaved necks as they drove him to the station in Chepstow Road. The detectives talked quietly to the uniformed officer at the desk, and he was taken though the glass doors into the back. He noticed nobody looked at him. As they walked along the corridor people nodded to the detectives, but never caught his eye. He began to wonder if he were in a dream. They came to a door and stopped.

'It's through here, Mr Latapy.'

Behind the door there was a man in a white coat who said he was very sorry. Jacob nodded, his heart beating like a fist inside his chest. They walked over to a large table in the centre of the room. There was a body under a green covering.

'You remember we said there were injuries to the head, Mr Latapy. Please prepare yourself. Just take your time.'

The man in the white coat rolled back the cover, revealing the head and shoulders of a young man. The top left-hand side of his skull was missing, as if it had collapsed inward. His mouth was open slightly and Jacob could see his two large front teeth, one slightly crossing over the other. Over his left eye was a scar he'd got from falling off his bike when Jacob was teaching him to ride in Gladstone Park.

'That not Dwaine. That not my little boy,' Jacob told them.

'We know it's difficult, Mr Latapy. Please just take your time.'

The bus stopped and the driver rang the bell. Jacob looked up and realised they were in the bus depot in Wembley. The bus was empty, but he didn't move. The driver unlocked his cabin and came down the aisle. Jacob told him he'd missed his stop and the driver said he'd have to get another bus back. He nodded, stood up, walked slowly towards the door, stepped down onto the pavement, and walked to the seats at the bus stop. Opposite workmen were re-laying the road, and the smell of bitumen washed over him bringing memories of the street he grew up in Laventille, the sound of the East Dry River, a vision of men in three-piece suits giving speeches in Woodford Square and he knew with sudden clarity that he'd never go home, he'd never see any of those places again.

SANTINO PRINZI

Plastic

After nine long months, my wife gave birth to a living baby doll.

'The box says her name is Suzy,' the midwife smiled, handing Julia our daughter – but she refused to hold it.

I took the bundle into my arms and fell in love with her in an instant.

Her eyes were candy beads with identical irises and her skin was smooth plastic, her limbs stiff. Her mouth was parted as if she were gurgling but only crying could be heard: recorded and placed on loop. Suzy was beautiful to me, perfect; my wife was not happy.

'It's his fault, obviously,' Julia told everyone. 'There's nothing wrong on my side of the family tree, if you know what I mean.' She couldn't take Suzy back to the manufacturers like a real toy, and she couldn't name her after her grandmother like she'd wanted to. I thought Suzy was a wonderful name, even if we didn't choose it ourselves.

Julia believed our daughter was defective, but I thought there was nothing wrong with her – what could be wrong with something so precious?

Only when Suzy was a toddler did we realise she had an alcohol problem. She'd grown a little bigger and could teeter around the house, though we always knew where we'd find her. Her favourite toy was our wine rack, and sometimes she'd pull out the bottles and play at working behind a bar. She'd pour wine into her cup, it didn't matter what kind, and demand money, real money, which she'd cram into her nappy. I never knew what she did with the money but it was always missing when I changed her. When it was Suzy's turn playing at being the customer, she swapped pouring out a cup's worth with suckling the bottle until she'd guzzled every drop. We'd tried to stop her, but she had a remarkable grip for a baby. If we were lucky we'd find her passed out in bed. Other times she'd run around screaming. Either way all I had to do was follow the wine stains in the carpet. Julia refused to clean up any mess. After a month of this, I ripped up the carpets and replaced them with wood-effect vinyl to make it easier to clean.

Soon Julia stopped buying wine for Suzy. She said she was sick of having a drunken daughter, that this was an act of kindness, but I knew she was tired of our friends and neighbours talking.

One morning I found Suzy dangling from the pull-down cabinet where we kept our spirits. I didn't mind treating Suzy to a little vodka every now and then – I couldn't see any harm in it, Suzy being a doll, of course. Seeing the happiness spirits brought Suzy, Julia poured them all away.

It was then that Suzy's continuous howling began. Our friends had warned us about the many sleepless nights, but they had no idea what this was like. Suzy didn't need to sleep, so her howling never stopped.

After the first week of sleepless nights we took her to the doctors. The doctor tapped Suzy's plastic torso and placed her stethoscope against her chest and back.

'There's no heartbeat.'

'What does that mean?'

The doctor booked Suzy in for an x-ray.

'Well, you'll be pleased to know she does have a heart.'

'But how do we stop the crying?' Julia asked, exasperated.

'Have you stopped giving her alcohol?'

The look Julia and I shared answered the doctor's question for her.

'She's going through withdrawal. She's a doll – she won't experience any long-term damage from excessive drinking. What does she like?'

'Wine.'

The doctor nodded. 'Had a couple last week whose baby doll would only drink Dom Pérignon; you're lucky to have a daughter like Suzy.'

I knew we were lucky, but Julia rolled her eyes and sighed. She wanted us to stop off at the nearest supermarket on the way home. We loaded the trolley with the cheapest wine Julia could find; she wanted to pacify Suzy for as long as possible.

When Suzy was ten she had a growth spurt. Her solid limbs stretched and softened, and blonde hair sprouted from her head. Each day she was taller, lighter. Her eyes lost their glisten and became flat, her irises and pupils solid blocks of colour. When she was sixteen all of her teeth fell out and her mouth wouldn't close. I took her to the dentist.

'Suzy's a grown woman now, Mr Ames,' the dentist sniggered. 'It's about time you let someone else look after her.' He didn't need to ask Suzy to open wide to inspect her gums.

I took Suzy straight home.

Julia worked everything out by the time we returned. I was to blame for Suzy's condition, again, because Suzy picked up all of her imperfections from my side. Julia was horrified by her own realisation: her daughter was a sex doll. I didn't believe her at first, but when Suzy started staying out until the early hours of the morning I wondered if my wife was right.

I felt bad about tying Suzy to her bed, but Julia insisted it was the only way we could protect her and we had to think about our reputation. I wondered if she cared more about our neighbours or our daughter. I complied, thinking instead about the dangerous situations Suzy could find herself in.

Julia wandered in with her iPad and showed me the webpage of a Christian conversion camp which she believed would fix Suzy. Nymphomania, alcohol dependency, drug addiction, kleptomania, and the rest – Julia ticked every box for good measure.

'They'll repair her and she'll return home as a normal person.'

I regarded my wife – she'd become a different woman to the one I'd married. I glanced at my blow-up-doll daughter writhing in bed. I knew what Suzy needed and this wasn't it.

'She is normal, Julia.'

'Nothing about this is normal. She's wrong, unnatural.'

'She's our daughter and she needs our help. There must be another way.'

Julia knew of another way. The next morning, I woke up alone, her side of the wardrobe empty, and the funds in our joint bank account gone. Suzy couldn't ask me where her mother had gone and, though her eyes were solid colour, I could feel the sadness behind them.

'It's not your fault, Suzy.' I caressed one of her inflatable hands. 'No one's perfect, but I won't give up on you.'

The weaning was tough on us both. By the time she was eighteen, Suzy no longer yearned for sex or alcohol. She retained what I considered to be a healthy interest in both, which I tried not to pry too much in to.

I replaced everything she wanted with everything she needed: love and compassion.

As the years passed her limbs hardened and lost their filmy bounce. Her blonde hair fell in synthetic strands, her eyes shone like oval emeralds, and her teeth returned. Her mouth formed a smile, content with the young woman she'd become.

Now she's a model for a Topshop window display down the high street. There she met a lovely male mannequin called Miguel; they're moving in together and getting married next summer. As her father, I couldn't be prouder.

P. T. WHELAN

Return to Winter

I don't think he raised his voice at us once. That can't be right, I know, but looking back it certainly seems that way. I think that's what I'll remember the most about him, and what is sad about my memory of him; it's typified by the lack of something. There was love, of course, I'm left with no doubt he loved us all. But when he lifted us up as children it was because we asked for it, reaching up with our arms. If we needed advice, or just attention, we learnt early on we had to request it. That was just the way he was.

We loved him. Sitting near to him, not needing to say anything, feeling safe next to him. As teenagers, if we needed money or a lift we always asked him, not Mam. He rarely denied us anything, as long it was somewhat reasonable. We tested this a few times. Sarah once asked for a ridiculously expensive coat she had seen in town, and Dad stared at her over his glasses, a slight smile playing on his lips. He didn't bother replying.

Mam made up for anything Dad lacked however, and then some. Her love was a fierce one. The type of love that drives mothers to seek a level of control over their children's lives that rapidly becomes contentious as those children grow older. We were not to be spoiled, we were to go to piano lessons twice a week, we were to get good grades and go to good colleges and get good jobs. I've lost count of the number of times she lost it and went berserk at us over sub-par grades. When we were young, after she teared into us for something or other, we ran to Dad and curled up against him while he put his arm around us, his calm a cooling balm for Mam's scorching touch.

I liked to think I was special to him, the way I sensed Sarah was for Mam. The way we could communicate our mirth, or lack of, with simple looks. Our mutual exasperation with the women of the family, their exasperation with us, bonding us.

The teenage years were hell for us all, I think. Mam's oppressive urges clashing with our expanding independence. Dad the gifted negotiator. It seems my youth at home boils down to one scene, repeated almost weekly in its many variants: Dad coming back into the living room having negotiated some armistice between Mam and Sarah for the fiftieth time that week.

He'd shake his head at me. 'What did I miss?'

'It's Indiana Jones,' I replied. 'We could quote this backwards.'

'Yes, but what did I miss?'

'He threw the Nazi out of the plane because he didn't have a ticket.'

He smiled. 'Classic.'

It seems we always knew he was a survivor. We were born with the knowledge of the Holocaust and Auschwitz. Like most of them, he didn't talk about it. We didn't talk about it, Mam didn't talk about it.

It's wrong to say it was taboo. You can't watch films, read books or talk politics without the Holocaust coming to the fore at times. I remember Dad wanted to go see *Schindler's List*. I think he preferred films to even reading, something he did vociferously. Mam didn't come, as was her policy. After the film, driving back, there was silence for quite a while. Sarah and I never really developed a good approach to the topic with Dad. But we had to say something.

'So,' Sarah asked, 'what did you think of it?'

'It's a survivor's film,' he said. 'The Holocaust wasn't about surviving.'

This, of course, made the uncomfortable silence worse, before Dad said, '*Indy and The Last Crusade* remains the best Second World War film of all time.'

'I think you're supposed to like the first one more,' Sarah sparked back.

'Doesn't have Connery.'

The Holocaust genre was never one he became pleased with, but he watched them all.

After the war, he left Poland and came to the States with nothing. He worked as a waiter for a while, then a barman, until slowly becoming a successful real estate developer. In Poland, before the war, he had been a rising lawyer.

He was old throughout my life, and I saw no real deterioration of his health, so I was shocked, when I shouldn't have been, when I got the call from Sarah. He had had a heart attack which had greatly weakened him. It was speculation whether he would survive.

I rushed back home, arriving a day behind Sarah. We went to the hospital with Mam, who refused to cry for some reason.

'He's been asking for you and Sarah,' she told me when I arrived, bags in tow to stay for the long haul. 'He goes into surgery later today.'

He had his own private room. Comfortable but not luxurious. There were some flowers beside his bed, but not many. He never had many friends, besides some fellow Jews in the city.

Sarah pulled up a seat beside him, taking his hand, and I stood beside her.

He opened his eyes and the wry smile I knew grew on his lips.

'How are you?' Sarah asked him.

He looked at her. 'Just fine.'

Sarah and I laughed. Mam shook her head.

We sat in silence for a while.

'Michael, Sarah,' he said, 'I want you to know I was a Sonderkommando.'

At first I thought he was speaking gibberish, that he had had a stroke and I wasn't told. I looked to Mam, but she was watching Dad.

'David...'

He clutched Sarah's hand.

Sarah looked to me. 'What...?'

I shook my head.

'What do you mean a Sonderkommando?' Sarah asked. 'What's a Sonderkommando?'

But he shook his head, and closed his eyes.

I had to take out my phone and Google the damn thing.

I passed it to Sarah. She read it and quickly handed it back.

The nurses came for him an hour later and we wished him luck, with the strange atmosphere he had injected into the room still there, still tainting the proceedings.

He died during the heart surgery. Mam allowed herself to cry, and I drove us home.

The next day we got the call from Carl Sunderburg and went to his office.

He was an old friend of Dad's, from his early days in the States when he reached out to the Jewish community.

The will was typical of what you'd expect, mostly concerned with the divvying up of his considerable wealth.

Then Carl stopped and cleared his throat. 'Now,' he said, 'the next part might be somewhat hard to hear, and come as a shock.'

We nodded at him to go on.

'Let it be known that it is my wish to be cremated, and my ashes brought to Auschwitz-Birkenau to be scattered in the crematorium.'

Carl put down the will. 'That's it.'

'That's quite the final flourish,' I said.

Carl smiled. 'Full of the unexpected, your father.'

'Why is he doing this?' Sarah asked. 'Jews don't even get cremated.'

'I can't answer that, Sarah,' Carl said. 'He never told me. He drew up the will himself mostly. He had an extraordinary memory of law from his lawyering days all those years ago.'

'I don't even know that I can get the leave to go to Poland,' she said, looking to us.

Mam and I looked back.

'Oh God.' She flushed. 'I didn't –'

'I'll book the tickets when we get back,' Mam said.

In the car on the way back there was an uneasy silence.

Sarah finally spoke. 'I thought I knew him.'

'Most people thought so too,' Mam replied.

I thought back to Carl's closet office, when Dad's final, dramatic wish was read out, and I watched as Mam caught Carl's eye, and some sad and intangible understanding passed between them.

I wished I had that understanding.

Our plane landed in Poland and we rented a car to drive to Auschwitz.

I drove, with Mam beside me, looking ahead. I glanced up into the rear-view mirror now and again to see Sarah staring out the window at our father's homeland.

It hit us when booking the trip that Dad had no family we could visit in Poland. He had been the only survivor.

'Did you know he was Sonderkommando?' Sarah asked.

'Yes, he told me on our third date. He thought it was crucial I knew for some reason.'

'What did you say?'

'There wasn't really anything to say, Sarah.'

On the drive, I grappled with my own thoughts. Dad knew what he was doing when he stole his death from us. He knew the pain and confusion he'd be throwing into the tumult of our grief. He weighed up the pain, and concluded it was worth inflicting. It was worth excluding us from his death; to insist we step outside to watch from the cold.

About an hour out from the concentration camp, Mam broke the quiet that had descended.

'He had a family before the war,' she said. 'Two girls with his first wife.'

'Oh God,' Sarah said.

'They all died in the camp.'

It was the frigid depths of winter, leaving Auschwitz with only a scattering of tourists.

At the gate, that gate, stood a man in a slick suit.

'Mr Nowak?' Mam asked, as we stepped forward to shake hands.

'I am indeed,' he said in a voice clinically sombre. 'I'm pleased to finally meet all of you. The site is ready, if you would follow me.'

'We have a Rabbi here,' he said, leading the way, hands held behind his back. 'If that is what you would like.'

'He wasn't religious,' Mam said.

Nowak nodded.

Nowak showed us the Sonderkommando quarters, separate from the other prisoner lodgings, and gave us a brief, polite tour.

'The Sonderkommandos did not kill, and their primary purpose was not even as manual labourers,' he said, strolling measuredly. 'The officers dropped in the chemical and then left, leaving the Sonderkommandos to deal with the aftermath. Their primary purpose was as a barrier, between the guards and the suffering they caused.'

He finished at the crematorium. Inside were multiple ovens, perfectly sized for a human body to slide into.

Nowak led us to one near the back of the building, whose door was open, ready.

Mam took the urn from me, reached in and threw a handful of his ashes inside. Sarah followed, then me. I then placed the urn inside, and Nowak closed the door.

That's it, I thought.

'Bye, Dad,' Sarah said.

We thanked Mr Nowak and left the camp. I got into the driver's seat and drove us away.

There was silence in the car, everybody sinking into their own thoughts.

Dad took his death from us. But he never really belonged to us anyway. We were the light at the end of the tunnel he must have dreamt of in the camp. But when he arrived in New York all those years ago, and met Mam, it probably dawned on him he'd never really left that place, that he was still in the tunnel. That he would always belong to those he left behind.

SUE LANZON

And It Is

She's involved with a man who works at the supermarket. He's approximately 27-years-old.

She's 51.

He has a receding chin, which bothered her at first, until she appraised his fine nose, and those lips, those dark eyes, that dark voice. She suspects, from the one time she heard him speak, that he comes from Eastern Europe.

His hair is dyed blond, the roots are also dark. He wears it in a ponytail.

She goes to the supermarket often, though it is tiresome having to pretend she doesn't notice him while he stares at her. Perhaps she reminds him of his mother, or he's just got a thing for older women, or maybe he thinks she's a vagrant, given that she's always wearing the same scruffy coat and a loud shirt of her son's that she borrowed because it is warm yet light. The shirt is recognisable from a distance. The coat has streaks of creosote down the front from when she was weather-proofing the shed.

He stares at her always, every time. She can't meet his dark eyes because she would then have to acknowledge her desire. Which would be futile, given the circumstances.

Her son finds her drunk and crying in the kitchen, though it is only 7.30am.

'What's the matter?' he asks.

'Do we need anything from the supermarket?' she replies, a glass of rum clenched between her teeth.

'No, I think we're fine for now.'

She goes to the supermarket anyway. And there he isn't, nor the next time, nor the time after that.

Maybe he's on holiday. Maybe he's been sacked.

Then, on a cold, foggy morning, she sees him behind the cigarette counter. It's early. The supermarket is quiet. No queues. She wants him to believe in her mystery, but the malign god who has put him in her way demands to be placated.

She grabs a bottle of water from the shelf next to the sandwiches and slams it onto the space between the till and cardboard boxes of chewing gum.

She learns from his name badge, now she is near enough – her spectacles having been broken when her son tore the old shed down – that his name is Kev.

Not an Eastern European then, or perhaps an abbreviation of something unpronounceable to English ears.

He asks her for 99p as if she was just anybody.

She fumbles for a pound coin in the dirty pocket of her coat. Her disappointment rages as he hands her the change.

I won't be coming back, she wants to say but, instead, says: 'And a packet of Chesterfield.'

'We're out of Chesterfield,' he says, having looked in the cupboard behind the till that is not allowed to advertise cigarettes. 'Anything else?'

'You,' she doesn't quite manage. What comes out of her mouth is, 'Who?'

'What?' he says.

'John Player Special.'

'Who?'

'Before your time,' she says. 'Let's call him JPS.'

'Blue, red or black?' he replies, complicating things further.

'Um, I think blue, though I'm not a Tory, far from it.'

'What?' he says again.

'No, not what, or who, or – well, just hand them over, motherfucker.'

He stares at her once more. It isn't provocative or even interesting, but merely a question she has forgotten how to answer. And that piece of chocolate her son left beside the washing-up rack. She wants to eat it now.

She puts the cigarettes and water bottle in her pocket and wanders into the hardware shop next door in search of a staple gun. There is still work to do on the shed. The bearers have been pressure-treated but the insulation is already falling apart. Her son is probably up by now, waiting for her return.

SUSMITA BHATTACHARYA

A Holiday to Remember

Rima looked around, feeling disappointed. So this was a caravan. It was quite flimsy and very cold. Certainly not worth the money, she thought.

'Look. Everything is fitted into this tiny space,' Anand said, pulling open drawers and waving a fork and spoon at her. 'Cooker, sink, microwave, fridge. Ingenious. It's got everything you need. Just sit back and relax.'

He sank into the couch and switched on the television. Anne Robinson's jibes filled the room. Rima placed Baby on her hip and went to inspect the bedroom. There was a bed and a wardrobe with some hangers. No cot. Hadn't they asked for a cot?

'Anand,' she called out. 'There's no cot here.' Baby wriggled and tried to slide down her hips.

'I know,' Anand said. 'I didn't ask. It's 50 quid extra. No worries, I'll sleep out here on the sofa-bed.'

Outside the evening was raw. It was grey and the wind had a bite in it. The bare trees heaved and strained above the caravans.

'It's freezing,' Rima said, covering Baby with her shawl. 'Turn on the heater, na.'

Anand jumped up and fiddled with the gas fireplace. It came to life with an orange glow and the warmth embraced them immediately.

'Aah-ha, that's wonderful,' cried Rima and tickled Baby's chin. She squealed back in delight. Anand tickled her some more, and soon they were all laughing together.

They had met in a suburban college in Mumbai; fallen in love in the canteen over oil-sodden samosas and sweet milky tea. They had argued over college politics and held hands in cinema halls. They were inseparable, only to part for their respective lectures and to return to their homes.

They should never have met. Anand, in his machine-washed, designer-labelled t-shirts was a misfit in a college where most students had their clothes bashed on the bathroom floor by their mothers and hung to dry in the sun. He had not got the required percentage to make it to the college of his choice. Besides, he had been holidaying in Australia during the admission week.

Rima was told to go to a college within walking distance of her home. So she set off to the end of the road, umbrella held over her head to prevent her skin from darkening.

To everyone's surprise, they got married. Anand did not abandon her to marry someone of his own class.

When Rima went to live in his home, she felt embarrassed: about herself, her family. Anand's family lived in a plush two-storey flat on Worli Seaface. The walls facing the sea were made of glass. There was art on the walls that was more expensive than the tiny flat her parents lived in. Anand was shocked to have to share a toilet with five people whenever he visited her family. He would have to sleep in his in-laws' bedroom with Rima, while her parents slept out in the living room with her grandfather. Eventually he stopped going.

It was hard on Rima. All this lavishness kept reminding her that she didn't belong here. All this was meant for someone else. Someone whose father was a neurologist or a diplomat. Someone who was comfortable with Italian furniture that had to be covered in bed sheets most of the time to protect it from the Mumbai dust and damp. She no longer licked her fingers clean after a meal. Her fork and knife clattered clumsily on her fine china plate.

It dawned on them both that maybe it wasn't so right, after all. But they both were still in love and worked hard to adjust to each other.

Then Anand landed himself a job in the UK. His parents were not so keen on their only son leaving. They begged him to reconsider. After all, whatever they had was his. They cajoled Rima to convince him. Life was so hard there, why were they ruining their lives fully aware of the consequences?

But this was an excellent opportunity for them to escape from their differences, where they could be on equal terms. It made so much sense. And so here they were, on their first holiday, and Anand wanted everything to go right for them.

He was very happy to get such a cheap deal. A hundred pounds for four nights. Off-season rates, no doubt, but who needed the sun? An outing to any place away from home was enough. A caravan holiday. How romantic was that!

'Let's have some tea,' he suggested.

Baby tumbled out of his arms and crawled towards the TV. Rima switched on the kettle and rummaged for the tea in the food basket. They had two types of tea. Anand only drank Darjeeling, and only Oxfam Fairtrade Darjeeling, which was nearest to the tea he drank in India. Rima preferred the strong taste of PG Tips, with lots of milk and sugar.

She dug deep into the basket, but couldn't find the Darjeeling. Her PG Tips was there, but where was Anand's tea?

Oh no. Rima bit her lip when she realised what she had done. Just before they had left, Anand had wanted a cup of tea for the road. She'd made it, and then left the box on the kitchen counter. She turned round to look at Anand, who was playing with Baby. She didn't want to spoil this holiday.

'Anand,' she said. 'I've left your teabags at home.'

He stared at her. Rima looked close to tears.

'It's OK,' he sighed. 'I'll have coffee, no problem.'

'I didn't bring any.'

'Oh.'

Rima wrung her hands in despair. Baby looked at her and stuck out her lower lip.

Anand swept Baby into his arms and smiled. 'I'll have whatever you have then. Good old English tea in an English caravan. Yes, Baby?'

'Ba-by,' Baby lisped and squealed with laughter.

So they sat huddled by the fireplace, strong tea steaming in the cups and they watched Anne Robinson insult one contestant after another until there were none left.

The next morning, they woke up stiff and thirsty. All three had squeezed into the pull-out in the lounge. The bedroom had been freezing and by midnight Rima had crawled under the duvet beside Anand, with Baby between them. Rima was awake most of the night, afraid of Baby suffocating under the duvet. Anand, being closest to the fireplace was hot and parched all night. Yet, he smiled and reminded Rima that this was a caravan holiday, not a five-star resort, so this was how it would be and that they should enjoy it.

Rima nodded and busied herself with making breakfast. She looked into the caravan in front of theirs. There was a white family in there. The children were having breakfast. The mother was carefully applying mascara. Rima looked at her watch. 8.07am. The woman needed to wear make-up so early in the morning? She reminded her of her mother-in-law. Never a hair out of place. Nails always manicured and covered in transparent varnish. Her mother's nails were perpetually yellowed by turmeric. She studied her own nails: chewed down to the skin. Ugly. She would have to buy nail polish when she got back home.

She whisked two eggs and poured them into the hot frying pan. She made up Baby's fruit purée and baby rice mix.

'So, what shall we do today?' Anand rubbed his hands together and then attacked his omelette.

Rima looked out, it was still blustery. 'It's very cold outside,' she said.

The family next door trudged out in t-shirts and track pants. Pink on the girls. Blue on the boy. They were giggling and talking excitedly. The mother had red lipstick. The father had a big paunch and a can of beer in his hand. Rima looked at the watch again. 9.10am. She rolled her eyes. Baby spat her breakfast on Rima's dressing gown.

'Let's go to the Entertainment Area. There's a heated indoor pool.' Anand picked up the dishes and put them in the sink. 'I'll do the dishes. You get Baby ready.'

The indoor pool was crowded. Children ran around, screaming and jumping into the water. Every inch of space in the pool was occupied. Baby was frightened and she wailed loudly. It was too cold to take her to the playground so they wandered around the pool tables and slot machines.

Soon, it was time for Baby's nap, and they returned to the caravan. Anand watched TV with the volume down and Rima padded about, preparing lunch. The TV had been left on in the other caravan, so she watched the *Eastenders'* Omnibus through the window, while stirring the noodles.

They passed the night cramped up on the pull-out bed once more. But feeling uncomfortable in this claustrophobic caravan made Rima feel very guilty. Her parents' flat was just as cramped, and they didn't even have the facilities so neatly fitted into every crevice of this caravan. She had been comfortable in her parents' flat, but now she knew things would not be the same again.

The next morning, they decided to go for a walk along the promenade. They trundled along the path, following the signs to the sea. Baby bumped along happily in her pushchair. Rima struggled to keep her hair out of her eyes. Anand faced the wind bravely, pushing Baby against the rebellious wind. When they reached the promenade, they were disappointed. In front of them was a great, muddy flatland, the water murky in patches here and there. It was low tide and the sea had gone right out.

Anand sighed. 'Nothing compared to the Arabian Sea.'

Rima nodded. The sea outside Anand's parents' home in India was different. Sometimes wild and hitting the promenade with such force that the glass windows would be sprayed with the salty water. Sometimes gentle and lapping softly against the rocks. Families, lovers, hawkers, policemen would cover every inch of the promenade. Balloons straining on their strings. Corn cobs roasting on white hot coal. Roasted peanuts in paper cones. People running, walking, laughing, holding hands, a stolen kiss perhaps, a knowing whistle.

None of it was here though. This promenade was very clean and almost empty at this hour. Bins with liners were set up neatly at equal distances. Benches with a few old men sipping their beers. A dog-walker who paused to smile at Baby. A bitter wind that threatened to blow all of this away.

Rima fiddled with Baby's blanket. Anand looked at her, his eyes questioning, what now? She didn't reply. She hadn't worn tights under her jeans and she was regretting that.

'Let's have some tea in there,' said Anand, pointing to a tea-room. 'Maybe they'll have Darjeeling tea.'

Rima's eyes stung and she bent down to adjust Baby's straps.

They walked back to the caravan in silence. The tea-room had *Twinings*' Darjeeling, and that was not the real thing. So they had coffee instead, which was also not the real thing. When they reached their car, Rima wanted mineral water from the boot for Baby's formula. She moved Baby's pushchair out of the way in order to open the boot.

Suddenly a man came rushing out of the caravan near them. 'Watch out,' he shouted.

They froze. Immediately they thought Baby was in danger and Rima moved the pushchair closer to Anand.

'Hey, stop. You're scratching my car.'

Rima looked at the man. What was he talking about? He was towering over them now, stubbing his finger on some scratch marks below the fender.

'Look what you've done,' he said, his cold eyes boring into her. His thin lips were snarling, baring yellow teeth and foul breath.

She leaned back. 'What have I done?' she said.

Anand stepped in front of her. 'What's the problem?' he asked.

'I seen it from my window,' the man yelled, saliva spraying into the fraught air. 'She pushed the buggy too close to my car, and scratched it.'

Anand stared at him. 'What? The buggy scratched your car?'

The man nodded, examining the scarred car with his fingers.

A woman came out of his caravan, pushing a wheelchair. A child was in it. His head was twisted in an abnormal angle and his tongue lolled out. He wore thick glasses, but the eyes were unfocused. Rima flinched on seeing him.

'We seen you damaging our car,' the woman accused in a shrill voice.

'Yeah, you need to pay us compensation,' the man shouted.

The boy grunted and twitched his head. He looked about ten.

'Two hundred quid. That's the deposit on this rented car,' the woman cried, her hand absently patting the boy. 'They won't give it back once they seen the scratches.'

Anand bent down to examine the car. Yes, there were a couple of scratches, but surely the plastic handles of the pushchair couldn't do that.

'Listen, sir,' he said. 'I can see the scratches. But I can assure you it's not our pushchair that did it.' He aligned the pushchair against the car and pointed it out. 'See, it doesn't even reach where the marks are. You've made a mistake. Those scratches were already there.'

The man's face turned red and splotchy. He shook his head violently. 'We seen you do it. We're going to sue you. I've got your licence number.'

The woman swore under her breath and wheeled the boy up the ramp into the caravan. The man jotted down their licence number and marched away.

Anand placed his hand on Rima's elbow. She was shaking. He guided her and Baby back to their caravan.

'What sort of people come here on holiday?' she asked, her voice unsteady. 'Bullies.'

He patted her gently and opened the door. Rima burst into tears as soon as they were inside. 'Did you see their boy?'

'It's none of our business,' said Anand, and switched on the television.

'But Anand, he could have been ours. Then we'd have been so angry and frustrated.' She held Baby tightly to herself.

'Don't be so melodramatic,' Anand snapped. 'Forget about them. Bloody trouble-makers.'

'But they'll sue us. What are we going to do?'

Anand laughed. 'Sue us? Saying what? A bloody push-chair scratched their car? Give me a break. That bastard wanted to pass the blame on to us. Try and get the money off us. But it isn't going to work.'

Rima continued to sob and Baby struggled in her grip. She held out her plump arms to her father.

'Ba-ba,' she said.

Anand gathered her into his arms and sprawled on the sofa. 'Make some dinner, Rima. Let's make it an early night.'

'I want to go home,' cried Rima. 'I hate this caravan. I hate this holiday.'

Anand stared at her, his ears went red. 'You are so selfish,' he snapped at her. 'I tried my best to have a nice break. I didn't complain that you forgot to bring my tea. I do the dishes every night. I've saved up for this holiday with our own money, not my parents' money and you don't appreciate it.'

'Appreciate what?' Rima retorted. 'Two sleepless nights on this pull-out bed? Wandering around aimlessly in this freezing weather? Is this a holiday?'

Anand stood up, his face glowering. No words came from his lips but Rima knew everything he wanted to say. Where did she think she came from? Since when did she start complaining about indecent accommodation?

He stormed out of the caravan, leaving Rima to sob loudly and Baby staring at her mother in distress.

After a while, Rima recovered. She fed Baby and played quietly with her. She regretted being so awful to Anand. He had meant only goodness. It was she who had a complex. She, who always saw the negative side to things. She played absently with Baby's toys and watched her giggle and crawl on the carpet.

Baby got on to her feet and held on to the coffee table. She looked at Rima and smiled. Two tiny teeth cradled delicately in her pink gums. She giggled and took a tentative step towards her mother.

Rima held her breath and watched. 'Come here, Sweety,' she cried and beckoned Baby to her.

Baby curled up her toes and tottered a step forward. Then another step. Slowly she went down on the floor and clapped her hands.

Rima clapped and laughed out loud. 'Well done, Baby. Well done. Once more, come on.'

Encouraged by her mother, Baby tried again. One step. Then another, 'til she was in her mother's arms. Rima picked her up and danced around the room. She looked out of the window into the deepening twilight. She saw Anand sulking outside. She opened the door and called out to him.

'Anand, come here quick,' she yelled and waved.

He looked up, concerned, and saw her beaming at him. He ran towards them.

'Baby's first steps,' she laughed. 'Baby just took two steps, then five. Where's the camera?'

Anand dashed to get the camera from his back pack.

'Oh Baby, show Papa what you did. Come on, come on.'

Rima placed Baby on the carpet and they knelt down in front of her. Then, with a look of great concentration, Baby teetered towards her father. He clapped and laughed and took a picture of his daughter. Rima leaned on him from behind to look at the LCD screen. Baby was there, one foot in front of the other, tooth shining in the flashlight, walking towards them.

'Take another one,' Rima gushed. 'Take another one.'

'You go in front,' Anand instructed her. 'I'll take one with both of you.'

Rima posed with Baby, giggling and victorious, just like her daughter.

'Now you,' she cried, and grabbed the camera. 'You pose with her.'

Anand kneeled on the floor, bending to be in the frame. Baby walked confidently towards her mother.

When Rima clicked she captured two pearly white teeth, out of focus, but evidence enough that Baby had walked right into the camera.

SILVANA MAIMONE

Map of the Streets

The map of the streets of this city,

The tangles and illogical flow
Match the pattern of the veins that run through me
That course through my body and make my heart beat
That curse my mind and let history repeat

This city is ancient
And so am I
I know every twist in every alley
Though I left here when I was barely five
This journey made me a foreigner to myself
How did I expect not to be a foreigner to anyone else?

I grew up with the notion that home was a faraway
place
Never here,
Never where I was
But a long way away

It was always a place I yearned for
Always out of reach

Ours was not a story of persecution
Not in the literal sense
But one of non-acceptance
Of non-acceptance of self
Of a family's love and expectations
Strangling and suffocating
Through tender cruelty and comforting guilt

Home is where I can be myself
Home is where I can speak my mind
Home is where I can feel safe
It's not a physical place
But a state of mind

Where are you from?
Where am I from?

Is that home?

This is what I have learnt about home

Home is the uncertainty I feel
Home is the discomfort
Home is the disarray, the chaos
Home is the conflict
Home is the fight to find peace

Only to disrupt it once you have found it
Because you have never known a home full of peace

Home is a memory
A smell
A song

Home is a photo you can't find
Home is all your ghosts in one place

Home is imaginary conversations
Battles un-won
Forgiveness not given

Home is your past
Wrestling with your present
Which you don't want to repeat in your future
But like a well-worn slipper beside the bed
You step back into
For some sort of comfort.

Home is a place in your head
A place in your heart
A place in your liver
Where you drunkenly try to obliterate what has been
Only to create the scars that remain

Home is faded photographs
Ordinary moments frozen in time

Given heroic sentiments and significance
Stories retold whenever they are reviewed

Home is always living in me

Home is all I am

POPPY O'NEILL

Siamese

Siamese, they call us. But Siam is another name for Thailand, and we're from Batley. Drizzle-glistened row upon row of terraces: the jewel of Greater Leeds.

Danaerys and Anoushka, named for strong women off the telly. Mum and Dad gave us a name each, and loved us enough for three. We lived a long time at home, a long time in hospital – things get complicated for a heart that's being shared.

Mum and Dad shuffled off into grey and beige death last year, so now we live here: 49 Christopher Road – it's an end-of-terrace. The woman at the housing office told us we'd get a specially adapted house, one made just for us. We pictured two of everything, a right telly and a left telly, a right toaster and a left toaster. A handcrafted vanity at a right angle, two mirrors surrounded by light bulbs, reflecting each other infinitely; smaller and smaller until we vanished. Turns out, that's not what they meant.

We did get a special bed, so we'll give them that. It dips in the middle and the mattress has a memory, so it knows how we're shaped. And a bath with a door to it, so we sit naked and shivering on the moulded avocado seat while it fills up.

The house is one room downstairs with a settee and telly and what the housing officer calls a *Kitchenesque*. There's a large front window with a sort of frosted glass which lets the light in, but folk can only see into if they insert their credit card.

We're the lucky ones – most folk like us are only troubled on the inside, or otherwise their troubles come from not being able to do something. No one'll pay to watch a man not walk, not dress himself, not breathe by himself. Single mothers are popular though – only second to us on the Leaderboard each Sunday. Plus they're the only ones with a suggestion box next to their credit card slot.

Folk bang on the glass and shout muffled questions. *Can Danaerys move Anoushka's hand? Can they read each other's thoughts? Who's in control?* The answer is: both. Like a trickling between two pools of water, a dotted line on a map, it is both. Yes, I can make Anoushka move her hand, if I ask nicely. Yes, we can hear each other's thoughts, but only when we think clearly, in sentences. The thoughts which arrive at once – not a procession of words but the thud of an idea – these are mine alone.

Sometimes I wait at the window for the glass to unfrost. I smush my nose up against it, and Anoushka kind of cowers away, or tries to hide in our cardigan. She's embarrassed by me. It gives the gawpers a fright. At least they're only locals. In America they have what's called Live Streaming. That is, cameras in folks' homes. I don't know if you can even tell when you're being watched over there. I sometimes think we'd like that better, but there's some law against it here. Some law saying you've got to see who's gawping for them to legally gawp at you.

Today is a school day, so pustulated teens insert their junior credit cards and make lewd gestures at us through the glass. Usually I look away when they start competitively exposing themselves, but today I take a picture on my phone. The semi-nude one shouts something muffled at me and they all laugh. Anoushka plucks the antimacassar from the back of the settee and draws it over her face. I reach my hand over the border between us and poke her where the nerves lead to her brain. There is a plain of skin where we both feel, where the nerves are crocheted. It's a gross and ghostly feeling, and we avoid that part of ourselves.

I poke her again. 'They've gone.'

She remains under the doily. 'I can't bear it anymore, Dan.'

'So you'll stay under there all day? Come up for air this evening, then down periscope when the drunks come stumbling past at midnight?'

'Why not? We could stay in bed all day like owls, come out at night while there's no one to see us.'

'All the good telly's on during the day, Nush.' I turn towards the screen, flick through the channels. NOW: *I Used to be Fat.* NEXT: *Shame on You – Kids!!* 'See?'

Nush is not that into telly. She pulls the antimacassar from her face and starts reading *National Pornographic.* It's not what it sounds like – the title is a marketing thing. A man in a smart suit unfrosts the window, glances earnestly in, pats his jacket where his wallet must be, and moves on. I wish we could have a day off.

A woman on the telly has not only lost half her body weight, she has also learned to paint. She's painted all the things that weigh as much as the flesh she has shed. A sack of flour, a pile of books, a microwave oven, a young child. All on huge canvasses taller than the presenter. She's good. I nudge Anoushka and she cranes her neck to see.

'She's good,' I say.

Anoushka nods and returns to her magazine. There's a pair of women at the window. They're wearing hats of ruffled fabric and brooches on their lapels. I stare back at them. They are holding hands and I see a small squeeze happen between them. The woman on the right unclips her handbag and draws a note from within it – old-fashioned money. Now they're both looking around for something, they see it, whatever it is, and disappear to the left as the frost descends. The paper money floats through the slit-thin letterbox and meanders down to the welcome mat. I look back to the telly. The presenter is offering constructive feedback on the woman's paintings. I think she's about to cry. The window unfrosts – a dog and its owner. Paws up on the windowsill, tongue lolling.

An idea comes to me in a thud. I string the words out like washing on a line, so Anoushka can hear it. She looks up from the magazine and grins. 'Yes!' she says aloud.

The idea is simple. I ask for paint with the next commissary drop. After dark, I stand in front of the window and take a picture of the downstairs room. A flash illuminates it, throwing shadows up the walls. Anoushka keeps an eye on the window. We pull a white sheet from the airing cupboard.

When the paint arrives – acrylic, top quality, with brushes of assorted size and coarseness – Anoushka starts to paint our downstairs room onto the sheet, while I offer constructive feedback and gently touch my phone screen each time the picture starts to dim.

We do all this in our bedroom for an hour at a time. If we're upstairs for too long in the day the housing officer will get complaints from the gawpers. They'll want their money back.

Anoushka paints the corners and edges of the walls first, all pointing towards the centre of the sheet, as if they are sinking. She doesn't talk while she paints, and her forehead scrunches into a fist of concentration.

When it's finished I think we could dive into the sheet, it looks so real. Anoushka has painted us in the centre, beached and casual on the settee. Laid out flat on the bed it looks like we are at the bottom of a pit. I am eating crisps and looking at the telly. She is reading *National Pornographic.* We sleep under the sheet, stiff with colour and light. We wake before dawn and pin it across the window.

A week passes, and it is working: no knock at the door. We watch the Leaderboard announcement between the news and the weather. There we are – Danaerys and Anoushka: #1 most observed for their 40th consecutive week! The glamorous assistant in the mermaid-tail dress claps. Behind her closed lips she runs her tongue across her teeth and the camera zooms in to capture this movement. We stretch out, relaxed and happy on the settee.

I think: *How long have we got?*

But Anoushka doesn't answer.

DAVID JOHN GRIFFIN

Maude's Bungalow

My job is to help clear houses of the overwhelming mess created by hoarders.

'We have had complaints of rat infestation either side of the house in question,' my supervisor at the charity centre had told me.

And so I visited Maude Ethelworth's rambling bungalow a couple of days after.

The garden was no longer a garden – a junk yard, more like. There were rusting washing machines and fridges, even a bathtub and a toilet pan amongst the other discarded objects. I was barely able to reach the front door with all the waste and litter.

It took a while for the door to be opened. Finally, there was Maude in a dressing gown and slippers. She was an elderly woman with bright eyes and intelligence showing.

'Come in, dear,' she said and I followed her into the hall, the passageway made thinner by piles of newspapers and filled black bags either side. I counted six doors leading from the hallway, half of them inaccessible due to the rubbish in front of them.

'This way, follow me,' Maude said brightly and led me down the cluttered hall to the open door at the end.

Upon entering, I saw a wall of magazines and books, paraphernalia and children's toys. Any furniture there might have been was covered with more of the same. Maude led me down the channel littered with paper until we reached a large wingback chair with plenty of cushions, on a dusty rug. To the left of it was a television set, seemingly set into the wall of rubbish. To the right was a bench with a tray upon it, and on that a teapot, a cup and saucer and milk jug.

Maude plumped one of the cushions and sat. 'I got your letter,' she said and leant over to sort it from a pile of newspapers beside the chair.

'You don't need to find it, Mrs Ethelworth,' I told her. 'We just need to discuss the clearing of your house.'

'But, you see, I don't want it cleared,' she replied. 'This is my home. I'm quite happy the way it is.'

'There are reports of a rat infestation, and we believe it would be in your best interests to make your house tidy again. We can put you up in a lovely hostel while we clear it. As explained in the letter, it shouldn't take more than a couple of days.'

'I don't know; what about Tibby?'

'Is that a cat?'

Maude continued without answering, 'Mind you, I haven't seen her for months now; perhaps she's gone to meet Maurice.'

'Who's Maurice?' I asked.

'My husband, dear. Died and gone to heaven.'

'I'm sorry to hear that. How long ago was this?'

'A year or more. But don't be sorry – he vanished and is in the best place, isn't he. Maurice and me never saw eye to eye anyway; always arguing. He often used to complain of my nagging. Do I seem the sort to nag?'

'I'm sure you're not,' I said. 'As for Tibby, we'll keep a look out for her while we clear. I can make arrangements for the cat when you stay in the hostel. They have lovely accommodation and fine food there.'

'I get all the food I want,' Maude replied, showing the first sign of distress since visiting her.

I guessed the kitchen would be in a similar state to what I had already seen, perhaps worse.

'Do you cook for yourself? You must find it difficult.'

'Oh no, dear, I haven't seen the kitchen for quite a while. It's been buried,' and she waved a thin hand over the wall of newspapers, magazines and books. 'I have my food delivered. A neighbour brings me food twice a day, and a pot of tea, just as I like it.'

I didn't recall any of Maude's neighbours mentioning that. 'Which neighbour, can you tell me?'

'I don't know. There's always a knock on the door, three times, then when I go to answer, there's a tray with food left on the side. Very grateful, I am.'

'And where do you sleep?'

'In one of the bedrooms, silly! I've made enough room.'

'There'll be all the room you could ever want once we've cleared for you,' I said encouragingly.

Maude Ethelworth wasn't convinced. It must have taken me another hour or more to persuade her to move out for a few days' stay in the hostel. But finally she agreed and a day after she left her bungalow, we started clearing.

Five full-size skips had been ordered and stood in line on the road outside the bungalow. And three helpers and myself began the hard work of clearing the garden first, at least up to the front door. Then while I cleared the hallway, the others continued outside before joining me to clear one of the bedrooms and then what used to be a dining room.

It took a day and a half for that; only then did we start work in the living room where Maude used to sit. I made sure her chair was kept safe for when it was to be returned to a tidy room. And finding a nice antique sideboard and table on the left-hand side of the room after moving the piles there, they were moved to one of the emptied rooms temporarily.

All four of us started on the huge wall of newspapers, books and toys. After one half had been taken to the skip, the television set and some of the books put aside, I saw an open door leading to the kitchen, which didn't look too bad a state after all.

It was after clearing the other half of the rubbish wall when we were taken aback: there was a man behind, sitting in an identical wingback chair to the one Maude sat in. He was elderly with silver hair but also bright-eyed, like Maude. He brought a glass of whisky to his lips to drink.

'Who are you, may I ask?' I said.

The old man sipped his whisky and wiped his mouth with the back of a hand. 'I'm Maurice,' he replied, then added, 'Can I have my wall back, please?'

MANDY BERRIMAN

How Wonderful You Are

You're angry with me. You stride up our road, your jaw set, eyes hard, fury radiating from the tempo and rhythm of your gait. Marching up Blueberry Lane, it pushes you to a pace that belies your age. A brown bird hops along the bushes, searching out the last of the berries but you scare it away before I can identify it. A female blackbird? A thrush? We don't see sparrows anymore. The blueberries make meagre pickings for now but in another month the brambles will turn dark and juicy. Will you harvest them this year?

It's a steep climb up the lane and you stop when you reach the stile to catch your breath and sweep your gaze across the valley. You're still not talking to me but I don't need you to; I can read your face. You are itemising the hills, South Head, Combs Moss, Eccles Pike, noting the loss of the old, iconic chimney, and how much of the green has been claimed by housing and industry and bigger, faster roads and railways. We fought every single incursion. Won a few; lost many.

You push on and up towards the shadow of Cracken Edge. There's the old quarry pulley. It looks the same as it did the first time we discovered it, decades ago: rusted and broken but still standing proud as a reminder of a past workforce. Do you remember? You don't even glance at it; not in a remembering mood. You stride on, reckless along the short, foot-wide section as if daring the hill to throw you off and then, safe on the other side, you push on faster still below the old quarry, over another stile and on and up and up, grabbing fistfuls of grass to pull yourself the last few metres and hopping over the narrow chasm that separates the hillside from the rock that juts out over the valley. You step right to the edge and I'm with you, embracing the precarious sensation of seeming to stand in mid-air above nothing. Cars, small and shiny like beetles, fly along the Hayfield road beneath us and a plane circles overhead on its descent to Manchester but you're looking to the hills again, past South Head towards the distinctive rock formations marking out the ascent to Kinder Scout. I try to read your face again but the emotions flit by too fast, too much. You are struggling and I want to hold you and tell you that you will be fine, that you will survive this, but I can't breach the barrier that has been built between us.

I don't know how long it is we stand there, you not speaking, me prodding at the silence. Finally, another plane circles and you say, *They're so quiet these days. I miss the old sound.* And then you breathe out a whisper, *Is this what you **really** want?*

Yes, I say. *Yes, it is.*

You wait until autumn has erupted in a riot of burnished reds and browns and golds and ochres. Then one morning, a crisp morning of blue skies and vapour trails, breath puffing from your mouth, you tell me you're ready. The flight and the hire-car are booked, suitcase located and cabin baggage allowance checked, and re-checked. *Just one more thing,* you say. You disappear indoors reappearing some time later with flushed cheeks and my old travel diary in your hand. *Must take this.*

Lifting off from Manchester on the last day of November, low cloud obscures any chance to wave goodbye to the hills. I see your shoulders slump a little, doubts creeping in, but soon we're flying high above a cotton wool carpet in dazzling sunshine, and while everyone around you settles down to films and games, you get busy with plans. You leaf through my diary, dreaming possible routes to cover the highlights of both islands. You use your Inflight Multimedia Console to calculate journey times, check if the old attractions are still there, research suitable hostels and guesthouses, but you book nothing except the first three nights in Akaroa, leaving the rest to chance, as we always did. I like that.

All the planning tires you out and when dinner has been cleared away, you sleep. For all the technological advances of the last few decades, it still takes a whole day and a night to fly to the other side of the world.

The plane touches down in Christchurch at dawn of the second day of New Zealand's summer. It's still the first day of winter at home. Predictably, Customs confiscate your walking boots for cleaning and you sit in the waiting area in your socks and I know you are remembering the first time: waiting hours while Grand Canyon sand was cleaned from inside and outside our tent.

Christchurch was our favourite New Zealand city but that was before the devastating earthquake of 2011. Decades of rebuilding and reinventing have passed since. There's a yearning in both of us to just go and see. Get it over with. But it feels too sad so you skirt around the city and point towards the Bank's Peninsula.

It's two hours to Akaroa, including a breakfast stop at a roadside café. I remember it being a winding, unpopulated road but Christchurch has spread, swallowing up outlying towns and villages. There's hardly any countryside left. But then to my relief, and yours I think, that first breathtaking view of Akaroa harbour from high up on the brow of the hill is unchanged and when we reach the town a little later, it is still pretty, still quaint, still Akaroa.

Three days pass in a blur of body clock and spiritual re-adjustment. The temptation is to stay longer but this journey has a purpose and it tugs you on. You drive in high spirits back past Christchurch and then down through Ashburton and Geraldine to the turquoise Lake Tekapo and out to New Zealand's highest mountain: named after Captain Cook by the Europeans but we always preferred its Maori name, Aoraki, 'Cloud Piercer'. Two nights' stay is enough to revisit the walk to Hooker Lake and sit, revelling in the tiny-ness of being human beneath the shadow of a giant and then it's southwards to Queenstown. You reminisce all the way about the cable car and the Luge and the Maori legend of Lake Wakatipu. You talk about driving out to Glenorchy to meander down the Rees-Dart Valley in an inflatable canoe on crystal clear water, flanked by steep mountains, and it's the most you have talked to me for months. I start to hope that I might be forgiven.

Queenstown disappoints; it has turned into a soulless Las Vegas. Worse greets you in Glenorchy: once a hidden secret at the end of a road to nowhere, now it seems to be the Tolkien Capital of the World.

You understand, you love Tolkien, but this was a place you didn't want to share with the tourists and I don't have to ask to know it's been ruined for you. The anger is back. You snap, *You shouldn't have asked me to do this. I can't do it. I'm too old and it's too much and nothing is the same.*

I whisper back, *You **can** do it. You **can**.*

You shake your head.

You leave in the dark and drive through the night. I ask you where you are going but you have stopped talking to me again. You drive for several hours and I lose track of where we're headed. Sometime in the middle of the night, you pull up in a lay-by next to a dark expanse of meadow and you get out of the car without a word, leaving the door wide open, and disappear. Silence and darkness wrap themselves around me and I wait. Five minutes? Ten? And then I hear you and the sound you make rips through me. I cannot go to you, I cannot make it better and I feel my heart shatter and shatter again. I shouldn't have made you do this.

Time passes. Sunlight peeps over the hills and I recognise where we are. Acres upon acres of lupins carpet the meadow, white in the pale light of dawn, but as the light strengthens, pastel shades of pink and purple mingle with the white. It is so beautiful and I am pierced with a longing to run through it, smelling the scent, feeling the petals brush my fingertips. Every inch of me hurts.

You return. Have you sat out there all night? You don't tell me. You start the car and drive back the way you came and I think you have decided to give up and return to Christchurch. Find a flight to Auckland. Fly home. But as we reach the fork in the road before

Cromwell, you don't head east, you take the road to the west, towards Wanaka and the Haast pass and, although you still won't talk, I allow a flicker of hope to catch light.

The weather is foul on the other side of the pass: a typical West Coast deluge. So when you spot a girl standing by the side of the road, thumb held out, bobbed dark hair plastered to her face, you stop. Of course you stop. You ask her where she's going and she tells you that she's making her way back to Auckland. You tell her you can take her as far as the glaciers and you nod to the backseat but she tells you she gets travel sick in the back. You hesitate, then I am relegated to the back and she climbs in the front. Her name is TK. You ask what that stands for and she laughs and tells you that it stands for nothing. That's it; just a T and a K. I have been relegated to the backseat for a pair of initials.

TK talks a lot, as non-stop as the heavy rain that accompanies us all the way to Fox Glacier. She tells you that she's never seen a glacier up close before. You tell her about the time we were almost stranded at the terminal face and had to wade a river, five-abreast, water up to our waists, to reach safety. She laughs and you, emboldened, tell her about the other time when we made it up on top of Franz Josef Glacier: the crevasses and seracs, the natural sculptures, the creaking and cracking of an ever-changing, ever-moving ice monster. I don't want you to tell her this; these are our memories.

You don't leave TK at the glaciers. You invite her to travel further north. You allow her to share every experience; she encourages more memories. Our memories. Sunrise at Lake Matheson to the backing track of a Tui's mechanical song, the blowholes at Punakaiki, the seal colony at Westport, a calm, evening crossing over the Cook Strait, a cable car ride in Wellington. You let her in; you shut me out.

In Wellington, you tell her that you plan to travel to the central volcanoes next, Tongariro, Ruapehu and Ngauruhoe, then on to Lake Taupo and Rotorua. She asks if you've ever been to Mount Taranaki in the west; it's her favourite. You haven't, so you go. Just like that. I shout at you, *That's not what this is about! We don't have any memories there!* But you refuse to hear me. When we reach New Plymouth, I refuse to look. I refuse to search out the volcano on the skyline. I refuse to be stunned by the beaches or invigorated by the vibrant city. I don't want to see somewhere new. I don't want to create new memories.

TK takes you on walks near the volcano, and on evening strolls along the beach. She takes you to museums and cafés and galleries and pubs. I do not come. I don't know what you talk about but I sense your growing closeness every time you return. When she flashes her eyes at you, you smile and blush. Am I losing you?

Then TK leaves. Says it's time to travel by herself again. Says she needs to find some bar work in Auckland for a while. She leaves you with a kiss on the cheek, an email address and a broken heart.

You stop going out, spending much of the day lying in bed, staring glassy-eyed at the wall, steadily emptying the mini-bar of its drinks and snacks, every action on auto-pilot. I preferred it when you were angry. I preferred it when you were sad. I preferred it when you were stoking my jealousy with a girl young enough to be your grandchild.

On the eighth day, you're listlessly flicking channels on the TV. You freeze. Sit up. Skip back two channels. The song croons from the speakers: that rich, deep voice filling the room. Your mouth parts a little, your eyes glisten and I'm right there with you in that sunlit room so long ago, dancing the first dance, feeling loving eyes all around and the promise of forever swelling between us.

You drive north and east without a break until you reach Thames: the gateway to the Coromandel. You stop to phone ahead and check it's still ok. A short nap clears your head. Then it's on and up the peninsula on coast-hugging roads, the sun sinking over the gulf, anticipation replacing fear and sadness.

The sky is velvety-black, speckled with stars, when you pull into the farm. A key has been left for you and you bump down the track to the caravan, let yourself in, set your alarm and then collapse on the bed, fully clothed, and sleep.

It is still dark when your alarm sings. You walk slowly up the track to the summit. Stiff, fragile, like the old man you are. You reach the top as the first hint of pink colours the Pacific and you sit and you remember that other sunrise in this same place so many years before and I know you are almost ready. I am ready too.

Then, as the sky catches fire, you speak. You speak of you and me, our family, our home, our life: the hopes and dreams we realised; the ones we allowed to slip away. *And that's the point*, you say, *we **allowed** them to slip away. We were happy in the place we built our lives. We could have come back here many times and each opportunity we had, we chose not to.* And you speak about the flight home and how afraid you are that if you leave a little bit of me here, you'll return home and discover you've left a little bit of you too.

The sun is blazing in the sky now and, at last, I understand how unfair I've been. You always were the wisest and the most patient. Always waiting for me to catch up. Never rushing me. Allowing me the time I needed to realise what was right.

I've caught up now, my love. I know what I want and I know where I belong: we are one tree.

Don't scatter me here. Take me up to the rock that juts out over the valley. Let me be carried by the four winds over Cracken Edge, South Head, Combs Moss and Eccles Pike.

Take me home.

LORRAINE WILSON

Echoes in Stone

Will you still remember me, if I leave? Will you remember the sound of my footfalls in loose sandals, the way my shadow danced between the trees? I have left my fingerprints trailed on walls and shaded windows, mapping out the pavements that I've wandered, but will you remember my laughter? The way it fitted in between the gazes of our grandfathers, rising up into your sky beside the birds?

You are the maps within my dreams, you are sun-heated stones, sharp edged shadows dense with childhood; warm-ripe fruit and precious water. My brother kicking footballs on white-painted trees, and days of indolence and freedom. You are the pulse at my throat, in the night. I have grown to fit the colours of your light and you have known me so well.

But we are changing, you and I. There are shadows in my heart and ghosts in all your doorways, we breathe deeply in your dust and darkened air, and we must contemplate our endings, you and I. Or our parting. Your skyline no more sings to me of star-light but heaves with hell and every ending, so do I flee your daily shatterings, your famine?

But will you still remember me, if I leave? If I walk no more past your bared bones weak with fury. I have gazed upon you fallen, your foreign landscapes dense with dying. I have felt your stones strain skyward to shield us, felt your fractured arms trying to console us as stone by broken stone, you have loved us. When I wiped the dust-trails of your tears from our lost children, I saw you. You have loved us so well.

But will you forgive me, if I leave? If I leave the ghosts of kisses upon your lintels, the last of my childhood on your floors. If I summon all the courage of my forefathers to journey to the sea, let lies and the tide guide me far from these shores. If I trail my dirty fingers in the salt-graves of our brothers and our sisters, will you forgive me?

You are the air in my lungs and the beating of my heart. You are all of my memory and how can I leave when you are dying? But will you forgive me, if I find myself in sordid kingdoms of cold earth and charity, if I take the pride of your ages and fold it beneath my hunger as I clamour at their walls? Or will you forgive me if the waves set their claws into my skin? If all the solace in your stones and all the hopes of my heart come to shadows on the sea. If I fall into the darkness and nothing of me reaches those far beaches but my despair?

Will that be the price of my leaving? Exchanging this death for the sea.

And if that is so, please, will you remember me then? Will my footsteps whisper down your alleyways once more? Will your sunlight search again for my smile? Will you hold me in your vast embrace and lay your dusty kisses on my skin?

Please. Let me be your tears, and your walls; let me cradle our sleeping children when the sky falls. Let me be echoes, in your stone. Let me come home.

CAROLINE HARDMAN

Straw Houses

Let's get one thing straight. I didn't *want* to build a house out of straw. I'm not a complete idiot. But they do say beggars can't be choosers, and after Mum kicked us out I definitely didn't have much choice. That's right, kicked out by our own mother. All three of us — William, Charlie and me — at exactly the same time, which seemed a bit harsh if you ask me. My brothers are both older than me and they already had jobs, earned decent livings. I was only sixteen. Still at school, although I wouldn't last there much longer. But Mum had met a new bloke — she's still with him, last I heard — and he'd never wanted kids, grown up or otherwise. So that was it. She'd been a single mum for half her life by then so you can hardly blame her for wanting more, I suppose. Doesn't everyone?

My brothers and I are… well, let's just say we don't see eye to eye very often. So there was never any question of the three of us living together. We all went our separate ways pretty much as soon as Mum sent us packing.

So there I was. Sixteen, homeless, and all alone in the world. And you work with what you've got, don't you? It would have been nice to have been able to build my dream home, brick by brick, but the reality was that straw, while not the most structurally sound building material, was readily available. Plus it was dirt cheap. And I do mean dirt. The stuff was filthy when I bought it, which is part of the reason I got it at such a good price, but after I'd hauled it down to the local stream, rinsed it out and laid it out to dry for a couple of days it was as good as new. Shone like gold, even.

And so I built a house. It wasn't much, but it was mine, you know? I'll admit, building it at the edge of a field of cows wasn't the smartest move I've ever made. They chewed away at sections, but I made repairs, and we rubbed along together in the end. And then I met Shelly, and she moved in with me. Perhaps a woman's touch was what the place needed, or maybe it's just what happens when you fall in love. Because all of a sudden that house – made of second-hand straw and regularly masticated by cows - became a home. We lived there for two years, or thereabouts. Happily ever after, some might even have called it. But then it happened.

I'd known Wolf since school – we'd been part of the same crowd, but I wouldn't have called him a close friend. When I first met Shelly, she told me that she knew him too. They'd been an item for a while but it had been months before we met, and was nothing serious – just a fling, she said – so I was as surprised as anyone when he turned up on our doorstep.

'Don't let him in,' said Shelly, and I should have known then that there was more to Wolf than met the eye.

I kept him outside, because of what Shelly had said, and we stood on the doorstep for a while. I listened as he huffed and puffed about how I'd stolen his woman and how she'd broken his heart, and how he'd get his revenge on the both of us someday. And then he left.

Shelly was pretty rattled by the whole thing. I promised her, swore by every hair on my own chin, that she had nothing to worry about. That I'd keep her safe. But it wasn't enough. She packed a bag and took off to her mum's the next day. I haven't seen her since.

So I was all alone when, at about midnight, I woke up to the smell of smoke and the crackling of dry straw. I ran out to the cow field, where I watched my house – our home – go up in flames. In hindsight I really wish I'd built it a bit nearer that stream.

I wasn't sure what to do after that. I sofa surfed for a while, staying with various friends, and friends of friends, but I didn't like to impose on anyone for too long. I tried a few nights on the streets, but that was pretty grim. People don't think much of you when you're on the streets, and I was kicked, spat on, and a whole lot worse. I spent a few nights on the buses, tried sleeping at the airport – anywhere I could get a bit of kip for a few hours. I did manage to hold onto my job for a while, but eventually that went too, and that was when I did what I swore I'd never do. I called my brother Charlie.

He's a bit of a hippy, is Charlie. Owns a business supplying organic mushrooms to local restaurants. He grows them in big tubs, full of old recycled coffee grounds. After Mum-gate, him and his partner (not his wife – they reckon they're far too 'unconventional' for marriage) built what they call an eco-house – all made from natural timbers. They were planning to build a tree house, apparently, but they had to chop all of the trees down to get enough wood. So it's a ground-floor treehouse. If you ask me, wood is no better a building material than straw, but slap the words 'eco' and 'environmentally friendly' in front of anything, and some people will be fooled. My hippy-dippy brother is one of them.

Anyway, after what was possibly the most awkward conversation of my life, he said I could stay with him for a while, and I turned up on his doorstep the same day. I only planned to stay for a month or so, just until I was back on my feet, but then one month turned into two, and two turned into two and a half.

Charlie casually asked me one evening if I'd tried calling our older brother. William lives in a fancy red-brick house in the city and I knew that I was the last person he, or his perfect wife, or their perfect kids, would want around. Charlie knew it too, but I got the hint. After all, that's the problem with being a house guest. You can never shake the suspicion that your hosts don't really want you there.

So I started going to the local bar at night, just to get out of their way. And one night, I saw Wolf there, sitting in the corner. Now the thing is, I can't say for sure that he was the one who set my place on fire. It could have been just a coincidence, the fact that he'd been on my doorstep making threats, just hours before that same doorstep, and the house it was attached to, went up in flames.

But I had a few drinks in me, so I went up to him. Let's call what happened next a conversation. I can't remember exactly what was said, but I think I might have let slip that I was staying with my brother, and even might have mentioned the whole mushroom business.

A few days later my brother received an official notice that his house was being condemned. Full of termites, allegedly. Not safe for anyone to live in. Again, I can't say for sure that Wolf was responsible. But it does seem like quite a coincidence.

And so that's how I ended up here. It wasn't easy to come in – I must have walked past half a dozen times first. I never thought I'd be the kind of person who asks for a hand-out. It's not the way I was brought up, you know? But I think it's time I found my own place. Got a good, solid roof over my head. Housing benefits would help with that, I guess.

I won't need them forever, just so you know. There was a bloke in the pub that night who overheard my 'conversation' with Wolf. He asked me all kinds of questions about the house I built –wanted to know about my weaving techniques, how I made the straw waterproof, that sort of thing. Turns out he's a builder. And after we chatted for a while, he offered me a job. Surprising the number of people who, after building their dream house, brick by brick, will pay good money to top it off with a thatched roof. I'm not complaining, after all a job's a job, and it sounds like it's going to pay pretty well. But building your house – even part of it – from straw? Well, it seems to me, you'd have to be a real idiot to do that.

GISELLE DELSOL

Day 89

Day 89

Drips coming through the blue tarp plunged into the metal bowl, their small pings barely audible over the incessant Calais rain. Tarek huddled, blowing warmth onto his hands. A visit to the food tent was in order to get some breakfast, but he was wary of leaving Amira alone, especially when she was sleeping.

As if feeling his thoughts, his wife whimpered and rolled to her side, a small, red coat clutched to her chest. Had it really been three months since its hood had covered their baby's face, framing his perfect, tiny curls? Amira rarely mentioned Ali, but she never let go of his coat, holding it tighter than a starving dog a bone. Of course they would see their baby again. They'd left him in a safe town, far from the bombs. They'd establish a home in Europe, and his cousin would bring him. All was planned.

Amira cried out and he leaned forward to stroke her cheek before stopping in mid-gesture, head tilted. The familiar early-morning sounds were replaced by shouts. He stood and pushed aside the tarp, narrowly avoiding a red-faced man who grabbed his arm, shaking it violently as he pointed towards the horizon. Yellow bulldozers had loomed there for days, a constant threat of destruction, but court orders and activists had kept them still.

Not anymore.

They growled forward, breaking and crushing everything in their path. A ragged parade followed close behind, jubilant locals holding up signs and crosses, cheering as the machines reclaimed the formerly-unused swathe of land. LEAVE! a sign announced. BUSINESS FIRST, screamed another, held up by a middle-aged woman whose diamond earrings, big enough to glint in the rain, probably cost more than he'd earn in a life-time.

Fighting back bile, he returned to the shelter and shook Amira awake.

'It's happening.'

'Then we must leave,' she answered, sitting up with a groan.

'Are you all right?'

'I'll be fine,' she said, accepting his outstretched arm to stand. Repetition led to precision, and she quickly folded their only blanket and stuffed their basic possessions in a small plastic bag. Outside they stood, together, as other shelters emptied around them, the rumble of machines mixing with screams.

'Come.' He made to move but Amira stayed put as a bulldozer arrived, ignoring the driver's angry gestures, her feet firmly planted, beseeching him with an extended arm. More gestures, more yells, and the driver shrugged at her, insinuating that he had no choice. The machine moved closer, its blade attacking their shelter. A small, red sleeve peeked out from the blue tarp. Tarek groaned. Ali's coat had fallen out of her bag.

'No!' Amira lunged towards the blade.

She was going to get herself killed! Tarek wrenched her backwards as the driver accelerated. The red fabric disappeared, buried in muddy ruts.

With a skewering look at the driver, Tarek placed his arms around his wife's heaving shoulders and followed the flow of distraught refugees towards the administrative tent. Form-filling civil servants tried to understand through the tears and shouts, urging those in the line to remain calm. They'd find a solution, their mouths said, eyes disagreeing.

Tarek and Amira reached a civil servant and started yet another interrogation, trying to ignore the woman's pursed lips as she looked at Amira's muddy pants. Pearls to swine, Tarek read on her face. Those nice pants we gave you yesterday, already ruined. He pulled Amira closer and gasped as her fingers tore into his upper arm. She collapsed without sound, her face whiter than frosted snow.

The civil servant stood, mouth open to protest. Instead she called for help and, when the paramedics arrived, turned to the next person in line.

Day 90

The hallway's fluorescent lights flicked and hummed as Tarek waited, the blanket clutched to his chest. They'd managed to save anything they could easily carry, but gone were the small luxuries they'd acquired over the past month. Gone was the thin mattress, gone was the wooden crate, gone was the small prayer rug and gone was the blue tarp that had covered their heads.

Just objects, he thought, we've already lived without.

Doctors and nurses bustled back and forth, their focus on paper files or telephone screens, seemingly oblivious to the people waiting with him, a group of haggard faces parked in blue chairs. His body called for sleep but he didn't dare close his eyes lest he miss a doctor's summons.

The hour hand on the wall-mounted clock turned five times before a doctor called out a rough approximation of his name. An infection, he understood from the surgeon's limited English. She could have died. Nurses guided him to the room where she was sleeping, peacefully, her face its normal colour. As she rested, a young nurse came in first with a cot, then with a bag she placed on the bed. Gesturing towards him, she pulled out a towel, a small bar of soap, a razor, a clean shirt and sweater. He bowed in thanks and, after a gentle kiss to Amira's forehead, followed the nurse's directions to the bathroom.

His reflection in the mirror was gaunt, his wrinkles deep, his hair thin. He shaved, as well as he could with his flimsy razor and long beard, stepped into the clean shower stall, turned on the hot water and stood, head bowed, as it pummelled his head, his shoulders, his back. After a great sigh he unwrapped the miniature bar of soap. Soft lavender rose in the air, transporting him to his grandmother's house, where small bags of the dried flowers had nestled between the clean sheets of her linen closet. Where did those little bags end up? he wondered, rubbing his skin until it turned bright pink. Someone in the family must have them. As his mind wandered, memories crushed his soul, bringing pain so strong it threatened to kill him there and then and he cried out, pounding his fist into the tiles until the pain in his hand overcame that in his chest.

Why! Why them? Why his family? What would they become?

No, he had to stop thinking. Magic soap was what he needed: magic soap to wash away the memories. He increased the hot water and lathered his hair, again and again, imagining clouds of darkness leaving his mind, memory-suds sliding down his body and into the drain.

As he dried off he felt lighter and returned to Amira, who welcomed his newly-shaved face with a wan smile and a kiss. She mimed scissors to a nurse and trimmed his hair, pinching her lips at the dark curls falling on the bed.

'I have something for you,' said an orderly who brought Amira's dinner tray. After glancing into the hallway, the orderly removed the plastic bell from a plate heaped to overflowing. She pulled an additional set of cutlery from her pocket, handed it to Tarek and left, pulling the door tightly shut.

Clean, dry and fed, he lay on the cot and held Amira's hand until she fell asleep, wondering how long it would be until daily warmth re-entered their lives.

Day 91

They had to leave before lunch, the night-nurse explained as she put down the breakfast tray and a plastic tub filled with Amira's prescribed medicine. She spoke quickly (information about the treatment, he assumed), writing the dosage on each box, and took her leave with an apologetic smile.

An orderly they hadn't yet seen came in for the breakfast tray and presented them with the contents of a battered gym bag: sweaters for each, bread and jam from the cafeteria, water, toiletries, and a backpack. The clothes they'd arrived in smelled of laundry detergent. How had they organized that? Tarek wondered. How many refugees had they helped? How many spare backpacks did they have?

When they were alone, he helped Amira dress. She was slow and stiff, but able to stand. They left the room and walked down the hallway, timidly returning the smiles and nods from some of the staff, ignoring those looking through them.

A dark-haired man left the hospital as they did.

'Is there a bus to the camp?' Tarek asked him.

'It far,' the man answered, pointing to the horizon with a shake of his head. 'No bus.'

'Then we will walk.' Tarek shrugged and picked up their bags.

'No.' The man squeezed Tarek's shoulder. 'Come, I drive. Follow me.'

Tarek followed, happy to have picked a winning number in this round of human lottery. Overall, he'd drawn enough winning numbers to have made it all the way to Calais. Not that the men with boats could be called winning numbers. Safe passage, they'd promised. They obviously didn't have the same concept of safety as he did, throwing sixty passengers into a dinghy with life-jackets so thin he doubted they'd float empty.

The man didn't attempt any small talk as he dropped them off at what remained of the camp; his eyes welling as Tarek thanked him said it all.

'We can do this,' Tarek said, when the dark-haired man drove off.

Amira nodded and followed him into the camp's administrative tent.

Yesterday's civil servant glanced at them, then did a double take. 'You're the lady who fell, yes?'

Amira nodded and the civil servant shook her head. 'Right. A shelter has room for two. Bus 5, parking lot B.' She jotted the information onto a piece of paper, had them sign a few forms, and pointed out the parking lot before tapping the face of her watch.

The driver, finishing a cigarette outside his bus, tossed their bags into the luggage compartment and waved them into the vehicle. They were still putting on their seatbelts when the bus lurched out of the parking lot and onto the road. Tarek wrapped his arms around Amira as she stared out of the window. Outside, what remained of the camp was replaced by an industrial zone, the bumpy road evolved into a highway. Night fell and the bus grew quiet. Tarek reminded Amira to take her medicine, pulled her close, and allowed himself to fall asleep after hearing her faint snores.

Day 92

'Everybody out!' The bus driver walked down the central aisle, tapping seatbacks.

Tarek stretched his arms upwards and moved his head in circles to work out the kinks, noting a landscaped park on one side of the bus and a three-storey stone building on the other. Amira's eyes were struggling to open and he helped her with a kiss. 'We're here,' he whispered. Wherever 'here' was.

The fifty-odd passengers filed out of the bus and collected their bags from the hold. Their driver was on the front steps of the building, talking with a woman who toyed with the lower edge of a blue, white and red sash. She nodded as he spoke, but her gaze was on the huddled refugees. As soon as he finished speaking she came over with the brisk walk of a woman already expected somewhere else, a young assistant trailing slightly behind.

'Welcome to Blancville,' she said, grabbing Amira's hand to pump it up and down, her smile too wide, her grip too tight. 'We are pleased to... euh... accommodate you in our town. My assistant will be by shortly.' The woman turned, shook Tarek's hand with the same ferocity, then saluted the rest of the crowd with a raised hand before disappearing back into the building.

'Shortly,' was four hours later, long after the bus had left.

'Sorry, busy day...' the mayor's assistant apologised as he waited for the refugees to gather. 'I will bring you to the gymnasium, and tomorrow we try to find you homes, OK?'

Homes? Tarek and Amira exchanged a frown. For a night? For two? For months they'd been leaves whipped about by autumn storms, never knowing where they'd settle, nor for how long.

The gym was warm, and Amira rested on one of the aligned army cots, rising only when the woman with the sash arrived with a television crew. The woman, the mayor, it would seem, made a show of ushering in two stocky women carrying a huge tureen of soup, then seized a ladle and filled and distributed bowls, talking and smiling into the camera. When the film crew moved off to interview a refugee, the mayor dropped the ladle and ran after them.

Tarek shook his head. Yet another politician using their story to appear on television. Well, at least they had shelter for the night.

Day 93

Severe stomach spasms woke him in the early morning. Not the well-known hunger pangs (last night's lentil soup had been the best he'd had in months), but the other pain which jumped to his chest and seized his heart. Breathe slowly and deeply, Amira always said when his eyes squeezed shut.

Breathe in. The claws tore into his sides. Breathe out. Breathe in. His chest managed to pull in more air. Breathe out. The spasms lessened, and stopped. He gazed at the wooden ceiling and shook his head. Barely awake and already exhausted. At least Amira hadn't seen him. He put on his happy face and left his cot for a quick shower, the second in three days. Luxury.

'So, it is time to meet your hosts,' the mayor's assistant announced after they'd all eaten breakfast, folded blankets and stacked the cots. 'Please do not leave anything in the gymnasium.'

As if they could afford to leave anything, Tarek thought as he filed into the bus behind the others, barely noticing as it wound its way along narrow country roads.

'The house on the left, with the green door,' the assistant called out, waving to Tarek as the bus pulled to a stop. 'You are staying with Madame Vaillant. Just knock, she is expecting you.'

Amil, who'd beaten Tarek at cards more often that Tarek would admit, looked stunned as the assistant ushered them off the bus. *You'll be all right*, he mouthed through the window as the door shut with a hydraulic hiss. Tarek forced a smile and tapped his heart with his right hand before raising it to salute familiar faces as the bus pulled away. When it drove out of sight, he and Amira turned towards the house.

The front garden had a rusty swing-set and roses trimmed for winter. Low-lying bushes lined the brick path leading to the door, which opened before they reached it.

'Madame Vaillant?'

The frail woman's broad smile and open arms pulled them inside, where she invited them to remove their shoes by pointing out a row of slippers. The furniture in the living room must have been stylish when purchased, Tarek imagined, taking in the doily-covered furniture and small figurines. Framed pictures lined the mantelpiece: a much younger Madame Vaillant playing with a curly-haired boy.

Madame Vaillant was asking them something but Tarek couldn't understand her chirping French. He simply shrugged with an apologetic grin, and she laughed, her stream of chatter barely diminishing as she showed them around the house, ending the tour in a large bedroom decorated with yellowing posters of soccer players he didn't recognize. A faded picture of the same curly-haired boy decorated the dresser. She opened a drawer and pointed towards their bags.

Tarek's heart shuddered as lavender tickled his nose. Sure enough, two small lavender-filled bags sat in the empty drawer. A sign, surely. But how long could they use the drawer? The son would come home on vacation, and they'd have to leave. They'd seen the house; there were only two bedrooms.

Tarek pointed to the picture and circled his finger to indicate the bedroom.

'Oui,' their hostess nodded, her smile fading. 'My son, Etienne. Accident,' she said, pointing out the window to the road. 'Eight-years-old.'

Amira stepped forward and took Madame Vaillant's hands in hers.

'When he dead, husband go. I alone for a long, long time.' Their hostess struggled to find English words. 'You? Children?'

'Baby.' Tarek removed a folded picture from his wallet and smoothed it out. 'Ali. Still in Syria.'

'Qu'il est beau.' Madane Vaillant reached for the picture. In total silence, she replaced Etienne's picture with Ali's and set the frame back on the dresser. She looked around the room, gave a great sigh, and began to remove one of the soccer posters.

'Please, it is all right,' Tarek said, moving to stop her.

'Non.' Madame Vaillant shook her head. 'Enough death. Time for life.' A few minutes was all it took to remove the posters, but once she had, Tarek could swear she'd grown a few inches. 'Now this your room,' she said, pulling a key from her pocket and pressing it into Amira's hand. 'And this your home.'

Amira eyes widened.

'Home?' she whispered, as if speaking the word too loudly would make the key disappear.

'Yes, home.' Madame Vaillant's eyes filled with tears as Amira and Tarek fell into each other's arms. 'Welcome home.'

JOAN TAYLOR-ROWAN

Never Knowingly

We decided to move into John Lewis in the second week of December. Spur of the moment, we said afterwards but I'd been thinking about it for months. We were sitting in Collections, a little bit like Argos but with manners and proper upholstery. Someone was thanking a member of staff for all the trouble they'd gone to, rather than all the trouble they'd caused. Roy just looked at me and I knew.

It's very busy in John Lewis in December and they take on a lot of temps. I know that because I worked there one Christmas, in bed linens. It was the best job of my life. There's nothing I don't know about tog values and interior baffles. Roy and I met in John Lewis; he did deliveries. He delivered me from loneliness I like to say and he rolls his eyes.

At first we packed a big suitcase and then Roy said, 'Why? They've got everything we need – even a food hall!' and I laughed and laughed.

It was a Saturday, early evening when we made the big move. We wandered about the store looking for the best place to hide until the shop shut. It was so busy. People seemed to burst in through the doors, their faces creased and angry, and one spray later, smothered in Dior, and riding on a smooth escalator, their faces had softened. I knew we'd made the right decision but still I was nervous.

'What about the security cameras?' I whispered to Roy.

He shook his head. 'Trust me they're all on the outside,' he said and tapped his nose. 'Everyone thinks they have those motion-sensitive cameras like in *Oceans 11* but they don't.'

We hid in the stairwell in a little recess that Roy knew about. He said some of the youngsters would go there for a snog in their breaks. Roy used to take my sandwiches in there – said he needed privacy for one of my cheese and pickle granary baps.

I could hear footsteps fading on the stone stairs, the muffled voices saying goodbye and finally the silence, except for my heart which was going like the clappers. Roy had his delivery man outfit on as a sort of disguise, although he doesn't do that anymore, in fact he doesn't have a job at all now.

It isn't nice to see your stuff on your front lawn especially when you've spent all weekend mowing it. But what really upset me was seeing how shabby it all looked in the daylight. Nothing looks shabby in John Lewis.

The first couple of nights were the worst. I found it hard to sleep. I'd forgotten about the cleaners; we had to hide until they'd finished with their vacuuming. It tied me up in knots that waiting.

Roy was so calm. 'They won't hear us. Industrial hoovers are noisy,' he said and he squeezed my hand. He's been like that since they put him on Prozac. It's marvellous, like having your own personal rose garden that your head is always stuck in. I'm tempted to get some of it myself, but Roy says one of us needs to have some perspective.

After they left, we spent two hours in the ladies' changing rooms until my nerves settled. We had such a hoot. You should have seen some of the things I tried on and Roy did too; he's got a good pair of pins has Roy.

We began to forget we'd lived anywhere else. We dined on delicious salads and cakes – things I'd never dream of buying, always past the sell-buy date of course.

'They'll only give this lot to the Sally Army for the homeless anyway,' Roy said. 'We're just cutting out the middle man.'

We got up early each day and straightened our beds. I was very careful to put back the evening dress I'd worn the night before. I even got a little cleaning job to keep my eye on things. It was all just perfect, the Christmas lights, the big tree on the ground floor all covered in gifts and the smaller one in the children's department hung with little trains. Roy sighed when he saw it. We had to put his Hornbys on eBay; it nearly broke his heart.

And then on Christmas Eve, I found the slippers. There were two pairs – his and hers, from the Comfywear collection on the ground floor. They'd been worn. They were tucked under a display armchair on the upholstery floor. I stared at those slippers for a long time.

That night Roy and I curled up on a swinging chair with our torch and I shared my suspicions. Someone else had entered our refuge. I blamed myself. We'd ignored upholstery and carpets – the heart of a well-kept home my mother would have said – and now we were paying the price. Roy wasn't convinced but he doesn't argue much these days.

At 11.00pm, wearing our black Damart all-in-ones and our faces dabbed with a bit of Cherry Blossom, we crept up the back stairs to the top floor. Roy looked like one of those girls on the Clinique counter with his tan shoe polish cheeks. I stood on the landing listening outside the door.

'I can hear them moving around,' I said peering in through the glass.

'Maybe it's mice.'

'With torches?' I scoffed. 'There is definitely someone in there, Roy.'

I could hear the quiver in my voice. I looked into his face and saw my own emotions reflected there. I thought he might cry because I know I wanted to and then that feeling was overtaken by another. It surprised me really because I'm usually so placid, so accommodating like one of those trees you see gripping onto the edge of a cliff in a high wind. Indomitable, that's what all the neighbours said when they saw my sofa loaded into the back of the DFS van and not a tear on my face. It was seeing that little tremble in Roy's chin did something to me.

I clenched my fists and I burst through the door shouting, 'What's going on?' in my best security guard voice.

Their flashlights went crazy. Then the floor was plunged into darkness. Roy thrust the Maglite into my hand and I scanned it around the rolls of fabric and the swathes of curtains before bringing it back to the floor where it stopped. I heard a grunt and then a, 'Shh,

George!' Four fingers poked out from behind a fixture, a cluster of rings on a wrinkled hand.

'Out!' I said.

She was short, permed, and huffing with indignation. George, her husband, was tall, stooped, about seventy I'd say, with tape on the side of his glasses, and shoes like a pair of battered tugs.

'You're not Security,' she said brushing off her fleece, and then burst into tears.

'Well you're not mice!' Roy said and he was right as usual.

I felt bad making her cry so I let George lead her to some nicely buttoned armchairs and waited for her to calm down. She wiped her eyes and blew her nose loudly.

'So what are you doing here?' I said still using my security voice even though I was no one important anymore.

'We've been here since December 15th.'

'It was that advert,' George added. 'You see we were relying on Doreen's pension for our home by the sea but she hardly got a thing.'

'It was crunched,' Doreen said. 'All those years in a job I hated. And then that advert came on with its lovely house and that Boxer dog and the sweet little girl in pigtails. I said to George, you know I think that John Lewis would understand – if we could just write to him.'

'Who?' I said, confused.

'Mr Lewis,' George explained patiently, casting his hand around the dimly lit space.

'There isn't one,' I said. 'It's just a name. They're called Peter Jones in Sloane Square.'

'Jones, Lewis, what does it matter?' Doreen snapped. 'He's a man with money and we've got none and we wanted a Christmas like on the advert. I've earned it.' She began to snuffle again.

'Well you weren't careful enough. I spotted the slippers. You were lucky it wasn't someone else. We keep ours high up – top of the fixtures is good.'

Doreen looked sideways at me. 'You too?'

'Since December 12th.' Then we all laughed, with relief I think.

'Our daughter is in Australia with our grandson. We were supposed to follow them but we couldn't afford it, and we couldn't bear the house without them.' George sighed.

'Roy and me, we lost our house.'

Doreen gasped. 'You poor dears!'

I felt sad for a moment just thinking about it then Roy looked at his watch. 'It's Christmas,' he said mournfully.

'No Christmas presents this year, Roy. No tree of our own,' I said looking up into his American tan face.

'No house to put it in,' he answered.

'No family,' Doreen sobbed. We were all silent for a moment.

'Well why don't you come down to us,' I said suddenly.

Doreen stopped dabbing her eyes.

'Garden furniture. We've got a table that seats six and we're not far from the food hall.'

'Oh, we couldn't eat the food.' Doreen said, appalled. 'That would be stealing.'

'You could stuff some money by the till – someone will think it got caught.'

'What a good idea,' Doreen said, and as she stood up I noticed the tag still hanging from her Gloria Vanderbilt jeans. 'We could go to Carvela and pick out some party shoes,' she said, her eyes all aglow, 'and there's a gold lamé dress I've been longing to try on.'

I gave her a look and she blushed. 'I'll wear a little top of my own underneath and we can put them back in the morning.'

I turned to Roy. His eyes had a glazed look in them and I knew exactly what he was going to say.

'I'll go get that tree from the kiddies' department.'

We had the Ratpack singing carols in the background and Roy and George rigged up some torches to give us the feel of candles – we didn't want to set off a smoke alarm. Doreen and I got Pictionary from the games department; the box had already been damaged in the Christmas scuffle. You'd never guess looking at George what a laugh he is; I nearly choked on my oak-smoked ham.

When Ol' Blue Eyes crooned, 'Have yourself a merry little Christmas,' Roy put his hand out and I got up. I rested my head on his chest and tried not to think of the blue chiffon catching on the unvarnished garden trellis. We moved slowly around the barbecues and the garden chairs feeling warm and safe and happy. As the song came to an end, George stood up at the table.

'Here's to John Lewis,' he said raising his glass of Harvey's Bristol Cream. 'Never knowingly under-occupied.'

ANGELITA BRADNEY

Golden Eyes

The wind pounced on Mike as he pushed open the door and stumbled into the gale. With one hand he held the torch and in the other he clutched the pan with its lid. The ground was uneven, but he knew the route by now.

A few more steps and he was outside the shed, its ramshackle form sheltering him as his hands, stiff with arthritis, struggled with the catch. The door swung open and he was out of the rain, which hammered on the roof like a beast deprived of its quarry. The torch beam cut a yellow swathe through swirling dust, highlighting odd-shaped shadows of tools, an old lawnmower, cobwebs many years old. Golden eyes glittered in the shadows. She was there.

'Here you go, girl,' he whispered, bending painfully and placing the pan down. He stepped back a few paces and lowered the torch.

She didn't make a sound as she approached on padded feet, head lowered. He watched the muscles move under her fur, her shoulder blades like pistons. She reached the pan and sniffed delicately, then started eating with a soft liquid noise. She turned her head this way and that, picking morsels of meat, licking the fat with her tongue, tossing her head to swallow. Mike watched her, making no sound. It had taken weeks for her to come near him. Even now, a sudden movement would send her darting back to the shadows. When the pan was empty, she glanced at him briefly, then turned and disappeared into the corner from where she came.

In the kitchen, Mike slowly washed up the pan, plus his own plate and cup, and placed them on the draining rack. He went upstairs and emptied the buckets that were placed beneath the leaks in the hallway and bedroom. Down in the living room, he lowered himself painfully onto the threadbare sofa. There had been a time when a fire had burned in the grate, but the hearth was now cold. Mike's thoughts returned to the cat in the shed. When he had found her a few months before, she was nothing but eyes and bones held together by matted hair, with only fear giving her the strength to hiss and spit. But he had persevered, and eventually gained her trust. He was proud of how she'd come on under his care. And, for him, life seemed to be gaining some meaning again, after a bleak year.

He sat with his memories until late into the night while the storm continued to crash through the garden.

Mike woke on the sofa to find daylight streaming clear and cold into the living room. He was slumped awkwardly; his back and shoulders ached. The rain had stopped and through the window he could see the wet garden with its vegetable patch tangled over with weeds. He could just about make out the weather-beaten estate agent's sign standing at an angle near the road. A rabbit lolloped over the grass and he sat up, fingers stiffening.

His old instincts prickled; where was that gun? But there was nothing worth saving in the vegetable patch. What was the point in defending it? The rabbits could take what they wanted.

Not long afterwards he heard tyres crunching on the gravel outside, followed by a car door slamming. He looked out of the window and saw Deborah striding towards the house, her ponytail swinging. He got awkwardly to his feet and opened the front door just as she was about to knock.

'Hi, Dad.'

'Hello, love.'

He gave her a brief hug. She smelt of shampoo and clean washing. He was painfully conscious of his furry mouth and slept-in clothes.

She looked at him, sniffed, then clicked her tongue disapprovingly. 'Did you forget to go to bed again?'

Mike said slowly, 'I might have.'

'Hmm.'

She didn't wait for his response but pushed past him into the kitchen. He followed, starting to feel the anxiety that Deborah's visits tended to bring on. He watched as she cleared the debris from the table and put the kettle on.

'I was thinking about you in the storm last night,' she said, 'with the leaky roof and everything.'

'I managed.'

'But still, Dad, the sooner you can move into Riverside, the better. This house isn't really fit for human habitation.'

Mike suppressed a sigh. He had been hearing this for months.

'And there'll be people to keep an eye on you, just in case. Out here you're so isolated.'

'In case of what?'

Deborah ignored the question. 'Living here is no good for your health. Look at you.'

Mike knew what she was seeing: gaunt face, unwashed hair, eyes dull with age.

'At Riverside you'll be around other people. It would be better for you. For everyone.'

Deborah had a way of making everything she said sound so convincing. But Mike wasn't ready to give up yet.

'Remember what we agreed last year,' he said, 'I'm not moving until this place sells, so...' He spread his hands. Waiting for the house sale was his strategy to avoid being bulldozed into a retirement home. The property had been on the market for over a year, and with its increasingly run-down state he was hopeful that no one could be persuaded to buy it any time soon. He opened the cupboard to reach for some mugs.

'Yes, I know that was what we said, against my better judgement,' said Deborah, acerbically. 'But in any case, I've got some news on that front.'

Mike turned around slowly. She looked pleased with herself.

'The estate agent phoned yesterday, and said that a property developer was interested in coming to look around. He's done up a few cottages in the area, so won't be afraid of the work, and the views from here really are fantastic – very attractive for the market he's aiming for.'

Mike turned back to the worktop and slowly dropped a teabag in each mug. The noise of the kettle reached a crescendo – for a moment, it was all he could hear. He flicked the switch before it turned off and poured boiling water over the teabags. A splash landed on the back of his hand and he was almost glad of the momentary pain.

'In fact, he's coming round this morning.'

Keeping his face turned away, Mike fished out the teabags with a stained spoon and dropped them in the bin. He tried to pour the milk but found his hand was shaking.

A rustle and a fresh scent told him that Deborah was by his side.

'Dad.' She took the milk out of his hands and carried both mugs to the table. Mike followed and sat down. 'We've been over this before. You know it's for the best.' She paused and took a breath. 'Mum wouldn't have wanted you here on your own, with the place falling down around you.'

Mike kept his eyes down on his tea. A dark brown film floated on top of the liquid, lapping the edges. He took a sip and watched the shape break into remnants which slid down the sides of the mug.

'It's too soon,' he almost whispered.

'Come on, Dad, don't be silly,' Deborah said. 'Tell you what,' she said, thrusting something into his hand, 'you read this, and I'll clean the place up a bit before the agent comes.'

She rose and strode purposefully out of the room. Mike looked down at what she had given him. It was a glossy brochure for the Riverside Retirement Home. He shoved it into his pocket as Deborah returned with a box full of cleaning products and a mop, bucket and vacuum cleaner that she must have brought in her car. Mike was brushed out into the garden, along with two months' worth of dirt, while she tried to make the place look presentable. He was powerless against her energy. There was nothing to do but to go to the shed.

Opening the door, foreboding rushed through him as if a beast were waiting in the shadows, but it was a miaow that greeted him. He stood still and waited until the cat emerged. She looked at him steadily with her golden eyes.

'I don't have anything for you yet,' he said quietly.

She stood still for a moment, then sat down where she was. Mike slowly reached behind for an old plastic garden chair, then sat down too, being careful not to scrape it across the floor.

The cat watched him. 'Later I'll be back,' he said, 'with your dinner.'

She seemed to understand, and started washing herself. There was something hypnotic about how methodical she was – first one leg, then the other, then face, stomach and hind legs. The minutes ticked by. He took out the brochure that Deborah had given him. It showed photographs of elderly people gardening on raised beds, laughing over a game of cards, or relaxing in their pastel-coloured 'individual en-suite accommodations.' He sighed. Sometimes, when the damp from the walls got into his chest and his joints ached so much he could hardly move, he could see the attraction of comfortable surroundings and help on call day and night. However, a part of him wondered whether accepting that life would mean letting something inside him, like a small burning spark, die out.

He heard a car draw up, then voices, but had no wish to leave the shed. He didn't want to meet the agent

– no doubt a sharp-suited type with a mobile phone. Better in here, with the quiet and the dust and the cat.

Who would feed the cat if he left?

The question rose with an urgency that sent adrenalin racing through his veins. He tried to relax, reassure himself. The property developer might not be interested. The cat could fend for herself. However, he was still worrying when he heard the agent's car drive away and Deborah's voice calling. As soon as the cat heard her, she fled back into the darkness.

It didn't take the property developer long to make up his mind. Deborah phoned two days later, her voice excited.

'Great news, Dad! He's made an offer. And I think it's a very good one, under the circumstances. I phoned up Riverside and they can take you next month. You'll soon be moving!'

Mike didn't say a word, just slowly replaced the handset.

He couldn't resist Deborah's willpower. Over the next few weeks, she and her husband came and sorted, packed and tidied. Mike watched morosely as his world was squashed into brown moving boxes.

'Shall we take this chair, or send it to the tip?'

'What about this electric blanket, it's a death trap!'

'Shall I take these clothes to the charity shop, Dad?'

He half-heartedly tried to get involved – to minimise the amount of meddling – but lifting a box made his chest tighten like a spring, so he stuck to trying to make sure that nothing of value was thrown away, like his fishing rods and his rifle.

As moving day loomed closer it was the cat that filled Mike's thoughts. Could she survive without him?

To answer this question, he had to try something. One day, at the time he usually gave the cat her food, he went to the shed empty-handed. She trotted out from her hiding place to greet him.

'Shoo!'

She didn't move.

'Shoo!' he tried again. 'I've nothing for you now.'

She just looked up at him with her wide, glittering eyes. Feeling like a traitor, Mike grabbed a broom and ran at her.

'No more, no more!'

He swung at her body, but she was agile and dodged the blow easily, flying back to the shadows in the time it took to draw breath.

'No more food, find your own!' shouted Mike hoarsely, stumbling like a drunk. He reeled out of the shed and slammed the door behind him.

The next two evenings, Mike sat in the kitchen, head in hands. He thought of the cat – the first time she had let him approach, watch her eat, then wash, thought of the delicate strands of trust that had been built between them. He couldn't bear the idea of her waiting for him, and him never coming. At night she paced his dreams, thin and starving. On the third day his resolve wavered and he put together a bowl of scraps. He walked slowly to the shed, almost praying that she would not be there. But she was waiting for him in the middle of the floor, miaowing desperately. She darted towards him as he approached with the pan, pounced on the food and began to eat, ravenously.

'I'm sorry,' Mike said, 'I'm so sorry.'

His heart sank with the realisation that she was completely reliant on him.

He hardly slept that night. He couldn't stay with the cat, but he couldn't leave her. He had taken away her ability to survive and now he was abandoning her.

By the next day, Mike had decided what to do.

As evening fell, Mike fried the steak he had saved, mixed it with a good dollop of fatty gravy, and let the pan cool while he went upstairs. He knew which box his gun was in. Outside, the dusk had started to unfurl and the clouds burned scarlet at the edges. As he walked the familiar path to the shed, his throat constricted as if something was digging its claws into his windpipe. He opened the door and she was there, of course, waiting. He placed the pan down and she trotted towards it on padded paws. What was that sound in her throat? It couldn't be purring. It was.

She lowered her head to the bowl. The gun against Mike's shoulder was familiar as an old cushion. The light was dim but he didn't have far to aim. He squinted through the sight, noting the fine shape of her nose, the fur undulating over her shoulder blades and haunches, her tail making tiny brush strokes on the floor. She was enjoying the steak. The pressure on his chest grew. Blood pounded in his ears. She wouldn't feel anything. It was the kindest thing to do.

The next morning Deborah arrived early to find Mike waiting for her outside. His eyes were bright and he stood upright and determined.

'Hi Dad, ready for the big move?'

'I'm not going,' he said.

Deborah made as if to laugh, but stopped as she saw the look on Mike's face. 'What do you mean, you're not going?'

'Call off the sale. I'm staying here.'

'What?' Deborah sputtered. 'But it's all going through next week! And everything's packed and ready.'

'No, Deborah,' said Mike. 'I'm staying.'

Several emotions flashed over Deborah's face. 'It's just cold feet, Dad! Come on, you'll feel better once we're on the way.' She smiled, teeth bared, and took his arm.

He shook her hand off. 'I'm not ready to move. I'm not giving up on this place just yet.'

Deborah's voice rose. 'But you said you'd move when we found a buyer.'

'I've changed my mind.'

Deborah took several deep breaths. Then she spoke softly. 'Dad, are you all right? Has something happened? Tell me what's worrying you.'

'I've just decided I'm not moving.'

'You can't stay here, it's not... safe!'

Her head darted around, taking in the roof with its missing tiles, the overgrown garden. The ramshackle shed.

'What about your chest when winter comes? Who'll mend that roof? What if you have a fall? It'll be days before anyone notices!'

Mike just shook his head slowly.

Deborah was at a loss for words. Mike had to stop himself from smiling at the sight.

'Dad, come on! There's nothing left for you here!'

Mike was unshakable.

Finally, all Deborah could do was retreat to her car and slam the door shut.

After she had left, Mike stood alone in the garden listening to the birdsong and feeling the breeze on his face.

A sound made him look behind. There was the cat, in broad daylight, her golden eyes glinting in the sun. As he watched, she sat down and gently began to purr.

ANOUSKA HUGGINS

The Turquoise Bottle

'How many, Papa?' Rufina rushes at him the second he comes through the door and into their tiny rented room.

He gently places the brown leather chest onto the table.

'How many until we go home?'

'Please, *cara,* a moment.' He tosses his hat onto the bed and removes his jacket. His white shirt has a round damp patch that clings to his back.

'Can I count them?'

He sits on the floor and lights a cigarette. 'Later.'

The warm smell fills the room as the orange flame shrinks to nothing. His smell. The one she longed for all the times he was away. The one she used to hunt for every night, nuzzling her face in his old jackets.

'But, Papa –'

'Hush.' He leans his head against the wall, the crumbling plaster sprinkling his glossy black hair with specks, like when Mamma has been kneading dough. 'It's siesta time.'

She doesn't want siesta time. Their tiny room is too sticky and it stinks of his rotten cigarettes.

Later, as Rufina sneaks down the narrow staircase and enters the street, the sun is already setting, the sky streaked with amber, violet, rose. The colours of the bottles in her basket. She weaves through the streets past the church. Papa, she is certain, will be on the other side of the village by now. He has gone to win money from some of the local men. Which means that he will return after dark with empty pockets, stinking of the sour wine that has stained his teeth black.

She leaps down the stone steps, feet together, feet apart, the bottles nudging each other in her basket, clinking in time with the chorus of the cicadas, as if they're calling across the village to Papa, threatening to give her away. She stops. Holds the bottles steady. Runs her finger across the tops, all ten of them. The other twenty-three are in their room, in Papa's leather chest.

While he'd been stretched out in the lumpy chair earlier that afternoon, snoring with a rhythm like Mamma's rolling pin running over their tiled counter, Rufina had clicked open the brass catches and peeked into the leather chest. She'd counted the bottles, moving along the rows, left to right, right to left. Checked it again. Thirty-three bottles. Five more than yesterday. Were they multiplying? Like the time Papa had brought her a pair of rabbits back from one of his trips and Mamma had called him a bad word.

Moving more slowly this time, keeping the basket steady, Rufina slips through the archway and across the piazza towards the fountain, choosing the side nearest the cafés. She lines up the bottles on the highest step, where they will glint in the candlelight, like the tourists' necklaces. In the centre, she places Papa's favourite bottle. The shape of a rose bud. Turquoise glass, the colour of Mamma's eyes. His treasure, he calls it. The one he never sells.

Rufina waits.

Eventually, a couple stroll by. They are English, like Mamma. The woman has shining gold hair. She stops and leans forward, admiring Rufina's display.

'What charming perfumes,' says the woman.

'You are Italian?' says Rufina. A line she has heard Papa use many times.

The woman glances at her husband and giggles. 'I'm afraid not.'

'Ah. But you have the style.' Rufina waves her hand with a flourish.

'Why, you are just darling.' She reaches for the turquoise bottle. 'May I?'

Rufina pauses. Papa will be angry if she sells it. But if they are to go home, she needs to get rid of them all before they get a chance to multiply again. She picks up the bottle and holds it aloft, as if it is something precious and fragile.

'I should warn you,' she says. 'It is not perfume.'

'Oh?'

'It is essence.'

'Essence?'

The woman's husband rolls his eyes but Rufina ignores him. She can tell by the neat hems of the woman's silk dress, the lustre of her long beads, that money will not be a problem.

'Do you have such a thing as a handkerchief, *Signora*?'

The woman rummages in her beaded purse and hands Rufina a delicate lace handkerchief.

Rufina drops a small dash of the scent onto the handkerchief. She catches a whiff of orange and rosemary, lavender and sandalwood. She looks at the woman. 'Now close your eyes.'

The woman glances at her husband.

'*Signora*, please,' says Rufina.

The woman does as she is told.

'Breathe in.' Rufina lowers her voice. 'And out. In. And out.'

As the woman's breathing slows, Rufina hands her the handkerchief.

'Now take a deep breath and you will see the rolling hills, the cypress trees, the dusty olive groves, the winding vines, the flaming sun.'

The woman is silent for a moment, inhaling the aromas from her handkerchief. She opens her eyes. 'Quite extraordinary.'

'You see?' says Rufina. 'Essence. Of this village. Of your trip. Something to transport you back here when you go home.'

Rufina pushes the roll of lire in her sock and watches the woman walk away with Papa's turquoise bottle. That will show him. She counts the remaining bottles. Nine to go. Plus the twenty-three in their room. She yawns, wishing she'd had that siesta.

Papa is standing over her when she wakes up. '*Cara*, what are you doing here?'

She looks around. The cafés are closed, the orange candle flames gobbled up by the darkness.

'I thought I could sell them.'

'And did you?'

Her eyes run along the nine bottles. 'Just one.' Hot tears pricking her eyes, she says in a small voice: 'The turquoise one.'

'Ah.' He sits down beside her. He reaches into his inside pocket and produces a bottle. Rosebud shaped and turquoise glass. 'Like this?'

'But how?'

'You think I'd only have one of these?' He laughs. 'It is my treasure. I have a stash of them. Of all of them. Stock.'

She shrugs, feeling silly. Of course perfume bottles can't multiply. They will never get home at this rate.

'Go on,' he says, waving the bottle under her nose. 'Take a sniff.'

She leans forward.

'Wait.' He snatches the bottle away. 'Close your eyes.'

'Papa,' she says with a groan.

'I am serious, *cara*. This is not just a scent.'

'Yes, I know, it's essence, elixir, whatever the tourists want it to be.' But she closes her eyes anyway and breathes in the vanilla and cinnamon of Mamma's kitchen, the lemons from her garden, the salt and bay of their morning swims together.

She remembers now. Mamma is counting on them.

Papa snaps the stopper back in place. 'OK, you win. Tomorrow we go home.'

'Hush, Papa.' Rufina jumps up and shoves the nine bottles back into her basket. Amber, violet, rose glass rattling against one another. They walk back past the church to their little room with Papa's warm cigarette smell and their stash of turquoise bottles.

SHELL BROMLEY

Desire is Poured upon Your Lovely Face

This landing was harder than it should be. I stumbled, catching myself on a side-table. The vase of violets rocked and steadied. That crimson bolt of pain behind my ribs flared and faded and I settled my feet into the deep pile of the carpet.

I scanned the room, chest still hurting from the transition, and picked up my clues: a wooden duck on the coffee table, so it was one of the Marks; a painting of a hillside above the fireplace, a figure striding away with a double-bladed axe over their shoulder, so it was one of the Marks who enjoyed history; silver trees on a black background on the wall, so it was the Mark I was already engaged to. I'd learned my cues ages back, and I never got them mixed up. Couldn't afford to. One slip, and I'd be found out. If there was one thing my kind couldn't be doing with, it was being found out.

That and pomegranates. Not a one of us could stand them. No idea why.

The click of the door opening brought me round with a smile on my face. You had to smile, when greeting the man who'd handed you a ring and asked for your hand. This had been explained to me many times.

He paused, his gaze flicking up and down before settling on my face, eyes wide. 'Cora,' he said, on a rising breath.

My name spiralled, golden and rich. It had never been that way from his lips before. The ring had been offered on a solid note of purple, not with this glowing light. Perhaps being engaged had engaged his affections, rather than his desire for an attractive partner.

Another detail: we were to kiss our betrothed. Quite why this mattered, I wasn't sure, but my aunt had been very clear. Kiss your fiancé or spouse. Do not kiss anyone else. We lived by our rules. We needed some certainty in our lives.

His lips were warm as I pressed against them, warm and still.

'Cora?' he asked, this time a curl of confusion.

'Mark,' I said through my smile. My lips ached, unused to the curve. Still, a rule was a rule.

His fingers settled on my shoulders, his brow furrowed as he looked at me. Inspected me. 'Are you all right?' he asked.

I found I didn't like the flakes falling from those words. It seemed wrong, all of a sudden, to see any of his words lose their gilding. I had never seen him speak gold before, and I disliked any of them being damaged.

'Of course. How are you?'

'Honestly? Kind of freaked out. Why'd you kiss me? And how'd you get in without knocking? Did I leave the door open?'

I should have known. The Mark I'd thought he was had never spoken precious words to me. But that wallpaper had thrown me, making me sure...

'Mark?' I asked, but that was useless. He couldn't hear the inflection in the name which said who I was speaking to. He only heard the name he was used to wearing. Human ears couldn't hear the distinction. 'You aren't the one who proposed to me,' I said slowly, each word dragging out like a blade of spring grass pulled from the earth, like flowers plucked of their petals.

'Uh, no. No, I think I might remember doing that,' he said. His eyes narrowed. 'Wait. Are you drunk? High? In shock? Did something happen?'

Yes. He wallpapered. He must have wallpapered. But that probably wasn't what he meant.

Now that I looked at him more closely, he had strands of honey-gold in his eyes. The Mark who had pulled out a ring box didn't have those. Perhaps I should have been less sure of my clues.

Still, the first rule remained. Next to that one, all of the others were guidelines. Do not speak of it. Do not tell.

'I've not been drinking,' I said, because that was a truth, and as far as possible we told truths. It was easier to deceive with them, in many ways. 'I just... wanted to surprise you.'

'OK,' he said. He didn't sound convinced. 'Consider me surprised.'

He pauses, frowning, and I take my chance to look around, to get my bearings. Behind me, through glass doors into some kind of garden room, I see the back door ajar. When I look back, he's clearly caught it too, and a rueful smile plays on his lips. He shakes his head.

'Had me thinking you could materialise out of thin air, there,' he said, and apparently put it behind him. 'Look, I'm going to get some drinks ready. Want one? Dinner's going to be a while, still.'

The drink he brought me was sweet and sparkling. I pretended to sip at it as he came and went, reporting on vegetables and meats and sauces. We were to share a meal then, but he'd not expected me to be in his home already. Confusion curled, white and cold, in my mind.

The silver peal of the doorbell was a relief.

Mark's voice echoed down the hall and then she was there, her hair as honey-gold as always and her eyes moss-green. Phil. Oh. I was in this world. I had hoped, in some ways, not to land here again. She was solid in a way nothing else in these worlds was, and all it did was remind me I could never have that, that solidity and safety. I was nothing but smoke until I persuaded someone to catch me in a net, and fate seemed to have determined it would be one of the Marks.

Violet and a white so pure as to be blue blossomed in my mind. Desire. It was harder to push aside than it should be, but I managed it. I had to. Had I known this was her world, I would have run, I would have avoided her.

'Cora,' Phil said, her hands out in welcome.

I smiled, and raised my glass, and avoided touching her. Better to miss out completely.

Behind her, Sean shrugged off his coat and took a drink from Mark. His hair was ruffled and his skin flushed, as it nearly always was, and I buried the thought he wasn't good enough for her. I wouldn't let jealousy taint me. If he made Phil happy, that was enough. I would make my peace with being with the Mark who was graphite-grey and royal purple.

We went where we were sent. Choice was for mortals. For as far back as my people went, we had known this.

The green and gold of her made me regret it, but desire was not for me. If I'd only realised I was in this world, I would have left, would have made sure not to see her. I told myself this over and over, almost sure it was truth.

'You sure you're all right?' she asked, as we sat down at the table.

Her concern cut.

'I'm fine,' I said, tilting the corners of my lips. A smile, however false, usually placated the Marks. Most of them.

Whatever sauce this Mark had used on the lamb, it was almost as sweet as the sparkling drink. I pushed a lump of meat across my plate, watching the smear it made. Other people had arrived, nothing but vague blocks of colour to me. Conversation swirled, snagging my attention now and then, but easy enough to ignore. Being this close and knowing I would soon be pulled away, that this might be the last time I saw her...

Her laugh drew my gaze, the spark of it richer than the gold this Mark had spoken. I set down my fork, the thought of food too much.

After, once I was released from the table, I fled out into the dark of the garden. It was possible, to an extent, to control the length of a visit, but I had yet to feel the currents shift to a point where I could leave. And I wanted to leave. Dreaded it.

'Cora?' Her voice tightened my shoulders. 'What are you doing here? Are you all right?'

'I'm fine,' I said, because I had to say something, and telling her how confused she made me wouldn't be right. 'Just feeling a little off.'

'Yeah,' she said. 'I can see. I wondered…'

But whatever she wondered, she didn't say.

When I turned around, she was gone, and shortly after I felt the eddies move in the right direction, and let them sweep me away.

The next time I arrived, she was sitting on the settee in front of that wallpaper, her legs curled up and a book in her hands. At first, I thought she hadn't noticed me. Not everyone did, not if I arrived in front of them. Some protection I didn't really understand.

'Mark's out,' she said, turning a page. 'I can get you a drink, if you want.'

'You… you can see me?' I asked.

Foolish. I knew how to move past these near-misses, when a mortal saw me coalesce in their world. Drawing attention to it wouldn't help.

'Cora,' she said, closing the book and meeting my gaze, the shock of it solid, 'I always see you. Now, how about that drink?'

That was the first time I sat next to her, the first time we almost touched. It was the first time I thought differently about what it might mean to find a home.

She took me out to the park in mid-winter, where trees with frosted branches arced across the fog-white sky. I walked next to her, saw her golden warmth push everything else to the background, and my fingers twitched to reach out and stroke along her skin.

She spoke words of amber and emerald to me, spilled her past and our shared heritage, a shock that eased into recognition in moments, and set herself in my heart.

When we returned to Mark's home, and Sean and Mark and their friends greeted us, we said we'd had a good walk and didn't mention our hands brushing as we wound around the trees.

The Mark with the ring grew more granite, his comments pointed as he told me I should be more grateful for his offer. I almost wavered, almost apologised and did as I was meant to do, but the thought of her had more weight than any rule or expectation.

He shouted sharp, purple words after me as I left the ring at his feet and let the tides tug me back to her.

One thing he had right: if I didn't find someone to complete a binding, I would never have one world to call home, though I doubt he meant that when he said I'd never find an offer like his. I found I didn't care.

Warm sunlight brushed her cheeks, gilded her hair, the first time we kissed.

'Sean doesn't love me,' she said. 'He never did. It's…he knows I'm from somewhere else. He thinks I needed to stay in this country. Can you believe that?'

'If you leave him,' I said, 'you'll be swept away, just like I am. What are the chances we'll be swept to the same places?'

'We'll have to see,' she said. 'Maybe it'll work out, if we make it clear we choose each other.'

I wondered, and worried, and argued she shouldn't take the risk.

She let me persuade her, but her golden warmth dimmed. I kissed her until she shone again.

Shades of fire ran through the leaves as she asked again. 'It has to be worth the risk,' she said. 'Do you really want to keep doing this? Keep seeing each other, knowing you're going to be dragged away?'

Putting off leaving as long as I could only got me so far. She was right about that. And it hurt, a crimson bright and blaring, if I fought it for every minute we could have. The most I'd ever managed was a few days.

'No,' I said. 'But we have no way of knowing if cutting you loose will mean we ever see each other again. We might... It might end all of it. I'd rather only see you once a year than never.'

'It might work out,' she said, as a breeze lifted a strand of her hair, streaking gold across her face. 'It might all work out, Cora. And I'd rather drift with you than have a home without you in it.'

And it might fail, but she felt more solid to me than any world I'd stood on, and I longed to believe her.

When she offered me a ring, I said yes.

We ate a last meal with Mark and Sean. Sean, because he was the one who'd be left, and she had to do it in a way that stuck, or it wouldn't work at all. Mark, because I was meant to stick to him, in some world or another. There may have been other people there. They didn't matter.

I drank more of that sparkling wine, ate more of the too-sweet sauce, and nodded as Mark explained he was bored of his wallpaper. It might have been a mistake. What did everyone think of him re-decorating entirely?

The meal dragged on and flashed by, and we stood in the living room with our hands close to touching and Mark leaking confusion.

'I don't get it,' he said. 'You two are breaking up?'

Sean shrugged. 'Not like it was love's true whatever,' he said. 'Anyway, there's someone at work. I've been thinking about bringing it up…'

And that was that. Good to know a bond we'd been taught should be eternal meant so little. I was pleased Sean was unhurt, that Phil had been so right about that, but it left me wondering what else our elders had been wrong about. I hoped they were wrong about needing an anchor, that at the very least Phil and I would drift together.

'So, how do we do this?' Sean asked, sipping at his beer as though organising something mundane. 'I guess you give me the ring back? Or do you keep it? I never know how that's meant to go.'

'You make it sound like you do this all the time,' Phil said, and the teasing light in her words was almost jarring.

I could see the affection in them, and knew again that I was taking her from a life which, if not brimming with love, was at least comfortable. She shook her head at my expression, and took my hand.

'Have the ring,' she said, holding it out.

It dropped into Sean's palm and we finished our drinks. There were no flashing lights, was no great tearing of the world.

Trees formed a canopy, the leaves gone and frost cutting through the thrum of my nerves.

Her fingers, laced through mine, webbed me into feeling we'd be together, we'd stay together. Waiting to see wore on me, the colours around me bright but distant. I was already detaching from this world, despite not being the one connected to it.

'We'll be together,' she said. 'We don't need solid ground under us as long as we're together.'

My longing for her words to be truth ignited, became desire. It burned gold and crimson, green and grey.

'We'll be together,' I said, a prayer.

Her fingers were still wound with mine when I felt the tug under my breastbone, when I spiralled out of that world.

I landed with a jolt, stumbling and catching myself against a tree, the bark rough against my empty palms, and the world almost entirely without colour.

She wasn't there.

In this world, Sean lived alone. He seemed as happy as he had done any other time I'd met him, the space never filled here not something to trouble him.

It was the same in the next world, and the next, and the next.

I fell off-balance, each and every time, my hand reaching for contact which wasn't there.

The wallpaper in this world was white, streaked with stars. This Mark must have moved out, leaving the house empty, and I sat with my back against the wall. My empty hands dangled over my raised knees.

There'd been more empty houses than full ones of late, and I hadn't landed somewhere I knew for some time. Whatever else we'd done, we'd knocked me out of my alignment. I couldn't go back to the royal purple Mark if I wanted to. I didn't think I wanted to.

But it was so lonely, so tiring, to keep holding out my hand and finding no one.

Perhaps what I should work on was curling my hand closed, and my heart with it.

Tracking the worlds was pointless now, and I had long given up trying to spot clues. Chances were, I wouldn't land in the same place twice, or if I did I wouldn't know it. I'd have been happy to circle back to the Mark and Sean who'd known Phil. I could talk about her with them, at least, and that Mark had been kind. It would be something. It would be a memory of home.

It may have been months, or years. Time was hard to hold with no anchor. I'd thought I'd caught a glimpse, once or twice, but it had always come to nothing, and now I was tired. I was so tired, and just wanted to be home.

But there was nothing I could do but drift, and search, and see.

This time, the bark under my palm bit, and I hissed, pulling my hand away, turning it, inspecting the red. A crunch of snow underfoot had me bracing my shoulders.

'You should clean that.'

This time, when I turned, the sun warmed my sight, glowing gold.

LEE HILL

Up the Garden Path

He'd gone out at six on a works do, having first filled the house with impatience and threat, intolerance and anger. By seven, each of us felt the tension glacier begin to thaw, sensed the lack of eggshells underfoot, realised there was no further need to second guess motives or reactions that night. It was December, and outside the cold gripped your guts and squeezed.

We sat in the warmth of the living room, my mother and sister and I, we sat and gradually we smiled. For once able to watch TV programmes we all agreed on, tentatively talking to each other, we unwound. The tension lessened further, we boldly turned on all four bars of the fire and defiantly increased the thermostat in the hall, knowing it would be smugly moved back down to 18 degrees before we went to bed. He'd never know, never rant about this particular house crime, never burden our ears and our hearts with accusation.

The conspiratorial mood grew, spreading like red wine on a carpet, thick, insouciant and undoable. Our programme finished and as the adverts barked their wares to us, we began discussing how he'd return. He'd be paralytic. He might piss in the wardrobe again. We all remembered the last time, a skid mark on his side of the bed in the morning, disgust and delight vying in a brown smudge of weakness. Cackling with spiteful glee by now, the conversation escalated. We all loved exposing and reliving those occasional little chinks in his armour, each one a shard of hope.

The leap across a lake of loathing to an island of an idea was mine. I take full credit. My thoughts had turned to him stumbling up the narrow path his car left spare on the driveway. He'd then turn right on the paving stones in front of the brick steps of the doorway. I saw him pawing at his pocket, then poking at the keyhole, unsteady, cold, shorn of any benevolent veneer. My first idea came then. Lock it from the inside, he'd be unable to get his key in, he'd be locked out.

However, I followed that scenario to its logical conclusion. Banging, swearing, rage. Someone having to descend the staircase with dread. Accusation and recrimination. Horrible argument if it was my mother, pushing, slaps or some other physical humiliation if it was me or my sister. Actually, my sister wouldn't have got out of bed, she'd have lain quietly weeping, terrified, silently begging one of us to go in her place.

No, that wouldn't be good. Funny, but ultimately not worth it. The idea though, the notion of fucking him over, of drawing revenge like pus from a boil, of applying a karmic poultice, that stayed. By the next ad break, the flicker had become a flame and I had it.

They got it straight away. My sister was worried, she was probably around seven then, and worried about everything. The shrill, slightly hysterical honks of delight that came from my mother balanced this, and so the plan was morally green-lighted. I went to the kitchen and filled a large pan with water. We converged in the hallway and opened the front door. Pausing to compose myself, I studied the glinting crystalline garden, bejewelled with heavy frost. Too cold to snow, as they say. Slowly, deliberately, I poured the water over the already frozen steps. As it spread and slipped over the surface I knew I'd need more water. I wanted to do the whole path.

So I did.

I still remember checking it later on, as I passed the front door on my way up to bed. The trap was hard to distinguish, but the slipper-clad foot I tentatively lowered shot off the step so easily and so fast I almost went over myself. A thin sheet of wonderfully smooth ice covered all paved areas of his walkway. His best black brogues stood no chance. Looking out from the threshold, visualising his impending downfall, a calming warmth unfurled inside me. After shutting the front door carefully, like a trapper loading a spring snare, I paused to turn the thermostat back to 18. No trace. I went to bed smiling.

LINDSAY FISHER

Rain

They came round the houses, knocking on the doors like politicians during election time. And they smiled like politicians, too, which is not really like smiling at all and is only brief. They shook Da's hand just as men at funerals shake hands, and they said that they was sorry, really sorry. It was bad news all round, they said.

Da thanked them for calling when they'd said their piece, and he nodded and said he understood, and thank you again, and Da closed the door – firmly, just like he did with the scruffy girls who came selling carpet brushes or clothes-pegs or pans.

Da called us together and, standing at the kitchen table, he reported on what the men at the door had said. Da's face was as long as a horse's and there was no music in his telling us what they told him. It was something 'bout the weather and the river rising faster than it should and the men said we was to leave our home just in case. All the farmhouses for miles around was the same, they said, and down in the village, too. When Da told us, his voice was hissing through his teeth, like he was telling us a bad thing and a thing he did not want to tell. Like he'd done when Lindy had given him a lie and he'd caught her out and he wished he hadn't.

It was the rain as was the problem is what Da told us. It'd been raining steady for days or weeks or forever, and the ground was wet as towels lifted out of the filled bath they'd been dropped in. Mam said it'd never rained like that here before, not 'less you went back to the Bible and the story of Noah and his forty days and forty nights. Mam said we should get to our knees and pray for forgiveness of our sins and for the sins of the godless.

Mam was always saying how prayer was the answer and she was always blaming the godless. Thing is, I think I'm maybe one of the godless myself, though I never would say that to no one, and specially not to Mam; and I think Lindy is one, too, which was part of the lie she'd told. Oh, I pray enough when Mam tells me to and I sing church songs when I'm busy and I read the stories in the Bible over and over – but I don't think I read 'em for the same reasons as Mam, because inside I don't believe in God.

I touch wood for luck sometimes, see, when Mam's not by, and I keep a rabbit's foot wrapped in a hankie and tucked deep into my dress pocket, and I don't ever kill spiders, not money-spiders leastways. I look in the meadow for four-leafed clover every summer and cross my fingers 'gainst harm or ill-fortune and none of that is godly. And I don't never open an umbrella in the house – but then Mam don't do that neither.

And now the rain has come. In buckets and bowls and bathtubs. Raining cats and dogs, Mam said, but that's just an expression she uses and it makes no sense really, none that I could see. Raining pitchforks, Da said.

Mam reads the story of Noah again and again, like there might be a clue hidden in the words or between the lines, a clue as to what we should do to be saved. And we all of us clasp our hands together, me and Lindy and Mam, and we mutter prayer-words like we'd been taught. Even Da prays, under his breath he does, and Da did not always go to church on a Sunday and whenever he did he didn't join in with the hymn singing, no way he did; and he sometimes swore oaths that was profane, which Mam says means is against God. I think I'm like my da in that and I think Lindy is, too.

'Not to tell,' Lindy said. 'Swear it. On Mam's life or Da's. Swear.'

And I did swear, an oath, not on the Bible or to God, but on things that was real.

'Cross my heart and hope to die. Stick a needle in my eye.'

And Lindy lay back in her bed and she confessed she'd kissed a boy called Howie, and more than kissing, she said. And I lay back in my bed and let myself be carried away with what Lindy was saying.

'Kissed him once and kissed him twice,' Lindy said. 'And his tongue in my mouth, just the bubblegum pink tip of it, his hands feeling under my blouse, and the brush of his fingers over the cup of my bra. It took my breath away, and his, too, and was unheavenly bliss.'

I touched where my titties would be one day and I opened my mouth and I sucked in the dark cold night air, tasted it on my tongue.

'Is it a sin?' I asked Lindy.

'It is,' said Lindy. 'Surely it is. But it's a sin like taking three spoons of sugar in your tea and sweeter than sugar, too.'

Da takes three sugars when he thinks Mam's not looking or counting, and he winks at me if he catches me watching, and he'd wink to God too, I reckon – if there is a God at the last. And I don't think God would do our da ill for his third sinful teaspoon of sugar.

'And sure, didn't He die for our sins,' Da says to Mam when she scolds him for something bad he's done. 'And if there was no sins at all, then wouldn't His dying have been just for nothing?' And Da holds his hands open like there are no tricks up his sleeve and his face is lit and lifted like he's found the answer to a riddle, and isn't it obvious? is what the look on his face says.

But Da didn't say that nor nothing like it when he found out 'bout Howie and Lindy and what they did in the barn after hay harvest. 'Lying is a sin,' he said. 'Lying with a boy and lying 'bout a boy and what a boy did when he thought no one was there to see, all of it an unholy sin.' Da hissing through his teeth then, like a cat when its back is up, or like geese when a fox is near. 'A sin under heaven it is,' Da said.

The men at the door were right 'bout the river. I'd watched it rising for the past two days. It was a great roaring rushing thing now, boiling and bucking, where before it was slow and slippy and sleepy. And the home-field was already sodden, and here and there were pools of water growing, the grey sulky sky mirrored in each of those pools, and in one there even a fish, a thin silver-dart minnow swimming between the blades of grass, blood in its eye and looking frighted and lost. Then suddenly – only it wasn't sudden – the river was just too big for its boots or its britches and it broke from its course with a kick and everywhere was water sloshing and gurgling.

Da said as how we should carry the things from downstairs to the rooms above. Everything, he said. And quick as quick and lickety split, he said. All the chairs and the sofa, and the carpets, too. And flour in sacks and eggs in baskets, and pots and plates, and Mam's knitting, and all else besides. And downstairs was shifted upstairs, bit by bit, and stacked just anyhow, Mam fussing over where the cat was gone to now, and how the milk-cows gathered into the barn would be and Milly the Saanen goat.

Da had filled hessian bags with sand and he piled the last of 'em slumped like dead things 'gainst the doors, pressing them into the cracks with the heel of his boot, back door and front door and side, and he shut all the windows fast, and he said a little praying couldn't do no harm.

We was on our knees in the kitchen when it started, on our knees on the cold flagstone floor helping with the sand-bags and praying under our breath. I could hear water, the small sound of sucking and slurping, like Lindy drinking through a straw and wanting every last drop, while Mam'd be tapping the table and scowling 'gainst the noise that Lindy was making; or like Lindy in her bed and sucking nothing 'cept her teeth so there was the wet sound of Howie kissing her with his tongue, or me pretending the same and licking the night air. And my knees was suddenly wet and all the lights in the house went out, like blinking and not opening your eyes again after.

Da said that we should maybe go upstairs and keep safe to our beds.

'And in the morning…' Da said. But he left what the morning would bring hanging in the air, like seed when it is scattered and the wind holds it up before letting it fall, just before; and so we was left like lizards to grow a tail to what Da had said, left to imagine.

Lindy crept in bed beside me and she held me close as ever holding can and we was as warm as cats or toast, and she whispered in my ear. And, 'Don't tell, don't tell,' she said again. 'Don't.' Lindy was thirteen – fourteen on her next near birthday – and what she told me was all the sinful things she wanted to have done before ever the Day of Judgement dawned and fell on our home, things she wanted to have done with Howie and with another boy called Kai.

I lay awake a while, listening to the dark rain falling 'gainst the roof tiles, and Lindy sleeping and breathing slow, and I could hear the water lap-lapping against the house. I thought again of Noah and his great and silly boat and all the animals herded into that boat and all the sinners left out. And animals can kiss and lick each other and it is no sin for they don't have souls – according to Mam they don't and according to God and the minister – not souls like people have souls. And I lay awake, all my flooding thoughts swirling like water trying to find its level, and me trying to make sense of Noah's story if there was no God in it, or even if there was.

'God is love everlasting,' Mam's always fond of saying. And the story of the drowned, and Noah saving cows before children, and camels before women and men, well, that was surely just mad and it didn't make no sense at all. And I wondered then if Da was not a little mad, too, for saying to the men at the door that a man's home was his castle and he was intent on staying despite the rain, mad as Noah building his 300-cubits-long ark in a dry place.

And when I slept at last, there was silver-dart minnows looking lost in all my dreams, and my bed was a bobbing boat endlessly adrift, and a boy called Howie or Kai said, 'God is love everlasting,' and he kissed me with his tongue, the pink bubblegum tip of it, and I let him, his hand fiddling under my dress; and still it was raining and raining all the way to morning and who knows, maybe all the way to rainbows.

MARGARET JENNINGS

A House of My Own

<u>*Preparing a rabbit for the table*</u>
Once table weight of between four and five pounds is gained at ten to twelve weeks, the young rabbit should be slaughtered. Do not eat old meat. Strike the rabbit a hard blow to the back of the head with your hand or a stick whilst holding the rabbit upside down by the back legs. To de-gut a rabbit a cut should be made in the abdomen, making sure that each cut punctures the skin and body without rupturing the intestines below. Extend the cut right up to the rib cage and down the vent so that the stomach, intestines and bladder are revealed. Remove these carefully, then cut off the head and feet. To ease off the skin break the connective tissue that holds it to the muscular wall using a small knife.

She is a regular daddy's girl. I watch her cuddle up on his lap of a night time, stroking his greying beard. She is too old to do that; it seems not nice somehow. I say nothing. I watch though.

One summer's day she is sitting by the well eating hot bread spread with butter. I cannot believe she is so unaware of the effect. The crumbs linger stickily on her chin as she licks the dripping butter with a smooth pink tongue. My hands are calloused from years of washing clothes in the icy waters of a nearby stream.

If I was to walk straight from the forest, I could walk until hunger or thirst stopped me. But I don't. I stay here. Fear holds me in an icy grip that allows me no freedom. The prison is of my own making. I watch a bear, fish in mouth walk away, hunched haunches lolloping downstream, careless and sleek, looking for more victims. I sit still and stiff. I trace the splits and cracks in my hands to the points where they pain me the most and realise I must act before the grave claims me.

Our home was made from trees cut from the forest. Tall, living communal trees smashed to the ground, hacked till they were limbless, prone, mud in their crevices dried by time, doing the bidding of lesser beings. Like me, I thought. Now I must make my own space.

My cottage is going to be a celebration of life and colour, the ultimate act of creation. I build in stolen hours. First my brick oven, which must be huge and womblike, a space to crawl into. Walls so thick they keep out the bird song. I scour soft clay from the bed of the stream, my hands sting and smart. I steal the butter pats and squish the clay into brick shapes, bake them in the blaring sunshine of the summer, then build them one atop the other in my secret place until they form a cavern that will let in the whole of my body.

I cannot tell you how much I love that oven. I wrap my arms around it, lay my cheeks against its smooth whitewashed plaster, feel the coolness on days when the oven is not used, feel my skin snarling on baking day. It is so huge it fills a whole corner of my cottage, the fire beneath it so ravenous that I spend precious hours searching for wood. Baking days are a luxury. Work is slow and time hard to find. My husband and his children demand and steal my hours.

My husband slumps in his chair of a night, staring at the fire. His daughter snuggles into his lap while a red point of blood stains the darning in my chafed hands.

I build my house from cakes and biscuits and sweets prepared in my oven. Turmeric dyes the food yellow and brown, lichen gives me green and buff, mimosa a constant yellow. But I am restricted by the colours nature can give me; I want more. I want vibrant red under the eaves, the whitest white for my candy floss curtains. I paint the eaves with the blood of the rabbit and the vibrancy of poppies. Cornflowers snapped from growth have the colour wrung from them. Slowly my cottage grows, throwing colour back into the world I stole it from.

One day I walk into the cottage and find a living shape growing there. Bees swarm around a queen, a huge mobile dripping dewdrop. I watch them awhile, amazed by the constancy of the shape when the bees are forever moving upward on the mound, mesmerised by the thrumming hum of women at work, women creating.

With my bare hands I scrape away the bumblebees. They mill down my arms, swarm around my head but they do not sting me. They are my fellow engineers; we are all champions of construction. They crawl around my eyes, down my ears. I can feel the tickle of their tiny limbs pressing on my lips. They are listening to me, listening to my thoughts and visualising the strengthening of my walls. Walls built like honeycombs, sweet and strong and straight. They set to work and soon the whole house is buzzing. In a few weeks it is dripping with the sweetness of honey, glowing with the brightest colours.

Then *they* arrive. They see my house. Stop their random search for fruit and mushrooms. The children and their father, *they* see my house.

I cannot own my creation for it would open me to ridicule but I watch from afar. Every biscuit pulled from the wall is an extracted finger nail, every colour smeared into another is food dripped onto my chin for public mocking. I am empty and desolate, feeling the roughness of the oak tree I cling to. Will they not go? Please go, please go. Their father laughs as he looks at my house; laughs as he pulls away a piece of wall and swats one of my bees.

'Just wait here,' I hear him say, 'I'll be back soon.'

Running, I am running through trees, through rivers, the sharp stones of the river bed catching at my bare feet, the splashed water darkening the rim of my skirt. I must be home when he arrives.

'You'll never guess what I just found,' he says cheerfully as he walks through the door. He's picking up his axe. God, he's picking up his axe. 'I've left the children there. More food than we could need in a month. I'm just going to bring it back.'

My house will die. Tears swim in my eyes. I try to look sensible. I try to look innocent, I try to think, I take a deep breath.

Running my finger slowly along the blade of his axe I smile up at him.

'Of course,' I murmur, 'while the children are away I could howl like a wolf.' Reaching up, I kiss the greying softness of his beard. He is sold. I howl like a wolf. I throw back the covers so that he can enjoy the fullness of me. The sweat runs like rivers to be drunk from and how we are drunk together, laughing at the damp hair clinging to our bodies. Finally he is asleep but this will not be for long. I must work quickly.

She, *that* girl, is pulling apart my candy floss net curtains. I can see the white stickiness around her mouth. *He* is unthreading the dark liquorice ribbon that is woven into mats.

'Hello,' I call amiably for I must keep their trust. 'What have you found?'

They are ebullient in their explanations, delighted in their showings and look here and look here and look here.

'But what is this?' I ask when I see the oven. 'It looks so huge – would you fit in it?'

Gretel laughs. Hansel explains that it is much too hot.

'But I think you would fit in. I don't think it is too hot.'

They look at me as if seeing the real me for the first time. 'Stop it, you are frightening us,' says Gretel.

'You look like an ugly old witch with your face like that,' says Hansel.

I laugh a laugh that causes birds to crash in multitudes from trees. Hansel and Gretel huddle fearfully together.

'Don't be silly, it's only me, you've known me for such a long while.'

'I'm beginning to think we've never known you at all,' says Gretel.

'Perhaps nobody ever has, nor ever will,' I replied.

The young rabbit should be slaughtered. Strike the rabbit a hard blow to the back of the head with your hand. A cut should be made in the abdomen just below the rib cage, making sure that each cut punctures the skin and body without rupturing the intestines below. Cut off the head and feet.

MOHINI MALHOTRA

Giving Thanks

My one-way ticket is in my bag, Washington DC to Bangalore. Two packed suitcases bulge like pregnant women in the bedroom. I wipe my hands on my apron and gaze at the yellow walls. We painted them soon after we moved in, to bring in sunshine, while snow was colouring the world white outside. The landlord said he will paint the apartment after I leave next week. I pause for the stories of each tenant pressed between each coat of fresh paint.

Last year I toasted my youngest brother and his new bride at their wedding back home via Skype. I couldn't go, my green card application was pending, it has been pending for nine years – and without it in hand, I feared I wouldn't be allowed back. So, we toasted his wedding like we toast every festival and all birthdays and every Sunday. We touch our glasses to our telephone screens and pretend to drink from each other's.

The green card still hasn't arrived. My employers have placed calls and tried to help – 'There's a backlog,' they get told each time. Father looks thinner each week and his cough sounds worse lately. The black has washed out of mother's hair over these years, although her eyes still sparkle like a girl's. She cries each time we prepare to hang up. They have not come to visit me, even though I saved up to buy them tickets. Visas denied.

The leg of lamb is in the oven. It marinated overnight in yoghurt, turmeric, cumin, with cloves and garlic nestled in its folds. This is the final large meal I will cook in this apartment, in this country. My sister and niece went back home last year. She was tired of waiting for the green card, and wanted more family eyes watching over her daughter with long lashes and budding breasts. No card – green or purple or rainbow-coloured – is worth this separation, I too have decided.

I spread my red straw placemats on the white dining table. Saffron and steam scent the room when I lift the pot cover to check on the rice. The roasting vegetables are tender – red beets, purple carrots, orange chunks of yams, white parsnips with a hint of my special curry mix and topped with grated ginger. I sprinkle fresh coriander leaves and squeeze lime juice over the green beans, sautéed with red onions and ripe tomatoes. The cranberry chutney smells of cloves and cinnamon and chillies.

I quickly shower and wrap on my special-occasion pink sari, pull my damp hair into a bun, wear my small pearl earrings, dab on pink lipstick. My employers will soon be here, tonight as my guests. Mrs Bock, Ms Beary, Mrs Romero-Follete, Mr Paulson, and Ms Janega, the people whose homes I have cleaned, whose Thanksgiving meals I have joined, and whose children I have raised and love like my own. Thank you for looking after me all these years.

J. A. IRONSIDE

Born at Ashfall

Jennet had always found the soft drifts of ash that clung
and coated everything – after one of the two or three
yearly falls – rather pretty. For a brief time it softened
the harsh lines of the stark landscape, blurring
boundaries and smudging the burnt, hollow carapaces
of the broken buildings. She had never mentioned it to
the others of her crate – she knew the ash was not as
innocuous as it appeared. Later she and her mates
would sweep the drifts away with whatever they could
lay their hands on to use as brooms. Left long enough
for the rain to fall on it, all the badness in the ash would
leach into the ground, killing the plants they gathered
for food. Or it might enter the water and cause sickness.
Worse it might kill the fish. It had happened before.
Jennet remembered a time, long before she became an
elder, when they had left the crate one morning to find a
shoal of fish floating belly up and lifeless in the ash-
murked water of the bay. She remembered the hunger
that had come after for many months because they had
not even been able to eat the fish. The ash turned
everything to poison in the end.

There was nothing pretty about the drifts of ash today; its softness was a deception. Jennet swallowed hard against the blockage in her throat. For all her words of comfort to Willow, her sister, she was not as sure as she had made herself sound that Willow's baby would live.

Born at ashfall
Dead by nightfall.

That was the old rhyme. It held true, at least as far as Jennet was aware. There was something in the ash that killed new babies and young mothers during or just after child birth. Willow had gone into labour just as the ash started to fall and there was nothing any of them could do. Babies came in their own time and the ashfall obeyed no one. So Jennet had sat with her sister and held her hand, swallowing back her tears as Willow bravely pretended that all would be well. That whatever evil came in the wake of the ash would not kill her and her unborn child.

Jennet scrubbed the back of her forearm across her face at the memory, knocking her goggles and the rough cloth tied over her mouth. Willow was resting now, and her child, a baby girl, had seemed healthy. If she lived through the day perhaps all would be well. It was rare but not unheard of.

There was a metallic clang and the lower door of the stacked shipping crates opened. Four figures, similarly muffled in goggles and face cloths, the rest of them covered in plastic over-suits duct taped together at the joins, clambered out.

They nodded to Jennet as she joined them, broom and tarp in hand. The sweeping took most of the morning. They shifted all the ash in the nearby vicinity onto the tarps, which were then emptied onto an old car trailer and covered with a thick sheet of plastic. It was hard work. Jennet's arms and back ached, sweat ran down the inside of the plastic suit, but she welcomed the distraction of the physical discomfort.

It took all five of them to get the laden trailer moving; the strain and the long walk added aches and pains to Jennet's legs to go with the throbbing in her arms and neck. After several miles, one of the others raised his hand and they let the trailer roll to a stop with relief and with that sense of accomplishment that comes from doing hard physical labour to its conclusion. They had dumped ash here before. Once it had been a road, or so Jennet assumed. She hadn't seen that ancient tarry surface used for anything else. Part of the bridge had fallen away long since and it was easy, if precarious, to balance the trailer at the edge of the gap and rake the ash out to fall down to the natural pit many feet below. The empty trailer was much easier to take back, and after they had peeled off their plastic suits and disposed of them, there was laughter and camaraderie on the way back. Only Jennet was distracted, trying and failing to hide her worry and join in. She saw two of the boys exchange a meaningful glance and change the subject, and bit her lip. She was grateful for their consideration but just then she would rather they had let her pretend. And then she was annoyed because she was an Elder now and Elders were supposed to admit the truth even if it was hard. They were almost home and suddenly it seemed to Jennet that she would go mad if she had to enter the crates straight away. The weight of her responsibility choked her.

'I'll be back soon,' she said firmly.

Her mates glanced at her. The oldest boy, Phil, gave her a searching look. 'All right then. If you're sure?'

Jennet nodded. 'I'll be back before dark.'

She watched them go and when they were out of sight, turned towards the charcoal-coloured stack in the distance. It had once been a collection of buildings where – according to her grand-dam's mother – you could *buy* things like food and clothes and games. The concept of *buying* was so strange that Jennet could not quite make it fit in her head. How did you *buy* something? What use were tokens of metal or paper if you could not eat them? Why would you exchange useful items for that? She had often wondered if the stories had become distorted in the telling. Still whatever those broken walls had once enclosed, it was a good place to sit and think. Or it always had been. Today Jennet found it eerie in a way she never had before. As if the past was very close and its ghosts whispered to her across the years, telling her tales of their strange, unthinking lives, blissfully unaware of what was coming. Even in the 'jewel' – a tiny corner of remaining building where high over her head a round window cast brilliantly coloured shadows on the ground from its tinted green and blue glass – Jennet felt the nearness of the 'others'. She huffed out a breath. Perhaps you were not supposed to be able to put off your responsibilities until you felt like facing them. And perhaps that was just as well. She glanced around at the derelict buildings. Perhaps that was what her ancestors, the others, had done. Then, when it was too late to change what would happen, had they realised what their neglect had caused?

Jennet thought they must have spent most of their long lives like children, except that all the children she knew were well aware of when to stop the game. The breeze shifted and she found herself starting to her feet before she realised what she had heard. A man's voice raised in a cry of pained protest, and the irregular *thunk thunk* of small heavy objects being thrown. Jennet peered around the side of the building. Three children, ten or twelve-years-old maybe, were harrying a fourth, much taller figure with hard flung stones. There was no element of play, nor did she think they were amusing themselves by tormenting an outsider. Wanderers always received a mixed welcome depending on which set of crates luck led them to first. Jennet didn't recognise the children. They weren't from her crate. But she did recognise the hard, determined expressions, the look of tightly controlled fear in their eyes. She had seen those things on the faces of her own folk. The look of those who have spotted a predator and are determined to drive off the danger despite being scared green.

This wanderer did not look dangerous, from what she could see of him. He was thin and unarmed. He carried no pack of provisions. She wondered how far he had travelled. A stone missed its mark and whizzed past her ear.

'Stop! Enough!' Jennet shouted. She pulled the scarf off her hair, so that it blew around her face in the breeze. Several hanks of her dark hair had been bleached white and it was cropped short at the back. The distinctive style of an Elder. The three children paused. A lean-faced girl canted her head to one side, watching Jennet suspiciously. She tossed a stone up in the air and caught it with the same hand, over and over in a single fluid movement. Jennet kept her expression calm, her stance relaxed, and waited. Finally, the girl narrowed her pale green eyes and whistled through her teeth. The two boys fell in behind her when she jerked her chin. Jennet caught the half-quizzical expression the girl cast her way. *He's your problem now,* it seemed to say.

Jennet approached slowly, holding her hands up where the stranger could see. 'It's all right, Friend,' she said, using the traditional greeting for a traveller. 'You may pass if you mean no harm.' She stopped a couple of feet away. The stranger looked up, his mottled hood falling back and Jennet gasped. He was the oldest man she had ever seen. At least fifty. Maybe even older. His eyes were huge and round in his thin face. Then she noticed a sluggish trickle of blood from one temple where a stone had cut his face. The stranger was grumbling to himself – something about 'bloody Lord of the Flies,' whatever that meant. Jennet wondered if he was confused from the stone hitting him or just confused because he had lived so long. She helped him over to the remains of a set of steps, then used water from her canteen to wash the cut. It was shallow, already closing.

'Are you OK?' Jennet said slowly. He hadn't responded to the traditional greeting. Maybe he didn't know the language of the travellers?

'I'm fine,' the man said gruffly. 'What are you doing out here by yourself? And why did those hooligans stop when you told them to?' He eyed her with suspicion.

Jennet frowned. Whoever he was, he clearly hadn't been well brought up although that had admittedly been some decades ago.

'They are children not hooli…what you said,' Jennet didn't know what 'hooligans' meant but the wanderer's tone had been unflattering. 'And they were merely doing their duty to their crate.'

'Stoning a man minding his own business is a duty?' the wanderer said incredulously.

Jennet shrugged. 'Sometimes strangers from other settlements attack. If there's hunger or drought or even if there's more ash than usual. People become desperate. Children learn early to fend off wild animals. If they are alone with no Elder to ask for help, they may try to drive off a stranger if he seems dangerous.'

The man gave a dark chuckle, then winced and pressed a hand to his ribs. 'And yet you told them to stop.'

'I can see you're not dangerous.'

The man raised a startlingly pale gaze to Jennet's face. In fact, under the grime and blood, all of him that could be seen was alarmingly pale. His skin was nowhere near as dark as her own. His hair was completely white, as was the stubble of his beard and his wiry eyebrows. Deep lines framed his blue eyes and there were grooves on either side of his mouth. Jennet gazed at him in fascination.

'What makes you say I'm not dangerous?' the man said.

Jennet shook herself. 'Because you are not. You are wandering without even a stick to defend yourself. You have no food or belongings. Your clothes are old and in bad repair.' She ticked off those things that she had unconsciously noticed. 'And you are sad.' The man started but Jennet went on. 'Deeply sad about something, in a way that goes beyond the sorrow of the moment. You carry your burdens on the inside.'

The man opened his mouth but said nothing. Jennet's curiosity got the better of her.

'How *old* are you?'

The man stared at her for a moment, then laughed. 'Seventy-four,' he said.

Jennet's ears seemed to be full of the sea at high tide. That couldn't be right. He must be joking or lying or confused. 'But then you must remember the old world,' she murmured.

A pained look crossed the wanderer's face and Jennet realised that he was telling the truth, and she knew then where his sadness came from. What if you lost not one person or two but your whole crate? Not just your crate but all the crates for miles around until you were sure you were the only living person in the whole world. What if you lost your world?

'Where are you from?' Jennet said with more urgency than she'd intended.

The man gave another short laugh. 'From the past, as you said.' He swallowed and seemed to come to some decision. 'Once I was a young man and the world was green and blue not grey. I never noticed the colours because I worked in a lab and did clever things with bacteria and viruses that older people – who I thought were wise but were really just clever enough to think they were wise – praised me and paid me a lot of money for. There were too many people, you see, and the things I made in glass tubes would sort that out.' The man laid his bony, withered hands out on his thighs, palms open to the sky. 'It worked too well and lots of people died. Other people – from other crates as you would say – became scared and tried to burn out the infection I had made and that those older wiser men released so thoughtlessly. They sent bombs that other clever people had made in labs. Now there is hardly anyone left and by the time the world is green and blue again, there may be no people left to see it.'

Jennet regarded him silently, then sat down next to him. 'That is a very sad story.'

The man gave her an irritated look. 'I am the reason you live like you do, kid. Don't you get it?'

Jennet shrugged. She felt certain of herself as an Elder for the first time since Willow had gone into labour. 'Maybe because you come from the old world you cannot see the colours in the new? In your mind, I do not think you ever did leave your lab. That makes your story ever more sad because what is the use of a story if you cannot learn from it?'

The man's white eyebrows pulled together. 'Just how old *are* you?' he demanded.

'I am an Elder of the crates,' Jennet said solemnly. She saw he didn't understand. 'I am fifteen-years-old. You have to be at least fourteen to be an Elder.'

The man gaped at her. 'But you're a child.'

Jennet shook her head. 'No. I haven't been a child for a long time.' She paused and then went on. 'Most lives are far shorter than the seven decades you have lived.' She saw he understood then and hoped he wouldn't take it as a reproach. The blood drying on his face was so bright a hue that it was almost a discordant note in the ash-coloured world. 'But as short as it might seem to you, we have many good things. Family, safety, children, friends. A place to belong.'

'I have wandered a long time but death never seems to catch up with me,' the man said wryly.

Jennet gave him an impatient look. 'Why waste so much time waiting for something that will happen anyway? You see a grey world but how many different kinds of grey have you counted? You look at all the wrong things. The old world will not come back in your lifetime, long as it is.'

The wanderer gave her an unreadable look. 'What do you want me to do?'

'I think you should come back to my crate and meet my mates. I think you should stay.'

'But why would you want me?' the man said in surprise.

'Because you must know other stories than the one you told me. Stories that make you laugh or cry or feel like you can do anything. I want you to tell them.' Jennet met that pale blue gaze again. 'Those children threw stones at you because they saw you were different and thought it meant you were dangerous. You *are* different but I believe different can be good. We can learn from different.'

'Are you sure you're only fifteen?'

Jennet smiled. 'Come back and meet my sister and my new niece.'

The man's wary expression softened into something Jennet didn't have a name for. 'All right. But I'm not house broken anymore. It's been a long time since I had a home.'

Jennet held out a hand and helped him up. 'Home is just the empty place we carry inside ourselves until we find the right thing to fill it.'

The man snorted as he fell into step beside her. 'Your niece is going to have to learn to navigate a lot of mystical bullshit before she's much older.'

Jennet half-smiled. 'She was born last night. You know the rhyme?'

'Born at ashfall, blessed by nightfall,' the man said. 'Of course. I've heard that one a few times.'

Jennet glanced sharply at him but he was serious. She could tell. And perhaps he was right. After all, Jennet herself had been an ashfall child. In her worry, she had forgotten. Hope, she realised. In his face, it was hope. We can all live in hope. We do so every day. Feeling lighter, strong enough to shoulder her responsibilities once more, Jennet took the wanderer's hand and led him home.

ANDY LEACH

It Was Only a Patch on the Wall

It was only a patch on the wall,
That only showed up when that afternoon squall
Tapped on the window, came in uninvited.
You blame yourself now for being shortsighted.
Remember you thought it was nothing, too small.
It was only a patch on the wall.

It was only a tickly cough.
They'd had worse, and besides, you were now better off,
Under a roof with fish fingers for tea,
You kept up their strength with some vitamin C
That you got from the chemist to add to some squash,
Before going upstairs, clean their teeth, have a wash,
Into bed, tell them stories, she laughed, he would scoff!
It was only a tickly cough.

It was only a polite request.
The patch had got bigger, you thought it was best
If you mentioned it now before things got much worse,
And you couldn't believe why the landlord would curse,
But he did, he made out as if you were to blame,
He made you feel small and he made you feel shame
And he said that he'd fix it; he didn't say when.

So after a fortnight you called him again,
And he said you made problems, he'd send you the bill,
And you tried to explain that your children were ill,
That the doctor had said that the damp was the cause,
There was mould on the walls, it was like the outdoors
Were creeping inside where they didn't belong –
He said you were lying, he said you were wrong.
He'd got you pegged down as the troublesome kind
And he warned you about the damned contract you'd
signed,
That if you didn't like it, there's others who would,
So now leave it to him and he'd do what he could.
And still your boy coughed, and your girl held her chest.
It was only a polite request.

It was only one half of a shift –
But you just couldn't leave them and so missed your lift
To the warehouse, but hopefully they'd understand
That both kids are sick, being late wasn't planned,
That they can't go to school or be left on their own
When they're like this. And so you had to phone
For your friend who came round, but it all took an hour
Then the bus wouldn't stop and your mobile lost power
–
And now two weeks later the work's running dry,
Your hours are down and as hard as you try
The ends just won't meet as your money is short
After rent, after food, and the shoes that you bought
When the others wore through. One more interview
To see if there's anything else you can do.
There's forms to fill in, someone mentions food banks,
And you're shuffling out and you're mumbling 'thanks'
While holding back tears so the children won't see.
This morning, no power, no electricity.

You're praying inside, please don't cut me adrift –
It was only one half of a shift.

It was only a zero hours job that you hate.
It was only some pay they refused to backdate.
It was only a cheque that arrived six days late.
It was only a landlord who owned the estate.
It was only a list on which you had to wait.
It was only a law that made you relocate.
It was only a system designed to frustrate.
It was only the lack of a fair Welfare State –

And now you're on a sofa, the kids with your mum,
Lying awake half the night, cold and numb.
Dreading tomorrow, another appointment,
With an officer dealing in hot disappointment.
You know the drill now as you've been there before –
(The smell of despair as you walk thought the door,
You're given more forms then they ask you to prove
Your predicament isn't a preconceived move.
Your temper will rise and you'll find yourself riled,
You've come for help, not to be Jeremy Kyled,
And you'll try not to lose it, you'll try to stay calm,
You'll try to explain how your kids suffered harm
In the last place you tried to make into a home –)
Staring into the night rendered bleak monochrome,
Wondering how to get life back on track.
Each glance in the mirror, a stranger stares back.
Evicted and jobless and feeling at fault,
Under a blanket and under assault.
Under the thumb of a state employee
And wondering how what's now one was once three.

It was only a zero hours job that you hate.

It was only some pay they refused to backdate.
It was only a cheque that arrived six days late.
It was only a landlord who owned the estate.
It was only a list on which you had to wait.
It was only a law that made you relocate.
It was only a system designed to frustrate.
It was only the lack of a fair Welfare State.
It was only a life that you now can't recall.
It was only a patch on the wall.

LEE HAMBLIN

Ballerina

Inside the box was a doll: pink-skinned, blue-eyed, her hair wire-like and unnaturally blonde. There was a pile of child's clothes: three plain cotton dresses flawlessly ironed and folded, three pairs of white ankle socks with pretty bows, a hooded blue overcoat that had wooden pegs as buttons. There was a silk dress as fragile as moth wings that I set down taking extra care, afraid it would crumble to dust if I unravelled it too quickly. And then there were the shoe-like slippers, rosy-pink with a satin sheen, hardened and scuffed black at the toe, with wide, long shiny ribbons for laces.

I heard the key turn in the front door, so hurriedly put the things back, and hid the box exactly where I found it, underneath the thick winter blankets at the back of the wardrobe. I skipped past her in the hallway and ran outside, to go play football in the park.

What you been up to, my boy? she called after me. But I was already too far down the road to hear her.

I have often wondered. But I never asked. And I was never told.

I pray for the rain to stop, if only for today.

Driving on motorways since dawn through a persistent grey. My mind lost in the mantra of the wiper's arc.

The letter, stonehearted official, lies open on the passenger seat. I keep glancing at it, unsure exactly how they found me after so many years.

Outside the house, under an umbrella, is a high-heeled stranger. She is wearing a dark trouser suit. She gives me refuge from the rain, sharing with me her canopy. I introduce myself and offer her my hand. I tell her that hers is icy, but she prefers to say that she is fine, and has just this minute arrived herself, which I think – no, I know – is not the truth. She is so very young and has a kind face, a trusting face.

From a bag she takes out a folder, crammed full of papers, some of which will need signing and returning when you have time, she says.

Here are the keys, she says. The cremation was last week. We had quite some trouble tracking you down. After a pause she adds, I am very sorry for your loss. Words she must often utter in her line of work, but they sound sincere nonetheless. She is closer to tears than I. She checks her wristwatch, and leaves me with a pot of ashes, a folder, and the rain.

It is fifty years since I was last here, and it looks much smaller than I remember.

There have been many other homes, and many others that I also called mother since I was last here.

It had started like any other morning, walking to school, and she waving me goodbye at the school gates, smiling the same smile as always.

But that day she never came to collect me. And I never got to go home.

I only ever saw her once again – a few weeks later – when she came to sign papers. She was led into the headmaster's office; he had made a point of not closing the door. I sat outside, as I was told to, my legs swinging to and fro, occasionally looking at her from the corridor, but she never caught my eye. I was aged seven, nearly eight.

Later on, when I asked my other mothers about her, they only ever told me that she was somewhat sick, or unwell, and they'd tell me it's best to forget about her.

Houses die too. Inside it's ice-cold and musty. I go to her bedroom, to the wardrobe, to the box. It's still there, in its secret place.

Inside is a photograph that I'm sure wasn't there before. It is of my mother. There is a young girl stood by her side. They are both smiling. It is strange and unsettling to again see my mother smiling; it's not how she left me. The young girl beside her is dressed like a ballerina and holding a shiny gold medal in front of her chest.

In my mother's arms is a newborn baby dressed in blue.

In a café now, percussive rain grappling with 80's synth-pop. In front of me: an empty teacup, salt pot, pepper pot, a glass ashtray that even after 25 years tempts me, and an A4 folder full of papers, that hold perhaps, if I really want them, answers.

JACQUELINE WARD

I Never Wore a Watch

When I was a little girl we had a cat that had kittens. Some of them were strong but the runt got runny eyes and kept sneezing. It was quite cute, to see it sneeze, until my mother's face did sad. The poorly kitten used to make the long journey down our hallway to the litter tray and the pobs. One day, my mother moved them nearer, but it still made the journey down the hallway, using all its strength.

That's a bit like me now. Still trying to do things for myself when it's all been arranged for me. Meals on wheels. I don't know why they call it that. The woman arrives every day with three containers. She's never introduced herself.

'Here you are, Annie, love. All you need for today. Melanie will be round later to warm them up for you.'

She wears a badge with her name on it. She's been coming for a while now. The other one, Melanie, has been coming for a shorter time and she's different altogether. She introduced herself right away, no messing about. She sits there for the allotted time, which I am guessing is twenty minutes or so, listening to me talk and doing bored and playing with her phone. I've got good at guessing time over the years because I never wore a watch.

I do get about a bit, even though I'm seventy-five or thereabouts. I go into the bedroom and switch on the radio and listen to that instead of watching the telly. I still like to keep my body going even if my mind isn't there anymore. I sometimes wonder if it ever was.

Oh yes, I've had psychiatric reports, you know. By order of the courts, no less. I was a little bugger when I was young, and not so young, come to that. Me and Ettie used to get up to all sorts, but breaking into that house topped the lot. Ettie Clark was my best friend. We'd concoct all sorts of adventures as children, but by the time we went to work in the ciggie factory we'd become more serious about things.

On our way home we'd pass Sam Bolton's house. Five bedrooms, it was. Huge. Been left to him by his father. He'd never married, Sam. One day Ettie had linked me as we walked past the beautiful red brick semi.

'I wonder what he does in there?'

I'd looked up at the windows. The curtains were always open and, in the top right hand window, there was some movement, but it was too far away to see what it was.

'I don't know, Et, but I bet he's up to no good.'

There's always someone in your neighbourhood, isn't there? Someone who has a few too many plants or cats or dogs? Someone who's a little bit unusual? To us, it was Sam Bolton. When he did come out, which was not very often, he'd wear a long dark grey mac and a flat cap. He'd go into town on the orange bus and sit upstairs. He never spoke to anyone and his face did nothing. It was that what egged us on. It was curiosity, I suppose.

Me and Ettie speculated for months about what he had in that house. Cats? Dogs? Rabbits? Mary Jennings told us that she saw the delivery cart pull up to his back gate and some sacks being delivered. And it wasn't coal. They were jute sacks, light enough for one man to lift easily.

After putting the scant evidence together we came to the conclusion that he was keeping someone prisoner. So we set about our rescue plan. One Saturday, when he was safely on the bus, we opened his back gate and pushed down on the back door latch. It opened. Ettie's face did surprised. We hadn't expected the door open and hadn't planned any farther than that.

So we ventured in. The kitchen was scrubbed clean, as was the lounge. Completely pristine. But there was a smell. An awful animal stench. Sawdust and lime. As we walked up the stairs we saw that he had erected a huge wooden frame with chicken wire stretched across it on the landing. Behind the frame were hundreds of pigeons. It was a bit disappointing when we'd expected to find a woman being kept against her will, or someone being blackmailed. We'd sat on the steps for a while, searching for a reason to be there.

Ettie said it first. 'It's cruel. Keeping them here.'

We were suddenly outraged. We set to work pulling at the chicken wire, breaking the edges first, tearing at the wooden slats until finally they came away from the wall. The back door was still open, and, in an urgent rush, all the pigeons made a break for it. We sat down on the stairs again, breathless. I looked at Ettie and her face did pure happiness.

'They're free!'

I felt joy. Liberation. Until I looked up and Sam Bolton was standing in the doorway. He didn't say anything but his face was doing angry now. He didn't shout or make a fuss. He just turned around and went out of the back door, locking it behind him. After a short while, during which Ettie and I reminded each other that we were just bothered about the birds and how they were being kept captive and how cruel it was, he returned with a Bobby. We were arrested and soon we were in court.

If my parents' shame hadn't been enough, what happened next was worse. I'd lived all my life timeless. I used to run over the crofts and moors, hair flowing behind me. Joyful. Free. I'd been to school and sat at the back messing about and apart from Ettie, I'd never had any other friends. I couldn't read and write and I'd never learned to tell the time. I don't know why, but it'd never sunk in. I'd always followed my brothers out when it was time for school and then work. I got up when it was light and went to bed when it was dark. That was just the way it was.

Now all sorts of people were asking me questions. The solicitor my father had paid for. The magistrate, who was really Mr Price from up the road in the big houses.

'What time did you leave the house, Annabel?'

'What time did you enter Mr Bolton's property?'

I'd always been all right when Ettie was there because she'd answer for me, filling in any gaps. I think she knew, really. But she'd already been seen, separately, because she'd said it was all her fault, which wasn't true.

When I said I didn't know the times they sighed, their faces doing big difficult. When they asked me to read an oath, I just stared at them. Eventually, after lots of time-related questions, Mr Price got up.

'Psychiatrist.'

That was all he said. I couldn't see what his face was doing because he didn't even look at me. But a strange thing happened next. My mother and father's faces, that had been very angry and hadn't really spoken to me since we freed the pigeons, suddenly did caring. Other people's faces did pitiful.

'Fancy that Ettie leading her on like that and with her being a bit strange.'

Me? Strange? I'd tried to tell them that we'd thought Sam Bolton was a bit strange, but my father told me that he was breeding racing pigeons and it was up to him what he did in his own house. All mine and Ettie's protests about cruelty were met with shaking heads, like we were children. But we weren't children. Ettie got sent to prison for three months. I got sent to the psychiatrist.

The psychiatric unit was quite nice, really.

'Sit down, Annabel. How old are you? Seventeen? And what have you been up to?'

I remember her face did a small smile as she read my notes. But I held onto the fact that she had told me my age. People telling me my age has been little milestones for me. Little stickers in my memory that I try to map onto my life.

'Pigeons? Eh?'

She was American. Told me she was from New York. Married a Manchester lad. First psychiatrist to work for the Manchester courts.

'So your notes say that you're difficult and you wouldn't answer any of the questions. But you weren't rowdy or violent. So why, Annabel? Why?'

I thought about it. I thought very carefully. Then I told her.

'I couldn't read the thing they gave me because I can't read. They were on about what time it was. And I never wore a watch, so I never knew. That's why I didn't answer them. Because I didn't know what time it was.'

She tapped her pencil on the desk. 'Tell me more.' Her voice did soft and not urgent and impatient like everyone else's.

'Well. I don't like the feeling of being tied down. I like to be free. That's why we let the pigeons go. Freedom.'

'And you feel tied down? You feel imprisoned?'

'I do. Not actually in prison, like Ettie is, but I feel like everyone wants to fit me in a box. I watch what they do. Their faces. Tells you a lot. I go by the light, me. I always have. When the birds sing, it's time to get up. Summer's summer, winter's winter. And the moon tells me when t' seasons about to change.'

She stared at me for a long time. 'What a wonderful way to live, Annabel.'

For a moment, I actually felt what her face did. The happiness. The freedom. Then it did sad.

'So. We've got a problem here. There's nothing wrong with you. Nothing at all. In fact, there's more wrong with me than there is with you. But if I tell them that you're saner than most of them they'll punish you for letting those birds free. So I'm going to tell them that you have a nervous disorder. OK?'

I nodded. She stood up and I took that as my cue to leave. As I opened the door she put her hand on my shoulder.

'It would do you good to learn to read and write. There's so much to love in stories. But never change, Annabel. Never change.'

So I got off with it and Ettie eventually came out. We both started doing work at the orphanage and I worked there all my life. I never did learn to read or write. Not because I didn't want to. My god, the joy in the stories Mel reads to me, I'd love to be able to read that. I just couldn't learn.

No, I never did change, and, by the time my body became autumn I'd become one of *those* people. You know, the strange ones. I think it stuck, that pretend nervous disorder. Eventually I'd got a little sheltered flat off the council and I'd filled it with plants. Because plants are another way of telling the time. I'd watch the birds outside my windows, the starlings getting ready to fly off in the autumn, and the baby magpies in the spring.

All the kids ran past the window quick because they thought I was odd; I could tell from their faces. Then I'd laugh, because it all reminded me of Sam Bolton and how me and Ettie thought he was some kind of monster when all he was doing was happiness, all on his own. Like me.

Now it's easy to tell what time it is. Meals on Wheels and Mel. They're my clock. After the pigeon incident was forgotten and my mother and father died, people forgot that I couldn't read and one bloke whose face did love even bought me a watch. I never wore it. I married him all the same and one day he brought home a bunch of flowers and said it was our ruby wedding anniversary. But I don't count in years. I still count in love and joy and light.

LIAM HOGAN

The Castle at Number 48

It is a street at war with itself. Not just the odds versus the evens, facing up across the no-man's land of black tarmac behind twin barricades of parked cars and net curtains. This street has found other battlegrounds over which to fight.

Each of the red-brick terraced houses has two front doors: one, leading to the ground floor and cluttered yards, the other – via a narrow stairwell – up 14 steep steps to the rooms above. 'Maisonettes,' they call them: 'Little houses.'

Only they're not; they're flats, without the sense of community that a proper block of flats might have. Instead they're treated as castles, drawbridges raised each evening. Because the enemy is at the gate. These are castles that share too many walls and floors and ceilings with their neighbours. Hardly the most soundproofed of castles, either.

The hot, dry summer isn't helping matters. Windows are thrown open, thumping music at pane-rattling volumes annoys even those who don't share a common wall. Bins overflow and fester, their contents redistributed during the night by rat, or cat, or fox. Tempers flare when stultifying heat robs the residents of their sleep.

Into this tinderbox of urban tension is dropped one Alfred Patrick Halligan: racist, homophobe, misogynist. These are his *better* character flaws – ones he was trained to have from an early age, passed down from father to son; unforgiveable, but explicable. Worse than these: he's a misanthrope, a bully. A mean-spirited son-of-a-bitch.

Sixty-years-old, he's a part-time worker at the sewage works beneath Alexander Palace. Of Irish descent, he keeps a permanent reminder of the Troubles in the shape of a smashed kneecap. He never says who gave him it, or why. At home he uses a walking stick to help him move around; its crook is a knob of black-gnarled wood, its tip solid brass. He's partially deaf. He's an alcoholic. And he really doesn't want to be on this war-torn street.

The housing block he's lived in for the last seventeen years is being renovated. All part of the council's New Deal. He was happy with the old one. The crumbling window frames behind the ground floor security grille didn't bother him, but he didn't have any say in the matter. The Council have found him alternative accommodation at Number 48, vacant after its previous occupants left in the early hours one morning, owing three months back rent. It's on the first floor. He grumbled and cursed, but it was what was available.

Each morning he clatters down the steps at 6.30; sewage is best handled before the heat of the day raises the stench to its full stomach-churning peak. Going down the stairs is the only time he really needs his stick, though he likes the feel of it by his side. Clump, clump, clump the stick and his heavy boots go.

Downstairs at number 46, his neighbour, Adriana Janowski: eight-and-a-half months pregnant, ankles swollen to balloons, sweat staining her poly-cotton sheets, turns over and tries to hide her head beneath the pillow until the heat forces her to break cover, just as the door slams shut.

She shudders, remembering her attempt to get him to be more considerate. She was pregnant, she said.

'So I see,' he replied.

She was pregnant, she repeated haltingly, and having difficulty sleeping.

'And I have difficulty walking. What exactly do you want me to do about that?'

She recoiled as if slapped, before muttering whether he couldn't somehow soften the end of his walking stick; a rubber cap, perhaps...

He laughed, harsh and braying. 'Oh aye, a rubber cap would solve both our problems. Bit late for you, though?'

She stared at him, disbelieving, before bursting into tears.

His leering grin softened a little. 'All right love, don't get into a state. I'll see what I can do.'

But he did nothing; the sharp tap-tap continues unabated. Alf is a creature of habit; she can set her clock by the tap-tap-tap as he goes to the bathroom for his 2.00am micturition. Tap-tap-tap as he gets up at 5.45. Tap-tap-tap when he comes home, going back and forth between the television – blaring out the Irish sports channel at maximum volume – and the beer-laden fridge.

The only respite is those blissful few hours when he is at work, before his thundering return, or when he limps out to the pub on the corner to watch something his chipped satellite receiver doesn't carry. But that is only a temporary reprieve; she knows that he'll return steaming drunk, the thuds of the stick more erratic, his voice raised in bellicose snatches of out-of-tune song. Eventually he'll quieten down, collapse in his armchair, boots still on, the rasp of his snore audible through the too-thin floorboards.

But it isn't just the noise from her upstairs neighbour that keeps Adriana awake through the stuffy, uncomfortable nights. It is the dwindling bank balance, no longer bolstered by her cash-in-hand cleaning job. It is the fear of what awaits her if she is forced back to her native Poland, the disgrace she will be in as a single mother.

And now, as if reflecting her concerns, worries, and shredded nerves, the city seems to be on the brink of an eruption. Sirens wail up and down Seven Sisters Road and flood through the open windows, shattering her dreams and waking the slumbering giant above her.

'Feckin' garda!' he bellows, his curses barely intelligible, 'Pigs!'

She doesn't know if he thinks they've come for him (oh, what bliss that would be!) or if he's just cursing in their general direction. She doubts he knows either.

The sirens are explained the next morning: an arrest gone wrong. Details are sketchy, but a youth has been shot. Was he armed? Black? Was he even a youth? Rumours that he shot first. Rumours that he was carrying nothing more dangerous than a table leg. Why would he be carrying a table leg? No one knew. Reports trickle down through the day, the local radio call-in is besieged by angry residents, by spokespeople for the community. A protest march is quickly arranged.

The following day is calmer; a lull before the storm, as though gathering energy for what comes next. Even Alf is quieter than normal, no doubt still feeling the effects of his drunken and disturbed sleep on top of a record-breakingly hot day's work. He still gets up at 2.00am, still slams the door at 6.30 and, even if he hadn't, the expectation that he will is enough to have her heart racing and her hand gripping the damp sheet that lies over her, as she feels the first heat from the morning sun burn through the thin curtains.

Adriana is eager for all this to be over; for the baby to be delivered, even though she knows that won't solve any of her problems, even though it hastens the day when she might be driven back into the disapproving arms of her parents. They will, of course, assume that the baby is Henryk's, assume that it is the unexpected and unwanted child that has driven him away. The truth is more prosaic; it's Henryk's, all right, but he left two weeks before that first pregnancy test, the one that revealed the little blue cross she is to be crucified upon.

The long day is even hotter than yesterday. The free newspapers on the oven-like underground blare impossible numbers as headlines and show pictures of young women sitting in deckchairs or paddling in Trafalgar Square's fountains. Yesterday's incident creeps onto the front page only as a redirection: North London Shooting – Page 6.

When she ventures out, the milk in the fridge having curdled, a gang of lanky youths sitting on the parched grass behind the pub heckle as she passes. They are surrounded by empty cans and bottles, tops stripped off showing taut, muscular frames. She pulls the beach wrap that is all that is still capable of covering the expanse of *her* taut belly tightly around her and walks – or waddles – as fast as she can.

She tries to snooze through the worst of the afternoon heat and wakes as the sun is setting, thirsty and with a dull throb of a headache. It is strangely quiet, no sign of Alf, no music blaring from across the way. She ducks her head out into the cooler evening; the street is empty, not even the younger kids haring up and down on their scooters and bicycles.

There's a spasm of pain as she gets up off the bed; needles behind the eyes, and suddenly devoid of breath she sits back down for a moment, before gingerly easing to her feet and stumbling to the tiny bathroom. But the cabinet is empty of Aspirin, empty of Paracetamol, the bottles and packets falling prey to the attrition of her last trimester. She switches the kettle on for a cup of mint tea and sits heavily on the arm of a battered armchair, breathing deeply, 'til long after the kettle has switched itself off. It's no use. She'll have to venture out, to once again struggle to the nearest convenience store.

She doesn't – *can't* – bother with the wrap, merely slipping her feet into a pair of Henryk's paint-stiffened work boots. If she bumps into a neighbour, so be it. They might at least run the errand for her, save her the trip. She's past caring.

But the street is as quiet as it was ten minutes earlier when she woke. She takes in great gulps of night air, steeling herself. It's a journey of a couple of minutes at most, just follow the curve of the street to the corner. Earlier, it took her five. Now though, it seems to take an age, the stabbing pain of the migraine preventing her from getting into a rhythm. Twice, she has to lean against a wall or lamp-post, holding back the tears.

When she reaches the shop on the Seven Sisters Road, the owner is pulling down the steel shutters. He starts when he sees her, a flash of something primal in his eyes before he takes in her state, before he recognises her as a regular.

'I'm closing–' he begins to say.

She begs him, calls him by name, pleads for painkillers: anything to stop the knives that make even the store's lights seem painfully bright. He ducks beneath the shutter and comes out moments later, a white and blue box in his hand. She fumbles for the coins in her pocket, but he holds up his hands to ward her off.

'Next time,' he says. 'You pay next time.'

She's halfway back before she thinks to look at her watch, the thin leather strap on its widest hole. She stares at it, wondering if it is broken; it says 9.00. She's been to Sanjay's store much later than that. As late as 11.00 or 12.00, in the days when she would take the crumpled notes from Henryk and exchange them for cans of Polish lager, while he showered the dust and dirt and paint out of his hair and skin.

She barely has time to register this before she sees a hooded figure running from the alley ahead of her. It serves as a cut through to the estate that flanks and dwarfs the row of maisonettes nestling in its shadow and, as she draws level with it, looking to see what there is to run from, a large group emerges: all male, all tall, many wearing hoods or bright scarves over the lower part of their faces. They spill out into the street, quickly fanning into a semi-circle with her at its centre and she feels the edge of the thin box she is clutching give as she tightens her grasp.

'What have we here?' an unfriendly voice asks.

She says nothing, tries not to look at them, tries to continue her slow progress back to the safety of her flat. But the crescent swings shut; her path is blocked.

'Please...' she mutters, 'Please, let me go.'

'Oh, it says *please*. And in English, at that.' The voice laughs, from directly in front of her, and the others join in.

There's a harsh smell, burnt plastic, spilt petrol, and she's aware that a number of them are holding boxes: shoe boxes, DVD players, electronic goods. Still she keeps her head down.

'Well, now, what have you got for us? Phone? Purse? What's that?'

A hand tug at hers, ripping the medicine from her grasp. She sways and stumbles, as the crowd hoots.

'Aspirin!' says a disgusted voice and the box is thrown down at her feet.

She begins to stoop, to reclaim her precious prize, the tears coming freely now, wanting to be home, wanting to free the little tablets from their plastic surround, wanting to curl up in bed and never again leave it. But as she bends there's a push – a blow – to her back and she collapses onto the still warm tarmac of the street, aware that the semi-circle is closer now, aware of a wall of trainers and legs in front of her.

But as she curls inwards there's a surprised yelp, a high-pitched laugh, and a 'Calm down, Granddad!'

'I'll calm ye, you feckin' lice.'

A clunk and a howl and suddenly there's space around her, a space into which a golden, gleaming cylinder at the end of a black staff magically appears. A strong arm pulls roughly at hers and she's up again, clutching at the shoulder of Alfred Halligan.

The crowd of youths hasn't gone far. A few are drifting off with their looted goods, the others hover just outside the range of the heavy walking stick.

'I know where you live, you dirty old bastard!' one spits, clutching an upper arm.

Alfred laughs. 'And I know you, Dominic Clifton. And you, Vinnie. I also know every ex-IRA hard-ass Irishman in the North of London. So get ye gone, ye yellow-bellied gobshites!'

For a long silent moment, neither side moves. In the near distance comes the sound of sirens. No doubt they have more pressing engagements than this one, no doubt none of the twitching curtains have bothered to call 999, but still, it's enough to break the stalemate. The rest of the youths disperse, hurling the occasional insult back down the street as Alfred helps Adriana to her door.

She's eager to be alone and she thinks she'll be able to manage from here. But the keys slip from her shaking fingers and it is Alfred who turns them in the lock, and then supports her into the darkened lounge. As she sits, he thrusts something into her hand. She's still staring at the crumpled packet of Aspirin when he returns with a glass of water.

'Yer man. He's not around, then?' Alfred asks.

She shakes her head, willing the tears not to return.

'When the time comes, give me a call, yes?'

She stares at him for a moment and gives a small nod.

He grunts. 'Ye'd best not go out so late. Ye'll be all right, now?'

She grins, like a fool, and nods again, and thanks him, her English having difficulty catching up with the sudden release of words, of emotions.

But he's already heading out of her front door, pulling it to and stepping over the broken fence to his.

And, as she sits in the gloom of the lounge, holding the glass and waiting – *praying* – for the headache to pass, there's a thump-thump-thump as Alfred slowly climbs the stairs of his castle.

TANIA HERSHMAN

Her Dirt

She keeps her dirt, and at first her dirt is enough. But then it isn't. So she takes to taking.

There is history here. A clean clean child. Or, rather: demands for a clean clean child. A pure-white home, a childhood washing and re-washing. Do you need to hear of distant mothers and of even further-spinning fathers?

She keeps her dirt in jars, in rows, on shelves, in rooms. She lives, of course, alone. Jars are labelled, jars are all the same. She does not touch the dirt, does not let it glister through her fingertips like stardust. The jars are sealed and left. If asked, she could not say why. But no one does.

She breaks into her neighbours' homes. She takes her own dustpan and brush and, no matter how many visits from their cleaner, finds something, underneath, behind. She labels, stares and sees no difference: Your dust or mine? His dust or hers?

Then she hears of Arthur Munby. A Victorian gentleman, he was obsessed, it seems, with dirt. Dirty women in particular. Part of her does not want to hear the rest, her insides long ago scrubbed of any thoughts of this. Of what he might want. With them. But when she looks down at her white white arms, her fingernails untouched, unbitten, the pale cloth of her shirt, she feels life spring up inside her.

She goes out for a walk, and at first she doesn't know what she's looking for. She wanders to her nearest train station, and when she is there starts to laugh because she realises she had hoped for coal. But there is no coal, no men kitted out in coal dust, no romantic muscled dark-faced men in this electric age. She will have to go elsewhere.

She takes to walking daily in search of this thing, this idea she could not name if asked, though no one does. It might be man or woman she is searching for. But everyone is freshly-washed. Even the cats are always cleaning, cleaning.

On one walk, she finds she's left the city. She did not notice, she had been humming to herself. The pavement has ended, she is on a path and by the path hedges are wild, no trimmers here, no neaten-uppers. She is not tired, which is odd, for she has never been that strong. She is not hungry either, although it must have been hours. Her legs keep moving her towards, towards.

The first puddle is a clue and she walks straight through it, no matter shoes or socks or trousers. A second puddle and a third, and she skips through them, off the path now. And then a barn, its door slightly open. Its door inviting.

What does she see when she walks in?

She sees a grey cube, in the middle of the floor. A large cube made of concrete.

She moves nearer and sees that it's not concrete. It's dirt.

She moves even nearer and sees that it's not just dirt. It's *her* dirt. All the childhood dirt she was forbidden. How she knows this she couldn't say if asked, though no one does.

As she approaches she sees:

- lint from pockets in a favourite summer dress that she was made to pick out with tiny fingers
- mud from their pond that she'd wanted to rub on her face and arms
- balls of dust from underneath the sofa, where she once hid and sneezed and gave it all away and was dragged out, dust-smeared, and afterwards was hit
- clippings from toenails that were never seen
- clumps of hair from the dog she was not allowed to have
- flakes of her skin from the mattress she cried into when the dog was taken away again

She moves closer still, towards this past-dirt monument. There is no moment when she thinks: How is this here? And: For me? No, there is just her reaching out one arm and then the other, sliding hands into the softness of her-dirt, up to her elbows and then further, to the shoulders, and then she takes that step and walks right in, into the middle of the cube.

As she does, her jars, in rows, on shelves, in rooms, burst open all at once. The dirt – her dirt and his, your dirt and mine – spills out, fountains, spurts, streams and gushes over everything. House dust and grime on every surface, every book, every fork and spoon and knife, every cushion, every shoe and every window sill, until there is a thick, thick layer. When it is done, the lids of the jars sigh closed, and everything is blanketed. As if no one lives here. As if no one has been here for years, for decades, for millennia. As if we were never here at all.

MARC DE FAOITE

Find Yourself

Find yourself. Alone in a strange city. Spend a long cold night outdoors: empty-pocketed/sober/deviceless/hungry. Use the safety net of a return bus/plane/train ticket. Or not. Add weather: cold/damp/rain/snow. Streets. Meet yourself in ways unexpected. Walk hours on end. Find warmth where you can. Find yourself, lost. Talk to strangers, but not to anyone you know. Or choose silence. In the quest for self-knowledge you double the stakes. Forty-eight penniless hours: dizzy with sleeplessness/weak with hunger/racked with crippling self-doubt. Walk. Feel the metallic weight of cold clouds and cold stares. Resist doing anything illegal. Or immoral. Let tears wash your illusions away. With cleansed eyes see the world afresh. See yourself now, finally honest. Find yourself, found. Return home. If you can.

RACHAEL DUNLOP

Emptiness in Harmony

The story of my birth could have been the stuff of family legend. First babies are supposed to take their time arriving; malingering in the birth canal, reluctant to leave the only home they have known. Or maybe it's the mother's body that holds them fast, unaware until then that the tenancy was always destined to be temporary. Either way, first babies are not supposed to rocket out into the carpeted foot well of a Ford Granada being driven with stately smoothness by a man wearing open-knuckled leather driving gloves and an expression of closed determination. That man being my father. I don't know he was wearing his driving gloves, of course, but given that he has done so each and every time I have seen him get behind the wheel, I think it's a fair assumption.

Late to the business of parenthood, neither he nor my mother realised things were progressing so quickly. The midwife was called and they were instructed to get to the hospital. 'We were so worried you'd be born at home, we didn't even remember to lift your mother's hospital bag,' my father said. 'Not that it mattered, in the end.'

'Would it have been so bad,' I wondered, 'being born at home?'

My father had looked at me across the top of his newspaper. 'Not the done thing,' was all he said.

So, the story continued, my mother was bundled into the back of the Granada and off they went to the hospital. But I was very insistent, apparently, on making my way out and, driven by instinct more than decorum, my mother swung herself around to brace her feet against the front seats.

'Cross your legs, Sofia!' my father instructed her, sliding panicked sideways glances into the rear-view mirror, wanting to know, but at the same time, not (I imagine. He retches if he finds the Sunday chicken has come with a bag of giblets secreted in its belly, I doubt he'd have dealt well with a view of my mother spread-legged and bloodied in the back of his precious motor).

So, to cut a short story shorter, out I came and my mother scooped me up, held me fast, still attached to her via cord and placenta. A placenta that refused to evict itself as it should and turned my mother inside out. She'd bled to death before they ever got to the hospital and the Granada was a write-off.

That's the story, more or less, oft retold, or variations upon it. And the thing is, none of it is true, not a word. Nothing bar the details my imagination provides.

When the phone call came it took me a moment to understand what the woman was saying. She announced herself as 'You Know, Linda!' and assumed I was familiar with my father's daily habits. And maybe most grown sons would be. But not me. I asked her to repeat what she'd said.

'Your father didn't come to dance class this morning, Guido. He hasn't missed a class in five years. Five years, can you believe it?'

It wasn't the five years I couldn't believe. 'Did you say dance class?'

'Yes, you know, his ballroom dancing. Every Thursday. You know!'

I didn't. I decided not to admit that. 'OK, so, um…'

'So,' You Know, Linda! continued, 'I phoned the house, to check on him, of course he refuses to have a mobile, and he's not answering. The community centre has you down as his emergency contact so really we just wanted to find out if he's OK.'

'OK.'

'So is he? He's OK?'

Now that was a question. 'I don't know,' I said.

I thought I heard a tsk from the other end of the line. 'Well, perhaps you could check? I know you're not very close. Close by, I mean. But could you… I mean, we're all a bit worried.'

Who? Who was worried about my father? I felt like I'd fallen into a parallel world, a world of opposites where my father had friends.

'If you're coming in by train, I could get my Pamela to pick you up at the station. I know she'd love to see you. She always felt bad about how things finished between you.'

'Pamela?'

'You know, Pammy!'

And then the penny dropped, a big old-fashioned penny-piece that dropped edge-on and spun in the deep recesses of my memory. Pammy had been my girlfriend when we were teenagers. From the age of fourteen to eighteen, right up until I went to university, never to return and (I assume) breaking her heart.

'Sure,' I said. 'Fine. I'm homeward bound.'

I stood on the doorstep of my father's house, Pammy teetering close behind me.

'Lordy, Guido, are you sure about this? It feels really weird.' Pammy poked her head around my shoulder. Pamela, as she likes to be called now. But always Pammy to me. 'What if he's in there, you know…'

'Dead?' I said. 'I doubt it. My father doesn't entertain either births or death in his house. This we know.'

Pammy gave me a poke in the back. 'All right, professor, how long have you been saving up that line?'

'I thought of it on the way down on the train.' I turned and gave her what I hoped was a wolfish grin but by the look on her face it was more of a grimace.

'Come on then, lover, let's get this over with.' Pammy put her hand on the small of my back. It's like we'd just seen each other yesterday, not half a lifetime ago.

I turned the key in the lock and opened the door slowly, waiting for the kickback from the security chain. My father never, but never, failed to put the chain on when he was at home. The door swung open.

'He's not here,' I said.

All the familiar smells of home hit me, like a madeleine on steroids: lavender wax polish on the parquet, rubbed to a soft sheen by the woman-that-does; the air thickened with the tannin of a thousand stewed pots of tea; the faintly vinegar odour that said a man lives here on his own. The plate rail that ran above the oak panels in the front hall still sported the maiolica plates my mother brought with her from Italy when she got married. Centuries of sunshine and lemons those plates had seen, to end up on a high shelf in an English 30s semi.

Pammy edged past me and stuck her head into the living room. 'No one here,' she said.

We headed to the back of the house, where the small dining room led on to the galley kitchen. I resisted the urge to take Pammy's hand.

Everything was neat and in order: the work tops scrubbed, the dish rack cleared, a line of washed milk bottles sitting on the window sill waiting to return to their maker. Nothing was out of place, not so much as a water-spotted coffee spoon with which to count out our lives.

'Maybe he's gone away,' I said.

'Like on holiday?'

I shrugged. 'Maybe.'

'When was the last time you were here?'

'When were we eighteen?'

Pammy pursed her lips. 'Fifteen years is a long time not to see your dad.'

'I'm here now, aren't I?'

'And he's not. Christ, you two are a pair.'

I turned from her, from the suggestion that me and my father had ever been a pair of anything. Two single souls under the same roof, more like. I surveyed the dining room, leaning my hands on the small fold-out table. I wondered if Pammy remembered us doing our homework at that table, shoulder-to-shoulder, knees pressed together under the Formica. I wondered if she remembered our first taste of alcohol; sherry and Dubonnet and lemonade filched from the cupboard on the wall, and mixed into a concoction with less potency than a lager shandy, but tasting to us like decadence and escape and growing up. I wondered which part of it she remembered, and which parts were mine alone to recall.

'Ah, baby Guido,' Pammy said, breaking my reverie. She was pointing at a photo on the wall. It showed a baby, dark haired and squint-eyed in bright sunshine, sitting on a headless woman's lap, her legs turned under her to make a seat of her skirt, grass and trees faded to brown behind her.

'Yes, that's me,' I said, 'You can tell by the dimple.'

Pammy leaned forwards and examined the photo more closely. 'Who's the decapitated lady? Is it your–'

'Babysitter,' I interjected. 'Probably.'

Pammy moved on, surveying the photos on the wall. Faces and people, faded and failed. The witnesses to our teenage fumblings all those years ago. 'Were all of these photos here before? When we were kids?' she asked.

I nodded. The things we don't see.

'I don't remember this one.' She was standing on tiptoe to look at a photo still in the soft cardboard frame it had come from the photographers in, fixed slapdash to the wall with masking tape. There were my parents, her young, him not so much, outside the registry office, her smiling, him not so much. But he looked happy, in his own way. It was the look he got when the last piece of the jigsaw puzzle snapped into place; when he locked up the shed for the winter safe in the knowledge he'd remembered to clean and oil his tools; when I'd passed my A-levels and my place at university was secured. It was the face of a man happy with a job well-done and no more to be thought about it.

Pammy had her head dipped to one side. 'That dress your mum is wearing in this photo. Yellow. Daisy print.'

'Yes?'

She moved back to the photo of me as a baby. 'Here.' She ran a finger over the bleached-out frock baby-me was half-cradled in. 'It's the same dress.'

I made a show of peering at the photo. 'I can't see it,' I said.

I felt rather than saw Pammy giving me a look. 'Shall we check upstairs?' I asked.

'It's your house, dummy,' Pammy replied. 'What are you asking me for?'

Pammy loitered at the bottom the stairs, hesitant. 'I'll just stay here,' she said. 'You go on up.'

That passing from downstairs to up in another person's house, it's a strange thing. Upstairs is private, the place where a family creates its own secrets. I remembered glimpses of Pammy's parents' bedroom as we had scuttled past, school uniforms already half cast off when we found the house empty and had the chance of a quickie. I had harboured secret fantasies of doing it in her parents' bed, the scent of her mother in the pillow, the soft stuff of her underwear spilling from drawers (or so I imagined. All my best memories are the ones I've supplied myself). To think my teenage fantasies were fuelled by You Know, Linda! I smiled to myself as I made my way up the stairs.

I don't know what I was expecting to find. My father clearly wasn't home. What was I checking for? Clues? What exactly was the mystery here? I stood on the landing, debating whether to just go back downstairs and call it a day. But then I saw the door to my old bedroom was slightly open. Of all the places I've lived, all the beds I've slept in, that is the one my subconscious defaults to when I dream of home. Sometimes when I wake from one of those dreams, I open my eyes and I'm still in my childhood bed. Brain and eyes don't always agree on reality.

Standing with my hand on the door handle, I felt like I was about to enter my own waking dream. The heaviness of the suburban afternoon deadened the edges of everything. I felt the presence of eighteen-year-old me passing the other way, a large duffle bag knocking sharp shards of gloss paint off the skirting boards as I dragged it down the stairs.

I was just about to push open the door and go in when I heard a key in the front door. The familiar jiggle necessary to get an old key to mesh with the slightly off-kilter tumblers in the lock. My father.

'Guido?' Pammy was leaning around the corner of the bannister.

'Yup, I'm coming.'

By the time I was halfway downstairs, my father was standing in the hallway, two suitcases at his feet. He looked up at me, opened his mouth, closed it, turned to Pammy.

'Pamela, hello, this is a nice surprise. Did your mother send you?'

'She was worried.'

'I should have anticipated that when I made my plans. Do tell her I appreciate the concern.' He couldn't have been clearer if he'd handed her her coat.

'Right.' Pammy cleared her throat, looked up at me, still standing a few steps up. 'Um, let me know if you need a lift back to the station, or...'

I hadn't taken my eyes off my father. Or rather, the suitcases at his feet. Pammy slipped out of the front door, hesitated at the threshold, and left the door ajar behind her.

'Nice girl,' my father said. 'Pity you couldn't hang on to her.'

'You have me as your emergency contact?' I asked.

My father gave a little shrug of his rain-coated shoulders. 'It's a requirement when one uses the community centre. I had to put down something and your number is written in the front of my diary. For emergencies.'

'So where have you been?'

'Where have *I* been? That's a bit rich, son. Where have *you* been? A Christmas card with a mobile telephone number poorly scrawled on the back of the envelope is all I've had from you since you left.'

'More than I ever had from you in the eighteen years before that.' And as quick as that, there we were, exactly where we had left off.

Movement behind the mottled glass in the front door. A splash of lemon yellow. The door opened, slowly, and in she came. My mother.

I remember the day she left. My father thinks I don't, but I do. I was five years old. Just started school and in trouble already for what my father and my teacher called lies and my mother called 'Guido's way with the world'.

There was a suitcase packed and standing in the hall. Just the one suitcase. I was sitting on the landing, cross-legged, concealed by a bath towel hung over the banisters to dry. Listening.

'Don't go,' my father was saying.

'I must,' my mother said. 'I am dead here.' Her English was often imprecise, her exact meaning skirting the outside of the words that came out of her mouth. She obviously wasn't dead, standing there with her coat on. I wondered what it was she really meant.

'Then take the boy. I don't know what to do with him,' my father said.

'I will send for him. But you must get him a passport. I am going home.'

'This is your home now.'

I heard the familiar little gasp from my mother that meant he had her by the elbows, squeezing hard in the places he knew hurt her.

I wriggled onto my belly to peer under the frayed edge of the bath towel and between the banisters.

'If you want your boy, you stay,' my father said.

Did he want me or not? I couldn't tell. I rested my cheek on the landing carpet, watching sideways as my father pressed his face close to my mother's, but not in a nice way. It was never nice when he got his face close. Not like my mother, who swooped in often to kiss my cheek, my forehead, the tip of my nose, or to take a ticklish sniff of the nape of my neck.

'If you leave, you're dead to me,' my father was saying, 'And to him. Dead.'

I should have called out to her, 'Mama!' But I didn't. I let her go.

'Mama, I thought you were dead,' I said.

My father snorted in the back of his throat, as close to laughter as he ever came. 'Nonsense. That's just the lie you've been telling everyone all your life. Such a bloody embarrassment, people coming up to me with their sympathy. And when I tell them my wife's not dead, just...'

And there my father's words ran out because my mother had her hand on his arm. 'Don't be too hard on the boy,' she said. 'I understand him. A lie so big people would never believe you made it up, that's the way to hide the truth in plain sight. I left you both. That's not a lie. The way of my leaving, that was the real hurt. So he made it a different leaving with his lie, one that he could more easily live with.' She shrugged and her shrug was different to that of my father. Her shrug said: let the pain of the past go. His said: hold fast to the hurt as if it's the only thing you own.

'Where have you been?' I asked my mother, resurrected as she was.

'I went home.'

'And what happens now?'

My mother looked at my father and he nodded. 'I've come home.'

'How many homes do you have?' I felt like I was building a new reality, question by question.

That shrug again. 'Just one home at a time,' my mother said. 'What more would I need?'

DAVE CLARK

The Tent

I am the master, the chief, el supremo, numero uno, king of my domain, emperor of my tent.

I can do anything I like in my tent. For ten hours a day I have no cares, I can sleep, eat, I can even read, I have a lamp I can burn any time I like, no one will stop me. I can read all through the night if I want to.

The tent is massive, a two-man tent, for just one of me. If I stretch my arms and legs out full-stretch I barely touch the sides. When I sleep I can choose whereabouts in the tent I lay out my sleeping bag, though in truth I always prefer the bottom left corner.

The tent is of the highest quality, thick as a fortress, said to be made from camel hide, whatever a camel is. It's water-proof, wind-resistant and completely noiseless; a bomb could go off outside my flap and I wouldn't hear a thing.

My choice of vocation is not for everyone. Working fourteen hours a day down the mine, the hardest physical labour there is. Some say the rewards for such labour are insufficient: food and water, a ten-minute crap-break and somewhere to lay my head at night; but it's a good life, my needs are simple and my reward is here, in the silence and sanctity of my tented kingdom. There is no prince, president or king anywhere in the world with a greater domain than mine.

For those ten hours per day I would willingly work my body and soul to their bare-bone remnants over the other fourteen. It's a fair exchange.

Terrible news! I'm going to have to share my tent. Following the expansion of the mine, there isn't enough accommodation for everyone. As a temporary measure, those of us with two-man tents to themselves will have to take in a lodger.

It's a blow to my entire way of life, but, I reconcile myself, even with another inhabitant the tent is still spacious and comfortable.

The only downside is that my new companion doesn't approve of all of my habits. He likes to return to the tent and crash out asleep, as soon as he's finished supper and his trombone practice. He complains when I light the lamp to read. I guess I shall have to get used to less reading time while he's here.

A third person has joined the tent, due to the closure of the West Field. The exact circumstances are unclear, but it is rumoured that the Governor's mansion is being expanded. At least I still have my own warm corner to sleep in, but it's decidedly cramped in here now.

The new contract is harsh. A sixteen-hour day. There are twelve of us to the tent now, rotating in shifts, four of us crammed into the tent at one time. My own little corner is no longer my own, being occupied by whoever sleeps there while I work.

Hank crashed through the doors of the saloon as loudly as he could, spurs jangling, feet clomping on the floor. Everyone pretended to ignore him, conversations continued, the piano didn't stop playing, but he knew that all eyes were on him.

'Where's the kid?' he shouted to the barman.

'I'm sorry, what's going on, this is my story. Why's it turned into a western?'

'It's not your story any more. You've had your 500 words. It's my turn now.'

'But it's my story!'

'Not any more, there isn't enough space in the world for everyone to write long stories. The new edict means that all stories must stop at 500 words. It's my story now.'

'The Kid's over here.'

Hank turned to face the centre of the saloon, where The Kid was standing.

JACKIE TAYLOR

QED

Baggage Reclaim. Granite-faced men in black combat gear, their trousers tucked into heavy-duty boots. Hard wear / hardware. Earpieces, mouthpieces and guns. In England? Really? Since when?

Sarah is quietly waiting for her Samsonite beside the carousel when a man behind her says, 'Would you mind stepping this way? Please, madam, sir, could you come with me?'

A group of them are gathered discreetly, gently almost, into this room. They are relieved of their hand luggage and the door is locked behind them.

In truth, Sarah quite likes the room they're being held in. She can imagine working here under different circumstances. White walls and white floors, both with a slight reflective sheen. Good, bright lighting. She can imagine doing excellent work here, perhaps even making her breakthrough.

No distractions. Perfect. Except...

'Looks like they've forgotten us,' a man, one of the detainees, says.

Sarah just wants to get home as quickly as she can. She is a mathematician; she approaches the problem logically. She still has plenty of time to catch her onward train. Whatever has happened to them will be sorted out soon, they will be released and she will get home tonight.

A proof must demonstrate that a statement is always true

'They've forgotten us,' says Derek. 'It's the only explanation.'

'You don't know that,' says Anne. 'They've probably just gone to have a bit of lunch.'

There were twenty-two of them at the start. Most of their fellow detainees have already been released, two by two like grateful ark-animals, but it's been a while now since the white door in the white wall opened to call anyone through. There are just four of them left now. Derek and Anne, both solidly three-dimensional and softly overweight. He is wearing knee length shorts with concertina creases and pristine white trainers; she's in a flowery blue dress with a repeated pattern which maintains a pleasing symmetry across the seams.

'We've been to visit our son,' Anne says. 'Silicon Valley. Computers. Doing ever so well for himself, he is.'

'Unlike our daughter,' says Derek.

The other person in the room, Michael, is a compass of a man, all acute angles, with dirty yellow dreadlocks and dirty finger nails. Sarah had noticed him, and done her best to avoid him, on the plane.

'My name's Sarah,' she says, in a voice she hopes will close down any further attempts at conversation.

'They've definitely forgotten us,' says Derek.

Theory is a contemplative and rational type of abstract thinking

Sarah removes herself as far away from the others as she can, four metres at least, she reckons. She sits cross-legged on the floor, which is clean and smells pleasantly of disinfectant. She scrapes her hair back into a ponytail and closes her eyes. Think. If her mind is fully occupied then she will have no spare processing capacity to worry about her dad, and getting home, or how the time is passing. It's a good working hypothesis.

The other three are talking, constantly talking, as if this will help. *What's going on? Why are we here?* Sarah doesn't understand why they're talking like this. It's obvious that they've been caught up in a security check, and they'll be released soon and be off on their respective ways. She'll still make it to the hospital tonight and everything will be fine.

Sine wave: a mathematical function that describes a repetitive oscillation

She would be able to think, if only they would all shut up. Every so often, the sinusoidal rise and fall of their speech resolves into recognisable patterns and once this has happened she is no longer able to tune them out.

Like now. Backwards and forwards, the dipole that is Derek and Anne:

'For God's sake, woman. You choose your moments, I'll give you that.'

'I can't help it if I need the lav!'

'Why didn't you go on the plane?'

Sarah's father used to tell her how much he admired the lavatories in England. Most excellent. She can hear his precise, earnest voice now. She remembers with shame how much these conversations with her father had embarrassed her.

A random sample is a sample in which each individual in the population has an equal chance of being selected

'I expect they just do this at random now,' says Anne. 'Pull people in. What with the way things are everywhere.'

The limit of a sequence is the number which the sequence tends towards

The conversation is tending towards the point Sarah thought it would.

'Well, there must be a reason for all this. What about her?' she hears Derek saying. 'She's hardly said a word. And she looks a bit foreign.'

The conversation continues along the same track. They must think she's deaf.

'She's very quiet,' Michael is saying.

'Sshhh – I think she's asleep,' says Anne. 'She said her name was Sarah. Pretty name.'

'Doesn't make her English,' says Michael.

'She did have a bit of an accent.'

QED, Sarah thinks. Quod Erat Demonstrandum: the phrase is written in its abbreviated form at the end of a mathematical proof; the abbreviation thus signals the completion of the proof.

Formula: a concise way of expressing information symbolically
Her father had insisted on naming her Sarah. It was symbolic of their new life. Her mother, ignoring the evidence of the birth certificate, always called her daughter Zarah. What a difference one letter could make.

Sarah/Zarah, 30-something spinster, and unmarriageable now, according to her mother, even to an Englishman. 'Always the clever one, heh?' Sarah can hear her mother saying. The clever one who is such a failure at the real business of life.

She knows that her father proudly tells anyone who'll listen that his daughter is a Doctor, working in America. She also knows that he doesn't correct them if they assume she is a proper Medical Doctor. Her father was always so proud that he worked in medicine, if only as a hospital porter. He loved the hospital – the order, the cleanliness. This at least is some comfort to Sarah now.

Extrapolation: To infer or estimate by extending or projecting known information
'So who's our chief suspect then?' says Michael.

'Well, I've got nothing to hide,' says Derek. 'I've always done the right thing. Parking fines. Tax. Always played by the rules. Doesn't get you anywhere though, does it?'

Formula: a concise way of expressing information symbolically

For Sarah, mathematics is sanctuary. She loves its ability to calm whole worlds of complexity and chaos with a few marks on the page, marks which can express nuance and subtlety in a way that words can't. Words are just too clumsy.

'I'm just trying to suggest...' says Michael.

He's going on about democracy and freedom and words are flying around the room, choking out the air.

They've been locked up for nearly four hours. She's not going to get home tonight. She won't get to the hospital tonight.

Inertia: the tendency of an object to remain at rest unless pushed

Sarah's father and mother had lived in the same house since they arrived in England. Her father would have been happy to stay at No. 47 all his life, minding his own business. Making polite conversation with the neighbours and choosing not to acknowledge the angry kids, the violence and the drugs.

A sudden vision: her mother eating alone, in the kitchen at No. 47. Until this time, in this cell, Sarah hasn't realised that a single thought can break your heart. She is surprised and she doesn't like surprises. Like father, like daughter.

In Sarah's work, the most interesting and unexpected events happen at the edges, where the normal rules don't apply. She maps this world out on paper and on computers and in lectures. But she doesn't want this uncertainty to have any place in her own life.

An inequality is a relation that holds between two values when they are different

Derek moves round the room, rubbing his hand over the architrave, smoothing over the satin surface of the wall as if he's feeling for a secret door.

'Tell you what, love,' he says, 'Maintenance, that's where the money is, now the developers have all gone to ground. If I ever get a chance at a government contract like this…set us up, it would.'

'Why don't you go for it then?'

'You must be joking. There's no chance for the likes of us,' says Derek. 'Poles, Irish, blacks. Anyone but us. There's nothing for us anymore.'

A linear asymptote is essentially a straight line which a curve approaches closer and closer but never touches

Sarah changes position, shifting her weight slightly. The others are silent; she knows they're watching her. Then:

'Do you think she's English?'

'Don't know. She's not said much has she?'

'Sshhh. I think she's crying. Don't stare, Derek!'

Infinity: something that goes on forever and has no end

What if she doesn't make it home in time?

Even if she gets a taxi, will they let her into the ward tonight? It depends, she thinks, on how bad… It had all been so well planned. She doesn't manage well when things don't go to plan. Another 'like father, like daughter' thing.

Probability: a way of measuring the chance that something will happen

Her father had been attacked, in his own street, outside his own house, a chance event. What were the odds of that? After the attack, it seemed that his whole story started to unravel. Sarah was surprised – she'd thought it was too well-constructed for that. As his physical wounds gradually healed, his silences became longer. Perhaps he had come to believe, as she does, that in words, true meaning is lost.

Sarah speaks. 'Why are they keeping us here?'

'Security,' Michael says.

'Can they do this?'

'They can do anything.'

'I've got to …' But she can't explain.

'Why don't you get off that cold floor and come and sit at the table with us?' says Anne. 'It's Sarah, isn't it?'

'It's Zarah.' She doesn't know what makes her say this, it just slips from her mouth. 'Zarah.'

'Told you,' whispers Derek to Anne.

QED.

Sarah thinks she can smell something on the floor, something under the disinfectant. She stands up, slowly, unsteadily.

'Our daughter's supposed to be meeting us, you know,' Anne is saying. 'I hope she's not waited, we can always get a taxi if we have to.'

'Do you think I'm made of money?' says Derek. 'She's probably forgotten anyway. Doesn't think, not about her mum and dad anyway.'

Don't talk about your daughter like that. You mustn't talk about your daughter like that. She never means to let you down. She's a good daughter!

Sarah doesn't know whether she's said this aloud or not, but the others are all looking at her so she thinks she probably has.

She begins to pace the room, slowly, metre by metre; measuring it out will give the room substance and anchor it down.

'Zarah, come along, sit here with us,' Anne is by her side, touching her arm. 'There, sit with us. Whatever it is, it'll all come out in the wash. Always does, mark my words.'

'It's my dad,' she hears herself saying. 'I've got to get home.'

Gently, Anne eases open Sarah's fists. Her nails have left white crescents on the soft flesh of her palms.

'Here,' Anne says, 'Let me sort your hair out, it's all over the place.'

Her mum used to brush her hair every night, one hundred strokes, to make it shine. Trying, against the odds, to make her beautiful.

A singularity is a point where a set fails to be well-behaved in some particular way

Sarah knows that events, once started off on a particular course, will reach a logical conclusion. She is moving relentlessly towards the edge of something, some boundary, some point of personal singularity at which everything will shift and change forever.

But not now. Please. Not now, not yet. She is a good daughter, she should be at home with her family.

She has to stop time moving on. She knows that time is flexible at the outer edges of things, where normal rules cease to apply. If only that were true in the real world.

The white door in the white wall opens. Derek and Anne, and then Michael, are called out. Two men enter. In words weighed down with authority and a certain pleasure, they tell Zarah that she will not be allowed to enter the UK.

'But I have to go home,' she shouts.

Silence.

Granite-faced men in black combat gear, their trousers tucked into heavy-duty boots. Earpieces, mouthpieces and guns. In England. Our home.

QED

The phrase is written at the end of a proof, thus signalling its completion.

KAREN ANKERS

Lydia and the Cat

Lydia had all sort of visitors. The red-faced Sunday school teacher. Her mother. Her husband. And Paul Newman. He was her favourite, with his intense blue eyes and slow smile and welcome gifts. Deep red roses, with velvet black tipped petals. Chocolate rich as silk.

She had been so pleased when he bought her the house. She'd had enough of the other place, where no one seemed to understand what she was saying. If she asked for coffee, she got tea. If she asked for red wine, she got tea. One day she asked for fillet of salmon with watercress and a glass of chilled champagne. When it arrived, it tasted almost exactly like weak, sugary tea.

She'd asked, excited as a child, how many bedrooms were in the house. Six, he drawled. Six? She'd started to panic. She couldn't hoover six bedrooms. And how long would it take, every Monday, to change the sheets on six beds? But then he'd explained that this was a magic house. One where the hoovering was done by magic, sheets obediently changed themselves every week (and washed, starched and ironed themselves) before putting themselves back into cedar-scented drawers.

'What?' she'd asked. 'Like the house my husband thought he lived in?'

'Exactly,' he nodded, before pulling her into his arms and doing things with his tongue and his teeth that she thought were impossible. Things her husband had never done.

When she first saw the house she had cried with happiness. It gleamed white as stripped bone in a huge garden, where peacocks strutted and called. Large, shimmering windows. It seemed to know what she wanted without her having to ask. If she decided she wanted fresh flowers, they would instantly appear on the mahogany table in a glittering crystal vase. Creamy lilies, usually, sometimes roses, filling the light-washed rooms with their musky scent.

Her mother had visited once. Lydia had been so proud, showing her the large kitchen and the comfortable lounge. The mother who had told her she would never amount to anything. Lydia had wanted to show her the collection of trophies she kept in the bedroom. Awards for singing, piano-playing, cake-making, all engraved with her name. But she hadn't stayed long.

'There's nothing for me to do,' she said impatiently. 'And you'll be getting into bad habits, my girl. The devil makes work for idle hands. It's Monday. You should be doing your linen.'

And Lydia had wondered if she ought to feel guilty. Was she the only woman in the world not hanging out her sheets on a Monday?

'And that's another thing,' her mother had tutted. 'Your sheets should be on the line. Lovely drying day and you've hung nothing out. A disgrace, I call it.'

But there was no need to hang them out. They were in the linen cupboard (Lydia felt very grand, having a linen cupboard), washed and dried, scented with lavender, ready to throw themselves over the huge, soft beds.

It was in one of those beds (the largest) that Paul had showed her what love meant. Her husband had sweated and grunted on top of her, usually after a few pints, and then gone to sleep. Paul did unspeakable things to parts of her body that she didn't even have a name for. Things that made her blush and caused the smiling doctor whom she visited once a week, to frown and check her pulse, asking in that irritating, slightly too loud, sing-song voice he affected, if she was all right.

'I'm fine,' she wanted to say. 'Only with Paul Newman sucking my nipples it's a bit hard to concentrate.'

He didn't understand, had shaken his head and gone away, leaving her to instruct Paul to lick the spot just below her belly button.

Sometimes, of course, he had to go and work on his films. And when he did, her best friend Myra came to stay. Myra and Lydia had been friends since their first day at school, when they were four years old. Lydia remembered Myra had on a red coat with a white fur hood. She looked like Father Christmas and Lydia had told her so. Since that moment they had been friends. Firm friends, who never argued, who shared their dreams and hopes with one another.

Myra loved the house.

'It's what you deserve,' she said. 'You've worked hard and you deserve a rest.'

She understood when Lydia confessed that sometimes she lost track of time, couldn't remember what had happened to her husband and couldn't remember what had happened to her children.

'Don't worry about it.' Myra helped herself to another large slice of the creamy chocolate cake that Lydia brought out every tea time. 'What does it matter? What's important is here and now. You and me.'

'And Paul,' Lydia reminded her.

'Ah yes.' Myra lifted a glass of champagne. 'We mustn't forget the gorgeous Mr Newman. How did you meet him, by the way?'

Lydia couldn't remember. There were lots of things she couldn't remember. And things she couldn't be bothered remembering. The smiling doctor asked her stupid questions. Like what day it was. Who the prime minister was. She couldn't understand how anyone had qualified as a doctor while being so stupid that he didn't know what day it was. And she wasn't going to tell him. He would have to find out for himself. Only she knew it wasn't Monday, because she hadn't seen anyone hanging out their sheets.

She wasn't sure why she still bothered coming to this place. Duty bound her to visit once a week. It was full of old people, who sat around in varying stages of decay. The ones who could talk had crackly voices and talked about the weather. The others dribbled while they slurped their tea. The walls were painted a horrible sickly green and there was a grey cat who insisted on sitting on her knee, even when she pushed it away. And there were people in uniform. Nurses, she supposed, for the old people. They always seemed to be busy. Too busy to talk or smile. Much like she had once been, when the children were small, with nappies soaking in a bucket in the yard, while her husband spent his days in the pub, squandering what little money they had. And then at night, he would do that thing that made more babies. More mouths to feed. More stinking nappies.

While he bounced and grunted on top of her, she used to wonder whether the next one would be a boy or a girl. It became a game to see if she could choose a name before he let out that ridiculous howl and rolled away to sleep.

She'd only had one boy. Edward. And he'd been sent away. Small, delicate as a daisy, with beautiful blue eyes and long lashes. Too pretty to be a boy, people had said. When he was three he'd caught a cold. Next day he was gone. But she'd always known he'd come back. The first time he had come to the house, she scarcely recognised him. A tall, handsome young man, with a deep voice and curly hair. But the eyes gave him away. He'd apologised for going away and she'd cried while she hid her face in his golden hair.

He came to visit once a week. Said how lovely the house was, but wasn't she lonely? And she'd explained about all her visitors.

'Even the nasty ones liven up my day.'

'You're wicked, mother,' he had grinned, waggling his finger at her.

Was it really wicked to tie her headmaster to a chair? Or to dress her Sunday School teacher in a lurid pink ballgown? She supposed it was, really. But so much fun. And she had a rule. She never did anything to them that they hadn't done to her. At school, she'd been tied to a chair because she couldn't sit still. And at Sunday School she'd been made to stand in a corner for insisting that God couldn't possibly have created the world in seven days.

The smiling doctor was asking stupid questions again. Asking if she could hear him. Of course she could. She just couldn't be bothered answering. One of the nurses was crying, splashing tears all over her blue uniform. Lydia wanted to tell her to stop making such a fuss. She would have to stop coming here. It wasn't as though the old people would miss her. She tried explaining that she wasn't going to come any more and now even the doctor had stopped smiling. Funny, she hadn't thought he would miss her that much. She wondered if she should invite him to the house, but decided he would probably be too busy to visit. And he would get in the way. The nurse was still crying. She wondered whether she ought to still come here once a week, since they were obviously going to miss her, but then the cat jumped on her lap and made the decision for her. Mangy creature. She'd never liked cats, ever since she'd watched one kill a baby mouse when she was a little girl, playing with it, batting it with its paw, tormenting it at its leisure. She remembered calm green eyes staring at her while a scaly tail hung out of its mouth and teeth crunched on bone and scraped across gristle.

The crying nurse reached out and stroked the cat's head.

'He knows,' she sighed.

Of course he knows, thought Lydia. He knows I'm not coming back. Why should I? There's nothing for me here. I'm not going to sit around drinking watery tea when I could be in my magic house getting sweaty in lavender sheets with Paul Newman.

Edward was waiting. He'd said he'd come and take her home. Not that it was a long journey. One thought and she was there.

Taking off her hat, she rang the bell in the hall for chocolate cake, which she ate sitting by the fire, laughing with Edward. She used a lace handkerchief to wipe the crumbs from her mouth and from the folds of her crimson silk dress.

'And now you have to go,' she smiled. 'Paul will be here soon.'

Stepping out of the rustling silk in front of her long, copper-framed mirror, she smiled. Sometimes she wondered if she was getting old, but her skin glowed smooth and pale as blue-veined marble. Paul was behind her now, his arms around her, his blue eyes smiling promises, and his warm tongue preparing to do those things that took her breath away.

ANTONIA HONEYWELL

The Tablecloth

Jazz expected them to give her a bin bag for her things, same as they gave everyone, but Roger the social worker said that she'd achieved something incredible and a bin bag just wouldn't cut it. He'd sort something out, he promised, muttering about special purpose grants and inspiring others, and she'd dreamed, briefly, of a suitcase in conker-bright leather, of stitched handles and corners and rose-coloured lining with pockets. But when Roger came again, he carried a battered navy blue canvas holdall with a white logo so worn she couldn't make it out.

'It's either that or my gym bag,' he said, 'and believe me, you wouldn't want my gym bag.'

Jazz didn't say anything. She took the bag.

The first thing that went into it was the tablecloth. Do-call-me-Gloria, the foster carer, had helped her choose the fabric and shown her how to use the sewing machine, for soon her mother would come and take her home, and Jazz was determined to prove that she would be, not a burden, but a helium balloon, lighter than a feather, lighter than the cake she was going to make for her last tea at do-call-me-Gloria's. When the day came, she found a recipe and followed it fiercely, shutting out do-call-me-Gloria's bleats that the butter needed to be soft and the oven door kept closed.

'Well, home-made makes a home,' do-call-me-Gloria said kindly when the cake was set ceremonially upon the gingham tablecloth, Jazz standing fierce sentinel as four o'clock became five, and six, and seven. The jam filling wept over the uneven layers; the checked lines of the gingham mocked her crooked seams.

The next day, Jazz and her tablecloth were moved to lucky-us-Lilian and Dave's, then to not-now-Jazz-Lesley's, and finally to *the* home and Roger.

Jazz had questions, but she swallowed them all. Perhaps that was why, when the new teacher swept into class all purple eyeshadow and clanking bangles and announced that Literature was about interrogating text, they came tumbling out of her. How come they only studied white writers, most of them dead? How come no one else thought Mr Rochester was abusive, or that Lady Macbeth was a fucking heroine? They read *Frankenstein*, who created a life then abandoned it, and Jazz excoriated anyone who dared to defend him.

'Fewer expletives, if you please, Jazz. Explain your views.'

And so she had explained, and Doctor Adoyo had argued, and the next book they read was called *Beloved* and it ripped at Jazz's heart so hard that she wept in class, in front of everyone.

'It's a powerful indictment of slavery, isn't it?' Doctor Adoyo said sympathetically.

And Jazz's tears dried instantly. 'Slavery?' she spat. 'Fuck slavery. The point is, that mother loved her baby enough to kill it.'

And the class fought with words that drew blood, and the essay Jazz wrote won a national prize.

One day, waiting outside the staff room, she overheard Doctor Adoyo on the telephone saying, 'It's Doctor, actually,' in a voice that made Jazz imagine the person on the other end reduced to a pile of ash. 'Not *that* kind of doctor,' Doctor Adoyo added impatiently, and the ashes of the idiot blew away in the wind.

And as Doctor Adoyo handed her piles of books upon piles of books, Jazz's dreams, like a well-mixed cake in a closed oven, began to transform and rise.

And then she'd got in, and now she was here. Around her, the ancient building bustled with a hundred families ushering their precious children into a new phase of life. Already Jazz had counted seven middle-aged women weeping, four blazing rows (two on the grass outside, one in the entrance hall and one behind the locked door of a toilet) and a bored younger sibling picking at the wall paint. The families were a mirror in which she could not see herself; she had lugged Roger's bag through them, alone and invisible.

Outside the room opposite, a grey-haired man in a soft jumper paced around a pile of leather suitcases. 'The room will do, but we'll need to get her a better mattress,' he said, as a flustered woman in a navy suit hurried up the corridor, carrying a plush rabbit in one hand and a wooden mugtree in the other.

Behind her, a girl with a rucksack rolled her eyes at Jazz through the open door. 'Why would I want a mattress?' the girl demanded. 'I'll be home by Christmas anyway.'

The mother smiled, but her knuckles were white around the rabbit's neck. 'You promised you'd try, darling. You promised.'

'Do what you want,' the girl said, 'but remember you're the ones who've got to come and pick all this crap up at the end of term.' She walked straight into Jazz's room and shut the door behind her.

'Sorry,' the girl said, pushing her hair out of her eyes, 'they were getting on my tits. And they won't fuck off until they've unpacked all my stuff and taken me out for dinner. Because God forbid I might actually want to get on with my life.'

Jazz stared.

A voice outside called, 'Frankie? Frankie!'

The girl looked at the blue holdall. 'Is this all your stuff? Everything you brought?' she asked.

Jazz nodded.

'That is so cool,' the girl said. 'My parents think I'll die if I don't have everything I'm used to at home. They've brought my duvet and a brand new electric blanket and, like, a million packets of tights. And I don't even wear tights.'

'Maybe they're trying to get rid of you,' Jazz said, and the moment the words were unreclaimable she wanted them back. Oh for a Doctor Adoyo, to teach her the right words, or parents with mug trees to shield her from the wrong ones.

'I wish they could, but they can't.' She shrugged. 'They've got my cat. She's like this hostage. A really cute hostage. I've got photos on my phone.' She looked at the bookshelf. 'Is that a tablecloth? Why on earth would you bring a tablecloth to uni?'

There was a knock at the door. 'Frankie? Are you in there?' The man's voice was impatient, but kind, like a big brother tired of playing hide and seek with a toddler who didn't stick to the rules.

'I don't have anyone to leave it with,' Jazz said slowly.

It was the girl's turn to stare at Jazz. The handle turned; the door opened slowly.

'Frankie,' the mattress man said, 'here you are. Making friends already, hey? That's good. I'm Leonard.' He leaned forward and held out his hand to Jazz. 'And this is my wife, Carol. Frankie, we need to be heading out for something to eat if your mother and I are to get home before midnight. Come along.'

'You haven't asked her name,' Frankie said.

'What?'

'You marched into her bedroom and told her your name, but you didn't ask for hers.'

'Neither did you.' Jazz hardly recognized her own voice. She felt her determination pushing into every corner of this little room, the corners of the tablecloth fluttering with its power.

Everything stopped – the laughter outside, the dragging of bags and trunks, the opening of new doors.

'I'm Frankie,' the girl said. 'For Francesca, you know? Come and eat with us. They can't help it, I brought them up really badly. But there's hope for me yet, I promise.'

'I'm going to be a doctor,' Jazz said, in that same alien voice.

'Good for you,' Leonard said heartily from the doorway. 'Good career. Help others. Give something back.'

'Not *that* kind of doctor,' Jazz said, and even though Leonard did not collapse into a pile of dust, Jazz grinned.

She just needed practice. She would let these people buy her dinner, and she would watch them, and listen to them, and learn what she could. She had her tablecloth. And they, too, had something to learn from her; that there is grace to be shown in lying on a bed you have not made; that a snail's shell is no less a home than the grandest nest, and that a girl who carries a tablecloth in an ugly, broken bag is not unworthy of love. Or worthy of it, either.

MIKE BLAKEMORE

The Globe

Daan tugged at his father's sleeve and tried to drag him towards a stall piled high with mirrors, vases, cups, candlesticks and ornaments of every shape and size.

'What's so interesting over there?'

'Old things, Dad, like we never see.'

Abram rose to his full height and put down the piece of fruit he had been squeezing for ripeness. 'You really are your mother's son, aren't you!'

The eight-year-old brushed away strands of his long blond hair and stared at the man he spent his every waking minute with and on whose every word he hung. 'Why can't we look?'

'It's not good to be seen looking at relics of the past.'

'Like Mother did?'

Abram looked nervously around him before replying in a soft voice: 'Yes, your mother looked at these things. Klara was curious; wanted to know where we came from. It doesn't do to ask questions about the past, about history.'

As they spoke, they had drifted towards the table that had caught Daan's eye and the stall-holder eyed them eagerly as they drew nearer.

'Come and browse, gentlemen,' she said in a voice that suggested she'd been a teacher before the schools closed.

'No, thank you.'

'Can't we just look a little, please?'

'I promised your mother… It was the last thing I said to her. I promised that I'd keep you safe.' He grabbed for his son but Daan was right beside the stall, his fresh blue eyes darting from one object to another.

Daan dodged his father's grasp, colliding with the stall and sending a pile of things crashing to the ground.

The noise caught the attention of two men in identical wide-brimmed hats at the other end of the market. They began walking towards Abram and Daan.

'Go,' said the woman on the stall and Abram pulled his son towards him.

Daan noticed that one of the items had rolled away from the stall, bent and picked it up. Abram cast the boy a look of both admonishment and concern as he snatched the item and stuffed it into his rucksack with a nervous glance over his shoulder.

It was several hours later when Daan finally dared to retrieve what he had picked up. Abram was sat in the living room of their cottage, simply and starkly furnished with armchairs, a table and a sideboard upon which the only ornament was a small picture of Klara, her appearance forever frozen in time as it had been five years earlier. Daan reached into the rucksack. It was lying by the back door, where his father had angrily discarded it as soon as they had come in. He carefully removed the object, not wanting to damage whatever it was and wary too of disturbing Abram.

Outside, the sky was turning orange as the sun set but its warm glow was strong enough to pick out the shapes on the globe, playing upon the strange beasts drawn so that their heads, their feet, their tails connected the lights of the night sky. Daan took the globe to his bedroom and gently placed it on his bed. He reached beneath and pulled out a wooden box Abram had made for him. He glanced anxiously towards his bedroom door, making sure it was closed before he removed the telescope and positioned it on its stand in front of the small window.

Darkness had fallen when Daan used the telescope to search the night sky. He saw no creatures.

When Abram awoke to find his son had gone he didn't worry. Daan would often take himself out for walks before breakfast but he knew not to go into the town alone or to try to cross the canals that provided a boundary to the flat lands that stretched far from their cottage. But when the youngster hadn't come back to eat he began to panic that their disagreement the day before had upset Daan. He wished that he had made things up with his son instead of sitting in his armchair moping about Klara while Daan took himself off to bed.

Now he stood in his son's small bedroom, looking for clues to where the youngster had gone. On the whitewashed walls the only pictures, apart from one of Klara, were those that Daan had painted or drawn himself. Abram had encouraged his son's artistic talents, which colourfully depicted his surroundings. There was the cottage, the flat lands, the canals and the walls of the town; all seen in summer and winter. If he had one criticism of his son, the artist, it was that he painted or drew only what he saw, but then this was not a time for imagination.

Abram turned to leave and took a stride towards the door but, as he bowed his head instinctively to pass through its low frame, he caught sight of the box poking out from beneath the small wooden bed.

'I remember making this,' he said with a smile as he pulled the box out and placed it on the bed. 'Daan was so thrilled with it.'

The varnish had become dulled and one of the hinges was broken so he opened the lid carefully and deliberately. Inside, a black cloth concealed the contents and Abram paused for a moment before removing it, quickly placing it on the bed as the contents of the box were revealed.

He picked up the globe and turned it in his fingers, admiring the craftsmanship. 'I should have hidden this when we came home,' he said to himself.

Then he picked up the notebook, opening its hard cover to reveal yellow-edged pages full of maps of the stars, painstakingly and beautifully drawn in ink. Abram wiped sleep from his eyes and stroked his unshaven chin. He consoled himself with his conviction that Daan couldn't possibly know what these constellations were. Finally, he glimpsed the telescope.

Daan thought Mrs van Deuren might be angry. They had taken the globe without paying for it, even if they hadn't planned to. She might expect him to be able to give her the money but, of course, he couldn't. And then there was the small matter of the telescope; he was pretty sure she had seen him take it all those weeks ago. At the time, he couldn't believe his luck when she didn't stop him and when he had managed to hide its beautiful form inside the sleeve of his jacket before his father could see it.

If his father would have been angry about the telescope, how would he react if he could see Daan now, dodging through the streets of the town all by himself? At the market he hid behind a huge pile of rubbish, close to Mrs van Deuren's stall. He gazed up at the orange sun and bathed in its warmth, wondering where it went when darkness descended and where the lights in the sky came from. He wondered whether there were strange beasts hiding in the sky, perhaps waiting to eat him, his father and all the people of his world. Had one of them eaten his mother?

'What are you doing here, young man?'

'Waiting for you.'

'Does your father know you are here?'

Mrs van Deuren peered down at Daan, a hint of a smile appearing on her lips. She was much older than his father, maybe 75 or more, but there was strength in her limbs as she stretched out both hands and pulled him from his hiding place. 'Come on, I want to show you something, somewhere. Feeling fit?'

The old woman and the young boy hurried away from the marketplace, through streets gradually filling with townsfolk spilling out of their modest homes and beginning their walk to work. The woman and her young companion stopped only when two men in wide-brimmed hats appeared from an alleyway, waiting until the men had passed before continuing their flight from the town and on to the flat lands.

They didn't see the men turn and watch them.

Daan was flagging and Mrs van Deuren had to encourage him on. 'You've done really well but now we have to cross the canal. Then climb the hill.'

Daan was already tired and hungry but now he was afraid too, missing his father and desperately wishing that he had not gone with this stranger to a place he knew was forbidden, but he had no choice now other than to do what she said, overcoming his fears to follow her across a fallen tree: their makeshift bridge over the murky water. Soon they were in the forest that covered the hillside and Daan was farther from home than he had ever been. Up they went, farther and farther up, and it was getting dark when they eventually emerged from the forest. Before them, in a clearing at the very top of the hill, stood a large building, but not like any that Daan had seen before. It was very solidly constructed from a different sort of stone from that used to construct their cottage or the buildings in the town. It had no windows and a dome for a roof.

'Come on,' said Mrs van Deuren. 'I know a way in.'

'I don't know why you didn't stop her when you had the chance,' said Abram to the two figures who now followed him into Daan's small bedroom.

'We thought she was harmless; an old woman full of stories of the stars.' One of them handled the telescope while the other thumbed through the notebook. 'But this is more serious; allowing your boy to have these artefacts.'

'I know, I know, but there have always been legends about the stars and nothing Daan can see through this instrument or read in these pages proves anything. These are ancient things, from a time, a place, when people believed their fate was ruled by beasts. By magic. There is no science here; nothing to threaten our simple life.'

The two of them gestured to Abram to accompany them, one of the men putting the artefacts into the box and carrying it downstairs, the other snapping at Abram: 'You of all people know how dangerous it is to ask questions. Your son mustn't start asking questions like his mother. You did the right thing when it came to Klara. But it may be too late to save Daan.'

For such a large building, the entrance was small and it was well-hidden in the undergrowth. Without her, Daan might never have found the narrow, low doorway but Mrs van Deuren confidently guided the boy through the trees and bushes and into a narrow passageway where they waited for their eyes to adjust to the dark before proceeding. At the end of the gloomy passage the old woman began climbing a spiral staircase. Her pace increasing as she ascended its narrow steps, she didn't bother looking back to check that Daan was still behind her but, as they neared the top, there was excitement in her voice as she shouted: 'Right, young man, we have arrived.'

They were inside the dome they had seen from outside. It was dark now but not too dark to see the huge telescope – a hundred, perhaps five hundred or a thousand times bigger than the one Daan had looked through in his bedroom. Mrs van Deuren, despite her age and the day's exertion, found the strength to turn a large handle on the wall and, to Daan's amazement, part of the roof began to open above them, allowing fresh air to enter the stifling atmosphere of the old observatory and revealing pinpricks of light in the night sky. She gestured for the speechless boy to approach the huge telescope, to gaze into its eyepiece.

Her attention momentarily shifted to a sound outside, voices perhaps, but she remained calm, smiling at Daan as he climbed upon a chair so that he could reach the eyepiece. She knew what he could see because she had come here countless times to gaze at it herself. There was blackness, infinite blackness, but within it, a tiny blue ball. A planet.

The voices were inside the building now, growing louder and accompanied by heavy footsteps. Finally, Daan stopped looking through the telescope and gazed instead at Mrs van Deuren, a look of wonder on his face and a look of pleasure on hers as infinite as the night sky above them.

'What is it?' the boy asked.

A word formed on the old woman's lips but before she could reply Daan clapped his hands over his ears to escape a loud bang like nothing he had ever heard before and Mrs van Deuren fell lifeless to the floor.

Abram emerged from behind the two men and rushed to his son, embracing him, pulling him close and whispering: 'Home.'

SHARON TELFER

Nomad

Home is always someone else's.

Someone else's sofa, spare room if he's lucky, someone else's floor more than once. Someone else's sheets, the sickly scent of someone else's washing powder. Someone else's postcode, tube stop, corner shop. Someone else's neighbour's cat. Someone else's front path, front door, someone else's spare key.

Someone else's cereal bowl, someone else's Man U mug. Someone else's wedding on the wall, someone else's daughter's drawings stuck to someone else's fridge. Someone else's choice of box set. Someone else's time for bed.

Someone else's clock ticking through the still small hours, someone else's radiator clanking into life. Someone else's window overlooking someone else's street.

Someone else's whispers in the next room, walking into someone else's silence. Someone else's invite down someone else's local, someone else's, 'I'll get these, mate,' someone else's quiet word, someone else's need for space – 'You know, if it was up to me, mate, but the wife...'

Someone else's name crossed off, someone else's phone number, someone else's favour called in, someone else's goodwill.

The bag and the pain though – they are his.

SYLVIA PETTER

The Fiction of Home

Once upon a time. That´s the way stories used to start. Today, they're meant to be as true as possible, but I´ve always distrusted autobiographies. Who can say if they're telling the truth? The storyteller? Just stories. Even when they're true? Memories don't tell the truth either, despite the storyteller. And what use is the truth if nobody's listening, or if you don't know where the story's meant to start? And what if it really doesn't matter? So let's see the story.

Once upon a time there was a little girl who didn't have a mother tongue. Her mother's tongue wasn't hers, or was it? Who can remember back that far? It's the memories of others that are told and we soon start believing that they're ours.

The little girl spoke English. OK. There was a time when she didn't understand English, maybe when she was four. When she was dressed up like a fairy and grabbed at the prize that was meant for another fairy and wouldn't let it go despite all the logical explanations of the adults and the emotional reaction of the other little fairy. That was Anna's only linguistic failing. Yes, let's call her Anna, since she does need a name.

Anna spoke English. Well, maybe she had a little accent since her parents spoke German before they migrated with her to Australia when Anna was about two, or was it three? She must have had an accent. Or was Mary Braddock, third-generation Australian of Anglo-Celt origin, great-great-granddaughter of those sent to the penal colony to keep the convicts in line, just jealous that Anna was better than her at tennis – Anna did practise every day hitting balls against the school wall.

'Dirty Nazi!' spat Mary.

Anna didn´t know what Mary meant, but it touched something in her heart, or was it her soul, or that spot deep inside where collective memories hid – is that what they´re called? – to unexpectedly raise their heads one day echoing questions.

'What's a Nazi?' Anna asked her mother, in English, of course.

There was no answer, just a Where? What? Who? Why?

Anna said nothing and thought: *Nichts*. Yes, she thought it in German and then said in English: 'It's OK.'

And it stayed OK until she was 16 and without being able to explain felt an urge, a desire to go to Berwang. Berwang? What's a village in the Austrian Tyrol doing in the middle of a Sydney bush suburb? Ah memories. Anna had been happy in Berwang. She wasn't sure how she knew. It might have been her Austrian grandmother in Sydney on a visit who'd told her. That was when Anna was nine, or was it eight? Funny. She hadn't thought of her grandmother. She didn't like her. Anna didn't understand the language she spoke and why she always wore black. Australian grandmothers wore Bermuda shorts and bright t-shirts in the Christmas heatwaves. Anna was sure that her grandmother would just melt into a black puddle. Funny, the things you come up with. What her grandmother did have though was a super bed with springs that Anna loved to jump on. So maybe it was her grandmother who told her that she'd been happy in Berwang. Or was it Anna's mother?

There are stories about Anna leaving her teeth imprints in a fresh slab of butter left to cool on a rock in the cellar of a mill. A mill? Yes, Anna lived in a mill in Berwang. And in summer she'd run around naked, abandoning socks, panties, singlet, tops, one piece of clothing after the other in the mountain fields. Maybe she was already practising for the heatwaves in Australia. The best of all possible worlds, that was Berwang, until the day Anna's father emigrated.

But where were we? Anna is already in Australia. She's Australian, yearning for Berwang. But she's too young to go to Austria all by herself. Wait. Wait 'til you're 21, said her father when at 19 she said she just had to go.

'I'll lose two years of my life if I wait.' Two years are an eternity when you are young.

Anna's German was fractured so she signed up for an accelerated course in the language and skipped over a couple of grammar rules on the way. Nearly there, she could recite some Schiller and Goethe and so at 19 – or was it 20? – she left Australia for Vienna, Austria.

Schiller and Goethe were of no use in Vienna where people spoke so differently to what she'd heard in her German course in Sydney. Her professor had come to Australia via South Africa after his favourite student had committed suicide because of *Apartheid*. Anna didn't understand what *Apartheid* was, although she guessed it had something to do with being different, until the day the woman in the paper shop asked her: 'Are you Yugoslav?'

'No,' she answered. 'Australian.'

'Don't believe you.'

'But it's true.'

'*Tschusch*!'

When was that? 1969. *Tschusch* was a common derogatory word for 'foreigner' used mainly for people from Yugoslavia.

Anna signed up for German for Foreigners at the university's interpreters' school. There were mostly girls in the class and they all wore fur coats. Even the recently fled Czech students wore them. Rumour was that the girls were trying to hook up with well-off law students.

Anna wore a duffle coat and fell in love with a plumber. She moved in with him in a one-room flat where they shared the toilet with a neighbour and on Saturdays went to the bath house for a shower. Anna tried to learn Viennese, but although she understood everything, she couldn't get her tongue around certain words.

'You have to be born in Vienna to speak Viennese,' her German teacher said.

'I was born in Vienna,' she replied.

He shrugged. She sighed.

Slowly Anna felt she might suffocate in the city of her birth. She had to get out. 'Come with me,' she said to her love. 'Let's go.'

Where? Anywhere. And so they went to France. 'Now you know what it's like to be a foreigner,' she said to her love.

Life went on to the pace of high heels clattering along corridors and eventually slowing down onto quiet soles. Anna had a daughter. The child grew up and went to Australia. Anna went back to Vienna.

Well, it wasn't quite as easy as that. Short trips to test the air and the water at first. Vienna had an underground train now; the UN was up the road. Vienna had discovered young people, was 'In' again after the Waldheim scandal, although the city had never really come to grips with its past. Austria was in the EU. Nobody asked if she was a Yugoslav. Yugoslavia didn't even exist anymore. People had other problems. Some focussed on scarves. But Anna didn't care about the scarves women wore. In the 60s all the old women had worn scarves, and young ones, too. The borders of *Apartheid* were starting to get fuzzy.

Today, Anna is old. She lives with her love on the border of two homelands – in the 'al' of Austr(al)ia: Australia, Austria, hot, cold, down under, up here. She has stayed in Vienna. She can live in Vienna. She can die in Vienna, a city of black humour, not just Mozart and cake.

Hey. All stories that start with once upon a time have a happy end. OK, then. It's just that what happens between the two is the story. You can always go back and fix it all up. So *Prost*, Anna says, and raises her glass of red wine.

'*Prost*, Vienna,' she adds.

'Cheers, Anna,' I say.

MAUREEN CULLEN

Home Baked

Jas was all smiles at breakfast. 'Mornin', Ellen,' he said, shuffling into his seat, black hair gelled in spikes.

'Happy Birthday, Jas,' I trilled. 'Ye're a teenager noo.'

He attacked his presents like a scavenging seagull. I was ladling batter when his smile crumpled and he burst out of the kitchen. The pan was smoking in the sink when glass smashed in his room.

I tore down the hall, not an easy feat for a sixty-five-year-old, and caught my breath at his door. The bedroom window was still intact. It was only another tumbler chucked, which was a blessing, because the neighbours weren't too enamoured with anything that lowered the tone. Specially at 8.45am, accompanied by the F chorus. Jas sat on the edge of the bed, fists bunched, jaw clenched.

I phoned the school.

'Of course, Ms McFarlane, we understand fully. He's best at home today. You know what he's like.'

His social worker said, 'See how you get on, Ellen, and if necessary we'll move him again.'

After me, it would be a residential school. Maybe that's what Jas needed. Authority, male influence. I phoned my sister to cancel the birthday tea, to give me some space with him.

'Ye need yer heid examined keepin that boy on, Ellen,' she said with her usual finesse. 'He's trouble. Big time.' Her words pistoned back and forth all day.

My first ever home-baked birthday cake, a squinty chocolate sponge circled with red ribbon, was caving in at the end of the worktop. I slipped it into the larder.

I stood outside his closed door. 'I'm… sorry… Jas. I should've tellt ye… I'm sure she didnae… mean tae forget. She's just no… always herself.'

That got a nice round of ripostes, one singled out for his mother that could've fired a nuclear warhead. I put my shoulder to the door but the damn thing jammed on the furniture and I could see in only an inch.

The morning crashed along with a litany of libel from his prize collection. I managed to stick the door open with a shoe and putting on my most severe matron's voice, the one I'd used for the most slovenly on the wards, I warned him, 'If ye close it, I'll have tae call the polis for yer own safety. I'll no come in.'

He did as minded but only after several suggestions as to the positions the constabulary might take.

I sat in the kitchen with my fags, a reserve pack kept back of the cornflakes. My heart steadied after the first drag. Was I right for him? A family was out of the question; he'd threatened his last foster carer's son with a dinner fork. I liked to think that showed restraint.

At twelve o'clock, furniture shifted and his door creaked open. He slunk past the kitchen to the toilet. Thank God for that. I'd found all sorts of fluids in all sorts of places. When the pipes growled with the flush, I stepped to the kitchen doorway and offered a half smile. He picked up my mother's Doulton figurine and threw it at my head. I ducked and it smashed against the wall. My fingers tensed, they wanted to choke him by the neck 'til dead. Instead, I picked up the phone to ring the standby social worker, but my mother's voice chided me, 'Well, yer own fault that, hen. Leaving it on proud display. Ye might as well have put a sign above it: "Smash me tae smithereens." He's jist a wean, he'll come round.'

Well, he might've just been a wean, but he was also a boy. I knew nothing of the male species. Avoided them my whole life, unless they were inert on a trolley awaiting a heart valve. My nieces were all wee darlings, affectionate and respectful.

I dropped the phone in its cradle and stepped into my bedroom, opened the wardrobe and slid out my old uniform, the watch still blinking at the breast. Pure stiff white cleanliness. We used to joke, *parfum de anaesthetic.* I stuck it back in. They all wore blues now. And trainers.

Mid-afternoon I placed a carton of orange at his door. 'Jas, ye need tae drink something. Here's a wee orange. And anytime ye want tae come out don't worry, I'll no talk tae ye again.'

A grubby hand shot out and retrieved the juice.

Later in the afternoon he ventured out and dumped himself in the living room pitching me a glare that said, 'Whit ye goin tae dae aboot aw this?'

I ignored that, though I could've skelped him. That wasn't allowed. Quite right too; weans like Jas would only hit you back and he was bigger than me. I busied myself with the soup, making sure the ham hock shredded with the spoon. I put a bowl down on the coffee table and he slurped it in, but still, whenever I looked his way, I was rewarded with one of his usual terms of endearment. But at least he was out of his room. I left him watching rubbish telly.

When I was making the night's meal, he came to the kitchen door and slumped against the jamb.

I sighed. 'What dae ye want tae drink wi yer tea?'

He sputtered an obscenity and a gob of spit landed on my scrubbed oak table.

'I'll ask ye one more time. What d'ye want tae drink wi yer tea?'

'Coke.'

'No.' He knew fine he wasn't allowed Coke with his tea.

'Ah want Coke, you.'

'No.'

The spark fizzled out of him. 'Awright then, ah'll hiv orange juice.'

I padded to the fridge, poured the juice into a precautionary plastic cup, and watched his Adam's apple work overtime. When he was done, he shuffled into his space at the table, laces streaming behind his black trainers. He laid his head on his arms, gelled hair in collapsed spikes.

As the kitchen darkened I stole peeks at him. He was picking his nose at the table. I decided not to follow the trajectory of the ping. Trying to appear nonchalant, I hummed a Frank Sinatra number under my breath. *I'll do it my way*. Lost on Jas of course. He wouldn't know Frankie Boy from the milkman. Despite the aroma of roast chicken, garlic and rosemary, a sour whiff came from Jas's direction. I'd come to know that well. It was that special *parfum de unwashed boy*.

The light was fading fast. I opened the fridge and it threw out an eerie glow. Moving the cheese for the fourth time I noticed he was watching me, mouth loose on its hinges.

I said, 'Would ye like some more juice?'

'Ye tryin tae droon me?' A joke at last.

'That'll be right, no much chance of getting you near water.'

He chuckled right up to his puffy eyes and I had to smother the urge to go over and hug him tight.

I said, 'Gies a hand wi this stuff, Jas.'

Puzzlement dented his features as, one by one, I passed him butter, milk, orange juice, tomato sauce and pickles. He placed them on the table and sank down.

'Ma mum'll be usin again, won't she?'

'Aye… I think that might be right.'

'Ah remember wance she fell right doon the stairs.'

'Aye…' I spooned fat over the roasties.

'Her heid wis aw bloody an her skirt wis up her arse.'

'Oh, dearie me…' I kept my back to him.

'Ah hid tae call the ambulance. Ah wis only wee. She's hid a load o chances.'

'How d'ye mean…?'

'The doctor keeps tellin her tae stop…' I turned. His face was shadowed by worry, and bereft of any bravado.

I held his cornflower blue eyes for as long as he could stand it. 'Well, Jas, I'm sure she's OK the now, or we would've heard. We can gie her a wee phone after tea, if ye like.' When he dipped his head, I put the tray back in the oven.

'Will you speak tae her, Ellen?'

'Aye, nae bother.'

I continued with the chores. He was working up to something else, kept slipping me sideways glances.

'She's no gonna get away wi it forever, is she?'

His shit detector was as finely tuned as my nurse's watch.

'No, Jas, she's no going tae get away wi it forever.'

I waited on tenterhooks for the next nuclear incident, and nearly dropped the brussels when his face cleared. He hauled himself off the chair, rattled open the cutlery drawer and started to set up the table. He smiled, turning his face into a wee boy's again, showing the space between his two front teeth and the dimple in his right cheek.

When he said, 'Hey Ellen, where's ma birthday cake?' I couldn't help myself. I clipped him one with the dishcloth.

JULIE HAYMAN

Motherland

Picture a woman about my height and build, with hair as fine as fishing twine and eyes the colour of salt water. Her hands are long and white and often cold, the ring on the third finger of her left hand much twisted and pulled. She has a white pet poodle which does tricks, walking on its hind legs, chasing its tail, biting the nose of the woman's husband.

This husband is a military man. Buttoned-up jacket, buttoned-up mouth, he cuffs the poodle whose name is Frou-Frou, and pulls wool from its coat which he stuffs into the ticking of the mattress on the big bed, alongside his medals, his Luger, his mention in dispatches. The man would like to mattress-stuff the woman, too, but she's too slippery for him.

Yet they have six children, all girls – let me tell you about them. The first daughter has golden-orange eyes wide on the side of her head. Her mouth is a surprised o, her name is Unimportant. The second daughter lies her way out of and into trouble, and will grow up to be a splendid actress in fishnets. She leaves home at an early age, and so we will not consider her much.

The third and fourth daughters are twins. Their names are Aurora and Isolde, and each twin knows what the other is thinking. They were born joined at the elbow, and Aurora's left hand clutches Isolde's right. They are in love.

The mother likes to smack the fifth daughter. Her name is Bunny and she has pink candyfloss hair. She lives enclosed by a pool of her own tears. One night soon she will drown.

The last daughter loves the smell of the face-powder on her mother's cheeks. She loves the smell of Frou-Frou which is like tunnels and secrets and warm hiding-places. She also loves her father when his back is turned. This daughter tells no one her name. The mother likes this daughter no better than the others and never asks what she is called, though Frou-Frou likes her and will often give her attention by growling and pissing on her feet. As you might have guessed, the story is mainly about this daughter, so it is a pity we do not know her name.

The family live in a peeling-plaster house, not far from the sea. The floors are covered in mottled turquoise linoleum, easy to clean after Bunny's tears and Frou-Frou's accidents. Easy, also, to learn to swim on. The sisters keep out of each other's way as far as possible, though the house is small and privacy is a lie like God. Frou-Frou sniffs the mother's slimy trail and follows her everywhere. The husband is locked out for most of the day, but let in after dark.

The youngest daughter is not much like the sea-creature, not much like the soldier. She used to be able to do the splits in cold weather, but now wears a long skirt because her legs are growing together. The twins tell her she is becoming like them, all by herself. The daughter looks at the skin between her webbed legs, and wonders.

The mother whose hands are nearly always cold finds the coldness spreading up her arms. Inside, her womb is unsettled and volcanic, spewing black lava through the halls and tubes of the inner labyrinth. Nobody, least of all the husband, knows this woman has been cultivating stone-flowers, ice-flowers, flowers formed in wax. Nobody knows she has an interest in flowers at all.

It is Unimportant who knows that the mother is ill. The mother slaps Bunny more and more, and more and more Bunny howls. Frou-Frou is bald in places from the amount of wool that is now pulled. The youngest daughter shuffles around the dilapidated house like a geisha, and nobody notices.

The mother is dying above the ticking mattress on the big bed under a snow-white sheet. Bunny weeps with joy, the twins watch only each other, the youngest daughter balances a ball on the tip of her nose and practises clapping her hands. The husband intends to shoot himself inside his ear but can't remember how to load the Luger, so he snatches more white wool instead and fills his head with that.

The mother takes a long time dying, but we must ask her to hurry up so that the youngest daughter has time to get down to the docks and kiss her way aboard a ship bound for Antarctica before her legs give way altogether.

Now comes the interesting part. The ship sails from Plymouth at midnight, pausing at Madeira, South Trinidad, Cape Town, Melbourne and Lyttleton in New Zealand before embarking on the final leg of the fifteen-thousand-mile journey to Cape Evans, Antarctica. The youngest daughter spends much of her time during the five-month voyage asleep on the ice-house or catching rats in the hold. For this, she is given all the fish she can eat: herring, tuna, cod, coley, haddock, sea bass and sardines, they all slip down her throat. She begins to put on a lot of weight, and her haunches shimmy as she hauls her lower body laboriously around the ship on short, strong arms. One of the seamen gives her a horn to honk, and she plays this night and day until the Captain orders it confiscated between the end of the last dog watch and eight bells of the morning shift.

Sailing through the Southern Ocean towards Antarctica, the ship is frequently rocked and bounced by storms. Cold, black, lacy-crested waves crash and swill across the decks, unscrewing railings, shifting cargo, sickening the crew. The daughter practises Eskimo-rolls in the sloshing ice which engulfs the ship, closing her nostrils beneath the breakers as waves suck and pluck at the planking. She watches the Captain lurch about the deck, unsteady as a nutcracker, and is glad she no longer has legs.

Now she is given an empty packing crate on the bridge in which to sleep. Icicles fringe it like the teeth of a sea leopard and the ribs of wood inside are as cold as bone. The daughter lies inside this case like a fat, bent sausage, and scratches her swollen belly with black horny nails. Not long now. The water has evened out under pack ice which scrapes and splits against the hull, while running leads like Chinese calligraphy sign the way. The light has changed and everything is in sharp focus. The daughter is surprised to see that the Antarctic is not white, but mauve, pink, blue, indigo. She tastes the air with her whiskers and smells the absence of smells.

When the ship reaches McMurdo Sound, the daughter is lowered in a canvas hammock, by order of the First Mate, onto an ice-floe. She flops and wriggles, and her eyes grow large and round looking at the big blue bergs and the smoking crater of Mount Erebus. She can't remember much about her family except that her father was a pink-haired, cold-fleshed sea-dog.

She sheds her past like a Selkie sheds her skin.

JACQUELINE PAIZIS

Safi

They had been warned by the camp volunteers to expect snow in a few days but here it was already: here it was, falling voiceless onto his narrow shoulders. His ten-year-old narrow shoulders. He watches it with curiosity as it stains into dark dots as soon as it touches his jacket. His jacket is too thin for snow. Shivers make his legs wobble and his hands dig their way into his pockets with a will of their own. He watches the snow gathering along the ridge of his tent and he is astonished at how quickly it mounts in shape and stays there without melting. He blinks when a snowflake chills his eyelashes like a frozen tear.

He stopped all that child's behaviour once his journey began. Mustafa had warned him to stop. From the moment they left their village he had to stop being a child. Those childish days were over. It became Safi's mantra.

'You are no longer a child. A child no longer.'

And it had worked. So far. Safi's mantra has got him over the mountains and into Turkey. It has nagged him across a river where he almost drowned. Then there had been Mustafa at his side. Always at his side.

He can't stand still. It is too cold so he walks a few steps, stamping his feet to get some feeling into his toes. His right foot is damp where the rip in his trainer is letting in water.

Safi hesitates opposite a group of men who are building a fire from the legs and arms of an abandoned chair. He doesn't know the men. They travel alone, no wives or children. Safi knows they aren't Syrian. He thinks they might be Libyan. One man, wearing a black shiny coat and grey jeans, is shouting at the man next to him. He bends down to light a cigarette from the newly sparking fire. Safi thinks he hears Mustafa's name but it isn't worth getting hopeful. He has been hopeful before, once when he thought he saw the back of Mustafa's head and once when he heard a voice that sounded like his brother's. The other man notices Safi standing there watching and he waves him over. Safi needs no encouragement. His little heart leaps like his step. Now he stands among them, in miniature, warming his hands over the lengthening flames. One of the men with a reddish hue to his hair, squats down on a rock, coughing. The man wearing grey jeans fishes in his pocket and pulls out a sweet that he hands to Safi and Safi takes it, his hand shaking. He remembers his manners. His mother would be proud that he remembers to say thank you. He smiles at the memory of his mother's face and he smiles when he tastes the sweetness of the sweet.

The snow is intensified by a gathering, spiralling wind, strong, insistent and silent. The men and Safi huddle closer to the fire, the flames hissing under the blizzard.

Safi looks over the roofs of the tents and sees some boys playing football. He knows one of them by sight, Hassan, a Libyan. He could keep warm by playing football. Hands in pockets, slight shoulders hunched, Safi wanders away from the men, quickening his pace.

It is late morning but the purple and pink clouds hang over the camp like heavy curtains. There was nothing to eat for breakfast today. The volunteers had run out of milk and soup so he had drunk some sweet, weak tea. His stomach has been replaced by a hollow. Ever since he'd lost Mustafa.

Kicking the football warms him up. Safi and the other boys laugh and shout and throw snowballs at one another. Safi aims one at Hassan but Hassan ducks and it hits a man standing behind him. Safi recognizes him as the man at the fire who had given him a sweet. The man fixes him with a cold stare. The snowball has landed on his jacket. He dusts it off but continues looking at Safi as he does so.

It is lunchtime. The children can hear the clang and bang of metal against metal. The soup kitchen is being set up. They abandon their game and head across the soggy wasteland towards the eating area. Safi's head is wet. Someone, he suspects the Afghan, has stolen his woollen hat that his aunt had knitted for him. Now he will have to steal a woollen hat from someone else.

The benches are lined up under the trees. A big tarpaulin is stretched over the branches above affording some shelter while they are eating their soup. They stand in line. Already about thirty people are in front of them. Safi imagines aubergines in rich tomato sauce, acuka, kibbeh and if he sniffs really hard he can smell thyme. He is handed his soup after half an hour. A thin potato mixture with some tomato but hot, at least hot. He looks across and spots the Afghan perched on a rock rapidly spooning the soup into his mouth, Safi's hat on his head. He plans how he will recapture his hat. He will go round from behind while the Afghan is eating and he will just whip it off and run. After all it is his hat and he needs it.

He hands back his tin mug to the girl wearing the red SOC bib and once he is assured there is no chance of a second helping he follows up his plan and executes it just as he had done in his mind. He is hurtling down the slope, skidding on the icy moguls, even before the Afghan realises what has happened. Safi runs, tumbles and gets up and runs some more. The running and the soup are keeping him warm. What was the point of heading to a freezing cold tent?

He runs straight into the arms of the sweet giving man but this time the man holds him firmly and claps his hand over Safi's mouth, marching him forward, his hands now pinned behind his back by the man's other hand. They are heading away from the camp towards a clump of trees: bleak, black skeletons silhouetted against the pink and grey skies. Behind the trees Safi sees a narrow ribbon threading away and disappearing into snow: a lane to the nearest village. Until this moment Safi hasn't thought about villages. He has somehow blocked out pictures of real houses, standing solid in the ground with trees and fields and animals grazing. It had been a long time, too much time to know how much, since he could remember anything but huge slabs of cement with rusted rods sticking out; rods that could trip you up and cut your leg when you tried to hop between the rubble.

There is a battered old white van at the edge of the road. Two men are leaning against it. Safi's arm is hurting from being twisted up his back so far. He tries not to cry. That behaviour stopped when they left

Aleppo but the tears are there, balancing on the edge of his eyelids like water pooling before it drops to a waterfall. He fights to keep them there. They are speaking Arabic but he doesn't understand their sharp accents. An intense, fuzzy snowstorm is whitening the landscape. Safi is bundled into the van, the doors slam closed from outside. He doesn't understand what he has done. Was it the snowball that landed on the man's jacket? Was he seen stealing his own woollen hat? He lies on a piece of old sacking and then he hears the two front doors closing and the engine kicks into life. Muffled voices come from the front cab. Smoke oozes through the cracks in the partition. Mustafa would have known what to do.

Safi feels very afraid. He gets to his hands and knees just as the van begins to slide sideways but the speed is too great and he falls down again and the spinning is out of control and he can feel huge bumps under the floor of the van and then he is hurled to the opposite side of the van and they are upside down.

All he can hear is the squeaking of the wheels as they continue to rotate in the air. Safi feels his throbbing head. He has a cut above his right eyebrow that is dripping blood onto his collar. He wipes it away with the back of his hand. He hears no voices. He crawls along the roof towards the doors. The windows of the doors are now upside down so he has to peer downwards to see out. But it is all white. He pushes against the door with all his weight but it refuses to open. He kicks it with his wet trainers but they slip at each attempt.

He knows it must be getting towards late afternoon and the light fading. He searches the van for something to smash against the window but there is nothing. And he prays to Allah even though it hurts his knee. He prays that one of the men is alive enough to get him out because even though he is scared of the men he is more afraid of being left in the van, alone, freezing, with night coming and only an old, thin sack to cover his legs. And maybe two dead men for company. Safi shouts and bangs on the sides of the van. Nothing but the silence of snow falling on snow and the smell of dusk.

Lying flat is impossible. The floor under him, that is really the roof, is sloping downwards making him roll to his right every time he turns his body. He curls up like a foetus trying to keep warm. Then he feels a different movement. The right side of the van begins moving and sliding again. Safi has nothing to hold onto, his little body being thrown around like a sack of potatoes. His head strikes something.

When he opens his eyes he can hear shouts and feel his body being lifted. What he hears is a foreign language. He's heard enough of it in the camp to know it is the local Greek but he can't understand what they are saying. He feels warmer. Something soft and heavy has been put over him.

They take him home to their house in the village on the big tractor. Despina tends to his wounds while her mother, Dimitra, makes soup. As Safi lies on the settee he watches the flames dancing in the old wood burner, its pipes snaking round the room and disappearing out through the wall.

When Despina has finished seeing to Safi's wounds her mother comes and sits beside him. 'Come,' she says. 'Eat this.' And she offers up the spoon to Safi's mouth.

He does as she beckons and is soon in ecstasy. The chicken soup has real pieces that he can chew even though his jaw is so sore where he smashed into the side of the van as it tumbled down the slope and hit the farmhouse wall. Safi takes in the room. He touches the soft fabric of the sofa under his body and feels the heaviness of the blanket laid over him. He is so warm he is almost falling asleep. A big black dog stretches out in front of the fire, its head between its paws.

Despina follows Safi's gaze and says. 'Iraklis,' pointing to the dog. She smiles at Safi.

He smiles back. She reminds him of his sister Amira. Curly chestnut hair. Eyes like almonds.

The family cat idles into the room to see what all the fuss is about and after circling round and round he chooses to sit on Safi's lap. Safi has no experience of cats but he likes the soft fur and he likes stroking it. The cat's name is Ektoras.

The first night in his new home Safi sleeps badly because he is in a real bed. He lies flat on his back with only his grazed chin poking out of the covers and he watches the blurry, metallic moon poking between snow clouds. Ektoras has no such problem as he lies curled up at Safi's feet. When Safi does sleep he dreams about his old Syrian home before it was bombed. He remembers the clay oven on the roof of the building and his uncle Sami stirring the food. Where is his mother? Why isn't it his mother stirring the food? He tries so hard to answer his own question that he wakes up with a jolt and frightens Ektoras who jumps off the bed and darts out of the room. Safi is sweating.

At first, Safi has many nights when he remembers his uncle being around the house but not his mother. He doesn't see her in his dreams where she always was: in the kitchen or on the roof hanging out the washing or returning from market with the shopping.

Safi is quick to pick up Greek. Despina helps him out. They have snowball fights in the garden, run with Iraklis around the lanes, hang about outside the village shop with the other kids. Then it is time for Despina to go back to school so she takes Safi with her and he is introduced to his new classmates and teacher, Miss Dukakis.

'Where do you come from?' some of the children ask. 'Where's Syria?'

'Go back to where you came from,' say others. 'This isn't your home. You aren't Greek. You don't belong here.'

'Don't listen to them, Safi. This is your home now. Ignore them. Refugees are welcome in our village and in our school,' says Miss Dukakis.

Safi can't ignore the voices and he can't ignore the traps the children set for him on the way home from school when Despina isn't with him. They throw icy snowballs at him; some of them have shards of stone inside. Sometimes he cries all the way home but he doesn't want his new mother to see him like that so he takes the long route.

He loves his bedroom. There is a small wooden desk under the window where he keeps his school books, his Quran and his pens. The walls of the house are so thick that he can make a window seat with cushions and sit curled up looking over the fields and hills beyond. He likes to look at the snowline of the Dyssoron mountains to the south-west because he feels at a safe distance.

One day Safi arrives at school and there are two new boys in his class, one from Libya and one from

Syria. He welcomes them. He welcomes the fact that he can speak to someone in his own native tongue. The same children call them names in Greek but Safi doesn't want to upset the boys more by translating. Instead he tells them to ignore the children, just like he had been told when he arrived.

After some weeks Safi's adoptive parents tell him that they had lost their son two years before. Dimitris was ten years old when he drowned in Lake Doirani, four kilometres from their village.

'I still miss my big brother,' Despina says.

Safi nods. 'I will pray every day for your brother and for mine.'

When they rescued him from the people traffickers Safi's adoptive parents saw it as a sign from God sending them a second son and they have loved him as their own ever since.

DAN MAITLAND

Click

So, how was the gig last night?

Well, you know Jamie…

Yes, I know Jamie.

It wasn't that bad actually for a while. We did lots of young people's tunes, which of course I had to learn. About two days' work prior. But I suppose that's partly my fault for being an old fogey.

Yes. That's completely your fault.

Anyway, we had to get there early to do a two hour soundcheck and rehearsal, which of course was fun. Middle of nowhere. I mean literally the middle of nowhere. Some posh school. No shops. No pubs. I tell you, I'm not really here for this sort of thing anymore. It's just such a ball ache. Also, he'd booked a girl singer, and I was just playing sax and keyboards.

Hmmm, I can see how that might be annoying to a diva like yourself.

It was.

Go on then; obviously something happened. You've got a face like thunder even now. I can see that you were hugely oppressed and victimised and that the world did you wrong in a very large way.

You may mock, my friend, but in fact the world did do me wrong. Though I must say that, after all of the nonsense, the gig was actually going pretty well.

For some reason Jamie was playing keyboards not guitar. So that was a bit bizarre, with both of us on keyboards, no guitar, Tim on drums, and my brother on bass. But actually it sounded OK, sort of worked on those dancey modern pop things. And also, and obviously annoyingly, the girl singer was really good. Really nailed it. Made me realise that there is a level in singing this sort of stuff that I just haven't reached.

Could have told you that...

Predictable, sir. Predictable. Do better. Anyway, as I said, sets one and two, pretty good. People dancing. Bad food eaten. Band get told off by Jamie for having a drink. I didn't mess up too many times. Diva strops more or less done with.

And then?

We're in the second break between sets and I've left it too long wandering around outside in my gig clothes with my sweat-soaked shirt. And suddenly it's cold –

Cold?

Yes. You know that summer evening cold when the day hasn't been that hot anyway but it's been clear and the sun goes down and suddenly it's cold. And you weren't ready for it. You know it being summer 'n' that. And there having been, you know, what's it called–? Ah, yes: sun...

OK. It's cold. But it's July. Can't be that cold.

Well, it felt pretty bloody cold to me. It was cold. Dark and cold. And I had my sweaty gig shirt on from actually working hard –

Lol.

From actually working hard. And we're just about to go on, and I realise that if I go on like this I will end up tomorrow with my normal post gig man flu.

Oh my god! You're so frail. How on earth have you made it to fifty-three?

Beats me. So me and Tim are heading back to the marquee after a quick fag break, and a sneaky glass of wine away from Jamie's headmasterly gaze, when I remember that I have another shirt in my car.

Always come prepared.

Exactly! So Tim is walking towards the tent; we are due on exactly now. I rush over to the car, open the boot, see my shirt, grab my shirt, put it back down again, put down my keys, rip off the sweaty one, put on the clean dry one – well clean-ish. And close the boot. Suit jacket back on. Start jogging towards the marquee. Tim waiting. I'm going to make it.

Then, suddenly it occurs to me: it's all going too smoothly, what could possibly go wrong? Only one thing at this juncture. Hand to pocket. Then to other pocket. Hand to jacket pocket, heart descending. Hand inside jacket. Turn around. Start walking slowly back to car. Being late can now bugger off. Jamie can now bugger off. Look forlornly and somewhat hopelessly at the dusky ground – the wet grass dewy from the evening frickin cold. Kneel by the back of the car. Nothing on the ground glints silvery in the moonlight. Mood, already fragile, descending at a frightening pace of knots. I don't need to, but I do, I look into the boot of the car, through the smug geometric, doesn't bloody work anyway, heating grille-dissected rear window –

Oh, you do turn a good phrase…

– to see them: gleaming maliciously and silvery in the retarded moonlight!

Ah…

Yes. Ah. Locked my keys in the car. What a twat. What a twat.

So now I am charging forlornly back to the marquee with my phone in my hand, which by the way has about twenty percent battery left –

You've got to get yourself a better phone, mate.

Well, that I do know. Anyway, remember the battery power as it's relevant later on.

Will do.

So, trudging back to the marquee, obviously trying to ring the RAC as I go.

Obviously...

And obviously they're not answering their phone.

Obviously.

If I can just get hold of them now, then by the time we finish the set they may actually show up.

If you can just get hold of them now...

Ten minutes later, I'm still holding. 'Thank you for holding, our operators are unusually busy at the moment, we will deal with your call as soon as we can. Please be assured your call is important to us.'

The emergency service.

Exactly. And rather predictably I have to go on stage without getting hold of them.

The Jamie Factor.

So there I am: sweaty gig shirt, phone lobbed somewhere behind me – still holding for all I know, grinding my way through the last set, putting on my rigor mortis stage smile and giving it the Old Pro one-hundred-per-cent for the punters, whilst my mind projects those effing keys grinning at me from behind the rear window... couched luxuriously, in fact reclining luxuriously, upon my coat – which also will become an important factor in the terrible tale of misery and tragedy that is about to unfold upon you, my friend.

I can't wait.

We finish the set. Encore, they cry. F off, I reply.

You can say the word you know. I'm over twenty-one.

I'm bored with the word. The word has no power anymore, it's been disenfranchised by spoken word artists and... and... well, me.

OK.

Band start breaking down. I clamber backwards and rummage for the phone. Redial. 'Thank you for holding our operators are unusually busy at the moment, we will deal with your call as soon as we can. Please be assured your call is important to us.'

Ouch.

Fifteen minutes!

Ouch.

It's cold. Band are getting it done. Marquee is emptying out. Sweaty shirt is damp and flu-like. Man-made fibre gig-jacket collar pulled up to pretend it's a scarf. Everyone steering a very wide berth round the icy pit of belligerent hell that is now my home. Then finally. Finally.

'Hello. May I have your membership number please.'

You don't want to hear my opening salvo.

I don't imagine so, no.

Suffice to say, she got the gist of my disappointment, and really couldn't give a...

Word.

Word. Exactly. Honestly, mate, nothing I said seemed to invoke, even slightly, any sense of compassion or empathy.

She didn't apologise?

She apologised. Like she'd borrowed my red crayon without asking in primary school... Like she'd misheard my coffee order... Like I was a crossword puzzle asking for a five-letter definition of, 'What you may say to someone you'd previously upset.'

Anyway, you got through. They gonna bash someone out. All sorted. Not that desperate a tale, mate, to be honest. I got worse than that. How about –

You are wrong, sir. This is not the end, this is merely the end of the beginning. Here's where the misery really starts.

'I'm afraid,' – she's not afraid – 'we aren't going to be able to get anyone with you for about an hour and half – possibly two. All our operatives are very busy. They will call you when they are near.'

What? etc. You have to be kidding me! etc. My phone battery, etc. It's really cold, etc. Middle of nowhere and so forth...

That worked?

What?

You know, the whinging like a little girl... Whining, maybe? No whinging. Whinging like a little girl –

F–

Careful.

So to recap –

Oh God, please don't.

I am now stuck in a diminishing marquee. Middle of a field. Middle of nowhere. It must, at this point, be approaching zero degrees.

It must not.

Clad only in my man-made suit and wet shirt and tie. Phone battery down to less than ten per cent. Band all packed up and ready to go. Keys glinting maliciously in the light of the bitter, gloating moon, behind their factory-tested, crash-resistant super-toughened glass – which also has a complacent mocking tinge to it, if you're asking me.

I'm sure no one was asking you anything at this point. I know this mood.

Well, my brother and Tim did stop by to advise against me poking the wire end of my sax cleaner up the jacksy of the back door.

In a pointless and inept attempt to trigger some more friendly response from the lock?

Yep. That.

Advice went down well?

Very. But fair play to them, they persevered. They then attempted to talk me into taking a lift home with them, and coming back for the car the next day.

Not bad advice.

No. But I had teaching the next morning. Needed the car for that. Also it was bloody miles away, in the middle of nowhere. How am I getting back? Also the school were going to lock the field.

Gotcha. Tricky.

Also the RAC were coming...

The RAC are coming. Just got to wait it out.

Just had to wait it out.

I stood and watched the tail lights, and all my other options, disappear in the night, two by two.

Like that joke about the flood, and the bloke on his roof praying to Lord to save him, and spurning the boats and the helicopter etc... The Lord will save me etc...

No.

So finally it's me and the caretaker in an empty field. Waiting for the RAC. Who, best case scenario, are getting there at 1.00. In forty-five minutes time.

Not so bad…

Did I mention zero degrees?

Yep. But it couldn't –

Well then. Caretaker potters about doing caretaker things, quite possibly avoiding me –

Quite possibly.

– while I head back into the illusion of warmth and security that is millimetre-thick canvas strung over poles with two huge apertures gaping into the Arctic breeze, saying, Come in, come in…

It's July…

I cast around for some source of heat and realise that I haven't packed away the stage light.

Ah.

Indeed. Filter off. Light on. Blaring at me like an escaped prisoner.

Warm?

Actually not so much as you'd think. Got me feet a bit better, but the ice-laden gale still had my torso.

Sigh… So?

So. Tablecloths, my friend. I grab two, wrap one around me – shawl-like, wind the other into scarf-width and jam it into the useless jacket, then resume my hunched position in front of five hundred watts of not so hot as you might imagine floorspot.

Better?

Yep. But I'm still getting man flu for sure.

No doubt.

So for half an hour I just sit there, turning off everything on my phone that isn't actually for phoning and waiting for the mercy call to bring me back to the world of light switches and radiators and laptops and whisky and a nice bedtime snack and the highlights of the golf.

They call?

1.00am on the nose.

Thank God.

You'd think, wouldn't you? But, 'Hello. Is that Mr Maitland? I am sorry to tell you that we are not going to be able to get to you.'

What? Not at all? Not ever?

Apparently.

You went mad?

What the F? I've been waiting. Sent friends home. Stranding me. Middle of nowhere. Freezing cold. Could actually die. How dare you?

I went mad. I actually began to feel a bit scared. What would I do? How would I get home? What about the golf highlights? What do people do? Would I ever again turn up a thermostat?

'The best I can say, is that we may be able to get to you within two hours.'

'Two hours from when I called you? Listen my phone is gonna run out any minute. You won't be able to contact me. Two hours from when I called you??!'

I was actually panicking now. This was a real thing. It was happening now. At this minute in time. One more in a long succession of horribly real minutes that constituted the last hour and a half of my, previously not nearly as shit as I thought it was apparently, life.

'No, sir. From now. We can't guarantee –'

Black.

That's it. Phone dead. Off. I'm alone. In the dark. In a marquee in a field. With just me for company.

Shit.

You have no idea, mate. It was desperate. I had no money – no wallet. No phone. No lift. No cabs. And could not stay where I was. No invitation. I was not welcome. Caretaker had promised to wait 'til 1.00. He had to go. Lock the field. I was now a trespasser. An illegal.

Wow. I can see it actually. That's horrible. What do you do? What would I do? I mean there's people... I mean the things we need... And then you don't have them... Just one absent moment... One click of a lock... What did you do? What could you do? Walk? Where? What did you do?

What I knew I'd have to do, right from the start; right from the moment I turned to walk back to the car, reaching into my acrylic pockets and knowing there would be no reprieve there. Violence. I did violence.

Eh? To who? You hit the caretaker?

No! Why would I hit the caretaker? Not who. What. The car. I did violence to the car.

Ah, I get it.

I now see how you are sitting in front of me sipping your third mug of tea and nibbling on your second slice of cake. Back in the bosom of us. And very welcome, my friend. Though I know your moods, no way you hadn't already violence'd the car.

True. A few new dents and the rubber seal on the boot is no longer with us...

You smashed the window.

I smashed the window. Or to be honest the caretaker did. As it turns out, I am too puny for that work also. My sax stand bounced off with every lunge, not even a scrape.

Not your field, for sure. So, let me see if I get this right. You smashed the window. Plugged in the phone. Nicked the tablecloths for warmth and to prevent man flu. Drove home.

Yep. All that.

At which point on the journey home did the RAC ring to say they'd just turned up after all and you weren't there?

You are good, sir. Ten minutes in. Twenty-five minutes after the, 'We'll be at least two hours if we come at all,' call.

Figures.

Ranting at them all morning on the phone, but no joy?

None.

Figures. Would you care for another cup of tea, that I shall buy with money? And that we shall consume in this warm, electrically lit, and reassuringly familiar beacon of civilisation?

Yes, please.

ISABEL COSTELLO

A Place to Paint Yellow

On my first day back, it hits me like an elbow in the face: my life adds up to less than ever now.

Thoughts like this fill my head almost the whole Piccadilly line, into town and back out to Hanger Lane. At the depot, they all think I can't drive because my commute would only take half as long round the North Circular. The examiner had to pass me after he called out, 'Maria Stegosaurus,' at the test centre and everyone burst out laughing. Poor man, he looked so uneasy as the handbrake disappeared under my thigh when I got in the car. Bit like these Tube armrests, wedged so hard into my side rolls it leaves deep red dents. There was that young bloke the other week who got up for me – but then he had to spoil it by saying, 'Would you like two seats?'

Of course, I wouldn't have moved out if I'd known Mum only had a year. She said living with her at 30 was the least of my problems and maybe it was, but it was the easiest one to fix. It was watching a programme about adults still living with their parents made me do it. I didn't fancy being in more than one group they made telly programmes about.

My flat was supposed to be the turning point. It was reasonable and only ten minutes from Mum's, but mainly I took it because the landlord said, 'Feel free to brighten it up.' I'd always wanted a place to paint yellow. But what with having to check on Mum each day after work and doing all her cleaning, washing and everything, the hours got swallowed up. Besides, can you see me up a ladder? I'll have to get used to turning left out of the station now. The Council want hers back by the end of the month.

Mum hollered, 'Is that you, Maria?' whenever she heard the key in the door.

Who else was it going to be? She'd scared everyone off. Don't know how I stuck it all those years, the two of us slumped on the sofa night after night, glued to the box, stuffing our faces like there was no tomorrow.

But here it is.

'My God, look at the state of you, Maria. You got to do something or you're going to end up like me,' she used to say. 'What's going to happen to you when I'm not around?'

The way she went on, you'd think she was a good influence. You'd think it was me started it. Her doctor said I'd be heading the same way unless I took action. This was when they found she had a leaking heart valve and they couldn't risk the operation.

When Mum complained she'd never done nothing in her life (apart from getting *morbidly obese*), what could I say, when I was the only evidence she ever existed? There's this lovely photo of her just after she arrived from Cyprus: young, *slim*, about to start a new life. About to screw it all up by having me before she could find a husband. Game over in five minutes round the back of the Coach and Horses in Enfield Town.

She really laid in last week when I turned up without the chips; called me a useless, pathetic waste of space. And maybe I am, not sticking up for myself. And maybe not, because I can get by on my own. Hold down a job, pay my bills, which considering how thick everyone thought I was at school…

Either way, I shouldn't have walked out without saying goodbye. But I wasn't to know.

Not until the morning, when I got a call from the ambulance crew saying it wasn't good. The North Circular was clear but by the time my cab got to the hospital she was unconscious. Two hours later her heart gave out under the strain. I sat there staring at the flat line on the monitor, like on TV, until it was turned off and went black. They had to ask me to leave when they wheeled her away.

'You can see her again if you want, at the ...' the nurse said.

She was really kind but I was embarrassed in case she'd heard me saying, 'Come back' to a dead body.

I went into Hassan's on the way home. He usually asked after Mum, but not this time – almost as if he knew. It sounds stupid, but he looked like a hero slashing away at the döner with his long knife, all that gorgeous juicy meat tumbling into the shovel. I had this weird feeling we'd both taken a wrong turn in life, like everything had been a big mistake and we were destined for greater things. Not 'wildest dreams'. Things which might actually happen. Normally I never eat in public – you should see the looks – but the day Mum died I just bit into the kebab and let the chilli sauce run down my chin, not caring who saw.

They don't know what it's like.

On the way out I put the greasy box and serviettes in the bin.

'You'll have to eat in more often, Maria,' Hassan called after me, 'Set an example to this lot!'

I managed a smile he wouldn't have seen. For the first time ever I was going to be able to watch *Silent Witness* without anyone yakking in my ear, in what was supposed to be my own home.

It was going to have to be, now.

I tripped over that loose tile in the hall and fumbled about in the wrong place for the light switch, like I was still at Mum's – even my few bits of furniture were from hers. She had never been here though. Come to think of it, nobody had. I started repeating out loud things I'd heard people saying to each other: 'Would you like to come over?' 'Shall we meet at mine?'

Saying the words is not the hard bit.

The arrangements had to be made quickly *for operational reasons* (meaning: *we don't have a big enough fridge*) and just when I thought it was all sorted out the funeral director called again.

'I'm sorry, Ms Steglioros, I have some upsetting news,' he said.

For Christ's sake, I thought, she's already dead. *For health and safety reasons* the coffin would have to be wheeled up the aisle of the Greek church on a trolley; his men couldn't lift it.

There were a lot more people than I expected on the day. Most of them I hadn't seen since before Mum got really ill, but at least they made the effort now. Greeks show respect to their own. Some hugged me and one or two thought about it and gave up. I tried to be polite, waiting for somebody to say, 'Your Mum was so proud of you,' like in the movies.

Hassan came. Funny how he was the last person Mum would have wanted there. 'That filthy Turk,' she used to call him, before wrapping her chops round one of his Charcoal Specials. She didn't mean it. Maybe she never meant any of those things.

Sandra was there too, from the charity shop on the Broadway. I recognised her behind the counter a few months ago, even though we're in the same extra-large boat now. She always had a pretty face, that one, and I don't mean the way someone once said I had a 'nice smile', as if the rest of me was horrific. Sandra doesn't seem to remember me as the fat girl she and her mates took the piss out of at school, so I never let on. She calls me if anything suitable comes in, and for Mum's funeral we were both wearing dresses from the shop's best ever donation, from an opera singer. Taffeta and velvet in July! God knows what Mum would have said about that.

I could ask Sandra round, maybe.

Hassan and Sandra both had to get back to work and all around me the mourners were speaking Greek now. Mum never bothered teaching me. Now and again I caught her name, Androulla, and the odd word but I had no idea what they were saying, standing in the middle of the hall as it emptied out. Lucky they thought it was enough to nod in my direction as they left, rather than go through the whole sodding performance again. All I wanted was to get back to my spreadsheets.

Nearly there now.

The best bit about the depot is that any woman would have stuck out. For twelve years there's just been me and Doreen, the old girl who answers the phone and does the typing. All day the drivers nip in and out of the office with their delivery sheets, asking, 'Just going over the caravan, get you anything, Maria love?' I hardly ever go myself because I hate crossing the yard.

The drivers take off so quick in reverse and the loud beeping noise is a warning all right, but I can't get out of the way fast enough.

Vince's burger van is in the layby outside the gates. We're his only customers so he knows everyone's favourite. The shifts keep him busy but when it's quiet I can just about make him out across the yard, hanging out the door by one arm, smoking, looking around like a food inspector might pop up in the van on the quiet.

All I want is a normal day, but it isn't, how could it be? One by one the drivers come into the office, patting me on the shoulder or making me struggle out of my chair for a sweaty hug. All my life nobody's ever wanted to touch me and suddenly they won't stop. And almost as strange, nobody offers to get me anything from the caravan, out of respect, I suppose. Doreen keeps checking the time then looking at me out of the corner of her eye. At midday she goes down the Tesco Local, and gives me one of those tiny freezing cold packets of sandwiches without saying a word. I'm not feeling myself at all and it takes a while to work out why. I'm not hungry.

It's a new week now. This morning I was watching Vince swinging off the back of the van, wondering if I'd ever leave this job. The boss says I'm worth my weight in gold, *ha ha!* The books were in a right state when I started, but it didn't take me long to get the Revenue off our backs. As I watch the foreman crossing the yard with my elevenses – bacon burger with fries – I realize I've not been thinking straight. I like it here. My life is not completely shitty. I don't have to change *everything*.

But it's true, I have to do *something*.

I'm going to paint the flat yellow.

And that's not all.

As soon as we have the office to ourselves I plonk my burger down in front of Doreen. You should have seen her face when I told her, 'I don't need this.' It was only right to let Vince know, and to settle up, even though it wasn't our usual day.

As I crossed the yard, the last lorry slammed into reverse. The alarm beeped but I did it, you know. I made it to the other side.

SAL PAGE

Real Comfort Food

Minutes ago we were walking through a stinging sleet storm, so cold it momentarily banished my sadness. Now we're home. Delicious warmth wraps itself around us. But the past few days still hang in the quiet air. John shrugs his coat off and goes straight through to the kitchen. Water droplets scatter onto the tiles. He grabs two leeks and a couple of spuds from the veg rack and lights the oven.

I nip into the bedroom to change out of my wet clothes, pulling on a fleecy sweatshirt and leggings then going in search of my slippers. I find them beside one of the bunk beds in the kids' room. I grab them, my mind snagging for a second on Thomas's bad dream when I got into bed with him 'til he went to sleep again.

Back in the kitchen John has split each leek down the centre and is splashing cold water through them. He's still in wet clothes and getting wetter. I glance up and he reads my mind.

'I know… I'll change once the soup's simmering and the scones are in.'

I put the kettle on then peel the potatoes. John lights the gas under a pan and adds a splash of oil. He throws in a clove of garlic and the roughly chopped leeks and potatoes and stirs as they begin to sizzle and spit. I crumble a stock cube into a jug of boiling water.

John adds the stock to the pan. I grate extra mature cheddar as John spoons flour into the big bowl. As he measures the baking powder, he looks up and smiles. I know we're both remembering Thomas calling it 'bacon powder'. We tried to put him right but he wasn't having it so we joked he'd invented something new. We thought of all sorts of things we could add the bacon powder to. Pizza, pasta, burgers, cheesecake. Even yogurt. Thomas got the giggles when I asked him next morning if he wanted bacon powder on his porridge. He settled for syrup.

John scoops up a bit of butter and rubs it into the flour; fine breadcrumbs through his hands, rain still dripping from his hair. I throw the cheese into the bowl and go to the fridge for milk. Pouring cold milk will always be a reminder. Milk and Jaffa Cakes. Thomas grinning through a milk moustache. So happy to just be sat at the table with us. Talking and laughing.

The scone mixture is gathered together and pressed out onto the work surface. I pass John a cup. He always uses feeder cups as scone cutters, despite the memories they hold. The red one Jennifer drank apple juice from. The twins' matching pink ones. They kicked up a right fuss if they didn't have the same.

Cut and twist. Cut and twist. I pass the buttered tray and John dips the scones upside down in a little milk, squishing a bit more cheese on top once they're upright again. Each scone gets this treatment 'til all twelve are lined up on the tray. I think about the the last time we made these when Thomas cut a few out then got distracted by nibbling stray strands of cheese. Thomas laughed when John kept asking if there was a mouse in the kitchen.

John puts the scones in the oven then pulls his jumper and t-shirt off together. I take them from him and throw them into the washing basket. As he stirs the soup, he reaches for my hand. I stand beside him as the soup moves towards a simmer, chunks of potato bobbing around and steam rising. John stares into the soup and I wonder what he's thinking. I know he feels sad and empty remembering Thomas, so recently gone. He turns the gas down low under the soup, puts a lid on then turns to kiss me. I wrap my arms around his waist.

'You need to get those jeans off.'

He grins and nods as he goes off to get changed. I peer in at the scones just starting to brown. They won't be long. I reach into the washing machine. What's this? Thomas's red jumper. I pull it out and place it on the radiator, recalling the feel of his hand in mine when I walked him to school on the last day. He'd been chattering away about *Spiderman* and let go of my hand as we reached the gates. His friends were waiting. He ran to meet them without looking back.

I'm still cold. I'm shivering and my teeth have started to chatter.

John's at the kitchen door. He's wearing the zebra-striped onesie his Mum bought him for Christmas. Zipped up to the neck. I'd said he was far too cool to wear it and can't help laughing out loud. He looks down at himself and puts on a puzzled, then pretending-to-be-hurt expression. I step nearer, pull the onesie's zip open slightly and put my hand inside, where it rests on his bare chest. I lean my head against his fleecy shoulder and feel his face in my damp hair as he rubs my back to warm me. We stand like this for a few minutes.

'Time to blitz the soup.'

I watch. I love to see it go from lumpy to smooth so quickly.

'Just look at it! A pale green pond of lusciousness.'

John peers into the pan and shrugs. 'It's only soup.'

I smile. Only soup. It's perfect.

I pull the scones out of the oven and slip them onto the cooling rack. They're gnarled, crusty-topped and overblown. They smell wonderful. I take spoons, peppermill and glasses of water into the living room. I move the fruit bowl and pick up the scattered pens and crayons. I gather up a bundle of pictures from the table. I stop at the one Thomas did of John lighting the Christmas pudding: orange and blue flames leaping towards a huge yellow sun. It's beautiful. For a few seconds I can feel tears pricking at my eyes. I blink, take a couple of deep breaths and pin the picture onto the corkboard with all the other pictures and photos.

John brings in two bowls of soup, each with a couple of warm scones on the side and I laugh at that onesie all over again. His hair's beginning to dry into irresistible curls. I expect while there's no kids in the house we'll be having a few early nights.

'You look like a big baby. You'd better take that horrible garment off soon. It's not doing it for me.'

He gives me that look. He's thinking the same as me about early nights. Good. Weekend lie-ins too. Coffee and bacon sandwiches. We tear up the scones and dip pieces into the hot soup. John adds pepper to his and I sneeze. I hope Thomas is getting food this good now he's back with his mum. She's out of hospital and getting her life sorted out again.

We know you can't get too attached to foster kids but neither of us can help it. When someone shares your home for several months you get used to them being around. You get to know them and love them. I remember the likes and dislikes of all eighteen children between the ages of six months and fifteen years who've lived here for a few weeks or months. Their favourites. Their funny little ways. Thomas liked my roast chicken and spicy potato wedges. He had to have a puddle of ketchup right on the edge of the plate. He loved John's chocolate mousse with raspberries but couldn't stand beetroot or broccoli. And crackers had to be round, never square.

I do really miss him. It's only been three days.

The soup and scones are delicious. Real comfort food. We watch each other through the soup-steam. The phone could ring at any time. A child needing a temporary home. But for now we eat, still missing Thomas like crazy but at last finally warm.

CATHERINE ASSHETON-STONES

Personal Space

Sex was the first thing to cross the guy's mind. Juliette had seen that look often enough to recognise it. Yes, he'd definitely like to sleep with her. He smiled at her, then faltered.

'Hello!' he said, with forced friendliness. 'You must be Juliette. I'm Jay. Come in, I'll show you round the flat.'

She hovered in the doorway for mounting seconds, unsure whether to go in or not.

He wasn't what she'd imagined from the ad on the flat share site. She'd been expecting older than this, and nastier. In a funny way this guy was almost attractive. He had a receding chin, which was more obvious when he turned his head to look back into the flat as though checking it was still there. And his teeth were yellow. But other than that, and too much hair gel, he was OK.

So what else was wrong with him? It was this question that made her reluctant to step over the threshold. She reminded herself why she was there and walked in past him.

Following, he overtook her in a tiny living room, coming up sharp mid-stride against the side of a brown sofa. Looking surprised it was there, he stopped and turned round to talk to her, as though that's what he'd always intended to do. He explained that this was the lounge and that the kitchen was just off it, leading her through to a narrow space with a gas oven, sink, draining board and small square of brown plastic surface for cooking.

'There's a mini balcony you can sit out on when it's sunny,' he said, brightening, and squeezing past her to go to the far end of the kitchen and crank open a sash window.

As he passed her, Juliette was aware of his body. It was young and firm. Maybe this wouldn't be so bad.

She wedged herself in next to him to look out, conscious he was eyeing her slim shape and fair hair as she did so. The balcony was two foot long and about a foot wide, with a square concrete wall around it. One person could probably crouch in it at a push; barely a balcony really. Traffic roared and whirred far below.

'You could keep plants there,' she offered.

He looked as though she'd suggested something shocking. 'I don't like plants.'

'Oh, OK.' Maybe she was beginning to find out what was wrong with the guy. OCD? She looked at the oven and surface as they left the kitchen. No. That wasn't it.

In the bathroom he showed her the shower over the bath, screened by a grimy curtain that he flicked back quickly. He told her to turn the water on so she could be sure it worked. She obeyed and it shot out with surprising strength, the head jerking in her hand, spraying them both with droplets, making them laugh.

He took her into the bedroom last. She stared around. Double bed covered in yellowing white duvet. Standard foot of space around it. Cheap wardrobe. Bedside table only at one side – at the other side there was a cardboard box with a different lamp sitting on it.

'And this would be our room,' he said, trying to smile and flushing instead. She met his eye, pleased at his discomfort. He should feel uncomfortable.

At the front door she could tell he was disappointed. He knew he was going to be rejected. Him and his scummy flat.

'Well, let me know... Text me!' he called, as she turned away.

Forty-five minutes on the tube later, she got back to the house, feeling the need to wash and cleanse herself of the experience. The family must be out. At this small relief, her spirits lifted. Things weren't that awful. Somehow, she'd find a way to carry on paying the rent here. She just wouldn't go out. Or buy anything. She remembered that pink top she'd bought last week. That was a whole £9 she didn't need to have spent. She'd take it back on the weekend. There were those letters about her credit card threatening her with legal action. They were shoved out of sight down the side of her bed. She'd ring the card company tomorrow if she could and see if they'd give her more time to pay. It'd be OK.

Juliette looked at her watch. It was later than she'd usually be cooking as she'd gone to see the flat after work. But as the family was out, she might get away with it. She put her pasta sauce into the microwave. She was in the middle of spooning it over the pasta when the front door banged.

Kate bustled into the kitchen, laden with bags for life. You're a bag for life, Juliette thought, making herself smile, but knowing what would come next.

'Oh, Juliette, you're still cooking. You know it's after 7.00? I am going to need the kitchen.'

A sensation of pure pain shot through Juliette's being.

'That's fine,' she said, surprised by how obliging her voice came out. 'I'll just take this to my room.'

Kate's face fell. 'Oh, no, there's no need for that. This isn't a doss house, or some kind of sleazy bedsit. We don't want mice. Just eat it here. We don't mind working round you for five minutes.'

'We' meant Paul must be in tow. In a minute he appeared, dancing paunchily round his wife in the kitchen area while Juliette sat at the table at the far end and ate her pasta. She could feel his eyes occasionally come to rest on her. Glancing up, she thought how fat he was. Not as much as his wife, of course. She stared at Kate's thick middle: rolls of flesh straining against expensive white linen. Kate saw her looking; she flicked her eyes away. The two teenage children could be heard going into their rooms and turning an Xbox on.

Waking up at 6.00am the next day to get ready for her shift, she went into the bathroom and found an orange oven cleaner spray sitting in the sink with a note on it: This bathroom should be cleaned daily. Thanks, K X.

Payback for being in the kitchen later than her allotted time. She didn't scream or cry. Instead, she ripped the note up and flushed it down the loo.

When Juliette arrived in her new home, Jay carried her suitcase upstairs, as though she was a friend arriving. He put it in the bedroom along the side of the bed. He looked excited. The musky smell of his aftershave was overpowering. At least it masked the faint damp smell of the flat.

He offered to make dinner and they ate burgers while watching the television. Juliette wondered if this was what arranged marriages felt like. Except this wasn't a marriage. Jay seemed so awkward that she wondered if he'd actually be brave enough to touch her. Maybe he wouldn't. If that was the case then this would be a pretty easy gig. But, she remembered a saying: there's no such thing as a free lunch.

And sure enough, once they were both in bed, he moved the fluffy teddy bear she'd placed between them out of the way, pulled off her pyjama bottoms, fumbled with a condom for quite some time, and had sex with her.

She didn't participate, just lay there with her eyes open staring up at him. Her ex-boyfriend had hated it when she did that. She'd done it to him to make him realise he wasn't exciting her. He'd called it her starfish impression.

This time, she really didn't know what else to do. The guy had no idea about anything. She wondered if he was a virgin. His breath was sweet, like liquorice, and he was damp with sweat. But, apart from that, it really wasn't any worse than a lot of guys. Well, of the ten or so she'd been with. When he'd rolled off her and turned away she looked at her phone. It had taken less than five minutes all in all. Not bad, as rent goes.

In his cubicle the next day, Jay glowed. He looked over the partition at his colleagues, all jabbering away into headsets. They didn't know he had a secret. There was someone to go home to.

He knew they all thought he was a creep; could tell by the shifty way they'd stop talking when he came into the kitchen, and the way the girls would avoid his eye if he tried to speak to them. But he had no idea what it was about him that marked him as untouchable, so he was powerless to change whatever social leprosy he carried.

Anyway, the worst shame was gone now. He'd done it: finally. He could hardly stop smiling. What was better, he'd get to do it again and again. And, it would cost him nothing. He'd often considered going to prostitutes, but the decent-looking ones were expensive, and he was frightened of disease. This way was so much better.

He thought of Juliette, with her wide blue eyes and her fair hair, and the fact she didn't seem to recoil from his touch. She didn't sneer at him. At least not openly. The arrangement they had made it feel as though the years of not going out and only ever shopping for bargains to scrape together the deposit for his flat had been worth it. He could hardly wait to get home.

Serving coffee in the station café for ten hours that day, Juliette had a lot of time to consider the move she'd made. On balance, she thought it was good. She kept calculating in her head all the money she'd save over time. She'd be able to pay the credit card people something. They'd promised an adviser would be phoning her about a debt repayment plan soon. And,

once she'd spruced it up, the flat might even be OK.
Things weren't so bad.

Jay got in when she was half way through cleaning the
kitchen. She looked up smiling from the oven to see
him frozen in the doorway.

'Are you cleaning?'

'Yes.'

'Are you using detergent?'

'Yes.'

'I never use detergent. I think it encourages
germs. Don't use it again.'

'Oh.'

'If you have to clean,' he looked as though he
felt this was an unfortunate habit, 'please just clean
with water.'

'Oh, OK.'

Jay cooked again for them that night. It was
some sort of chili. It was too spicy for her and she
didn't enjoy it, so she offered to cook for him the next
evening.

'That's so kind of you!' he exclaimed, turning
to her, as though no one had ever done anything so nice
for him before. 'Just nothing with shellfish in. I'm
really allergic.'

Juliette zoned out while he started going on
about anaphylactic shock and what the doctors had said
last time he'd accidentally eaten some crab two years
ago. She got it. She wasn't thick. No sea food.

That night the sex took a full ten minutes.

Juliette lay there after, listening to his breathing,
and thinking about money. Maybe if she'd stayed in
school longer and got a proper education and things,
she might not have found herself in this position. Still,

there wasn't much she could do about that now. She opened her eyes.

An orange glow from street lights below lit the room. At intervals, passing car headlights bathed the wall next to her in white light. All the previous places she'd lived rolled through her memory in a procession. A dozen different flavours of irritation and humiliation. Always more rent than she could afford, and never worth the price.

There'd been the place with no fridge for three months, the one where her flatmate had stolen money from her purse if she left it in her room, and the one with no heating. But the worst flat was the one where the guy must have been watching too much porn, and when he realised she hadn't moved in to be his girlfriend and shag his brains out, he'd waited until she was out and slashed her bike tyres and pissed all over her bed. At least here she knew what the deal was. And, really, it was a good deal. But, if she'd known how things would be, she wouldn't have been in such a hurry to leave home at 16 to escape her mother.

The korma she cooked the next night was a success. She promised to cook more. Another few days passed. Jay seemed to be developing stamina in the bedroom. Juliet wondered if there was anything to do to stop this happening. He'd started moving her about to do it in inventive new positions: doggy style down on the scratchy carpet, with her draped over the back of the sofa, or her legs over his shoulders. One night she felt ill and told him so. He accepted it tamely and fell asleep beside her, with nothing but his hand resting on her hip. But she knew not to push her luck.

After a few weeks, she bought up the idea of plants again.

'I don't like living things in the flat,' he explained.

She was learning his idiosyncrasies now. It had been a while since she'd annoyed him by trying to tidy. She'd also learnt not to move his car magazines. It just wasn't worth the fallout. They watched what he wanted to watch in the evenings; that was never in question.

They settled into something like a sham relationship. Jay returned home from the call centre walking more upright by the day. He'd smile for no reason, and often be heard singing round the place, off key.

By this time, an idea had presented itself to Juliette. Such a brilliant and simple idea that she carried it with her like a lucky charm all day and warmed herself with it at night.

At Jay's work, people were sometimes disconcerted by how his appearance could vary. One day he'd look like a drug dealer's cousin; another, hang-dog, beaten; another, he'd look confident, smooth, as though he should be your boss.

The boss look was more frequent now. This particular day, he looked handsome. Dark hair, dark eyes, and the features all seemed to be working together, harmonising, doing their thing. Without gel, his hair had somehow fallen into place of its own accord. You'd hardly notice the lack of chin at all. His colleagues weren't to know that he was excited about the evening ahead. It was his birthday, and he was celebrating it at home.

Juliette too was familiar with his changing looks. Often, she hated the sight of him, but sometimes caught herself with a pang of something like desire. Then she'd feel disgusted at herself. Especially if it happened while she was looking at his shadowed face during sex.

She'd never seen him looking as good as he did tonight.

The table looked beautiful, she had to admit. He had no objection to offer to the white table cloth and candles she'd arranged. She laid the plate of rice in front of him and gave him a ladle to help himself from the cauldron-like pot in the centre of the table.

'What is it?' he asked.

She thought again how much he looked like a romantic hero right now. 'Thai green curry,' she said, smiling at him.

'My favourite.' He helped himself and picked up his fork.

She smiled some more at the thought of the small addition she'd made to the dish since the last time she made it for him.

It took longer than she expected. She looked at her phone a couple of times, wondering if she'd made a mistake. Maybe it wasn't crustaceans but some other kind of shellfish, or, he'd exaggerated how allergic he was. She tried to recall what exactly he'd told her the doctor had said. But, at last, he gulped, frowned, spat out the mouthful on to his plate, and continued to choke. She put down her cutlery and watched him as he turned red then white then blue.

Holding his throat, he croaked at her, 'Ambulance.'

He stretched an arm forward to reach for her before collapsing back into his chair, which broke with a crack, landing him on the floor. His head hit the discoloured vinyl and he lay there twitching.

Juliet didn't want to be there anymore. She got up and went out for a walk.

Hours later, she was impressed by the sound of her own voice on the phone. 'My flatmate... I just came back and found him. I don't think he's breathing...'

When the men arrived she was glad of her naturally wide blue eyes. It was fortunate for her, she thought, that she'd been born looking innocent.

After they'd gone she cleared out all the rubbish and scrubbed the flat with bleach spray. It took her all night. She called in sick to the café and slept all morning.

Waking up in the empty bed the flat seemed too silent and larger than before. Without Jay's aftershave, the smell of damp was more apparent. She told herself not to be silly. It was sunny, a beautiful early summer day. And the flat was hers now.

She went through the kitchen to the balcony, opened the window, and looked out at the pot plants she'd bought the night before. The balcony was full of them, green and healthy. Fetching a jug, Juliette began to water the plants, enjoying the way the stream of water glinted and flashed in the sunlight, singing to herself under her breath.

F. J. MORRIS

When You Said Nothing

You asked me: *Where you from?* And I told you but you asked again: *No, where are you from-from?* I was more puzzle than man at that point, because I don't always remember that I'm black any more than I remember I have feet. *Your parents, what about them?* Same place, I said, and then it clicked – problem solved. My grandparents are from the Caribbean, I said, and you didn't have to say anymore, because you'd already said it.

This is not your home.

You said it when you jabbed me with your elbow for a bit o' the stuff – you know 'the stuff'. You said it when you followed me and my mates round Tesco in your uniforms and insisted on searching me for a stolen doughnut – as if I'd stick all that loose sugar in my pockets. You said it when you moved your handbag to your other shoulder as I walked to College. You said it with police stops, rejected applications, with reams and reams of stares, and deciding to stand up on the bus when the last seat is next to me, and asking, *Can I touch your hair?* And then grabbing it anyway. And worst of all you said it when you said nothing. When you did nothing. When you watched and said: *That's terrible, that's not me.*

But the night tells me something different. Down the streets, and rivers and docks, I hear my heart beat on the pavement. Here I open out, I can lift my head and shoulders and walk with no shackles. Here I am a free man. I hang up my skin on the peg of the moon and rest my feet on the silence. I reclaim my city under the roof of night that's leaking starlight. They tell me that these streets are not mine but they are etched onto the back of my hand like fingerprints. They twist and turn to spell my name, and down the road there is a footprint where I planted my shoe in drying concrete – forever telling you I was 'ere.

This is where I'm from.

This is my home.

SOPHIE WELLSTOOD

East, West

A group of people are gathered, shivering, outside a small town registry office. They stamp their feet and hug themselves; some try to smoke a last minute cigarette, cupping hands over lighters, the little metal wheels spinning *tchh tchh tchh*. It's a grey English morning, autumn, 1962.

Bernard's jaw aches from the smile he has managed to fix in place since the day dawned. He checks his watch again and again, looks up to the heavy October skies. Dear God, do something now, he urges, anything. A lightning strike, a meteorite, a Commie missile. Yes, yes, that would do. Stop the damn world. Blow it all to hell.

Thirty minutes later, Jean is standing beside him, her hair piled high, her cream suit and stockings smelling of rosewater and mothballs. She squeezes Bernard's hand. Behind them, sitting stiffly on green velvet chairs are Jean's parents, Mavis and Ken.

The council registrar is close enough for Bernard to smell his breakfast breath. He squints at the teenagers standing in front of him, the boy licking his guilty lips over and over, the girl a little slip of a thing, clearly knocked up. The registrar has seen this all too often before, but do they ever learn? Do they heck. He recites the vows and the laws in his most solemn voice and the teenagers respond like little parrots. In no time at all rings are on fingers, they're all drinking in the function room above the Swan, and Bernard and Jean have their whole lives ahead of them.

Bernard takes a sales position in the Ford showroom on the Solihull Road. He's popular with his clients and earns a reasonable commission. When he returns home in the evening, he sits with Jean at the kitchen table. They eat from the dinner service gifted to them by Bernard's parents, their conversations mirroring the cautiousness of Jean's cooking. After supper, Bernard goes to the front room and lights a fire. It's a cold house and if Bernard had his way he'd have a fire burning all night and day, even in the summer.

He sits back in his chair and smokes a couple of cigarettes while Jean washes up. Hanging on the wall above the fireplace is one of Mavis's needlepoints. Five carefully stitched words curve like a rainbow over an embroidered country cottage: *East, West, Home is Best*. There are other needlepoints hanging around the house, too – in the bedroom: *Home Sweet Home*; in the kitchen: *Home is Where the Heart Is*; and in the hallway by the telephone table: *God Bless This Home*.

Bernard can hear Jean in the kitchen, the clatter of cutlery being put away, the wireless playing the theme tune to *The Archers*. He blows his cigarette smoke hard at the needlepoint and the little stitched house, the little white fence, the pink roses, and the carefully sewn ducklings and kittens momentarily blur in the blue-grey fug.

The house is on the outskirts of town, a draughty three-bedroomed terrace in a street of others exactly the same.

It has a small square of muddy lawn at the back which Ken insists will do very nicely for a bit of veg. Potatoes, runner beans, onions. Sweetpeas in the summer. The house is not in a desirable neighbourhood by any stretch, but Ken stumped up half the deposit and Bernard has made his bed, and he should be damn well grateful, considering. Bernard is certainly grateful that when Ronald Kenneth arrives the following February, everyone agrees he has inherited his grandfather's extremely handsome nose and luxurious hair. This goes a fair way towards building some sort of bridge between the two men.

Bernard has a degree of affection for Jean, but wears his marriage heavily. It is an overcoat born of lust, fabricated from duty, buttoned in monotone. It hangs in every room mocking him, goading him, challenging him to run into the summer sunshine bold and brilliant and bare-chested.

And there is no passion in their marriage. Bernard knows now that the distant Saturday night when Jean mewed like a little cat, asking him if he loved her and his breathless lie that he did – that Saturday night was the only time he has ever, fully, gone the whole way. Not even on their honeymoon was there any union. Jean undressed in the boarding house bathroom, slipped into the nylon sheets then turned her back to him, nauseous and tired and scared of hurting the baby.

Now, three years later, at the age of twenty-two, Bernard has been making do. Before Jean wakes and can frown at the shape of his pyjama trousers, Bernard is in the bathroom, gripping the shower rail, losing himself in the swirl of soapy water and shaving foam. By the time Jean is up and has put her face on, he is in the kitchen feeding Ronnie milk and cereal. Ten minutes later he kisses them both, puts on his overcoat and drives to the Solihull Road.

Bernard meets Lizzie one Friday evening in the George, half a mile from the showroom. His colleague Derek is celebrating his thirtieth birthday and the whole team is there, even Tom the hom. Lizzie is known to provide discreet, affordable services for the men who travel and sell, men whose sniffy, critical wives approach the marital bed in hair curlers and face cream, men who buy top shelf magazines knowing that there is a world of pleasure out there hidden from them. Men with the cash and the courage to spend it on women like Lizzie.

Bernard drinks quickly. Lizzie is sitting over by the fireplace. Bernard catches her eye and realises she's smiling at him and oh, suddenly he's smiling back at her, and oh, suddenly he's brave, he's wiggling his hand and raising his eyebrows to indicate an offer of a refill for her. Yes? Lizzie laughs and nods, and when Bernard has managed to get the barman's attention he orders a large gin and tonic, plus another pint for himself. He moves carefully through all the elbows and cigarettes, then places the drinks on the table mats and Lizzie pats the empty space beside her.

They lie on Lizzie's bed, the blinds drawn, the sounds of Friday night on the Solihull Road filtering in: scooters revving, young men shouting, girls shrieking, all emboldened by drink. Lizzie's pillows smell of lavender and soap, and are patterned with tiny daisies. Bernard has undone the buttons on his trousers and stares at the ceiling, his heart threatening to bash its way out of his chest.

At the touch of Lizzie's hand Bernard shudders and it is over. Dear God, he cannot help it, but Lizzie smiles and shushes him, gives him a tissue and lets him rest for a while. They will try again. She goes to the kitchenette and pours a couple of gins. A couple of stiff ones? she laughs. She has a wide, soft backside and the bed bounces as she sits down. Her hair is dyed, and the lines around her eyes describe many years lived without fancy creams or powders. Bernard walks his fingertips over the dimples in her shoulder blades, over her bra strap, inside the top of her knickers. Her skin is puddingy and smooth. He leans forward and rests his forehead on her back, breathing in the smell of her, then she turns and kisses him with her beautiful, beautiful mouth which tastes cool and of lipstick and lemons.

Then at last he is there.

She coos and soothes him, says his name, says, 'My love, my love.'

He tries to keep his eyes open but he can't, so intently is he focusing on the sensation enveloping him. He is in an ocean of heat, hopelessly adrift, until suddenly and uncontrollably he must push faster and faster. A white light spreads out behind his eyes and with a great sigh like a whale breaking the waves he is free.

Jean is waiting up for him. She is at the kitchen table, sobbing, a handkerchief crumpled in her fist. Bernard has prepared his lie, but before he can feign exhaustion and being drunker than he is, Jean tells him that her father is dead, a heart attack at home half an hour ago. Why has Bernard taken so bloody long to get back? Why? He's four hours late, four hours, for God's sake. He must drive them over there now, is he listening to her? Now, now, now. Bernard can feel his own gloriously living heart thumping, nourishing him, and is aware of the smile trying to take over his face. He forces it into hiding, forces his arms around Jean and kisses her forehead. Ten minutes later they are in the car, Ronnie on the back seat, whining and confused. Jean is babbling: she knew he wasn't right last Sunday, she said so, didn't she? He was only fifty-two, for God's sake, fifty-two.

Ken is on the floor in the front room. He looks absolutely wrong. Huge, ridiculous, a fallen tree. It is almost embarrassing. There is a smell, too, which no one mentions. Mavis is sitting on the couch, wet-eyed and trembling. Someone has made her a cup of tea but it is untouched. The ambulance staff talk to Bernard in low voices, take details, shake hands. Within the next hour, Ken is stretchered away and when all that can be done for now has been done, it is two o'clock in the morning and Bernard drives back home alone and elated.

Jean and Ronnie continue to stay with Mavis long after the funeral. Bernard visits every weekend. On Saturdays he takes Ronnie out for fresh air and on Sundays they have lunch together around the dining room table, but they all agree that it is best for Mavis if she is not alone for the time being.

Every Friday night Bernard is with Lizzie. He calls her his angel, she calls him her love. He has touched every part of her body with his hands and fingers, and, most exquisitely, his mouth. She is a landscape he cannot stop exploring. He begins to visit on a Tuesday, then a Wednesday and Thursday. He brings groceries, flowers, chocolates, gin, a toothbrush, his washing. She opens the door before he can ring the buzzer, and when they are ready to get out of bed it's usually late and the walls have turned warm and orange from the city lights.

After Christmas, Jean decides that it makes no sense at all for Mavis to carry on living in that house with the memory of Ken on the carpet, and that she must sell it and move in with them. Ronnie needs his father and there's plenty of room, isn't there? And think of the money, they could have a real summer holiday, couldn't they? All of them together, at the seaside. Bernard cannot argue, or at least he cannot argue truthfully against them all returning.

The change is a shock for him. His evenings with Lizzie must be curtailed, and the noise, the mess, the constant presence of Mavis, is an intense annoyance. She is like a portrait whose eyes follow him wherever he goes. But the worst of the changes by far is that Jean has returned to his bed.

Bernard watches her on her first night back. It has been almost a year since she slept in this house, in this room. She has showered, is wearing a pink negligee and some sweet, market-stall perfume. She sits at the dressing table with her back to him, brushing her hair very quickly. She is slim – much too slim, he thinks; her spine is a bumpy sea creature and her shoulder blades are sharp triangles. She turns to him and smiles, and it's a different kind of smile, her head to one side. Hello again. Shall I get in? I've missed you. Bernard's stomach somersaults. She is expecting him to make love to her.

It is over in minutes. Bernard groans and collapses and for the first time in his marriage he feels a wretched stab of infidelity. He moves to the edge of the bed and turns onto his side. He cannot stop tears from creeping down his cheek.

At 6.00am he abandons the bed and goes to make coffee. The sun is rising and he takes his mug and cigarettes into the back garden. There's a robin hopping around the nettles and brambles, dark-eyed and quick, and another bird too, absolutely tiny but very noisy. He doesn't know its name.

He'll go to Lizzie's straight after work, he'll tell Jean he has overtime, a meeting with Tom, a new vehicle being delivered, he'll – his thoughts are broken by the sound of a little dry cough, and he is shocked to realise Mavis has been standing on the doorstep behind him. She says good morning, dear, did he have a good night? She smiles a small, tight smile and raises her eyebrows.

Good God, did she hear him? Them? The woman is quite insufferable. Bernard stares at Mavis, unable to find any words, then pushes past her, goes upstairs, dresses and leaves the house within ten minutes.

At his desk, he calls Lizzie. There's no reply. At lunchtime, he jogs to her flat and rings the buzzer. Nothing. He shouts through the letterbox, waits, knocks on the door and windows. After fifteen minutes, he gives up and turns to go back down the concrete steps, and then Lizzie is there, walking towards him, carrying shopping, and he laughs, sprints towards her, wraps his arms around her. She tells him to come in, she's got a bit of news.

Riddled. It's a word Bernard literally cannot say. The words he has for Lizzie are ripe, earthy, yielding; words that are not even words but are imitations of words, or the beginnings of words, or are sighs, or just silences, which are not the silences of absence, but the silences of completion. They sit at her kitchen table and she explains what will happen. When she can explain no more, they lie on her bed and listen to the boys and girls of the Solihull Road and watch the walls turn orange.

Bernard visits the hospital every evening between work and home. He eats the grapes he brings, holds Lizzie's hand, tells her about his day.

The changes come swiftly and unkindly. To the unquestioning Matron, Bernard is Lizzie's devoted nephew. To Jean he is working longer hours, lining himself up for promotion ahead of Tom, and so as a surprise and a reward she has booked a real summer holiday for them all in Weston-Super-Mare.

Bernard has Ronnie on his shoulders. He is waist deep in the choppy sea, the thin July clouds blowing high above them. Jean and Mavis are sitting in deck chairs. Jean is flicking through magazines, Mavis is stitching a new needlepoint. Jean's stomach is tight and swollen and she won't step into the sea in case germs affect the baby. Ronnie is a delight, a skinny strip of energy and chatter, and Bernard is glad of his uncomplicated company. They stroke the donkeys on the beach and play the one-armed bandits on the pier.

On the Friday morning, after breakfast, Bernard says he's very sorry but he really must make some important work calls, so could Jean possibly please –? Jean tells him she's exhausted, the baby is going to be a bloody footballer, she's sure of it, and Mavis looks up from her needlepoint and agrees, oh yes, a footballer, and so Bernard must take Ronnie with him.

They walk along the seafront. Bernard finds a café close to a telephone box and leaves Ronnie there with cheese on toast and a comic. The young manageress has a nephew, he's Ronnie's age and a proper little scamp, aren't they all? And she promises to keep an eye.

Two hours later the young manageress has run out of patience. She has had to close the café and there will be consequences. A mile further down the seafront, Ronnie points to a solitary figure sitting on a bench.

There he is, that's him, that's him.

He lets go of the manageress's hand and runs, shouting, waving the comic.

I read it three times, Dad, all the words. She's really cross with you, you're a bloody bugger.

Bernard fumbles for his wallet, whispers an apology to the manageress, and presses notes into her hand. The manageress takes the money, and Bernard needn't bother coming anywhere near her café again, that's for sure.

The seafront is packed with people: families, grandparents, teenagers, girls eating candy floss, their arms linked, boys in sunglasses, bold, bare-chested, drinking Coke. The July sun is hotter than ever.

For a few long moments Bernard continues to stare out to sea. The funfair plays songs from the hit parade and then Ronnie's small hands are on his knees.

You're a bloody bugger, Dad.

Bernard closes his eyes and pats the empty space beside him.

DAVID COOK

A Tap on the Door

There was a tap on the door. Peter frowned. He took off his glasses, cleaned them on his shirt tails, and put them back on. Yes, the tap was still there, just above the letterbox on the outside of the door. Hesitantly, he reached out and turned the handle. Water gushed onto his loafers and pooled over the doormat, forming a lake in the 'o' of 'welcome'.

'Sharon!' he called to his wife. 'Is that plumber still here?'

'He's gone for his lunch I think, love,' came a voice from upstairs. 'Why?'

'He's put a tap on the front door.'

'A what?'

'A tap!'

'Are you sure?'

'No! I'm imagining a blinking great stainless steel tap! It's all in my head!'

Sharon came downstairs to take a look. 'That's odd,' she understated. 'I'll give him a call.' She jabbed at buttons on her phone and went into the living room. Peter glared at the tap.

A minute later, Sharon returned. 'He said, "Did you not want that?" And I said no. He seemed a bit flummoxed. He's coming back round now.'

A few minutes later, the plumber – known locally as Ron the Wrench – wandered back up the garden path. Peter was waiting on the doorstep and tapping his foot, which was making a squelching sound.

'You didn't like the tap, then?' asked Ron.

'No.'

'It's just that when you called me yesterday, you said, "When you get here, give us a tap on the front door."'

'Eh?'

'So I did what you said. I think I got confused. I once had this terrible mix-up with an old man and his stopcock.'

'Just take it off and go away.'

'Will I still get paid?'

'No!'

Ron scowled, reached into his box of equipment, selected a little metal tool, and took to jemmying away roughly at the tap with it.

'Don't faucet,' suggested Peter.

Ron scowled further. The tap fell to floor with a clunk. A fountain of water sprayed Ron in the face, which Peter enjoyed enormously. Ron scowled for a third time, scooped the tap into his bag, then skulked away down the street.

Peter retreated indoors, stepping over the puddle that had formed on the doormat.

'I'd better check if he's fixed the toilet,' he said to Sharon, who was watching *Countdown*. 'That was what we actually wanted him to do.'

He climbed the stairs and walked down the corridor to the bathroom. The toilet's flush mechanism was in bits on the lino.

Grinding his teeth, he picked up the phone and called Ron. 'Why haven't you fixed the toilet?' he demanded, when the call was answered.

'I tried my best,' said Ron.

'So what happened?'

'I just couldn't get a handle on it.'

BRITTA JENSEN

Three Fingers

A simple lark's call snagged my attention away from translating an English soap opera for my bunkmates. We'd never had a bird inside before. I peered over the edge of my hammock in the 8th bunk in block Q dormitories for the *Super Sporty* factory workers. Everything had been painted from dull grey to vibrant green after the visitors came.

The song of the lark transported me beyond the fresh paint, old ladies playing mahjong and the flickering of an old projector below. I was back in my old family house in Macau, birds swooping over my favourite spot on our flat rooftop.

'Shut up, Birdy!' a girl called out from the bunk under mine.

I tried to locate who or what Birdy was, but no one had moved below. I climbed down the rusty narrow pipe ladder connecting the various bunks and jumped the last two levels to the unfinished cement floor.

'Ruofan!' one of the old ladies yelled at me, upset that I'd stopped translating.

I caught a retreating figure of an older boy who had been staring at her in the doorway.

'Out, Birdy!' another woman screeched and I followed him, not caring that I was barefoot.

He didn't seem to notice me at all. Birdy's eyes were searching upward in the dim corridor that connected all the windowless dormitories: metal boxes with stacks of people in bunks of eight levels high. Women and men often bickered for the best spots. The top bunks used to be referred to as the 'penthouse' until adults started falling through the canvas hammock bottoms. Children like me were forced to the upper levels.

Birdy stopped at the last dorm. It was smaller than the others with mostly men and some kids my age. Birdy ignored me peering around the doorframe to watch him. He opened a rusty locker that squealed with age. There was nothing inside except a tin penny whistle and a book. He slammed the locker door, spinning the lock, and ran past me.

I followed, not caring about the dark empty corridors, the fact I was now lost, or our final exit out of the factory complex. Birdy climbed a small building made out of three storeys of old shipping containers. Once we were on top of the 'roof' I tested my weight before joining Birdy on the other side. I expected such shoddy workmanship to topple, but it didn't. A small bridge connected the back part of the building to the factory's main warehouse. I headed toward the bridge, eager for a shortcut back inside. Birdy played a soft melody on his pipe and I turned around.

It finally hit me that I was outside. Cranes and stacks of shipping containers obscured some of the view. I concentrated on the sea beyond that sparkled in the sunlight peeking through dense clouds. Birdy's song danced in rhythm to the bits of light refracted from the ocean. I pulled my knees to my chest and imagined the working men below stepping in time to the jig Birdy played. Instead of yelling at the crane drivers, they were twirling as the cranes moved along their tracks, some prancing atop shipping containers being loaded onto barges.

When the song stopped I felt cold. The wind whipped up from the bay and I had to pull my shirtsleeves down. We were always indoors, so no one had a coat, except the head overseers who went home.

'Birdy?' I asked.

He turned to face me and handed me his tin whistle.

'I can't. Please, will you play another?'

He stared at me, his thin black eyebrows unmoving, then put the pipe down and stood, closing his eyes. He began to whistle. His song transformed to a variety of birdcalls, then back to a tune I thought I'd heard my father play before he died.

'Blackbird singing in the dead...' I started to sing the words. But, the melody became something else completely and I was glad because I didn't want to remember how my life had been, only a short year before.

Birdy's song ended in a grand finale of starlings, blackbirds and other birdsong I couldn't identify. A sea hawk soared overhead and tipped its great wings at us, as if to approve of the music, then was gone.

'Where did you learn to do that?' I asked.

His black hair was sticking straight up, despite his efforts to smooth it down. His eyes didn't meet mine, then he turned away to watch the cranes.

'What is your real name? I'm Ruofan,' I called to him, but he acted like he hadn't heard me. I waited awhile. We were missing supper, but the fresh air here was better than burnt, salty soup with onion and plain rice.

Someone called out to us across the bridge and Birdy grabbed my hand, indicating for me to go first down the ladder. He made sure I was several rungs down before he joined me. I wasn't sure where to go, once we were at the bottom.

'Hey, you two! You're not allowed out here!'

We sped back into the building, the aroma of steamed dumplings assaulting us. Birdy led me to the overseer's dining room. We snatched two dimsum, stuffed them in our faces and continued running.

Birdy brought me into the kitchens, where a grate floor below one of the trough sinks poured the raw sewage below. A young woman, who looked about Birdy's age, raised an eyebrow. She held a small knife in one hand and an onion in the other.

'You are Little Sister?' she asked Birdy, indicating with the blade.

'Hey, I'm not little, I'm nine!' I yelled.

Birdy clamped a hand over my mouth.

'Little Sister…' The girl rubbed the top of my head. 'I knew you were hiding her somewhere.' The girl handed him the onion and grabbed me by the back of my shirt. 'Chop these, will you?'

Birdy followed, inclining his head for me to listen to the older girl. There was no use protesting.

Even if I was dizzy with exhaustion, too tired to peel potatoes or slice onions after twelve hours of threading and fixing cotton looms, when I heard Birdy's lark call I would meet him straightaway by the kitchens. In the summer, we often fell asleep outside, a discarded sailcloth our only protection from the swarms of mosquitoes and flies.

I became Little Sister and he remained Birdy.

Machines have a predictable rhythm when they're working right. The hums, whirrs and hisses become lullabies that drown out snippets of gossip and the music you aren't singing yourself.

The day I severed two fingers, the machine barely registered it had eaten part of my hand. Without sound, the pain was delayed: my fingers a pulp mashed into the pristine white cotton cloth headed to the dye vats. My bones finally halted the clanking of the enormous weaver. A rusty stain spread across the middle of the newly knitted fabric and thousands of spindles stopped. The pack of ice sealed to my hand with duct tape felt like someone else's appendage. I wanted to travel onward with the fabric and block out the frozen grimaces of the girls who still had all their fingers.

Then I heard his familiar starling warble above the din. I fought against the two teenagers pushing me toward the sick bay, but I couldn't find Birdy. No hospitals necessary for me; I wasn't any good to them damaged. The sound of the birds calling to each other magnified.

Birdy stood in front of them, almost blocking my helpers rushing me through the double glass door of the infirmary. He didn't look at the blood pooling under the ice pack. Instead he whistled a song the entire time they cauterized my wounds, holding me in his lap.

For once, no one told him to shut up.

His song echoed in my ears for months after I was thrown onto the streets. With only three fingers on my left hand I wasn't employable. No one needed a maimed twelve-year-old weaver, even if I did speak and write English. A jumped-up orphan of a former Macau Magistrate meant nothing in Shanghai. I longed for the days when all I had to think about was school.

Sometimes I sang Birdy's old songs while begging on the streets, rain pouring down in monsoon season, hunkering under the scaffolding of new high rises outside Shanghai. Foreigners mostly gave me money. I lived off discarded food, often half-rotten. I stopped counting the insects and held my nose.

I scavenged my way out of Shanghai, surprised by the lack of vegetation in the open country as I searched for river water to wash myself. I was quickly growing out of my clothes and I had lost count of the years since our family's prosperity.

Was I thirteen now?

I didn't dare look at myself in the smoked glass of the abandoned office buildings I walked past. I had figured that I could walk for a week on a can of Coca-Cola if I travelled during the rain and avoided the heat of the day. The muddy country roads subsided once I was on the pavements of Keqiao, which had large electric signs boasting of the New Textile City. Tall steel and glass buildings lifted their rectangular fingers to the muddy sky.

Waste sites contained plenty of workable scrap yarn, linen and cotton. North Korean migrant workers welcomed me to live in their camp of ancient shipping containers. I made clothing and bags for them out of the scraps from waste sites. Within months I had a growing group of customers and traded items at the night market. I liked hearing the occasional English word, trying to translate it in my head to Mandarin. The words gave me hope.

I was at my sixteenth place of interview. The same drab linen sat in front of me. I was lucky to get to this stage. Normally the minute I whipped out a left hand missing two digits I was turned away. The sign for this place at the night market said, 'Sanitary conditions/good pay.'

I took the fabric out and fed the edges together through the machine, minutes ahead of the others, my half of a long linen blouse finished. The two suited women monitoring us stared at my left hand.

'Doesn't it hurt?' one lady asked kindly. Maybe my hunger was getting to me.

'No. I can knit and crochet too,' I responded in English.

They quietly motioned for me to follow them into the next room, which was filled with colour-coded stacks of yarns. I wanted to feel the fibres, but I was afraid. I had never been to this stage of interviews.

'Show, show,' one of the darker ladies said in poor Mandarin.

'Do you want I speak English?' I asked, my tongue halting over the words.

'Oh, no. It's OK,' the older woman replied.

'What do you want I make?'

I inspected the patterns and after thirty minutes at each sample I had a variety of knitted and crocheted flowers. I couldn't tell if they were pleased. Instead of taking me by the back of my tunic and giving me my marching orders, I was escorted to another place, a room on an upper floor with a window outside. I could see the sky beyond the towers of skyscrapers.

'We need you to work here, as a supervisor,' the woman said in Mandarin.

The room only had a desk and a shelf full of coloured files and boxes. On the wall next to the window was a soft wall that had papers pinned to it.

'Supervisor?' I scratched my head. 'Like little boss?'

'Yes, exactly,' she clarified.

I think I passed out, because when I opened my eyes a small crowd was gathered around me. A young man pushed through. There was something familiar about his face. I tried to sift through the hundreds of faces I'd worked with. Nothing was coming clear to me until he put his hands to his mouth and made the call of a lark.

'Ru…o…fan…' he stammered. It was the first time I heard him speak.

I reached for him, not caring who was staring, holding him so close I was crushing us both.

'Big brother,' I whispered into his shoulder.

'Little… sister.'

JAMES LAWLESS

A Voice from an Attic

There's nowhere else safe. I tried it down below for as long as I could but it became impossible. Marjorie thought it a bit odd at first, but she knew the circumstances and after a while she just accepted it.

There was already a bit of a chipboard floor over part of the fibreglass – the part you can stand up in. And I've thrown sacking over the rest of it so I won't get any itches: sort of funny stuff that, air and glass trapping air above to keep hot air down below. Come to think of it, our school meetings were a bit like that. But it was more than hot air that drove me up.

It was like a farewell at an emigrant ship when I ascended the ladder with my suitcase. Marjorie was there of course, and her sister Linda (whom Marjorie had phoned) came along to see me off. They actually waved from the base of the ladder, and for a moment there was a hint of a tear. But there was no turning back. I knew that as soon as I had cleared the third rung. *No turning back now*, I said to myself.

Of course I have photographs with me, of Marjorie in her younger days – a great figure, and eyes so full of promise. And now, well, nothing ever stays the same.

I am settling down up above. Marjorie sends up meals to me on a pulley system which works quite well.

I have an electric light which I use for reading, and thanks to the fibre glass I have no fear of rodents. And silence? – the boon of teachers. It's not totally silent though. I mean I can still hear the launches and tiddlers and the odd cry from the deep, but the noise is so removed it can't touch me now; it can't get inside my head.

Marjorie won't come up, not even for conjugal rights. Can't say I blame her at the moment. Things are in a bit of a mess up here. Of course my going down is out of the question. All those nights without sleep: the calls and door bangs at all hours; the smashed window; the wear and tear on the nerves; the nightmares about the school. No way. Man's first instinct is not for food or sex, but for safety.

I am trying to make the place more presentable to persuade Marjorie to relent. She does her bit from base. She passes me up pieces of wood so I can extend the floor space. I use glue to stick the pieces together. No hammers for me. I have a bed and a bedside locker but no window. I'd be afraid of a window.

Marjorie says if she came up there would be none of us then with our feet on the ground. 'One of us has to have feet on the ground,' she keeps saying, and I suppose she's right.

You might think me cowardly to abandon Marjorie like that, especially after the window of our house was smashed, but *she* didn't crack; she's stronger than me. Of course, the juvenile shoals which swarmed around our house were something new to her, but for me it was the final cut that snapped my synapse. I mean the school had done the groundwork – a quarter of a century of violence inflicted upon oneself, the gradual wearing down, *detrition*, you know from Geography.

By the way, I brought my maps up with me. I hung some of them on the gable wall. We can all frame our own world really. It doesn't matter where we are. Sometimes I look at a map of the Balearic Islands, at Menorca especially where Marjorie and I spent our honeymoon many years ago, and I am transported there again. I see the sunshine and the blueness, and I don't hear the wind blowing through the rafters, or the roar of hydroplanes, or the taunts of sea urchins rising from the stormy waves. No. Up here I can control things.

That's what happened down below. I lost control. Teaching adolescent sea creatures is a funny business. One invests so much of oneself. But as the years go by, they get stronger and you get weaker. It's a law of diminishing returns.

The first mistake I made was the day I turned my back to write on the blackboard. The normal thing, the thing that was drilled into us in our teaching practice, time after time, was that information was always to be disseminated laterally. You never, *ever* turn your back. It was a cardinal rule. The day I turned my back I had a lot of writing to do. I had nearly covered the entire board with wave definitions when perky young crabs (obviously bored) sneakily advanced and clawed at the legs of my chair, and when I turned around shark bucks were snapping dangerously close. While I was warding them off and ordering them back to their crawls, one of the bucks snapped a piece off my pointer stick. And then a grinning octopus wobbled up and, before I could gauge what he intended, he had wrapped his tentacles tightly around me and squirted me with his ink. He then lifted me up and dropped me into the icy water where I was prodded by a hyperactive sword fish.

And when the sea creatures saw my predicament they boomed their approval in a deafening roar.

'Just another day at the office,' that's all I could say to Marjorie when I got home that evening, when she enquired about my dishevelled state and wet clothes.

'But–' she said and I said, 'No more.'

I didn't want to admit that I had broken one of the cardinal rules of teaching. I didn't want to admit to Marjorie that maybe I was losing my grip.

After that incident, matters got worse. I began to notice things I hadn't noticed before: the noise from outside the house; a lot of traffic hadn't bothered me before. But now it was like a new channel had opened in my head, and all this traffic – motorboats, hydroplanes, drifters – came noising through, all night long. And two and three nights would go by without any sleep, and then in the mornings into the school...

The second mistake involved forgetfulness. I hung a map of the Mediterranean on the blackboard to which I was standing laterally (of course). I caught sight of the Balearics and just for a moment I forgot the class was present. I forgot the tension. I had always carried the tension (a prerequisite for alertness) all those years. But for this short space of time I inhabited a different world – it was so easy when you were a Geography teacher with imagination.

I was in Menorca walking by white buildings towards a blue sea. In some distant courtyard a guitar was being strummed so soothingly, it was like a balm; I could feel an oozing-out, a melting of all that was gnarled and caked inside me.

And then something struck my head.

I looked around to be confronted by a class of grinning sea monsters, waiting with gleeful expectation to see what I would do next.

A spiral conch lay at my feet.

Perhaps it was due to the lack of sleep but I was confused momentarily. The music in my head soon faded however and I could see where I really was: in a grey oily seaschool with suffocating clouds above.

I looked again. Not all were monsters. No. It has to be said. There were a couple of friendly dolphins and a pod of quiet seals. They weren't all grinning either; it was just the usual few ringleaders with their little runs of sycophants.

Can I have me conch back, sah?

It was then I made my third and final mistake.

I gave the grinning octopus his conch back in the same place he had given it to me. It wiped the grin from his face.

The sea erupted. Even creatures from the deep were roused from their slumbers.

You can't touch us.

We'll have you in court.

We'll get you for this.

We fuckin' will.

The octopus complained of sleepless nights, of headaches, of lapses of memory, of failing examinations.

That's when the shoals started coming. Random night raids on the house. The smashed window. The taunts and jeers. Sure, we called the police and Beachwatch, but no one was ever caught.

And the phone calls at all hours of the night!

We're watching you, sah.

We're waiting for you to come out, sah.

They even called Marjorie a *slut*. We grew to dread the merciless cacophony of that damned machine. We became isolated – Marjorie lost touch with her sister because we disconnected the phone; neither one of us could face that lethal weapon which had turned inwards upon ourselves.

Sure, I could have sought support through official channels, but you see it's all committees and subcommittees now, all blank and anonymous, no personal touch anymore. I would have had to go back and forth like a beach ball being tossed in endless motion in a current of hot air. And a lot of those sea creatures knew more than their rights. Oh yes, some of those weatherwise sharks or litigious crabs snap or snip at you like surgeons just for the fun of it, just to see you squirm. And then they continue to provoke you in the hope of retaliation so that they can claim against you. Oh yes. It happened. One of those brazen Brachyura twins got a whole new play benthos out of a previous action, and the unfortunate teacher – a gentle soul near retirement – was dismissed.

Oh yes. I know what I'm saying. A quarter of a century is a long time.

Anyway, I'm safe up here now. The court case will be coming up I know, but they'll have to find me, won't they? Cowardly, yes, maybe I am, but I just can't face that sort of thing – having to justify one's actions. Actions should always speak for themselves, don't you think?

Marjorie has relented a little about where her feet should be and will be coming up at least to visit as soon as I finish tidying the place.

No. It's not bad at all up here now. I'm even exercising (on a rowing machine) and I have made a little hiding place behind cases and boxes and things, just in case they ever tried… well, not that they would...

One can adapt to any environment once there is no aggro. Once there's nothing there to upset the equilibrium. That's why I'm on the tablets. It will only be for a short while, just until I get the equilibrium back again. Man is a finely tuned machine. That's what the doctor said when he came up to see me. It can't take too much meddling or interfering with, especially by amateurs.

'Especially by young amateurs,' I said.

'Yes,' he said. 'They're a different species.'

LINDSAY BAMFIELD

The Importance of Shoe Laces

What was I thinking of, joining this group? Every time the speaker mentions the word empowerment, the more I feel out of my depth. The women here already have more empowerment than your average stealth bomber. They call themselves the Mother's Group, but they're accountants, lawyers and lecturers simply disguised as mothers. They may have given birth but I bet each was issuing orders to her minions on her mobile in between contractions.

I reach the safe embrace of home and sit at the kitchen table deciding whether to leave the group.

'Oh Annie,' I whisper, 'do I stick with it or just give up?' Thinking of Annie makes the tears well up.

The front door slams as Maxie bursts in followed by Tallia who has just fetched him from his school bus. I hastily wipe my eyes but Maxie notices.

'Mum sad?' he asks. He hugs me and pats my arm. 'Mum all right now.'

Tallia peers round the door. 'Mum? What's the matter?'

'Oh nothing,' I say, 'I'm just being silly.'

'Let's have some tea.' She comes into the kitchen, fills the kettle and gets the tea mugs out.

'Mum cwy,' says Maxie.

I hug him back. 'No, Maxie I'm fine, I feel much better now I've had a Maxie hug. Tell me about school and we'll all have some tea. There's cake too, for a treat.'

Maxie's face lights up but Tallia frowns.

'From the Women's Group, not one of mine,' I reassure her.

'That's OK then.' She puts plates on the table.

The front door slams again, and the clump of Ross's size tens on the stairs half drowns the tinny whine of music escaping from his headphones.

'Mum cwy,' Maxie yells, knowing he has to increase the volume for Ross to hear.

The footsteps stop. The music blares then muffles.

Ross slouches into the kitchen. 'Crying? Why? What for?' He pulls out a chair and flops down, limbs all over the place. 'Gi's one as well, Tal.'

Tallia brings over the mugs two at a time while I slice the cake. It's lemon drizzle with perfect sugar frosting on the top. I take a piece and savour its delicious moistness and look at my three gathered round the old, scratched pine table.

Ross is stuffing down two chunky slices of cake as if he hasn't eaten for a week. Tallia has cut hers into three and is nibbling on one piece while Maxie has reduced most of his to crumbs. I cut him another slice.

'So what's up, Mum?' asks Tallia.

'Crying?' Ross puzzles over the word as if it's newly coined. But in truth the children have rarely seen me cry. Most of my crying has been in secret and I'll never let them know how many tears I've shed. Tears of worry, frustration, and sometimes sheer exhaustion.

'I was missing Annie,' I tell them. They all nod. They miss her too.

'Annie in heaven,' says Maxie.

I'm not sure if he can really remember her, my best friend and link to sanity. Whenever I had a crisis, Annie would always help me see what I had to do. She claimed the support was mutual, but Annie had great belief in herself that was distinctly lacking in me. I think back to the day we visited the park so Maxie could feed the ducks and geese.

'You can do it, Kate,' said Annie. 'I know you can and I know you better than anyone.'

Somehow her faith in me transmitted the confidence I needed to take on the biggest challenge of my life.

'Yes, Maxie,' I say now. 'Annie's in heaven but I was just wishing she was here with us. That's all. I'm all right now.'

After our tea and cake I gather up the plates. Ross gives one of his habitual grunts and disappears upstairs and Maxie announces he has to practise his writing for Miss Harris. I settle him at the living room table with his lined paper, pencils and a fat india-rubber which, knowing Maxie, will get plenty of use. The little rubbery peels will litter the table like the crumbs that Tallia is sweeping up as I come back into the kitchen.

'Were you really just missing Annie? Or was it someone in the group?' Tallia has developed an acute perception in these past few months. My stroppy teenager is growing up.

'Not exactly,' I say. 'It's just that I don't fit in. They're all very nice but everyone is so, well, competitive. Laura and her cakes,' I say, pointing to the mess of crumbs left by Maxie. A giggle bursts from me.

'She'd have a fit if she saw those two eating her precious lemon drizzle. I shouldn't think Ross even tasted it and Maxie's left most of his on the table and floor. I should have taken a picture of you eating it as she would see fit. Daintily, piece by piece.' I doubt Laura would be as impressed by Tallia's bright green fingernails and multi-coloured hair.

'But if it's not Laura's cakes,' I go on, 'it's someone's flower arranging and somebody else's marvellous home-made curtains. And Jocelyn's a soloist in the choir and her daughter's got a grade eight, whatever that is, in piano. And some of them are lawyers and teachers and nurses and...and I'm just a dinner lady at Maxie's school.'

'I thought you liked doing that.'

'I do. I do,' I say. 'It's just that they're all so brilliant and I'm not. I think I might just give up going.'

'Mum, you can't.' Tallia's voice shoots up an octave. 'You never give up. Never.'

'I gave up baking.'

'Only because we begged you to stop.'

'Mmm, that coffee sponge was terrible,' I agree.

'It was the banana cake that did it.'

We exchange a grin as we recall the blackened brick that emerged from the oven. Ross, in a surprising fit of articulacy, had defended my effort, saying it would make a very good doorstop.

'And I gave up the pottery class as well...' I glance at the misshapen pot on the windowsill. It houses odds and ends that don't belong anywhere. If you want a pen top, a stray bead or a book of matches that don't work properly, just look in my pot. I tell myself I must throw the bits of junk out. And the pot.

'But why give up?' persists Tallia.

'If it wasn't bad enough everybody going on about all the clever things they do, today's meeting was all about empowerment. We all have to write down our achievements in the past year and then pick the three most important for somebody to read out to the group next week. What have I achieved? I haven't launched a business, like Laura, I've not leapt out of an aeroplane for charity or won a prize for my begonias. What can I say? That I've taught Maxie how to tie his laces? No one's going to be impressed by that, are they?'

'Maxie was though,' Tallia points out. 'He's dead proud of his lace up trainers.'

She's right. It was an achievement but would these women understand what it means for a twelve-year-old with learning difficulties to tie his own laces? Their children are all so articulate and talented with their dancing classes, music lessons and straight As in their exams.

I used to imagine that I would be like them and have the perfect family: a husband and well-behaved children and we'd do fun activities that broadened their minds. I'd be a wonderful mother with little paragons. Instead I'm a frumpy, exhausted, single woman with what feels like a full scale battle on my hands.

I think of Ross and his almost unintelligible grunts as he wolfs down his food, absorbed in his own world. And Tallia's mere three GCSEs, none of them an A star, not even in her best subject, drama, although she should have an A with a dozen stars, the dramas I've had with her. How many nights have I lain awake, crying my secret tears, worrying about Tallia?

When Laura asked me about Tallia's exam results, her eyebrows nearly shot off her forehead before she rearranged her face into a sympathetic and patronising smile and hastily changed the subject. I heard her telling someone else that her daughter had six A stars but had let herself down in science with only a B.

Still, Tallia is right, I don't give up. That's my mantra. Every time one of the children has a set-back, and they've had plenty, I tell them to pick themselves up etcetera so of course I must do the same.

'You're right. I mustn't be such a wimp. Annie would have said the same.'

To my surprise Tallia comes over and hugs me. Never demonstrative, her arms wrap around me and I hold her taut, thin little body to me and plant a kiss on her spiky pink and blue hair.

'Thanks,' I whisper.

She slides away from my grasp and says she has some homework to do and is off upstairs.

I check on Maxie's homework, and help him select a DVD to watch while I get the pizza in the oven. The children are much more appreciative of my pizzas than my cakes. I sit at the kitchen table with one of Maxie's discarded pieces of paper and a pencil and start to jot down my successes. The list is slim, but I mustn't allow my small triumphs to be overshadowed.

At the next Women's Group meeting, I read out Jocelyn's list of achievements. They are impressive. She has sung to great acclaim in the choir, completed an Open University course, run a half marathon, as well as taking on extra hours at her job in the library.

'Now,' I add as decreed by Laura, 'please join me in congratulating Jocelyn in all her achievements and let us wish her greater empowerment for the forthcoming year.' I feel silly saying these grandiose words. There is a smattering of applause while Jocelyn sits smiling graciously.

Laura stands up with my paper which will break the mould. I feel my hands dampening. She waves it at the expectant audience.

'I'm not going to read this.'

My face flushes with embarrassment. Of course, my list is pathetic. Laura turns to me. 'I'm going to read this.' She holds up a piece of pink paper covered with Tallia's large, round, childish handwriting.

Laura clears her throat. 'Kate's daughter wrote this and brought it round to me before school today and asked me to read it. "In the past year Mum has achieved all sorts of things. She helped Ross stand up to the boys that were bullying him. She stayed up all night making me a costume for my drama presentation when someone lost mine. She spent two weeks teaching Maxie to tie his laces so he didn't have to wear Velcro trainers when he wanted grown-up ones with laces. These things might not sound terribly important to you but they were important to us.

'But Mum's three real achievements are us. Maxie, Ross and Tallia. Mum doesn't give up. Mum never gave up even when we were difficult and horrible to her. Specially me. Most people joke about not being able to give their kids back, but Mum really could have. She could have given us back to Social Services to go to another foster home. But she didn't. People aren't impressed when they hear I've only got three GCSEs but I hardly ever went to school until four years ago. Mum taught me to read and persuaded me to stay in school. Mum never gave up on me even when I gave up on myself."'

In my mind's eye, I see each of my children when they first came to me after Annie said, 'You can do it.' Tallia, five years ago aged twelve, angry, defiant with scarred arms and a record of truancy. Eleven-year-old Ross two years later, bruised and terrified, with nightmares every night and a wet bed in the morning. And two years ago, Maxie, my best friend Annie's foster son.

I tune back to Laura's voice. '"Mum took in three children, gave us a home and made us into a family."'

I'm fishing around in my bag for a tissue to wipe my eyes but I can't find one.

And it doesn't matter.

ROSE McGINTY

The Nightingale's Song

Yarl's Wood. Femi thought it sounded like the kind of place where nightingales would sing. Through the sealed shut window the little brown bird on the sill wasn't singing though. It perched there just a moment, cocking its head, looking at Femi, then flew off. Femi didn't know it was a nightingale at the time. She had never paid much attention to birds before, other than the scrawny hens that scratched around the market. She knew a tender hen for the pot, for sure. Or one that would lay tasty eggs. She had an uncanny knack for picking a good layer. Her Mama always sent her to the market when a new hen was needed. When she came back, dangling the bird upside down by its claws from her bicycle handlebars, her Mama would push out her considerable chest with pride.

'My clever daughter,' she boasted to all the neighbours.

Femi couldn't eat the grey, congealed omelette that was served on the square plastic trays in the canteen.

The little birds that flitted overhead, those were just up in the sky, like the clouds. In those days, she didn't look up much. All life was on the ground, in the market place, by the milling stone, round the well, pulling up weeds in the fields. She asked Mr Clarke the name of the little brown bird.

'A sparrow, most likely.'

But a couple of days later he bought her in a *Pocket AA Guide to British Birds*. Later, back in her room, she flicked through the pages. So many little brown birds. Page after page. Femi liked the pages; she couldn't understand the words, but she traced the lines of flight from England back to Africa. She knew her map from Sunday school, after church. While Miss Mercy read the parables, Femi would gaze at the map on the wall behind her. She liked the colours: gentle pinks, lilacs, creamy yellow, pale green. The colours in the village were all riotous: watermelon ccrise, preacher purple and blazing oilcan gold. The sky was so blue it hurt her eyes and even the ground was red. The map was a square of cool serenity.

When the red earth ran black with blood, the day the blue sky turned grey with smoke, as she and the other children hid silent in the Sunday school cellar, she tore a strip of the muted colours from the map and put it in her pocket. She held the scrap of map in her clenched fist as the screams echoed into the fields, the forest, the dark night.

'This one, you say?' Mr Clarke tutted and drew in his breath over his teeth. 'Maybe, maybe. It's been many a year though, but anything is possible.'

Mr Clarke was Femi's favourite. He wasn't like the other warders; his eyes had a wrinkly softness still. The others weren't unkind, but they weren't kind either. They were just doing their jobs. They liked shouting a lot, 'You there.' Mr Clarke never shouted and he called Femi by her name. Mr Clarke's daughter, Julie, was working in Africa. She was a nurse. His eyes went all watery when he said her name.

 'Our homeward step was just as light
 As the dancing of Fred Astaire,
 And like an echo far away
 A nightingale sang in Berkeley Square.'

 Mr Clarke's voice was as damp as his eyes as he sang. 'Ah, listen to me, silly old fool. I used to step out with my Iris to that one down the dance hall.' He wiped his eyes.

 'Where is Berkeley Square please, Mr Clarke?'

 'It's in London.'

 'London. So my Papa will see nightingales like me here?'

 'You won't find a nightingale in Berkeley Square these days, or anywhere else in London, for that matter, Femi my dear.' Mr Clarke shook his head. 'It's been a great many years since there was a nightingale in London.' The bell rang. 'Back to your room now, Femi dear. See you tomorrow.'

Femi stood by the windowsill, willing the little bird to return. She looked up at the mottled sky; rain was drizzling against the windowpane. The little bird would most likely be up in a tree somewhere now, wrapped under a leaf. Femi only looked up these days. If you looked down all you saw was concrete and wire fencing. She thought about what Mr Clarke had told her. Nightingales were as 'rare as hen's teeth,' he said. She was lucky to see one. Not many people could say that. She was a bit confused about the hen's teeth. The hens back home never had teeth, but maybe over here they did.

Papa had said that too, 'Anything is possible, once we get to London.'

Only nothing seemed very possible inside these brick block walls. If she could just see the little bird again.

'Mr Clarke, please tell me more about the nightingale,' Femi asked when she next saw Mr Clarke, handing him the pocket book.

'Have you seen him again?'

'No, I'm waiting, every day.'

Mr Clarke thumbed through the pages of the guide. 'Let's see. The name has been used for more than a thousand years. It means night songstress. Early writers thought the female sang, when it is in fact the male. Its song is particularly noticeable at night because few other birds are singing.'

Femi smiled. 'My Papa liked to sing at night. After we put out the fire, he would sing. All the pots and pans stopped banging about then, the talking stopped, everyone in the village listened. He sang hymns. Miss Mercy said his voice made the angels weep.'

'The day Thou gavest, Lord, is ended,
The darkness falls at Thy behest;
To Thee our morning hymns ascended,
Thy praise shall sanctify our rest.'

Papa was singing in the church the day the guns started. No one heard the guns at first because Papa and the organ were so loud, rousing the saints. When they did, it was too late. Mama's chest was ripped open.

Mr Clarke was squinting at the small print in the book. 'Here we are, they arrive in April. They leave again from July to September. So, it is possible you saw a nightingale, Femi. Just arrived from Africa.'

Femi counted on her fingers, five months. Surely in that time the little bird would find her again. She would look every day. He wouldn't go back home to Africa without trying to find her.

Scabies. Scabies. Femi didn't know the word. She hadn't heard it before. But today everyone in the camp was saying it. The bulldozers were coming soon. Femi didn't know what a bulldozer was either, but she knew from the way everyone said the word it meant trouble. Femi wasn't scared. Since that night in the village nothing scared her anymore, and there had been plenty on the long journey to Calais that should have scared her. But when the worst thing that could ever happen to you has already happened, what is there to be scared about? The cold rain made her numb.

Where was Papa? He had told her to wait in the shack with some women while he got them food. There weren't many women in the camp and Papa had been glad to find these few. Desperate men from Syria, Iraq, Sudan, Somalia, Afghanistan; those were the main inhabitants of the camp. He didn't like to leave Femi alone, but he couldn't take her with him, he said. Femi had started to argue, begged to go with him. She didn't want him out of her sight for even a moment. All this way together and never a second apart. But one of the women pulled her over to the battered mattress where she sat and told her to hush. After Papa had gone the woman told Femi she had to be brave; she couldn't go to the food queue. There were too many fights there, sometimes with knives. Papa might have to throw a punch to get them some food, he couldn't do that with a child about his legs.

'I'm not a child,' Femi said.

'Hush child, you are, don't wish away your life.' The woman lay back and closed her eyes.

Femi wasn't hungry, even though they hadn't eaten for over two days since they arrived here at the port. Eating just made her feel sick. Papa seemed to have been gone for a long time. And now all the women were talking about scabies and bulldozers. She poked her head from under the tatty, blue plastic sheet. The cold winter wind bit her immediately. She looked about, but her eyes didn't know how to make sense of the scene. Everywhere the fierce young men were running about, snatching up dirty old duffel bags, ripped up trainer shoes, muddy blankets, and black bin bags that they wrapped around themselves to fend off the rain. It was like when the mosquitoes swarmed over the lake.

A thunderous roar ripped across the camp. Femi was pushed out of the opening of the shack as the women rushed past her to see what was happening. They screamed, 'The bulldozers.' The men were all running in the same direction now and shouting, throwing stones, bits of wood, anything that came to hand. After them ran heavy lines of bulky beetles all in black. Femi couldn't see their faces; their heads were hidden inside black helmets. They ran with big, shiny shields held up in front of them, deflecting the shower of rocks. Behind them, the mammoth metal crunching machines.

Guns, the beetles had guns at their hips. Femi started to shake. Papa, the word formed on her lips, but no noise, not that anything could be heard above the tearing of the machines through the shacks and tents. Papa. In the corner of her eye she saw the rock. The tarmac was black with blood.

When Femi woke up she was in the back of a windowless van. She was soaking wet, freezing cold. Her head was sore, she rubbed it, blood flaked across her fingers. She looked around the van. There were about fifteen women and a few small children with her. Some were groaning, others just clasped their little ones close. She didn't recognise any of them. She opened her mouth, but she could not speak. Once the van pulled up at the centre, and the women and children were emptied out, a woman with a red cross on her apron asked Femi her name; but she could not speak still. Every day the woman in the red cross apron, or another like her, asked Femi her name. Every day she could not say. Every day she tried to mouth the word, Papa, but her voice was gone.

Femi didn't know how long she had been at the centre with the women in the red cross aprons. Too long, however long it was. She had to find Papa. London. That's where he said everything would be possible. The other women in the centre, the ones who came with her in the van, and others who came in the days and weeks after, all talked about London. They were all going there, one day, somehow, soon. They knew a man who could get them there and there were good jobs in London, in hotels and fancy houses. Soon they would be earning enough money to send for their other children. He promised through his gold teeth. Femi knew where London was on the map. It was creamy yellow.

Nothing was creamy yellow at Yarl's Wood. Not even the eggs. Everything was grey, especially the eggs. The plan to get to London had gone wrong as soon as they got across the sea, bumping over the waves in the back of the lorry. The man with the gold teeth was nowhere to be seen. More beetles with guns. Another van, another centre. This one didn't have women with red cross aprons. This one was called a 'removal centre.'

'Went clean past London on your way here, so you did,' Mr Clarke told her when she asked about where London was.

Her voice had come back in Yarl's Wood. Not at first. But once Mr Clarke started to sing when he made his rounds of the rooms of an evening. He sang hymns.

'The day Thou gavest, Lord, is ended,

The darkness falls at Thy behest;

To Thee our morning hymns ascended,

Thy praise shall sanctify our rest.'

The little bird on the windowsill had flown three thousand miles, Mr Clarke told her. Across desert, over seas, through storms, past hunters. 'Just a tiny handful of feathers come all that way, all by itself.'

Femi had been glued to that window every minute she could be for the last five months. She knew the little bird would come back. Even as every day went by and Mr Clarke tried to distract her from her vigil with photos of robins, blue tits, green woodpeckers.

'Look at these lovely birds, Femi, look at their colours. Like the parrots back home in Africa, eh?' His crinkled eyes welled up as he watched her stand by the window every day. 'You know, it might not have been a nightingale, Femi dear, maybe it was just a sparrow.'

But still she stayed looking up to where the clouds drifted and darts of little brown birds speckled the sky.

On the last day of September Mr Clarke brought her a picture of a nightingale in a small silver frame. 'There, you can look at this one during the winter. Put it by your bed, dear. Maybe your little friend will come back next Spring.'

Femi opened her mouth to say thank you, but nothing came out. She tried again. Nothing.

'Oh Femi, dear.' A tear rolled down Mr Clarke's rough old cheek.

Femi took the picture frame from him and sank onto her bed. She curled up and held the picture close to her heart.

'Femi, look, look, quick.'

Femi looked up. Mr Clarke was pointing to the window. Head cocked to one side. The little brown bird opened his beak and sang.

RACHAEL MCGILL

Full Powers

The Brexit vote was a management nightmare at Quick 'n' Tasty Chicken™. My staff were all from the EU, except the ones from countries we hate more than the EU. Portuguese Bruno came in the day after the result and announced he was now a wizard called Edgar. He insisted I change his name on the rota to Edgar.

I said, 'That's not going to help, mate. If they decide to deport people, wizard won't be a protected occupation. Anyway, Edgar's got a German ring to it.'

'Idiot!' he shouted. 'It's an old Anglo-Saxon name!'

'OK, OK.' I held up my hands. 'You have five degrees, I'm Tom Thumb, we all know that.'

'You're the only person in this room with no degree, and you're the manager, because you're English,' said Celeste. Then she gave her sweetest smile. She knows I fancy her so rotten she can slag me and my country off as much as she likes.

'Anyway, I didn't choose it!' Bruno spat. 'It's my wizard name, simple as.'

Bruno started wearing a leather pouch, scarily like a gun holster, strapped to his calf. There wasn't a gun in it, but there were various different-shaped bulges. He wouldn't let me look and he wouldn't take it off. I tried having a word in his ear between shifts one day in the staff room.

'Look, mate, you have no idea of the bollocking I'll get from head office if those are terrorist items in there.'

Unfortunately it was four o'clock, so it was like Piccadilly Circus in the staff room (OK, it's a cupboard), everyone drinking their builders' tea with milk and eating biscuits. I'm not sure if they find soggy digestives delicious or if it's 'cause there's a tea drinking test for British citizenship (Celeste told me there was, but she might've been winding me up).

Pietr said, 'Keep your hair on, Gavin, is just his hobby.'

I said, 'You're not the one who has to implement the health, safety and anti-extremism policy.'

Five heads turned away from me to snigger into their tea cups.

'I need only one more thing, then I'll have my full powers,' said Bruno.

'What thing's that, mate?'

'I can't tell you. No one must see my things.'

'Is it Theresa May's heart?' asked Celeste.

'Is it Boris Johnson's dick?' That was Pietr. 'If so, I can –'

'All right, let's give it a rest!' I shouted. I was going to miss this gang of over-educated multicultural no-hopers if they got expelled from our shores.

'It's lonely being a wizard, you know,' said Bruno. 'Especially when you're one of the first to approach full powers. You'll be laughing on the other side of your faces when we all reveal ourselves.'

I taught them that phrase. I started teaching them all a weird English phrase every day after I noticed

Celeste was really into them. It was when I said, 'You're barking up the wrong tree,' to the bloke from the Border Agency who came in looking for Syrians.

Celeste eyeballed me and said, 'Your language is full of that kind of stupid crazy shit.'

'Yeah, yeah,' I said, 'Stupid compared to yours, the language of…' I was too embarrassed to say 'love', so I said 'garlic', which made her laugh at me, as usual.

'No, no,' she said. 'I really like it.'

I imagined she'd said 'you' inside of 'it'. It gave me a warm glow for a minute.

We all kept taking the piss out of Bruno, 'til Romanian Luca announced one Friday after closing: 'It's time to let the cat out of the bag. I am a wizard too, name of Adolfo. And I have attained my full powers.'

'I too have now attained my full powers,' said Bruno/Edgar. 'And I'm champing at the bit.'

They gave each other a meaningful wizard look that actually gave me the willies. I thought maybe it wouldn't hurt to test this wizard thing out. I took the two of them for a pint in the George.

'OK, guys,' I said. 'I have a mission for you.'

They gave me serious looks. 'Spill the beans,' said Bruno.

'Can you make her fancy me?'

Spookily, they didn't need to ask who I meant.

Luca snorted, said, 'Piece of cake.'

Bruno looked a bit disappointed, like he'd been hoping I wanted someone in the government turning into a warthog.

The next day, Luca brought in a book. 'Just read that,' he said.

'Oh, right. In front of her, you mean?'

'No. I mean actually read it. Cover to cover. And when you've finished it, read this.' He handed me another one. 'There's more,' he said. 'If necessary.'

'But these two might be enough?'

He said, 'That depends if you can *embody* them, Gavin,' like he thought I was the wizard.

One Saturday, Celeste said, 'Finally finished my PhD, Gav. I'm a fully-fledged dangerous expert. You can call me doctor.'

I said, 'Oh wow, hats off! Will you let me buy you dinner?'

It popped out my mouth before I had time to shit myself. I think she answered before she had time to think about it too.

'OK, why don't you take me to a really good British restaurant?'

I said, 'Uh...'

'Ha ha, joke!' she said.

We went for tapas.

She told me over the patatas bravas that she was leaving the UK. 'I'm not welcome here anymore,' she said.

'Oh no, Celeste, that's not true. Brexit's not about people like you not being welcome. It's a crisis engineered by the neo-liberal elites as a cover for their elimination of the public sphere. Please don't go!'

She gave me a sideways look. 'Have you been reading something?'

'No!' I shouted, like she'd asked if I'd been wanking under the table.

'I've lived here since university,' she said. 'All my adult life. I thought it was my home.'

'It is your home!'

'It's not,' she said. 'Don't you see? That's what they're saying.'

I was thinking it wouldn't feel like my home either without her in it. But I said, 'They're only saying that based on an idealised, gender and culture normative concept of "home" that's basically a fiction, and a fascist one at that.'

'Oh Gavin,' she said. 'You're as sweet as a nut.'

That was around the time when all sorts of people had started coming out as wizards: the Mayor of London, Jarvis Cocker, that girl who won X Factor even though she fell over, a really high proportion of the old ladies who work in charity shops. One of JK Rowling's companies tried to sue them all, but they lost, because wizards were invented in the Middle Ages, whenever that was. They've been biding their time since then, gathering their magical items and waiting for us to fuck up so badly they have to intervene.

They convinced the non-wizard population they were serious by infiltrating an episode of *Masterchef* and turning the contestants into owls, and handing out money in the street. Then they got to work sorting us out. They nationalised the railways, gave everyone a free house, reduced the working week to 15 hours, and got us making electricity out of potatoes.

I'm no socialist or green or member of a radical left post-Pasokification anti-austerity alliance, but things are better round here. People have become quite a lot less like tossers. I'm not just saying that 'cause Quick 'n' Tasty Chicken™ turned into a sanctuary for abused goldfish and me and Celeste finally got it together after I gave her the first lettuce from my allotment. Most of us in London have Euro mates and a penchant for French or Spanish or whatever birds/blokes, so we thought Brexit would have no advantages except getting to eat British bananas.

Turns out we were wrong. It was the thing that finally prompted the wizards amongst us to reveal themselves.

BIOGRAPHIES

Andy Leach has previously had both poetry and a novel (Blow Your Kiss Hello) published under his alter ego, Andrew James, a soubriquet adopted for reasons of previous professional discretion, despite not being a spy. He is currently working on a new poetry collection. When not writing, he works in wine, largely for charities, and lives in South West London. He can also be found on Twitter at @4ndrewJames.

Angelita Bradney is the winner of the 2017 National Memory Day short story prize and has also been shortlisted in several other competitions including the Fish Prize, Shooter Literary Magazine and Writers' Forum. Her fiction has been published by Litro magazine, Alerion Books and performed in New York. She lives in South East London. Twitter: @AngelBradn.

Anouska Huggins lives in North East England where she squeezes in the odd short story between the day job, family, and grappling with a thing that might eventually resemble a novel.

Antonia Honeywell's career began in the Education Department of the Natural History Museum, where she ran creative writing workshops for children. She went on to become a teacher, eventually running the English department of a three-site Inner London comprehensive school. She wrote her first novel when she was eight, but it took over three decades and many millions of unread words for her to achieve publication. She is an active mentor for the Womentoring programme, which offers feedback and advice to aspiring women writers who struggle to afford conventional courses. Her debut novel, The Ship, is published by Weidenfeld & Nicolson. Twitter: @antonia_writes.

Britta Jensen grew up in the south Tokyo bay area and lives in Germany. Her first novel, Eloia, was longlisted for the Exeter Novel Prize. Her short stories have been shortlisted for the Henshaw Press and Fiction Factory prizes. For the past thirteen years she has taught secondary English to the sound of artillery from the NATO training base next to her school. She's on Twitter @Britta_Murasaki and writes at murasakipress.com.

Caroline Hardman has lived in London for 15 years and was born and raised in Western Australia. Her short stories have been performed at spoken-word events and published in print and online.

Catherine Assheton-Stones has lived in London, Wiltshire, the Lake District, London again, and now in the beautiful city of Edinburgh. She has wanted to be a writer since the age of 12. She's so far had one other short story published, has a novel-and-a-half firmly shut in a drawer, and is currently working on a new one. Twitter @CatherineAsshet.

Writer and musician **Daniel Maitland** released his debut solo album, Rumours of A Nice Day, on Folkwit records in 2008. His Christmas single, Taken In, has recently gone choral – as can be evidenced on YouTube. He has written three novels plus a miserable-ist's travelogue, The Black Diary. His poetry has been featured on Sky TV and in UK magazines, and was shortlisted in a number of national poetry competitions, including Faber and Faber. His words have been set to music by the North Sea Radio Orchestra and other artists, and his poetry collection, Even Bad Dogs do Good Things, is available online and at gigs.

Dave Clark lives in Cambridge, England, where he works at the university. His stories have been published in the charity anthologies 50 Stories for Pakistan and 100 Stories for Queensland. In his spare time he and his partner run the UK Pie Party, which involves taking pies in the face to raise money for cancer charities and hospices.

David Cook's stories have been published in a number of places, both online and in print. You can find more of his work at www.davewritesfiction.wordpress.com, and he's on Twitter @davidcook100. He lives in Bridgend, Wales, with his wife and daughter.

David John Griffin is the author of the gothic/magical realism novel, The Unusual Possession of Alastair Stubb, the literary/psychological novel, Infinite Rooms, the magical realism/paranormal novella, Two Dogs At The One Dog Inn and Other Stories, all published by Urbane Publications davidjohngriffin.com @MagicalRealized Facebook

Debi Alper's first two novels, Nirvana Bites and Trading Tatiana, urban thrillers set among the sub-cultures of South East London, were published by Orion. She has since set up her own imprint and has re-published both novels as e-books, along with the next ones in the series. For the last twelve years, Debi has spent most of her time helping other writers to perfect their novels through critiques, mentoring, Book Doctor sessions and creative writing workshops. Debi also runs the phenomenally successful Writers' Workshop Self-Edit Your Novel course, together with Emma Darwin, as well as acting as a short story competition judge. Twitter: @DebiAlper Facebook... www.debialper.co.uk

Freya Morris is an award-winning flash fiction writer from Bristol. She has been published in a variety of places including the Bath Flash Fiction anthology, Bare Fiction, The Fiction Desk, Popshot, Halo magazine and two National Flash Fiction Day anthologies.

Giselle Delsol is a Franco-American living in Paris with her husband, three children and various animals. She's currently juggling a few different manuscripts on which agents have nibbled and – being the eternal optimist – keeps pursuing the writing dream. This story, her first in an anthology, stems from her frustration about not being able to 'do enough' about the refugee crisis in Calais, and her admiration for all those extending a helping hand. Find her on Twitter: @DelsolGiselle.

Isabel Costello is a London-based author and host of the Literary Sofa blog. Her short fiction has appeared in magazines and anthologies including the first volume of Stories for Homes. In 2016 her debut novel, Paris Mon Amour, was published in digital by Canelo and she has since released a paperback edition under a new Literary Sofa imprint. https://literarysofa.com/ @isabelcostello

Jackie Taylor lives in rural Cornwall, where she works from home and writes whenever she can. Her short stories have appeared in journals including Mslexia and QWF and have been placed in several competitions. Her first play, Boomtown, was produced by Sterts Theatre in 2015. www.jacketaylor.org.uk.

Jacqueline Paizis was born in Hythe, Kent but spent many years living and working in London and Athens. She now divides her time between Hove in East Sussex and Greece. Jacqueline is currently editing her second novel set in contemporary Greece at the beginning of the socioeconomic crisis. She also writes a blog about Greek life, politics and literature. The Cleaner of Kastoria is Jacqueline's first novel and is available from Lulu.com and Amazon kindle. Jacqueline is also the author of a number of short stories including Albanian Mothers and Anti Valentine, the latter published by Centum Press in Volume 1 of 100 Voices. Find her on Facebook at @writingjacquyp.

Jacqueline Ward is a Chartered Psychologist and her debut psychological thriller, Perfect Ten, will be published by Corvus Atlantic Books in Spring 2018. Jacqueline is the author of the DS Jan Pearce crime fiction series and a speculative fiction novel, Smartyellow, and enjoys writing short stories and screenplays. Her short story, Brick Heart, featured in the first volume of Stories for Homes. She holds a PhD in narrative and storytelling which produced a new model in identity construction. Jacqueline has worked with victims of domestic violence and families of missing people as well as heading a charity that deals with the safety and reliability of major hazards, and received an MBE for services to vulnerable people in 2013.

James Lawless' poetry and prose have won awards, including the Scintilla Welsh Open Poetry Competition, the WOW award, the Cecil Day Lewis Award and a Hennessey award nomination for emerging fiction. Two of his stories were shortlisted for the Willesden (2007) and Bridport prizes (2014). He is the author of six well-received novels, a book of children's stories, a poetry collection, Rus in Urbe, and a study of modern poetry, Clearing the Tangled Wood: Poetry as a Way of Seeing the World, for which he received an arts bursary. Born in Dublin, he lives in Kildare. www.jameslawless.net.

Jan Carson is based in Belfast, Northern Ireland. Her first novel, Malcolm Orange Disappears, was published by Liberties Press in 2014, followed by a short story collection, Children's Children, in 2016. Her short story, Settling, was included in the anthology, The Glass Shore; Short Stories by Women Writers from the North of Ireland, published by New Island in 2016, which won the BGEIBA Irish Book of the Year in 2016. She has had short stories aired on BBC Radio 3 and 4. Her flash fiction anthology, Postcard Stories, was published by the Emma Press in May 2017. Her stories have appeared in journals such as Storm Cellar, Banshee, Harper's Bazaar and The Honest Ulsterman. In 2014 she was a recipient of the Arts Council NI Artist's Career Enhancement Bursary. She was longlisted for the Sean O'Faolain short story prize in 2015 and shortlisted in 2016, won the Harper's Bazaar short story competition in 2016, was shortlisted for the Doolin Short Story Prize in 2017 and was shortlisted for a Sabotage Award for best short story collection 2015/16.

Joan Taylor-Rowan is a prize-winning writer. Her work has been broadcast on Radio 4 and her stories have appeared in a number of anthologies including London Lies and Stations (Arachne Press) and Tales of the Decongested. Her work has been shortlisted for The Asham Award, and her stories have been finalists in the ChapterOne international short story competition, SLS international short story competition (SLS is based at Concordia University, Montreal) and the Writer's Village international short story competition. Her novel, The Birdskin Shoes, was a winner of the Spreadtheword novel pitch competition and her young adult novel was longlisted in the Mslexia children's novel award. She has recently moved to Hastings after years in London and loves it.

J. A. Ironside (Jules) is the author of the YA paranormal mystery series, Unveiled. She co-authored the historical fiction Oath and Crown duology – centred on the political intrigue leading to the battle of Hastings – with fellow author, Matthew Willis. The duology was published by Penmore Press in 2017. Jules is also a founding member of the Random Writers and has co-edited their current three anthologies. She lives on the edge of the Cotswold Way with a small black and white cat and her boyfriend creature. jaironside.com... @J_AnneIronside

Julie Hayman works as a university lecturer but she has also been a dancer, dog-trainer, secretary, waitress and writer-in-residence at a school. Her short stories have won and been shortlisted in many competitions, including being 'highly commended' in the Costa Short Story Award 2016, and have appeared in numerous anthologies and magazines, as well as being broadcast on radio.

Karen Ankers lives in Anglesey. She writes stories, poems and short plays, in which she tries to give a voice to those who would usually not be heard. Her plays have been performed in the UK, US, Australia and Malaysia. She is currently working on a novel.

Lee Hamblin is originally from London, now living in Greece. He has had stories published with F(r)iction online, Flash Frontier, Spelk, Flash Fiction Magazine, Platform for Prose, Sick Lit Magazine, STORGY, and some other places. He occasionally tweets @kali_thea and puts words here: https://hamblin1.wordpress.com.

Over recent years **Lee Hill** has got into chopping wood and then burning it. He also likes cheese and backgammon. Sometimes he worries he may be mistaken for a hipster.

Leigh Forbes lives in rural Sussex with three children, a cat, and a coffee machine. She works as a page-designer to feed her book-buying habit, a charmingly circular way of life exacerbated by living 400 yards from an indie bookshop. She spends her free time running, hiding in the kitchen eating chocolate, and being unable to move because there's a cat on her lap.

Liam Hogan is a London based writer and host of the award winning monthly literary event, Liars' League. Winner of Quantum Shorts 2015 and Sci-Fest LA's Roswell Award 2016, his dark fantasy collection, Happy Ending Not Guaranteed, is out now from Arachne Press. Find out more at happyendingnotguaranteed.blogspot.co.uk, or tweet at @LiamJHogan.

Lindsay Bamfield has written a number of short stories and flash fiction pieces and has been published in Greenacre Writers' Anthology, Voices from the Web 2012, The Best of Café Lit 2012, Mslexia, Writers' News and Writing Magazine. She has won prizes in The Great British Write Off 2017, Writers' News, Writing Magazine and Words with Jam competitions and has been shortlisted in several others. She is currently re-working her first novel with advice from an editor and has a second novel on the back-burner.

Lindsay Fisher was third in Fish's flash fiction competition in 2016. In 2017, he was third in Fish's short story competition and won Fish's flash fiction competition. Published in Stories for Homes Volume 1, he is thrilled to now be in SforH2 and to know that his story is helping to do good in the world.

Lorraine Wilson writes 'book club' fiction, usually with a touch of the fantastical. Before settling by the sea in Scotland, she worked in various remote corners of the world and so the wilderness bleeds into everything she writes. She has published several short stories with the Random Writers and can be found on Twitter @raine_clouds.

Mandy Berriman was born in a British military hospital in Germany and grew up in Edinburgh. She studied music at Sheffield University, where she met her husband, and then trained to teach in Glasgow before moving and working as a primary school teacher in the Cambridgeshire fens. She's now a specialist music teacher at a primary school in Oldham and lives on the edge of the Peak District with her family. Her story, A Home without Moles, featured in the first Stories for Homes anthology. Her debut novel, Home, is due out from Doubleday in February 2018.

Born in Dublin, **Marc de Faoite** lives on an island off the west coast of Malaysia. His short stories, articles, and book reviews have been published both in print and online. Tropical Madness, a collection of his short stories, was longlisted for the 2014 Frank O'Connor International Short Story Prize.

Margaret Jennings writes poetry, short stories and novels. She has an MA in Creative Writing and has read her work at many venues. Longlisted in the Bare Fiction short story prize and shortlisted in the Bridport Prize for flash fiction, Margaret is currently finishing her second novel.

Matt Barnard is a poet and short story writer. He has won and been placed in competitions including the

Bridport Prize, the Ink Tears short story competition and the Bristol Short Story Prize. His debut poetry collection, Anatomy of a Whale, will be published by The Onslaught Press in spring 2018. He was born in London, where he still lives with his wife and their two sons and two dogs.

Maureen Cullen has been writing poetry and short fiction since 2011 after early retirement from her social work career. In 2016, she was published along with three other poets in Primers 1, a collaboration between Nine Arches Press and the Poetry School. She won The Labello Prize for short fiction in 2014, and has stories published in Scribble, Prole, and the Hysteria Anthology. Her stories have been longlisted and shortlisted in various competitions. Maureen lives in Argyll & Bute where she is working on her first short story collection.

Michele Sheldon lives in Folkestone, Kent. Her short stories have been shortlisted for different prizes including the Bridport Prize, the Colm Toíbín International Short Story Award, Wells Literary Festival, Frome Literary Festival, HG Wells Short Story Competition and others. They have also been published in different anthologies including the first Stories for Homes, and magazines including Rosebud, Storgy, Here Comes Everyone, Kent Life and Woman's Weekly. She co-hosts live lit events in Kent with Hand of Doom Productions. www.michelesheldon.com.

Mike Blakemore trained and worked as a journalist before switching to public relations. He has held senior roles with Amnesty International, the BBC and the

National Health Service, before setting up his own consultancy, Blakemore Communications. Over the last three years, Mike has been researching and writing a biography of a Nepalese woman mountaineer as well indulging his love of creative writing. He lives in Folkestone with his wife and twin son and daughter.

Mohini Malhotra is from Kathmandu and lives in Washington DC. She is an international development economist, and founder of a social enterprise (www.artbywomen.gallery) to promote contemporary women artists and invest in causes that better women's and girls' lives. She loves language and her fiction has appeared in Gravel, Silver Birch Press, Blink-Ink, Flash Frontier, 82 Star Review, A Quiet Courage, Writers' Center, and forthcoming in other journals.

Paul Whelan is a student in Maynooth University, Ireland, studying law and politics. He has been writing short stories since he was young and has worked hard to hone a unique voice in his writing.

Poppy O'Neill's writing has been featured in Oh Comely, The Dangerous Women Project and Halo magazine, as well as short story anthologies from Mother's Milk Books, A Room of Our Own and National Flash Fiction Day. Her work has been longlisted for the Bath Flash Fiction Award. She is currently writing her first novel and studying for an MA at the University of Chichester.

Rachael Dunlop is an award-winning writer of short stories and flash-fiction, and has recently completed her first novel. Despite living in a very big house, she has given up on having a room of her own and seeks the Muse from her kitchen table.

Rachael McGill was born in the Shetland Islands. She lives with one foot in Britain, the other in Lisbon. She's a playwright and translator and has recently finished her first novel. Short fiction has been published in Shoe Fly Baby (Bloomsbury), Shorts 5 (Polygon), New Writing Scotland 35 (ASLS), The Frogmore Papers and online.

Rose McGinty is the author of Electric Souk, published in 2017. She lives in England and works for the NHS. She studied at Trinity College, Dublin and is an alumna of The Faber Academy. Follow @rosemcginty.

Sally Swingewood has over 20 years of experience in publishing, both as an editor and a writer. Beginning her career on business-to-business magazines, she survived employment with the Maxwell group to become Assistant Editor of Time Out's first venture outside of London, Time Out Amsterdam. Sally has written for local and international newspapers, edited film and theatre scripts and contributed to a number of books. Also an internationally exhibited artist, Sally studied Fine Art & Art History at Goldsmiths' College before gaining an MA in Creative Writing, the Arts and Education, from Sussex University.

Sal Page has a creative writing MA from Lancaster. Her stories appear in various places online and in eleven print anthologies, including three National Flash Fiction anthologies, three FlashDog anthologies and Stories for Homes Volume 1. She won the Calderdale

Prize in 2011 and the Greenacre Writers' Short Story Competition in 2013 and has been placed and shortlisted in many more. When not distracted by the lure of writing, reading and performing flash and short stories, she's working on a novel, Priscilla Parker Reluctant Celebrity Chef. She works as a nursery cook and lives in Morecambe. When not writing she can be found swimming, cycling, watching sitcoms, listening to Squeeze and trying to join in on Twitter as @SalnPage.

Santino Prinzi is the Co-Director of National Flash Fiction Day in the UK, a Senior Editor for New Flash Fiction Review, an Associate Editor for Vestal Review, and the Flash Fiction Editor of Firefly Magazine. His debut flash fiction collection, Dots and other flashes of perception, is available from The Nottingham Review Press. His short stories, flash fiction, and prose poetry have been published or are forthcoming in various places, such as Flash: The International Short-Short Story Magazine, Great Jones Street, Litro Online, and Bath Flash Fiction Award Volume 2. To find out more follow him on Twitter @tinoprinzi or visit his website: tinoprinzi.wordpress.com.

Sharon Bennett has been shortlisted for The Yeovil Literary Prize, The Exeter Flash Competition, Fish Publishing Flash Fiction Prize, and twice shortlisted for The Bridport Prize for Flash Fiction. She was awarded second place for Words with Jam First Page of a Novel. She is published with Platform for Prose and the Bath Flash Fiction Anthology and is especially delighted to be part of Stories for Homes, supporting Shelter. She can be found on Twitter @sharonbennettme.

Sharon Telfer won the June 2016 Bath Flash Fiction Award and the 2016 Hysteria Flash Fiction competition. As a non-fiction writer and editor, she translates social policy research – including work on housing and homelessness – into everyday English. She tweets @sharontelfer.

Shell Bromley is a writer of fantasy fiction. She is a founding member of the Random Writers and has co-edited their current anthologies. Generally, she's lurking around in Yorkshire with a small pack of border collies and plenty of tea.

Silvana Maimone is a London-based actor/singer and theatre deviser, and 'secret writer' for some time. Born in Sicily, at the age of six she and her family sailed across the world on a month-long voyage to Melbourne, Australia, to start a new life: a modern-day Odyssey in keeping with the ancient mythology associated with her Sicilian heritage. The question 'Where/What is Home?' has been one that she has asked herself ever since. Silvana is extremely honoured to be part of this anthology, and to make a small contribution towards helping to answer this question for others, who like herself, still seek it.

Sophie Wellstood grew up in rural England in an unconventional family. Her fiction was first published in Stories for Homes Volume 1. Since then her debut novel has won Triskele Books Big 5 competition and was shortlisted for the Caledonian Novel Award. Her story, The First Hard Rain, was shortlisted for the 2016 Manchester Fiction Prize and appeared in the Best

British Short Stories anthology, Salt Publishing, published in June 2017. Sophie lives in London and is working on a short story collection and her second, third and fourth novels. sophiewellstood.com.

Sue Lanzon lives in London. Her first book of short stories, Something in the Water & Other Tales Of Homeopathy, is published by Winter Press. She is currently at work on a second collection, which has nothing to do with homeopathy and everything to do with love.

Susmita Bhattacharya's debut novel, The Normal State of Mind (Parthian), was published in March 2015. She is the winner of the Winchester Writers' Festival Memoir Competition 2016, and her writing has appeared in Stories for Homes Anthology Volume 1, Structo, The Lonely Crowd, Litro, Wasafiri, Mslexia, Commonwealth Writers, Tears in the Fence, and on BBC Radio 4 among others. She lives in Winchester where she teaches Creative Writing at Winchester University and facilitates writing workshops for young writers with SO: Write at Southampton. She tweets at @susmitatweets.

Sylvia Petter, an Australian based in Vienna, Austria, writes short, long, serious, sexy and fun. Her stories have been published widely and in her collections, The Past Present, Back Burning, Mercury Blobs, and writing as AstridL, Consuming the Muse – erotic tales. She holds a PhD in Creative Writing and is revising two novels, of which one was awarded third place at the 2016 Yeovil Literary Prize. She blogs at her website www.sylviapetter.com.

Tania Hershman's third short story collection, Some of Us Glow More Than Others, is published by Unthank Books, and her debut poetry collection, Terms & Conditions, was published by Nine Arches Press in July 2017. Tania is also the author of a poetry chapbook and two short story collections, and co-author of Writing Short Stories: A Writers' & Artists' Companion (Bloomsbury, 2014). Tania is curator of ShortStops (www.shortstops.info), celebrating short story activity across the UK & Ireland. www.taniahershman.com.

Ted Bonham is James Horrocks, a writer and creative writing researcher from Birmingham, England. He was awarded an ASA Bronze Award for Swimming in 1999 and was the John Moore Mathematics prize winner for his year group at Bishop Walsh School in 2002, 2003 and 2004. His first novel, Drawing Hands, is not available in all good book shops (for very good reasons). Find him online @TedBonham.